A Sword and a Cross

Also by Douglas Fain

The Phantom's Song

2040 American Exodus

Anarchist for Rent

Why Projects Fail and How to Succeed

A Sword and a Cross

Douglas Fain

Bergen Peak Publishing, Evergreen, Colorado

This book is fiction, but a great deal of research went into the political landscape and customs of the time. I was amazed at the amount of material that was actually available, thanks to the work of ancient Hebrew, Roman, and Greek historians. Some of the primary reference books are listed at the end of this novel.

Douglas Fain's *A Sword and a Cross*.

For information contact Bergen Peak Publishing
2964 Elk View Dr.
Evergreen, Colorado, 80439.

Cover and book design by Lorna Clubb

ISBN: 978-0-578-70981-9

Second edition: April, 2024

For Susan
She was music to our world.

Acknowledgements

I would like to thank all of those in my life who have helped me try to understand the wonders of our God and the great gift of His Son. My parents, my wife, my pastors, and many friends have walked with me along this path. The truth they helped me understand was the greatest gift one could receive. I will be eternally grateful to them as I continue to stumble toward the light.

Once again I send a salute to the artist, Lorna Clubb. Her art adds much to this book. Also, to my special readers: my wife Mary Jo, my special friends, Tom Calandra, and Lou Henefield, and my sister-in-law, Shirley Weaver, thanks again for your critiques and your encouragement as I struggled through the process of writing a story I felt drawn to tell. A special thanks goes to Andrea Mansor for her excellent editing. It made a great difference in this book. Finally, to my friend Jack Kintner, thanks for loaning me a book that inspired me to pursue this endeavor. I found it to be a great inspiration along the way. God bless you all.

Ask and it will be given to you;
seek and you shall find…

Matthew 7:7

Characters: A Sword and a Cross

Archelaus — one of Herod's sons, Ethnarch of Judea and
Samaria after Herod's death

Augustus — (Caesar Augustus) Roman Emperor 27BC—14AD

Caiaphas — (Joseph ben Caiaphas) Jewish High Priest who
presided over the trial of Jesus before the Sanhedrin.
Appointed to that position by the Roman procurator
Valerius Gratus.

Coponius — first Roman procurator of Judea after the rule of
Archelaus

Cyprianus — Roman centurion, friend of Nathan

Darius — Roman soldier killed by Nathan in Bethlehem

Decima — Procula's friend

Doran — Sabina's son/Gilad's adopted son

El'Azar — aid to Caiaphas and Commander of the Temple
Guards

Gilad — Commander of the King's Guards/Palace Guards

Herod — last King of the Jews, puppet for Rome

Kalev — guard and friend of Nathan and Tobias

Lealius — Decima's husband, changed after seeing Jesus

Matthias — friend of Nathan and Samuel, gave Samuel a
vineyard

Nathan — member of the King's Guards/Palace Guards

Pontius Pilate — Roman Prefect sent to rule Judea, condemned
Jesus

Procula — Pilate's wife, a believer in Jesus. Considered a saint in the Eastern Orthodox Church

Rebecca — mother of Samuel and wife of Nathan

Sabina — concubine for Herod, gift from Herod to Gilad

Samuel — crippled boy from Bethlehem, Rebecca's son/ Nathan's adopted son

Sejanus — (Lucius Aelius Sejanus) Chief administrator of the Roman Empire under Tiberius (appointed Pontius Pilate to his position in Judea; executed by Tiberius)

Tiberius — (Tiberius Caesar Augustus) Roman Emperor 14AD—37AD

Tobias — one of the guards and Nathan's best friend

Vitellius — (Lucius Vitellius) Roman Legate in Syria

Sanhedrin — Jewish administrative/judicial council in Jerusalem

---

Abba/Aba—Hebrew for father or dad

Ima/Eema/Ema—Hebrew for mother or mom

Chapter 1

Bethlehem, Judea, 6 B.C. (For reference, most scholars agree that this would have been the year of Jesus's birth. Herod's death is documented two years later in 4 BC.)

* * *

He was seventeen years old, a member of King Herod's Guards, and he was holding a sword above the crying baby before him. The sweat on his forehead had puddled into his eyebrows and had already invaded his eyes, blurring his vision. The young woman kneeling before him was desperately crying and pleading, but he could not hear her. Her mouth was open, but the sound was lost in the voices screaming obscenities in his own mind. How does a man slaughter a baby, a Jewish baby born to his own countrymen? He looked at his right hand and tried to move the sword, but he could not. He had no control over the shaking sword or the hand that held it. In desperation he turned to his fellow guard for help. What he saw was a face even more distraught than his own. Both young men were traumatized in the drama of that one moment in history, a drama that would play out in their lives and change the world forever.

* * *

The bitter wind blowing from the northwest matched the solemn file of dark silhouettes as they trudged along the north-south ridge road in the Central Highlands toward Bethlehem. What was left of the sun's presence was fading quickly as the soldiers' shadows grew longer on the dry, parched, soil. The pending darkness hung poised in the gathering clouds, ready to flow across the landscape and mask the somber men as their column marched slowly on their unwelcomed journey. They had walked the six miles from Jerusalem along the dusty road in a disorderly gaggle. They did not look like a military detail; their heads were not erect; and their demeanor reflected shame. They stared at the dirt below their feet and glanced furtively at the people who watched them moving down the road. They were Herodians, members of the King's Guard, normally a proud and respected group of men, until today when King Herod had ordered them to accompany a group of mercenaries who were being sent to Bethlehem with orders to kill all male babies under the age of two in the village. The mercenaries, unlike the King's Guards, were hired soldiers from Greece, Gaul, and Syria who fought for whomever would pay them. They were violent men who valued life even less than King Herod, himself. But the Herodian guards were Jews, like the people in the village and the babies they were being sent to murder. Several Roman soldiers also accompanied the group to ensure the order was fulfilled and to assist if the men from the small town decided to fight, at least that is what the chief centurion in Jerusalem had told Herod. Actually they were there to observe and report back to the centurion for his report to Rome. Unlike the Jewish guards or the mercenaries, the Romans led the column, marching together with their heads high. They were above the petty Jewish king's orders. They fought men—not babies.

Nathan looked over at his friend Tobias and shook his head. They both were members of King Herod's Guards, and they were unsure how to follow the orders they had been given. More importantly, Nathan knew he would *not* follow those orders. He could not. How does one slaughter babies? These were children—Jewish children. And what about the men in the village? Wouldn't they fight? Their sticks and tools would be no

2

match for the weapons of the King's Guards, the mercenaries, or the Roman escorts, but still they would fight. Nathan was sure of it. They were Jews, like him, and he knew he would fight if he saw men slaughtering children. Nathan was tall, almost six feet in height. He was also very strong and a handsome young man. He had just turned seventeen, and his dark beard was not yet full. He was young, but he was also one of the expert swordsmen in the King's Guard, a position of great honor for any young man in Judea.

The men walked more slowly as they approached the small town. Nathan pulled his cloak around him and stared into the heavens above. Only a sliver of the moon was climbing across the sky as the sun slowly sank into the hills to the West. He studied the stars that were just beginning to peek from the dark heavens. The large one they had been watching for several weeks was gone. Perhaps it was an omen. It had been the topic of conversation of most everyone in Jerusalem, and what a magnificent star it had been. From Jerusalem, it had hung in the sky to the Southwest, in the direction they were now going. Night had been swept away by the bright light as the star covered most of the countryside with a brilliance as bright as day. Where did it come from; where had it gone? His mind kept returning to the task they had been given by their cruel king. Perhaps it was best that the star was gone. How could such deeds be done in the sacred light of that star?

Tobias cursed the cold and stepped aside to retie his sandals. He was shorter than his friend, Nathan, by several inches, but both young men were strong and well trained in their role as protectors of the king and the palace. While not as large or as strong as Nathan, Tobias was gifted with a quick mind and a strong will. Unlike Nathan's scraggly dark beard, Tobias already had the beginning of a full, manly beard, light brown in color and the envy of all the younger men in the guard unit. He pulled the leather sandal straps tightly, nodded to their commander, and rejoined the group as they slowed their pace even more. They were not tired; they just wanted more time to consider their predicament. They were about to enter a Jewish village and kill children. How would they ever face their kinsmen again? Perhaps more importantly, how would they live with themselves with such a stain on their hands? It was a stain they all knew could never be washed away.

Gilad, the commander of the King's Guard, raised his hand, and the men stopped. He was a large man, towering over his men with arms almost as large as most of their legs. His beard was dark and full, touching his chest and flowing over his cloak. Like his beard, his eyes were dark and piercing. It was said that he could win any sword fight by simply looking into the eyes of his enemy and turning him to stone. His reputation was known across Judea; no one had ever bested him in armed combat. He was the leader of the famed King's Guard, and he was the idol of every man who wore that uniform. The men loved him, and they knew he loved them in return. They were his family; he had no wife nor children, just a group of young men who had sworn their lives to protecting their king and his palace. Gilad watched and waited until the mercenaries had passed then stepped before his men and spoke quietly. There was a pained look on his face as he looked over his shoulder toward the south at the little town. The day was fading, and lights could be seen in the small houses bunched together on the plain. It was so different from the city of Jerusalem where the king lived in his resplendent palace. "Bethlehem is just ahead. We all know our orders, and none of us like them. Cover your faces with a piece of cloth to hide your identity, and remove all indications that we are from the King's Guard. That is why I told you not to wear your official cloaks. We do not want to be recognized. It is getting late and the moon is not full; that will assist in our efforts to remain unknown."

One of the men in the back of the group spoke up. His voice was filled with emotion. "How do we do this? How can we kill babies—Jewish babies?"

"The order came from a Jewish king, and we follow those orders."

"Herod is no Jew; he is an Idumean. No Jew would issue such an order."

"Quiet, we do not want our Roman escorts to hear us. They already say we are weak."

"This is not about weakness. There is no honor in killing children, Gilad, only shame. We will live with this blood on our hands for the rest of our lives."

Gilad hung his head and spoke even more quietly. The men could see the pain on his face and understood the dilemma he faced. "My heart aches as much as yours, so let's be about our business here and leave as soon as possible." Gilad waited until he was sure he had the attention of all his men then continued. "Herod assigned us to this detail to ensure it takes place as he ordered. I am to report back to him as soon as we return to Jerusalem. We are his eyes and ears for this night. We were directed to participate, but I'm directing you to let the mercenaries do the killing. They have no conscience about such things." He bowed his head a moment. "There will be much blood shed tonight; just be sure when we re-group you have some on your swords. During the night, go to a house the mercenaries have left and put some of the blood there on your swords. But be aware that the Romans will be watching. They, too, will issue a report tomorrow. It must appear that we were participants in this deed."

The man in the back spoke again. "What if the townsmen fight back? What do we do then?"

"The Romans are here to take care of the villagers. I'm sure the mercenaries will join them. Let us hope the men who live here do not interfere."

"Of course they will fight. Was it not Jair, a son of Bethlehem, who killed Golaith, or his father Elhanan, one of the thirty mighty men who guarded King David? David, himself, was he not from Bethlehem? These were brave men. The men of Bethlehem descended from such men. Surely they will fight. What would *you* do, Gilad?"

The large man ignored the question. They all knew what he would do. Gilad was a brave man, and also a strong leader of men. But he was also the commander of the King's Guard. They knew he had argued against the orders, but, in the end, he would follow them, or at least make it appear that he had.

The men were aware that Herod had received notice from foreign visitors that a new king had been born in Bethlehem, and that was something Herod would not allow. His scholars had studied the scriptures and predicted that the birth would happen in that small village. That prediction agreed with the direction of the star the visitors were following. The Romans had put Herod on the throne in Judea over thirty years ago, and he had already murdered many who had tried to wrest that title from him, including some of his own sons and Mariamme, one of his ten wives. Herod had waged wars to maintain his crown; certainly no baby from Bethlehem would be allowed to challenge his throne. At sixty-nine years, Herod's health was failing rapidly, and he could feel the winter of his life surrounding him with a cold embrace. Still, he was Herod the Great, King of the Jews, and he would claim that title until the day he drew his last breath.

Gilad raised his hand, and the conversation stopped. The men were staring at the ground in silence; when they finally looked up, he gave final orders about their unwanted task. He also reminded them that to disobey one of Herod's orders would be to suffer instant death. It was a fact they all understood; their king was a cruel man, a man feared by all. They were to split up and go into the tiny houses in pairs. "When you return tonight, be sure your swords have blood on them; the Romans will be checking." A flash of lightening crashed through the darkness and lit the entire sky, shocking the men as they cowered from the sound. Lightening on a clear night—it was an omen that forebode ill for them all, a foreboding that accentuated the shame they were about to claim for their lives. Were Gilad not such a strong and beloved leader, they would have killed him and fled. Instead, each man struggled with the confusion in his own mind and weighed the alternatives he faced. The wiser ones recognized Gilad's subtle message. It was a possible escape; it only required blood on their swords. But there were also grave consequences should they be caught. Each measured his soul and made his own decision and, in doing so, banished the confusion in his mind and heart. Each man's choice was then wrapped carefully in his cloak of duty, and finally resolved, they all marched on, following their leader.

Nathan and Tobias had been friends from childhood. They had been raised in the same village and were chosen as guards together. They shared everything. Today they would share a deed that both knew would change them forever. As the men paired, Nathan grabbed Tobias for his teammate. It was the only possibility of finding a way to avoid the assignment he had been given. He needed time, and he needed someone he could trust. What to do? Nathan looked at Tobias' face. It was white; Tobias looked as if he were in total shock. He was obviously also struggling with the orders they had been given. Nathan closed his eyes and began a quick examination of the alternatives available. Run? Swear there were no babies in the house they entered? State that only girls were found? How often could any of these excuses work? When he looked up, Gilad was looking at him and pointing to a small house on a corner of the road.

Nathan and Tobias stood before the worn door for several minutes, frozen in place. The little house was poorly built of mud bricks covered with a white plaster. The roof was constructed from wooden planks supported by long logs and covered with straw and dirt. There was a small window on either side of the door, covered with heavy woolen drapes that let in a small amount of light and prevented some of the cold during the winter months. It was obviously a poor working man's home. The door was made of heavy, rough wood, held together by two cross beams that were attached to rusty iron hinges that held the door perpetually at an odd angle. Finally Tobias nodded and opened the door with a loud screech from the rusting hinges. They quickly stepped inside the small dwelling and crouched defensively in the main room, searching for any men who might be present. Inside, however, they only found a young woman. She was holding a baby wrapped tightly in gray cloths. It was cooing softly as she rocked it back and forth in her arms. Outside, shouts from the villagers echoed down the small streets as they became aware of the soldiers' purpose. The shouts became screams, and then there was the sound of fighting. Nathan closed his eyes, but he couldn't close his ears. He didn't want to hear the death of good men outnumbered and with only farm tools with which to fight. Sticks and knives were no match for the heavy swords of the Roman soldiers. As they stood in the entry, the young woman turned from them, protecting her baby. She began to scream and moved to the corner farthest from the door as they advanced toward her. It was a small house, and she had nowhere to hide. Nathan looked at the woman, she was no more than fourteen or fifteen, only a few years younger than he. On her face was the look of fear and disbelief. What were these masked men doing in her home, and why were they trying to take her child? As Tobias grabbed the baby, she began screaming and tried to fight the man before her. Nathan stepped between the two as his friend raised the child before him, his sword shaking in his hand. Nathan looked at the sword and then at Tobias's face. Tobias's eyes were closed tightly; there was panic on his face; and his lip was trembling. The woman was pleading and crying; her screams joining those of the entire neighborhood. Suddenly she turned to Nathan and looked directly into his eyes. He could feel her gaze penetrate his very soul. "Please, kill me, but not my child."

Tobias had paused; he was frozen in that moment. He turned and looked at Nathan for some sign, some way to escape the fear and disgust that overwhelmed him. Then Nathan raised his hands into the air. "Stop!" He turned to his friend and took the baby and unwrapped the cloths, hoping to find a girl. The child was a boy, but he was deformed. One of his legs had not fully developed in his mother's womb. He would be a cripple for life. A look of relief was on Nathan's face as he carefully wrapped the baby with the cloths that lay on the floor and handed him back to his mother. "This is clearly no king." He said it very deliberately. She quickly took the baby and turned from the men to shield her son. There was fear on her face, in her eyes. Tobias looked at Nathan with a thin smile on his face and simply nodded. Very slowly he began walking backward toward the door, his eyes locked on his friend. Finally, both men turned and walked out into the night air. Nathan put his sword back into his leather scabbard and began walking toward the edge of the town.

Tobias caught up with his friend, his eyes on the dirt before him. "I can't do this, Nathan. I just can't."

"Neither can I."

"What can we do? How will we answer to Gilad? To the Romans?"

"I don't know. Let me think."

The men had walked for only a short distance when they heard the angry sounds of a fight on the small road before them. As they approached, they found a Roman soldier standing over the body of a man from the village. The soldier was wiping his blade on the dead man's worn cloak. There was a broken staff lying beside the body and a large bloody stain in the center of the man's tunic. Blood was slowly spreading across the body and into the dust in the road. "Where do you two think you're going? Are you afraid of the children?" There was an ugly sneer across his face. "I figured some of you would try to sneak out the back way. Let me see your swords. I'll bet they're still clean." He stepped forward and reached for Tobias's sword, but Tobias pulled it away before the Roman could reach it. "I said give me your sword, you toad." The Roman pulled his sword and swung it toward Tobias who parried with his own. The Roman's sword was like no sword either of them had ever seen. It was longer and heavier and swung with such force that when it struck Tobias's sword the force of the impact alone knocked him to the ground. The soldier raised it above his head. "You don't threaten a Roman soldier, you cowardly Jew."

Nathan rushed forward shouting "No! Stop!" But the soldier swung his sword and cut Tobias's arm as he rolled away from the blow. Laughing, the attacker raised his sword again for a killing blow, but he had made one major mistake. He was concentrating on his victim and did not see the shock and the fear on Nathan's face behind him or the small Jewish sword that Nathan rammed into his back as the Roman stood with his sword raised above Tobias. Nathan could hear his blade as it entered the man. He could feel the ribs crack as the blade sliced through the soldier's leather vest. In less than a second the blow had been delivered; the deed had been done. The Roman slowly turned his head and looked at Nathan. His eyes were large; he said nothing. He only stood for a moment staring at the Jew behind him. Slowly his hands fell to his side as his sword banged on the rocks by the path. Then he crumpled with a thud to the ground. He tried to speak, but only a gurgling sound came from his mouth. Then there was silence. Nathan stood there motionless, staring at the dead soldier bleeding into the same dusty road as his victim. Slowly Tobias climbed to his feet, holding his injured arm. He stood trembling before his friend as darkness moved across the village.

"He would have killed me. You saved my life."

"I had no choice." Nathan stood, still looking at the bleeding corpse. "What do we do now?" As the words escaped his mouth, two Roman soldiers ran from the clearing beyond the town. They stopped when they got close enough to see their comrade on the ground. "What happened?"

Tobias stepped forward and spoke quickly. "We heard fighting and ran to help. There were several men attacking your soldier when we arrived."

"You're bleeding." The man handed Tobias a strip of cloth that was carried for just such wounds.

Tobias wrapped his arm as he continued. "There were at least five of them. Nathan killed that one." He pointed to the villager's body beside the road. "We tried to help Darius." He nodded to the dead Roman. "But it was too late. He fought well, but there were just too many men in the ambush." Tobias tied the cloth around his wounded arm and picked up his own sword that lay in a puddle of blood near the dead soldier. "I wounded one of the others as well." He turned to the dead villager and wiped the blood from his sword on the corpse.

The soldier glanced at the dead man beside the road and then at Nathan's sword, also covered with blood. "You did well.

11

We'll find the others. A wounded man cannot go far." One of the Roman soldiers knelt beside Darius and examined their comrade. "Darius is dead. One of them must have sneaked up behind him. But there is blood on his sword as well. He must have fought even after they stabbed him." He turned to Nathan. "Which way did they go?"

"They ran down that path and disappeared into the darkness." Tobias pointed to the east. Nathan was still clearly stunned and only shook his head.

The Roman looked at the two and nodded toward the dead soldier. "Take Darius back to the deployment area. We will look for those who ambushed him."

The Roman was far heavier than expected. It took both Tobias and Nathan just to lift the man. When they stopped for a rest along the way, Nathan took Darius's sword and scabbard and hid them in some bushes growing alongside a small dwelling. The darkness had covered the village, and he was confident he had not been seen hiding the weapon. He made a mental note of the location and carefully covered the sword with limbs so that it would not easily be found. He wanted to study the weapon carefully; he also knew that kind of sword would be a prized possession for any man in the King's Guard.

As they deposited the body at the edge of the village, several of the soldiers were lighting torches around other bodies lying there as well. The gruesome sight was made even more alarming as the garish light of the torches flickered over the bloody corpses. The men in the village had fought bravely, but the battle had been brief. Six Jews were laid side by side in the sand, left as a message to any others who might want to challenge the soldiers in the future. Nathan looked at them and grimaced. They were brave men who had fought injustice in their village; now they were dead. Among them was a boy, probably no more than twelve. He was young, and he was clearly too small to wield a sword, but he had fought. Nathan considered that the boy might well have more honor than any other person in Judea that night. He wondered which of the mercenaries or Romans had done such a deed. He would never know, but he wished he did. Nathan was a large man, and he could wield a sword very well. He would have liked to challenge the coward who could kill so small a boy. He stood silent for a moment, then walked over to the dead Roman and carefully removed the cloak that had covered the body. He wanted the townspeople to see that they were not the only ones to pay a price that night. At least one of the Romans had been killed as well. Nathan glanced at the torches, then into the sky. What had happened to the large star that had given so much light just a few nights before? It was gone now, and like the deeds of the night, darkness had returned.

* * *

The sun had just begun climbing into the Eastern sky as the detail packed their things to leave. High above them the sun's rays were painting a bright red color in the clouds that drifted overhead. Like the blood puddled around the bodies still lying in the street, the bright clouds would shock the people, then soon they, too, would be gone. Darius' body was placed on a commandeered donkey and tied securely for the trip back to Jerusalem. Nathan and Tobias had joined the hunt for the purported wounded attacker and had avoided the slaughter that continued through the night. As they were preparing to leave, Nathan decided to check the magnificent sword that he had hidden. As he approached the bushes where the weapon was stashed, he heard weeping behind him. Turning quickly, he saw a young woman trying to pull the body of a slain man down the side of the road. She was crying and talking to herself as she struggled with the bloody load. Nathan recognized the voice

13

immediately. It was the mother of the deformed child. He pulled the cloth across his face and tied it securely. As he approached she slipped and fell into the dirt. She could go no further. He looked at her for just a moment. She was exhausted, covered in blood, and numb from the horrors she had witnessed. In the light of day he could see her face more clearly. She was, indeed, as young as he had assumed. She had long dark hair and large eyes. Even in her pain and covered with dirt and the blood of her husband, she was beautiful. When she raised her head, her eyes were red and blank. She had cried all of her tears, and now she simply sat on the side of the road, unable to move. Nathan walked over and lifted her to her feet; then he lifted the man's body. It was the man Darius had slain. He was much older than the young woman; Nathan guessed him to be in his early thirties. He was also very thin. Nathan was surprised how light he was, unlike the Roman soldier. "Where shall I take him?" The young woman barely looked in his direction. Finally she wiped her eyes and began the sad trek to her home. Nathan carried the man into the small house and placed the body on the floor in the center of the main room. He glanced around for the child, but the baby was not there, well hidden somewhere else. "Your husband?" She only nodded. "I'm sorry." He could think of nothing else to say, so he turned to leave. She said nothing as her eyes looked into his once again. As he stared into her face and witnessed such pain, he sensed a sadness that was unimaginable; exceeded only by a strength he could not comprehend.

Chapter 2

The following morning after the men returned to Jerusalem, Gilad had them all standing in formation outside the palace walls. They were dressed in their King's Guards uniforms and looked more like professionals than they had the prior evening. Slowly and deliberately he walked up and down the rows and stared into the eyes of each man as he questioned the teams about the events that had transpired in Bethlehem. As he anticipated, they all lied about the number of babies that had been killed; they doubled or even tripled the actual numbers. Gilad nodded somberly with each report. When he finished his review of the men, he dismissed them and called a young slave who served as his scribe. The commander lowered his head for several minutes in thought. Those nearby could see his eyes closed tightly as he considered his report to Herod. After a moment he tugged on his beard several times then looked up and doubled the already exaggerated number and ordered the young scribe to send the report to the king. The entire detail had actually been surprised at how few babies they had found. It was almost as if someone had warned many of the mothers in advance, because most of the children had been taken out of the small town before the troops arrived. Gilad looked at the final number and grimaced. Any number was painful to acknowledge. Thankfully one of the mothers in the village had received some kind of warning and had alerted the others. Most who had been warned had left, and many babies had been saved. Herod was briefed on the slaughter and was content that his orders had been accomplished. What he did not know was that the particular baby he sought was the first to be taken away before his troops arrived.

Gilad walked deliberately back to his office in the palace. Once inside he poured fresh water into a large bowl and washed his face and hands. A bright ray of light shone through his window and caught his attention for several minutes. There was a deep furrow between his full eyebrows and a dark frown upon his face. Finally, he diverted his eyes and stared at his hands. How much blood would he find there? How deep was the stain that Herod had forced upon him and his men? And another dark thought crept into his troubled mind. His men; how would they ever forgive him? How could he ever regain their trust? Would they understand the situation he had been forced to accept? Gilad walked to his desk and picked up a piece of bread that had been soaked in honey. He looked at it then slowly put it back on the plate. His appetite was gone. That was his state of mind when the young scribe walked into his office and announced he had a message from the king himself.

The commander frowned as the young man read the note from Herod. The king wanted to speak to him immediately. He stroked his beard repeatedly as he paced the room while the message was read a second time. His right hand massaged his forehead as he continued his pacing. He could feel the adrenalin being pumped through his body and the sharp, knife-like pain in the pit of his stomach. Gilad seldom knew fear in his life. He had fought in many battles and had challenged many men, but fear had never been a problem for this warrior. But this was different. This was a summons from King Herod, a powerful man who could threaten the only things Gilad treasured in his life, his command and his men. Was it possible that Herod knew the numbers Gilad had reported were false? Was Herod's singular fixation on his throne driving him toward even more despicable acts against his people? Were his men safe from the king's madness? His relationship with this man was complex and one he feared. "Fetch my cloak, the blue commander's robe."

"Yes commander; as you wish."

"And bring my brush. I need to look like a commander when I meet the king."

"And your sword?"

"I always carry my sword. I am the commander of the King's Guard after all." He forced a small smile for the young man helping him into his robes.

Gilad found Herod talking quietly with a man he did not recognize. Their conversation was obviously not about pleasant topics. Both men were speaking privately with eyes narrowed to mere slits. Finally, Herod glanced to his right and noticed Gilad standing across the room, waiting by the door. He lifted one finger as a signal and continued the conversation for several minutes. Then the unknown man bowed and backed away from the king. When he was at a proper distance, he stood, turned and left the room. Two slaves met him at the door and ushered him down the hallway. Herod stood with his head slightly bowed with his chin resting on his right fist. Then he straightened and turned toward Gilad. When he did he had a smile on his face. Gilad returned the smile, and a huge shadow disappeared from his troubled mind. "You requested my presence, my King?"

Herod thought for several moments before speaking. It was obvious he was finalizing a decision in the back of his mind. "Gilad, my commander." Herod stepped forward and put his right hand on Gilad's left shoulder. "I have been advised that some in Bethlehem are fomenting trouble as a result of the raid. Rome would be very displeased if we were to experience an insurrection there." Gilad nodded and the king continued. "So I think a show of force there might be in order. You know, have some troops there for a few weeks. What do you think?"

"My King, I think any presence by either the Romans or the mercenaries might fan those flames. I would suggest some of my guards instead."

"I see, and why would that make a difference?"

"I had my men disguise themselves during the raid. The Romans and the mercenaries were easily identified and are therefore hated by the villagers."

"Good. If the villagers don't know the guards were involved, they would not be seen as a threat. That was masterful thinking. You always surprise me with your well-planned strategies."

"Thank you, my King." Gilad paused for a moment, then continued when Herod did not reply. "My men will not be welcomed either, I suspect. But they will not be seen in the same light as the mercenaries or the Romans. We have a far better chance of observing the mood in the town without inciting violence from the citizens."

"How many men would you take?"

"We must not make it appear that we came to fight, so I would send only one of my units. Ten to twelve men should do. We'll tell the townspeople they are there to protect them. Some of the people will probably believe us." Gilad stroked his beard several times. "Perhaps we can spend some money in the market and share some supplies with the right people. That generally helps as well."

"You are a wise commander, Gilad. I always value your recommendations." Herod raised his hand and signaled for a slave who immediately brought wine and two goblets. "I'll tell my administrator to supply your men with some extra funds for the trip. I like that idea of spending in the market. That will gain us some support for sure." Herod's eyes narrowed again. "It is important that we ensure that Rome not become nervous about recent events in Bethlehem. We would not want that, would we?"

"No, my King. My men will handle this with utmost skill. I'll send my best guards to ensure that is the case. You need not worry further."

"That is good, Gilad. I knew I could count on you." Both men took a goblet of wine that the slaves proffered and raised them in a toast. As the two silver goblets clinked in unison, Gilad felt a moment of great relief. His fears were gone, and all he had to do was arrange a unit of his men to travel back to Bethlehem to demonstrate the king's insistence on stability and order in the realm.

* * *

Two weeks after the killings in Bethlehem, a small group of guards was sent back to the village to ensure that order had been restored and to report any remaining problems. Any talk of rebellion against the king was to be promptly stopped; Herod wanted peace, but he was more than willing to use force when necessary to demonstrate his control. A great deal of work had also been done to convince the population that the killings had been carried out by rogue soldiers and mercenaries. Some accepted that explanation; most did not. Either way, Herod wanted all to know he would accept no insurrection without bloodshed.

Nathan and Tobias were among the group selected to return to scout the small town and gather intelligence on the mood of the people. Since the King's Guards were Jews, they could mingle with the population more easily, and their observations should prove more accurate. Gilad put Nathan in command of the squad and gave them a day to prepare and pack for the trip.

The walk to Bethlehem was a short trek, and they planned to camp on the outskirts of town for two weeks, a symbol of the king's power.   Herod wanted all to know that there would be no insurrection, or more blood would flow in the tiny village. Gilad's instructions were somewhat different. Try to blend in with the villagers; make some friends; spend money and support the merchants; and do everything possible to avoid conflict.

Only three of the men selected for the trip to Bethlehem had participated in the unconscionable killing of the babies. They changed their clothes, wore different sandals, trimmed their beards, and wore their cloaks denoting they were the King's Guards. They did not want to be recognized by anyone in the town as having taken part in the massacre of the children. For this trip their pace was different from the last time they entered the small town. They stood tall and walked with the authority of the King's Guards. They passed citizens along the way who walked by without speaking; the townspeople were understandably suspicious of anyone who was not from the immediate area. Nathan had the men pack extra food rations in case they needed to stay longer than anticipated. He had planned for two weeks maximum, but provisions for almost a month were brought, a wise leader with an ulterior motive. The supplies could also be used to buy favor from the population if needed.

Initially the day was sunny and clear, but as they set up their camp, the weather turned cold with a strong wind blowing from the north and gathering clouds in the East. The men pulled their cloaks around themselves and sought shelter from the approaching storm. Everywhere people were distributing large clay jars to catch any rainwater that might drain from the small homes in the village. Men and women alike walked quickly through the village with armloads of sticks and firewood to provide warmth. Nathan was looking for a good spot to do the same when he spotted her. It was the same young woman with the deformed son. He paused and watched as she passed. She obviously did not recognize him and walked by without even a glance. He was thankful for that. As she continued down the street, he observed her carefully. She was dressed in a worn blue cloak and looked very thin. Her face was pale and drawn. Streaks of dirt lined her forehead and ran across her face, interrupted only by lines where tears had stained her cheeks. It appeared she had been ill, but Nathan knew differently. He could see quite clearly that she was starving. Without even thinking he turned and followed her down the road to the small house he had visited twice before. She had a few small sticks for fuel in her left hand. Her right held the child as she walked slowly toward the door. Nathan passed the house as she stepped inside. When she was out of sight, he stopped and turned around near the front door to leave but stopped suddenly. Inside he heard the cries of a small child, then the beautiful voice of a young woman singing a lullaby to the tiny voice crying in her arms. Nathan stood silently listening. It was soft, and the notes were more beautiful than any he had ever heard. Then the singing stopped, and he heard the muffled sounds of crying. The mother tried to sing again but dissolved into tears. Again she tried to sing, but again the music would not come. Instead, there were tears he could not see, but tears he understood. He looked down for only a moment as the cold air blew under his cloak and chilled him. Then he looked up, resolved, and turned and walked quickly to his men. He gave them orders and told them to stay out of sight as much as possible. If anything arose needing his attention, they were to contact him or Tobias immediately. Then he left. He had an urgent chore to complete as he stared at the dark clouds approaching. The sun had vanished, and the rain clouds grumbled in the East as the wind shifted and became colder. A few drops had already begun to fall. Nathan looked up at the clouds rushing through the heavens above, a mixture of black and several shades of dark gray. The darkness spoke of evil and frightening visions of thundering chariots racing across the open landscape in the sky. He pulled his cloak close around him and turned into the windblown rain; he was on a mission, one that had nothing at all to do with darkness or evil.

* * *

When Nathan stepped into the small house, he was not recognizable. All she saw was a large bundle of sticks and wood, with two legs extending below. Finally, he dropped the fuel onto the dirt floor beside the small fireplace. Then he turned to face the young woman clutching the child to her breast. She recoiled in fear, scrambling to the corner where she sat huddled, protecting her baby. "I will not harm you. I just brought some wood for a fire. It will be very cold tonight." As she looked deeply into his eyes, he stepped to the middle of the room and displayed his cloak so she could see it clearly. "Do you recognize this cloak? It is the cloak of the King's Guards. You need not fear me." He looked at the fireplace and put his hand over the coals. They were cold. He searched the small dwelling and found no food at all. "I'll be back." He walked into the street and looked around. Smoke was rising from several of the small homes, and he could see the light from a fire dancing in the windows of a small house across the street. Nathan knocked on the door and held a small stick to the man who opened the door. "May I have a light from your fire?" The man looked at him for a moment and said nothing. "Please?" Still nothing. Nathan frowned, slid his sword around so that it was visible in the evening light. "You can take this wood and light it, or I will take it and shove it through your ear. Which works best for you?" He smiled as he spoke. The man, older and smaller than Nathan, took the stick and returned in a moment with fire climbing along the wood. "Thank you, neighbor."

In a few minutes a fire was blazing in the small fireplace and the room was becoming warm. The young woman remained huddled in the corner watching Nathan with wary eyes. He searched the room and found a jug for water. It was empty. "Which way for water?" She pointed down the road. He left and returned later with a full jug. He smiled at her, but she simply watched him carefully. She did not seem afraid, only wary. As he unwrapped a sizeable portion of meat, her eyes broadened. It was the first time she turned her eyes away from him. He knew she was hungry. He felt the baby must also be hungry since he had not stopped crying since Nathan first arrived. Nathan set the meat aside and unwrapped a large loaf of bread. It was not fresh, but it still had the smell of Jewish bread. He smiled as her eyes skipped between the two. He tore a large piece of the bread and handed it to her. "Take it; I know you're hungry." She looked at him for several moments before taking it, but finally she reached and grabbed it, putting a large piece into her mouth immediately. The sword he carried served as a fine skewer to roast the meat over the open fire. As the smell of roasting lamb permeated the room, he watched her face. Her eyes were glued on the crackling meat as it hung above the fire. When it was cooked, he handed the entire portion to her. "This will make you stronger."

Finally she spoke. "What about you?"

"I've already eaten today. I'm fine." She tore a piece of the bread and a portion of the meat and handed it back to him. He smiled. "Thank you." Suddenly he realized he had forgotten something important. "I'll be back in a few minutes."

Nathan walked quietly along the road between the small houses and found the location where he had left Darius's sword. He stepped into a dark shadow of one of the houses and peered carefully in all directions. When certain he was not being watched, he retrieved the sword and hid it under his cloak as he walked back to the small house. It was beginning to rain and the wind caused him to shield his face from the blowing debris. The dark night would suddenly light up with the flashes of lightening that sent large white bolts flashing from the dark clouds to the earth below. For a moment the entire town would suddenly recoil from the crashing sound and the flash of light, then as quickly it would be dark again, and people would catch their breath and resume their daily routine. Once inside the house he laid the sword on a small table in the corner and began inspecting it carefully. The young woman slid back into the corner at the sight of the sword. "Don't worry. I will not harm you." The sword was wonderfully crafted, but it was not a ceremonial beauty; it was a fighting man's weapon. There were small nicks along the blade, reminders of past battles. It was big and heavy; it was also surprisingly dull. Nathan had not expected that. Obviously Darius had relied on his brute strength alone to wield the blade with great power to ensure success in battle. Nathan carefully slid his finger along the edge, feeling each of the nicks that he would remove with a thorough sharpening. How many men had died from a blow or a thrust of that sword? Probably many. It was regrettable that he had to kill Darius, but he had been left with no choice. Tobias was his best friend, and Tobias had needed his help. Nathan then examined the belt and the scarf that was tied around it and found a small leather pouch. Inside were a handful of coins. Nathan breathed in suddenly; to him it was a fortune. He looked quickly to see if the young woman was watching. She was talking to her baby as it tried to suckle her. Nathan knew she was unable to nurse the child. She was barely surviving herself. He counted the coins carefully then tucked the pouch into his own belt. It was an unexpected benefit from a contest he had not chosen, but one he had been forced to join.

When Nathan rolled his bedroll out onto the floor opposite the fireplace the young woman looked startled. "What are you doing?"

"Preparing a place to sleep."

"You're going to sleep here?"

"It's cold and wet outside, and, besides, I need to sleep here."

"You do? Why?"

"I have a roof to fix tomorrow." He pointed to the water dripping onto the floor in the corner of the room. "I'm Nathan. I will not harm you. I promise." She nodded and glanced at her baby. "I won't hurt your child either. I promise."

"Thank you for the food."

"Your neighbors wouldn't help you?"

"My child is not normal."

"You love him; don't you?"

"How did you know he's a boy?"

"When you spoke to him. You called him your little boy." Nathan smiled. "You also called him your little pumpkin."

She blushed slightly. "I call him that often." She paused for a moment, then looked into Nathan's eyes and continued, almost reluctantly. "The people in the village told me to leave him in the desert."

"You have no one?"

"My husband was killed in a raid."

"I'm sorry to hear that. It must be difficult without him."

"He was a good man and took care of us as best he could."

Nathan could see the sadness in her eyes and changed the subject. "I think the child is hungry."

She frowned. "I have no milk for him. When he cries it hurts my heart."

Nathan walked over to the two and put out his hand toward the child. She pulled the baby to her breast immediately. Then she looked into his face and slowly moved the child toward the smiling man. He folded the cloth back and saw a beautiful little boy, with one exception. His left leg was not fully developed. "He's beautiful."

She beamed. "Yes, yes he is."

"What is his name? And what is your name?"

"His name is Samuel." She looked down at the child. "And I am Rebecca."

The food soon brought sleep to the tired young woman. She was laying on a thin blanket on the floor, her baby cradled in her arms. Nathan stood and looked at her. He studied her long dark brown hair and when she finally opened them, her beautiful eyes. They were dark and very large. He could see that she was quite thin. She had not eaten well even before the loss of her husband. He guessed her to be several inches shorter than he, but then, he was a relatively tall man in his society. Unlike her, he had been well fed as a guard in the palace. He had watched as she tried to feed the baby the bread he had given her, but it was just too young to eat regular food. Nathan lived among men, but he also knew a few things about families. His own mother and father had been significant in his life. They had taken care of their son; they had taught him everything they could—everything except the ability to read and write. That was something they could not give; neither of them possessed that gift to offer their son. Rebecca tried to watch him, but soon sleep returned and her eyes closed. As he watched her fighting to keep her eyes open, an idea began to form in his mind. The child needed milk, and perhaps he knew where he might secure that.

The wind outside blew harder and the rain fell upon the roof and dripped into the dwelling. Nathan could feel the cold and put extra wood on the fire. He then took his cloak and placed it over the young woman and the child. As he did, he slid his own bedroll closer to the flames. He lay there and surveyed the small house. Her husband must have worked hard for little return, but he had taken care of his family as most poor men attempt to do; he gave them everything he could, even when there was little to give. Nathan wondered what profession he had followed. The only thing he knew for sure about this man was that he was brave. So too was his wife. He glanced over at her face and fell asleep to the sounds of dripping water and an occasional cry from a hungry baby.

* * *

When Rebecca awoke in the morning she looked up into a smiling face. "I have something special for Pumpkin." Nathan held up a small jug. Rebecca sat upright and peered into it. "It's milk. When we were coming into town yesterday, I saw a field of goats. I went down this morning and got some milk." He smiled at the baby. "It's for Samuel."

She looked up and a small tear ran down her cheek. "Thank you, Nathan." She tested his name carefully, for the first time.

"Give the baby all he will drink, but also you should drink some as well. It will help you to feed him yourself." He smiled at the two. "I'll get more this evening." Rebecca looked at the cloak that had covered her during the night. More tears escaped her eyes. Nathan knelt beside her and just smiled. Then he reached and touched her arm. "I must leave to see my men. I will return in the evening. While I'm gone I need you to hide this for me. It belonged to one of the Roman soldiers who was killed here. I don't know what to do with it yet, so no one can know I have it. Will you hide it for me?" He handed the sword to the young woman who took it with both hands and studied it carefully. After a moment she nodded and put the weapon under the blanket she slept on. "Hold out your hand."

"Why?"

"Just hold it out." She studied him carefully and finally held out her right hand. He placed his hand over hers. When he removed it, several coins were in her palm. She looked at them carefully and then up at him. "Go to the market and get whatever you need: food for you and the baby, a new blanket to keep you both warm, whatever you need. If anyone asks where you got this, tell them it came from the king. If that is not sufficient, I'll discuss it with them later. Her eyes filled with tears again as he walked out the door.

Chapter 3

The smell of rain still permeated the air as the three men walked through the streets of Bethlehem, stepping around small puddles that spotted the road and reflected the hot sun that would soon provide the heat to dry them. With only one day in camp, they were already gaining some insights into the small town and the people who lived there. As expected, there were angry people in the village, and the loss of the children was still evident in mourning families, but any idea of a revolt was far from anyone's mind in Bethlehem. Tobias and Nathan were joined by another friend from their youth, Kalev, as they prepared to scout the town. They enjoyed having Kalev along. He was always animated and always excited about something. They made a good team. Nathan was always calm and thoughtful; Tobias was the thinker and strategist; and Kalev was the energy of the adventure. Tobias was watching Nathan carefully as they walked slowly through Bethlehem, noticing everything. Unlike before, they were all wearing their King's Guards robes. They were emissaries of the king, and everyone knew who they were. The people also understood quite well why these men were walking through their town every day and gave them wide berth.

Tobias had grown up with Nathan and knew him well, but he was beginning to notice a very distinct change in his friend. It was as if today were his birthday. It was a day of celebration. Nathan was happy; there was a perpetual smile on his face. What had changed him so suddenly? Nathan glanced down a small side street as the men walked along. About a block away several men were leaning against a wall, talking. Then one of them laughed loudly. Nathan nodded slightly and proceeded, increasing the pace. He had ordered that the men would travel in groups of no less than three. If they were attacked, three could form a defensive posture and drive most civilians away if necessary. They all carried small swords under their cloaks, much easier to conceal than the larger Roman blades, but the size of their swords didn't bother Nathan or Tobias. They didn't anticipate encountering adversaries with Roman armament. A knife or a farming tool was about the worst they could face in this small town.

The sun was rising in the east, and the morning coolness was beginning to change to the dry heat of the semi-arid desert. The men stopped at a small well to refill their water containers, small jugs that had to be carried in small packs on their backs. As Tobias filled his, he glanced at Kalev and smiled at Nathan. "You seem in a good mood today. Are you that happy to be away from Jerusalem? And where were you last night? We worried about you out in that storm."

"I spent the night on a dirt floor."

"Well, I hope it was at least dry."

"It wasn't. The roof leaked."

"You must have slept in your cloak. I saw how dirty it was this morning."

"Actually, a young woman slept under my cloak last night."

A quick smile spread across Tobias's face. "Aha! So you were with a woman last night. Was she pretty?"

As Kalev filled his water jug Nathan pulled Tobias aside and spoke quietly. "Remember the woman with the deformed child."

"Yes."

"I've stayed at her house several times this week."

Tobias's eyes widened. "You did? Why are you staying there?"

"She was starving. The neighbors shunned her because of the baby. She hadn't eaten in several days. I had to do something."

Tobias looked down and nodded. "Is there something I can do to help?"

"Actually, I do need your help. The men will start to question where I am on occasion. Tell them I am staying with one of the town leaders to build confidence in Herod. I don't want them involved in this. And when I need your help, I'll let you know."

"I can handle the men. But how long will you be away from the detachment?"

"I'll be here most days and on occasion I'll return to sleep with the men. But some evenings I will disappear until daylight the next day."

"So you'll be spending your nights mostly with her?" There was a playful tone in Tobias's voice.

"It's not like that. She is alone with a crippled child. If we can help her for a while, then I feel we should. Her husband was the man Darius killed by the road." Nathan looked at his friend to gauge his response. It came quickly.

"Damn that bastard. I'm glad he's dead." Tobias unconsciously rubbed his old wound and glanced over his shoulder as Kalev finished stuffing his water jug inside his pack. "But now we have to clean up the mess he made for everyone else."

"Maybe tomorrow evening you can accompany me to the *town leader's* house and meet *him*." Both men became suddenly quiet as their comrade joined them. "Are, you ready to go?"

"Set."

"Let's pick up the pace a bit. I'd like to visit the market today before it gets too hot."

"Good plan." Kalev grinned at his friends. "And I'd like to sample some of their local wine."

"Just make sure the sample is only a sample. Don't forget you are wearing the robes of the King's Guard."

"Oh, I brought another cloak, just for situations like this." All three men were laughing as they proceeded along the narrow road bantering as only a group of young men can.

* * *

The sun was slowly sinking in the late afternoon sky, sending golden rays across the few clouds that lingered over the dry landscape. Far off in the distance a lone cloud rose high above the hills reflecting gold and red hues back across the countryside. The men looked up and marveled at the colorful image that towered into the blue sky. The warmth of the day lingered and sent small trickles of sweat down Nathan's forehead. He had been working with his men and was tired. Mostly, he was hungry. His mind traveled from the bright sunlight on the clouds to the dark room where he had slept the prior night. A smile crept across his face. The contrast was dramatic, but both caused him to smile. Nature's beauty painted across the sky had caused him to stop in awe to look, but the beauty he had found in that small house had no less of an impact on his heart. Both were gifts to remind him that even in the midst of a troubled and bleeding world, beauty and love prevailed. The sound of Rebecca singing to her child echoed through the darkest corners of his mind, and he found himself smiling and humming the same lullaby. He looked quickly to see if any of the men might have heard him.

As the men began their chores to prepare their evening meal, Nathan nodded slightly to Tobias and slipped quietly out of the camp and hurried to the small house on the edge of

Bethlehem. He hoped Rebecca had gone to the market and had purchased enough food to include him. Then a sudden realization flashed across his mind. He did not know if she could even cook. But all Jewish girls were taught to cook, weren't they?

Nathan's smile disappeared when he entered the house. Two men were standing in the middle of the room. They had knives and sticks in their hands. Rebecca was crouched in the corner on her bed. When she saw Nathan she rose quickly and moved between him and the two armed men. She began to shout. "Go away. Leave my home. This is a good man. He has not harmed you."

The taller of the two spoke slowly, watching Nathan carefully. The man was shorter than Nathan by several inches and much lighter. "You are one of the King's Guards. We know who you are. You protect Herod, the baby killer." As the man stepped forward with the knife extended toward Nathan Rebecca stepped backward and continued to shout at the men. That was when Nathan saw what she had hidden behind her back. It was the Roman sword, and it was out of its scabbard. Nathan grabbed the sword as the man lunged forward. He pushed Rebecca to the side and moved quickly to his right, striking the man with the flat side of the blade. The sword did not cut the intruder, but the impact knocked him to the floor. Very quickly Nathan stepped forward and put the point of the sword on the neck of the second man. "On the ground! Now!" The trembling man did as he was told. Nathan kicked him and shoved him beside the other prostrate man. "Turn over and sit up, both of you. Don't rise!" The man lying on his stomach groaned as he rolled over and sat upright. "I could have easily killed both of you. You attacked a member of the King's Guard. There would be no questions." He paused as the two men winced at his words. "But I'm not going to do that. Do you know why?" When the men made no response, he said it again, louder, holding the large sword in the air above them. "Do you know why I'm going to let you live?"

"No."

"What did you say?"

The man forcibly spoke more loudly. "No, I don't know."

"Well listen very carefully and take this back to all your friends." He paused to ensure their attention. When he spoke, he spoke very slowly and deliberately. Both men leaned forward to hear his words as he began quietly. "I'm going to let you live because I have never killed a Jew—never! I know you have problems with the king." His voice rose as he continued. "But you have no problem with me. I have not harmed Bethlehem. I am a Jew like you. We believe the same things." He paused for emphasis. When he resumed it was much louder. "But, if I am attacked again, I will kill you both. Is that understood? There is no rock under which you can hide. I will find you and violate a vow I took long ago to protect Jews and the king." Again he paused, then in a much lower voice he continued. "Do you understand what I have said?"

"Yes, yes."

"I can be a friend when needed, or I can be the worst enemy you can imagine. It is really your choice. And when you leave, you will treat this woman with respect. You are small men to abandon her after her husband was slain. Unlike you, he was a man of honor and courage." Nathan paused to let his words sink into their consciousness. "Her husband was courageous. He fought for his family. What did you do?" He paused again for emphasis. "Perhaps you can try to measure up as well." Both men were staring at the floor. "Now leave. And I don't want to see either of you again unless you come as a friend, or next time I won't use the broad side of my sword." Nathan lowered the sword and stepped back two steps. "Now, go!" The men scrambled to their feet and ran out the door.

"I'm glad you didn't kill them."

"I understand their anger. It was just misplaced." Nathan smiled at the woman standing beside him. "And thanks for handing me the sword."

"You used it well."

"It is a beautiful weapon, if one can call a weapon beautiful. It was well made. I hope I can keep it."

Rebecca reached and took the sword from his hand. She lifted it above her head and then swung it in front of her. "It's heavy." She smiled quickly, "and very uncomfortable when you sit on it for half an hour."

"Yes, the Romans design them that way, big and heavy. Our swords are smaller and lighter, but ours are sharper." He studied the sword carefully. "I need to do some work on this one—if I am allowed to keep it."

She stared at him for several moments before speaking. "What do you think those men will tell their friends?"

"Most likely, lies. They will tell them how they frightened us. But their friends will know they're lying." Both smiled. Then Nathan did something he had never done. He reached out and touched her cheek. She closed her eyes and turned slightly away from him. "Thank you, Rebecca. I see I was right about you."

Her head snapped back immediately. "What do you mean you were right about me?"

"I knew you were a very brave woman. You don't quit when life is difficult." He put his hand under her chin and raised her eyes to his. "I like that about you—very much." Suddenly it was Nathan's cheeks that were turning red. Rebecca put her hand on his cheek and laughed out loud. "Nathan, I think you are blushing."

"You are a silly girl, and Pumpkin is crying for his dinner."

"Well he can just have his dinner while we have ours." She scooped the child into her arms and settled him on her left hip as she began serving the food.

Nathan sat on the floor and watched the two. He determined two things as he smiled at the scene before him. One, he had never been happier in his life, and two, tomorrow he would purchase two chairs and a small table. He was tired of sitting on the floor.

Chapter 4

The commander of the Temple Guards walked through the Double Gate and down the steps on the south side of the Temple. He scanned the crowds and unobtrusively joined a group of Jews heading west towards their homes for the evening meal. Unlike the commander of the King's Guards, El'Azar was heavy by Hebrew standards. His arms were not muscular, but that was not a problem for him. His weapon was his mind, not a weapon he might wield in battle. He walked with purpose and took note of the two men who walked up beside him and assumed his pace. El'Azar smiled as he watched each of them glance back carefully at the two armed men who followed at a distance of twelve feet. The two were obviously unnerved by the presence of armed men behind them. "Don't worry about my guards. They are very capable and take their orders from me."

The older man was having difficulty keeping up with the commander's stride. "Can you slow it down a bit? I'm not as young as you."

El'Azar slowed perceptibly and began speaking in a very conspiratorial voice, causing both men to strain to hear his words. "Tomorrow afternoon Herod will be showing a very important centurion his new creation. They meet first at the palace, then they will have to walk across the empty field to the theater."

"You are certain?"

"It is on his schedule."

"Will they be guarded?"

El'Azar slowed his pace and turned to look at the man who asked the question. After a moment he spoke with derision. "Of course they will be guarded. Have you ever seen Herod without his guards? He probably has guards in his toilet."

"And the centurion?" The Temple Commander turned again and stared at the questioner. He shook his head in contempt but said nothing. "Any idea of numbers?"

"You might ask Herod. I'm sure he could answer your concerns." With that El'Azar motioned to his own guards and turned right, leaving the two men standing in the path.

Chapter 5

The soldiers stood in two rows; Romans on the left and the King's Guards on the right. Herod was meeting with the Primus Pilus, the leading centurion of the first cohort of one of the most decorated legions in the Roman army. All troops were at attention. The position of Primus Pilus was the epitome of success for any Roman soldier. He was a man respected by soldiers and leaders of the Roman Empire alike. He was the epitome of strength and honor, a man his soldiers would die for. Slowly the king and his entourage began walking southeast from the palace toward the newly constructed theater, about three hundred yards away. It was late afternoon and the heat of the day was dissipating slightly as they walked along the small, dusty road. The king and the centurion chatted affably as the entourage proceeded slowly toward their goal. Nathan and three other guards walked in a parallel line with four Roman soldiers. The dignitaries were protected inside the guards' formation. All were armed and alert. When they had walked about half-way, a group of citizens stood beside the road watching, and some were waving at the king. The guards and the soldiers watched the crowd carefully since they would pass very near the group. Nathan was scanning their eyes, cloaks that might hide weapons, and unusual groupings. Something didn't make sense. Why would this group have a wagon with them? Then it became apparent as they neared the crowd. A man suddenly stepped back and threw off the cover on the small wagon. It was filled with weapons. That is when the attack took place. Men on both sides of the road rushed forward from the crowd with swords and spears and surprised the entourage. In total there were almost two dozen men charging toward the king and his guest.

The attackers had depended upon surprise to catch the guards unprepared. That was their first mistake. The King's Guards walked with their hands on their swords at all times. Withdrawing their weapons was quick and efficient. The Roman soldiers walked with spears and shields as well as their swords. That gave them an advantage over any enemy rushing toward them. What the attackers had as their advantage was their number. Twenty against eight meant that some of the attackers would undoubtedly reach the two men the guards were protecting. The king was their primary target, but the Primus Pilus would be a welcomed bonus as well. Both represented the power of Rome over Judea, and both were hated equally.

The Roman soldiers immediately raised their shields and charged forward, initiating a fierce battle. The spears took out the first line of attackers and their swords challenged the remaining men before them. Nathan and his men, unlike the advancing Roman soldiers, fell back and formed an arch around their king and the centurion. Twelve men rushed around the ensuing battle and charged the king. As they approached, the guards stepped forward and met them with ferocious combat. Men screamed, sometimes in anger, sometimes in pain. The fighting was difficult, and the guards began a slow pace backward toward the king and the centurion as the fighters advanced. Nathan dodged a sword and struck the attacker under his right arm. The man went down and another stepped into his place. As the fighting intensified, Nathan looked quickly to see where the king was located. It was then that he saw three men advancing on the centurion who held only a dagger. Nathan quickly stepped back and tossed his large sword to the Primus Pilus. He then drew his smaller Jewish sword and continued with the battle around him. Suddenly the attackers backed away and began a slow retreat. Nathan turned his attention again to his charges. Two of the King's Guards stood on either side of the king, poised to fight. Ten yards to his right the centurion was fighting three men with the sword Nathan had thrown him. Nathan rushed to challenge the third man, while several of the Roman soldiers were running toward their leader. With consummate skill the centurion dispatched both of the men before him with the large sword as Nathan finished the one behind him.

It all started so quickly, and so quickly it was over. Nathan took his defensive stance and carefully assessed the battle scene. The attackers left as quickly as they came. Two Roman soldiers were killed and three injured. One of the guards was also injured but not seriously. Enemy dead were scattered around the site of the battle. The king walked among his men and saluted them. The Primus Pilus did the same for his soldiers. In the distance they could see a detachment of guards running toward them with Gilad leading and outpacing most of the younger men. As the additional guards formed a new defensive position, Gilad rushed to the king. "My King, are you injured?"

Herod stepped forward and put his hand on the commander's shoulder. "No, your men did an excellent job of repelling a much larger force. You should be proud of them, Gilad. They fought well."

The centurion walked forward and joined the conversation. "Yes they did, and that man saved my life." He pointed toward Nathan. "In the midst of the battle he gave me his sword to defend myself as the rebels broke through the ranks. Without it I would have fought three of them with only my dagger." He motioned to Nathan to approach. "Thank you. You saved my life." He looked at the bloody sword in his hands. "You even furnished a special sword, a heavy one that would feel familiar." Nathan said nothing but bowed slightly. The centurion nodded to Gilad. "As his commander, I return his sword to you." Gilad took the sword that was proffered but handed it back to the centurion. It was obvious that there was a measure of respect between the two. Both were military men; both respected men of the sword.

"This is a Roman sword and a strong weapon. It rightly belongs to you."

The Primus Pilus studied it carefully. "I recognize this sword. We lost a man in Bethlehem, Darius. He had a very special sword, one from far away. Is this that sword?"

Gilad looked at Nathan. Nathan answered quickly. "Yes, Centurion."

Gilad spoke quickly. "Nathan fought beside your soldier in Bethlehem. They were fighting together when he was killed."

The centurion stood silently studying Nathan. Finally he spoke. "You are a very capable swordsman. You are also a man of honor. You gave me the better sword in the battle today and fought with a smaller one." Nathan's Jewish sword was still in his hand, covered with blood. "You prevailed against several attackers even though you were fighting with an inferior weapon. That must never happen again." The centurion studied the sword for several moments. "It was carried by a professional soldier. You shall carry on that tradition. The sword is now yours."

Nathan bowed slightly. "Thank you, Sir."

"And if any man questions why you have this sword, show him this." He handed Nathan his own dagger with the seal of the Primus Pilus on the handle. "Your bravery has earned you this honor." The leader of the first cohort in the Legion raised the sword high above his head and spoke to his soldiers who stood at attention listening to his words. "Men of the First Cohort, I raise this sword today and salute it and the man who carries it." He struck his clinched fist sharply against his breast armor. "Warriors so recognize men of honor. I expect you to do the same." He handed Nathan the sword, and all of the Roman soldiers saluted.

Nathan returned the salute with a clenched fist to his breast, then turned and took his place in the ranks. As he departed he could feel the weight of the sword as it bounced against his thigh. It was heavy, but now he could wear it without fear of detection. He had much to tell Rebecca that night.

Chapter 6

Herod walked onto the palace patio and promptly ordered wine. He was beginning his second goblet when his wife approached. "My Lord, you look disturbed. I heard there was an attack on your party today. Were you harmed?"

"I'm fine. There were about twenty rebels, but between my guards and the soldiers with the centurion, we fought them off."

"I'm glad you were not harmed." She poured herself some wine and sat opposite the king on a large, soft pillow of red linen. "Did you catch the attackers?"

"We killed most of them; the others ran like rabbits."

She caught the word "we" and smiled to herself. She was trying to imagine Herod wielding a sword in battle. "Who are these people? What is their grievance? Why would they attack their king?"

"Let's see. Just who could hate the king of Israel?" Herod smiled at his wife. "Let's count our enemies. The Saducees hate me because I terminated the rule of the old royal house—their people. The Orthodox Jews hate me because I have Greek tastes; even my name, Herod, is Greek. The Pharisees despise anyone who doesn't consider their law supreme for the country. Now let's see, who else hates me. Oh yes, everyone else hates me because they think my Idumean heritage is not truly Jewish, even though John Hyrcanus forced us to convert to Judaism. They see me as a half-Jew whose mother was actually an Arab, and, oh yes, I also impose too many taxes; there are even rumors that I have had David and Solomon's tombs scavenged for their gold." Herod poured more wine. "And we cannot forget the Parthians. They are sworn enemies of the Romans, so they hate me since I am allied with

Rome." Herod smiled. "I think that about covers it. I guess I probably have a few friends, but they only want what I can give them."

"You are certainly a popular man, my dear. But you forgot one major transgression."

"And what is that?"

"When you put the Roman Golden Eagle over the entry to the temple—that was not welcomed by many. That gained you no points with the priests."

Herod laughed. "You're right. That did aggravate a lot of people." He looked off into the night and took another drink of his wine. The heat of the day had given way to a beautiful evening with thousands of stars blinking from the heavens. That, and the wine, relaxed the king and caused him to pause briefly. "You are right, of course, but that Golden Eagle did assure our Roman friends that we recognize the emperor, and, after all, they are the ones with power. I always seek the source of power in choosing my allies. And for now, the power in this world is Rome."

Chapter 7

It was just after dark when the men began arriving at the fashionable house located in one of Jerusalem's nicer neighborhoods. It was a large house with many rooms on two floors. It was made of carefully cut stones and fine tile floors. In the courtyard just off the road, there was a large water fountain that fed an even larger granite pool below it. The smell of freshly baked bread and roasted lamb permeated the entire dwelling. The visitors came in pairs or individually, never in groups. Each was met at the door and allowed entrance. It was obvious that all of the men were well known to each other. There were no strangers in the group. After the last man entered, two young men walked outside and sat at the entrance of the home. There were two others at the rear of the house. They were not armed, but each had a hand carved whistle to alert those inside if needed. The young men appeared to be simply sitting in the warm evening talking, but all four were alert and watching for anyone who approached. Inside, things were different. The men greeted each other a bit more emotionally than usual; the conversations were a bit more subdued. Their meeting for the evening was not a pleasant one; their purpose was to discuss the attempt on Herod's life, an endeavor they had supported with money and men, an endeavor that had failed. Many of their men were now dead. After they sat down, the leader stood and surveyed the group. He nodded to the youngest man in the group as he spoke. "How many men did we lose?"

"Nine plus two injured."

"How bad are the injuries?"

"They will recover."

"Where are they now?"

"We have them hidden in Jericho."

The leader stroked his beard in thought. "That's good. Herod's men will be looking for anyone with a sword wound. Keep them out of sight for the time being."

One of the other men with a graying beard nodded to the leader and spoke. It was obvious the others paid him deference. "What happened? Why did we fail?"

The younger man turned to address the question. "We expected the King's Guards and also the Roman soldiers, but we underestimated their strength."

"How many men did they have?"

"Eight."

"Only eight?" The old man rubbed his forehead for several moments. "And we had twenty?"

The younger man anticipated the next question and spoke before it could be uttered. "They had superior weapons. Our small swords are equal to those of the guards, but they were no match for the Romans' spears and shields. They blocked our initial charge, and that gave their men the ability to counter-attack." He paused a moment remembering the slaughter along the road. "Three men broke through, but the guards had formed a defensive position around the king and the centurion."

The older man climbed to his feet slowly and walked across the room to the younger man who had been speaking. He looked at him for several minutes then reached and pulled back his cloak. There was a blood stain on the shoulder of the young man's tunic. "How bad is it?"

"I will be okay."

"You lost friends yesterday fighting bravely for the Jewish people. You have the respect of every man in this room." As he returned to his seat he said aloud. "We failed this time, but Herod's days are numbered. We are not finished with him."

The titular leader of the group waited until the older man was seated then addressed the group again. "We learned something important yesterday. We are not military men; we are merchants and farmers and men of business. We must learn to think like Joshua. We must learn to fight with skill." The men murmured and nodded. "One other lesson we learned yesterday is that numbers of men alone will not achieve our goals. We also need strategy, tactics, and weapons, especially weapons. Better weapons and lots of them."

In the back of the room a man slowly rose to his feet. He held out his hands for help. It was obvious he was blind. "I think I may have a contact who can help us with weapons." Immediately the group turned to listen to his words. "This must be kept in utmost confidence, but I am working on a contact with a highly placed person. If I can convince this man of our purpose, he is in a position to help with information and perhaps even weapons. We need both."

Several of the men spoke at once. "Who is this man? Can he be trusted?"

"I will not divulge his name yet, for his protection, and I have not divulged any of your names as well, for your protection. I will follow this lead and see where it goes." He nodded in the general direction of the leader. "I will keep our leader informed, but no one else should speak of this." Slowly, and with effort, he sat back down.

The leader turned to the young man, still standing on the far side of the room. "Who do you have who is an expert on weapons? I fear my knowledge in this topic is very limited."

"I have such a man."

"Bring him to this house tomorrow evening. I will select a few of us to question him." He thought a moment. "Would he also have knowledge of tactics in battle?"

"Perhaps some."

The blind man waved both of his arms in the air. "The man I spoke of is an expert. He understands such things. When he is ready, I will ask him to speak to us."

"Be sure he can be trusted first. We must keep this group secret, as we pledged the night we agreed to cooperate in this endeavor." The blind man nodded affirmatively with exaggerated gestures. "Okay, we are agreed." The leader turned to the young man standing across the room. "We grieve for the losses we had yesterday, but they did not die in vain. We will get Herod. It may take weeks, months, or even years, but we will get him and place his head on a pike before the temple." There were exclamations of agreement from every man in the room. "Wine and food will now be served. When you leave, do so individually, and watch for anyone taking note of your passing along the road."

Chapter 8

The eight men walked slowly along the hot, dusty road toward Jerusalem. They were tired, and all were ready for a rest. Physically it had been a challenging day, even for strong young men. They were nearing the outskirts of Jerusalem when a detachment of Roman soldiers approached and confronted them. "And where are you going?"

Nathan stepped forward as the senior guard in the group. "We are traveling to Jerusalem."

"What is your purpose there? I see you are all armed."

"We are members of the King's Guard." Nathan stood straight and stared back at the Roman soldier. He pulled his cloak around to show the distinctive markings of the king's personal guards. "We have been on assignment for the king."

"What king is that?"

"King Herod."

"Herod is not your king. Your king is Augustus Caesar." The Roman soldiers had been watching the Jewish contingency carefully, especially their weapons.

"Herod is our Jewish king; Caesar is our Roman emperor." Nathan looked quickly at his men. All eight had their hands on the handles of their swords. The Roman squad was equal in number and they, too, were clearly getting ready for a fight. "Now let us pass."

"You will pass when I say so. Now turn and return from whence you came." The Roman commander pulled his sword and glared at Nathan.

"If you insist." Nathan pulled his own sword and stood his ground. "I will ask you again, let us pass."

The Roman soldier was shocked as he studied Nathan's sword. "That is not a Jewish sword. Where did you get that? Give me that sword."

"It was presented to me by one of your centurions, the Primus Pilus himself. I yield it to no one. If you want it, you will have to take it." By now all of the soldiers on both sides had their swords drawn. Nathan stepped back a step. "If you insist on a fight, I propose it be between just you and me. There is no sense in our men fighting as well. Will you accept those terms?"

"Accepted!"

"Then all of the remaining troops -- put your swords back in your scabbards. As professional soldiers we are agreed." Slowly all of the men returned their swords to their scabbards, carefully watching the men of the opposing force. With a nod each man signaled his crew to back away; slowly they complied. As they did; the Roman soldier rushed Nathan, swinging his sword at waist height. Nathan quickly stepped aside, and the arc of the blade missed him by inches. "You fight like a coward, not a Roman soldier. Normally we step back and begin together. Both men hold their swords out straight and nod to each other. Only then do both men point their swords toward the other." The Roman, surprised by Nathan's demeanor and skill stepped back and let him talk. "Now we fight as equals. My sword is as good as your own." The Roman rushed forward and swung his sword, but Nathan blocked his blow, knocking the man to the ground. The soldier quickly rose to one knee, but Nathan was upon him too quickly, knocking the sword from the man's hand. Quickly Nathan picked up the sword and threw it behind him. Then he advanced on the soldier, his sword high above his head. The man scrambled backward and fell to the ground. The Roman soldiers stepped forward, but the Jewish guards stepped quickly before them. For a long moment Nathan stood over the fallen adversary, his sword high in the air above the fallen victim.

Then Nathan stepped backward two steps and sheathed his sword. Holding his hand out, he helped the man stand. "I have no desire to kill you. We may fight side-by-side someday." Nathan watched the man's hands carefully. "It would be unwise to pull your dagger. Have you seen mine?" He raised the Primus Pilus's dagger high into the air. "As I said, it was a gift from your Primus Pilus, given to me in Jerusalem."

"I have heard that story. Was it you who saved his life?" The Roman soldier stood, carefully watching Nathan. "You are a worthy warrior. I salute you." The soldier hit his right fist against the armor on his chest. "I have heard the story of your sword, but I did not recognize it."

Nathan turned and watched as all of the men moved their hands from their swords. "Men, we have a long walk ahead of us, let us be on our way."

"Before you go, won't you share our water, and we have food as well." The Roman soldier put his hand out to grasp Nathan's. "We passed an orchard down the road. Come, let us sit in the shade together and eat."

Nathan looked at his men then nodded. They were hungry, and their water was running low. Together, as would be the case so often in history, fighting men stopped to share their food and conversation. "What is your name?"

"I am Cyprianus, leader of the third unit in our cohort."

"And I am Nathan. I would prefer that we be friends rather than enemies. We both seek the same goal. Peace along these roads."

"I agree, Nathan, my new ally."

Chapter 9

Nathan, Tobias, and two other men stopped under the shade of a sycamore tree to rest as they approached Bethlehem. Their initial assignment had lasted over a month, and they had returned on several occasions to ensure the town was not a threat to the peace Herod demanded. The sun was beating upon the earth, and the water in their jugs was hot from the waves of heat that rose from the burning sand on the rocky road. But even hot water was welcomed by their sweating bodies. Nathan looked toward the north. There were small clouds in the distance; otherwise it was a clear sky, the sky they all knew so well. Tobias downed the last of his water and turned to his friend. "Are you going to run the rest of the way to Bethlehem?" Nathan said nothing but smiled as he stared into the distance. He estimated they were only about another hour's walk to their destination. "The rest of us have had difficulty keeping up with you this morning. I personally think you are in love." Tobias watched his friend carefully to see his reaction.

"I think you're right." It would be difficult to discern which man was more surprised at the comment. It was the first time Nathan had admitted his feelings about Rebecca; it was a fact he had finally discovered himself.

* * *

After the team was briefed, Nathan made his excuses and left. It was a short walk to the little house he had learned to love. He hefted his pack onto his back and noted that it was heavy, far heavier than those of his men. He had gifts inside.

Nathan heard the shouting as he turned the corner a stone's throw from the house. Then he saw the crowd. There were over a dozen villagers standing outside, and Rebecca stood beside her door clutching Samuel. The shouting voices were a cacophony of anger, all directed at the woman and the baby. Nathan tried to shout above the din from the crowd, but to no avail, so he pulled his sword and held it high in the air. A ripple of silence flowed over the crowd, and soon everyone had turned to stare at the man with the weapon walking into their midst. As he approached Rebecca he turned and spoke loudly to the silent crowd. The sword in his right hand now hung loosely by his side. "What is going on here? Why are you shouting at this woman?"

An older woman in the group stepped forward and spoke, her eyes on the sword. "In our culture women do not sleep with a man who is not her husband."

"What does *our* culture say about widows with children? Does it tell you to let them starve?" He used the word "our" to emphasize that he, too, was a Jew.

"But the child is..." the woman glanced at Rebecca and the baby. "Her child was marked from birth."

"Would you kill such a child?" He offered his sword to the woman. She stepped back, looking at the ground at her feet.

"Our culture has rules. Rules, rules, rules. But it lacks something important. It lacks love. You know Jewish laws, but you know nothing about love." Nathan's eyes glared at the small crowd.

Someone in the crowd shouted back. "And you do?"

"Yes, I do. I took care of this woman and her child while you condemned them. I fed them and protected them when you abandoned them." He raised his head high and looked at the crowd. "I know about love." He glanced back at Rebecca. "I love this woman, and I love the child she holds. The boy is from another father, a good and brave man. I will honor that man, and I will raise his child. And why wouldn't I? This child's mother

54

is my wife." The crowd stepped backward in unison, but their surprise was small compared to the look on Rebecca's face. *Wife?* Nathan stepped forward toward the people. "Who among you can read?"

A Pharisee stepped forward. "I can."

"Then read this." Nathan handed him a small scroll. The scribe took the document and studied it for a moment. When finished he looked first at Nathan, then Rebecca, then the crowd. "Read it—loudly!"

"In case of death all possessions of Nathan, son of Adonais, a guard in the service to Herod the King, shall be given to Rebecca, daughter of Jahin." He stopped and looked at Nathan.

"Continue Scribe; read the remainder."

"...his wife."

Nathan looked at the Pharisee and demanded. "Who signed this document?" Nathan glanced at Rebecca and noted that her eyes were suddenly very large.

"The Commander of the King's Guards, Gilad."

"Now, is there a man among you who would like to challenge the word of the Commander of the King's Guards? Anyone?" Nathan stepped forward another step as the crowed retreated. "Anyone?" He looked into the eyes of everyone in the street. "I thought not. It takes no bravery to shout at a woman and a child. It takes courage to face a man." As he spoke Tobias and two other guards walked through the assembly and stood beside Nathan. "Go back to your homes and think about the laws of Moses. And when you realize how empty your hearts are, try to find even a spec of love for others. Don't we have enough who oppress us? Are you no better than they?" Slowly the crowd began to disperse, leaving the tall man standing beside his new wife, alone in the small street with his friends.

Tobias returned his sword to its scabbard. He stood for several minutes just looking at Nathan before he spoke. "Is this true? You are married to this woman?" His face was a mixture of both surprise and pain at the same time.

"Yes, that is true. Gilad has approved it."

Tobias looked at Rebecca then back at Nathan. "We'll be heading back to the camp. I think our work here is done." He turned quickly and left.

* * *

He found her sitting at the small table nursing the baby. Her eyes were glued on the child. "You could have talked to me first." She did not look up.

"That was my plan. I'm sorry. That crowd...."

"What if I refuse to be your wife?"

"Is that what you want?"

"I can't be your wife." Tears were streaming down her cheeks when she turned to him.

"Why? You know I love you." Nathan sat across from her and took her hands in his. "Surely you know that. And I can take care of you."

"I don't need you to take care of me."

"I know you don't need that, but I do. I need to take care of you. When a man loves a woman, he wants to take care of her. That's just the way we are made."

"Samuel and I are just a burden to you. To everyone. You deserve a better wife, your own child."

"I couldn't find a better wife. And you know I love little Pumpkin. He's my son now." Nathan stepped forward and pulled her up. "I will take care of him and love him as if he were my own child." He put his hand under her chin and raised her face to his. "And who knows, perhaps we will have our own children as well."

Rebecca buried her head in his chest. "Nathan, you are a good man. Are you sure this is right for you? I would not want you to wake up some day and realize you had taken a poor woman with a crippled child and regret what you had done."

"You silly woman. Look into my eyes." He paused a moment. "Don't you know how much I love you? Really?"

"Yes. I knew before you did, and it frightened me."

"Frightened you?"

"I knew what joy might enter my life. And then I feared I might lose it. I also realized what I might be doing to the first man I ever really loved." Tears streamed down her face. She stepped back and stood before him. "Look at me. Look at me, Nathan. I'm a poor woman. I have nothing. I am not pretty. I cannot read. I barely know how to cook. But you work for the king. You are beautiful and strong..." She stopped, overcome with tears. "And you are kind." It was almost a whisper. After a long pause she looked up, right into his eyes, his soul. "And I love you so dearly. But you deserve a better woman than me, and I love you enough to let you go."

Nathan pulled her close and lifted her face with both his hands to peer into her eyes. "When I wake each morning, the first rays of the sun remind me of the joy I will experience that day with you. When you sleep at night, I struggle to remain awake so that I can look at your beautiful face. I am just a man, just a guard in the palace. Nothing more. But your love gives me purpose and a measure of joy that I have never known before. Now I have meaning in my life." She tried to look away, but he held her face and continued to look into her eyes. "You talk about needing me, do you realize how much I need you?" He embraced her gently as he wiped her tears and then kissed her. "You are a strong woman, Rebecca, and you are beautiful.

I will be the luckiest man in Judea to have you for my wife. I'm thinking that you, Pumpkin, and I will make a great family, so you better just get used to that idea. Besides," He held the small scroll before her. "We are husband and wife now—the Commander of the King's Guard says so." As she hugged him, the baby cried. He smiled and kissed them both.

Later that night they both sat watching the fire send sparks up into the chimney. He nervously looked at his blanket in the corner several times. Rebecca put the baby in a small cradle, then rose, took his blankets and placed them atop her own. "If we are husband and wife, I guess we should sleep together. We will need less firewood that way."

Nathan rose, took her in his arms, and kissed her gently. "Rebecca, you have been married before." He paused and spoke with some difficulty. "There are things I know little of."

She grinned, understanding his remarks. "Then we will learn together. I was very young when my father gave me in marriage. I fear I didn't learn much of love then." She kissed him again. "But now I am anxious to know everything. I want to be a good wife—in every way." She turned from him, placed a small candle on the table, and lit it. As it spread its rays across the room, she adjusted it several times. Finally satisfied with its light, she took his hand and led him to their bed. As they lay beside each other she smiled in the dim light of the candle. "I am anxious to meet this commander who has decreed us to be man and wife. He has changed my life completely." Before Nathan could respond she rolled over and tickled him, and that is how their life together began, with love and with laughter.

Chapter 10

When she awoke the next morning, she opened her eyes to see him studying her carefully. He spoke softly then kissed her gently. "I love you, Rebecca."

"And I love you too."

He glanced at the cradle. "Samuel is still asleep."

"Then we must be quiet; not like last night."

"Last night was wonderful."

"Yes. Yes it was." Her cheeks were red as she rolled over on top of him.

Later as they ate their morning meal, Rebecca looked out the door into the clear morning air. It was the time of day she loved best. The air was cool, and the heat of the day had not yet driven the people back into their homes. Far off on the horizon she could see puffy white clouds that appeared to be racing along the tops of the distant hills to the west. "Do you think we will ever be accepted here? It is difficult to live in a town where people look at us with hatred every day. They hate you because you are from the King's Guard and protect Herod. They hate me because I have a crippled baby." She paused then returned to the small table.

"It doesn't matter at all." Nathan was smiling as he watched her response.

"How can you say that?"

"Because we are moving to Jerusalem. I've been ordered back to the palace." Nathan watched her carefully to see her response. After all, Jerusalem was a large city, and all Rebecca had ever known was Bethlehem and the neighboring villages.

"We're going to Jerusalem? When?"

"We leave later this week. It will be a long walk; do you think Samuel will be okay for traveling? He seems to be a strong boy." He paused for a moment, then continued. "Other than his leg."

"Well, since he's too small to walk anyway, it doesn't matter. I will carry him. I'm strong."

Nathan grinned. "Yes, you are." She blushed and kissed him on his forehead. "We have two donkeys to carry our belongings; you can ride on one of those if you wish."

"What about our home? Our things?"

"We'll pack whatever we can carry on the donkeys. The rest we leave for the next people who live here. I have spoken with the Rabbi; he will take care of everything here." He looked around the small room. "We have very little. We can replace what we need when we get to Jerusalem. Oh, Rebecca, you will marvel at the city, the palace, the temple. There are so many people and so many things to see and learn. You will love it."

"It will be good to have a new home. Bethlehem was the joy of my childhood. Then it became a place of nightmares for me. I am glad to leave." She lifted the baby from his small cradle. "Hi Pumpkin. Did you know you are going to live in a big town?" She turned to Nathan. "Will the trip be dangerous?"

He tickled the baby as he spoke. "My dear, you will be escorted by a contingent of the king's very own guards. They are armed and brave. No one would dare bother us on this trip." He suddenly turned and walked quickly into the back room. When he emerged he held the leather pouch with the coins. "I can't forget this. As soon as we get settled, I intend to buy you a beautiful cloak and new sandals. And when everyone sees how beautiful you are, I will be the envy of every man in the city." Nathan put his large arms around Rebecca and the baby and squeezed them both until she pushed him away. Then he turned to the door. "I must go and relay our plans to the men.

Start thinking of what you want to carry with us. And also think of all the adventures that await us as well." As he walked out into the bright sunlight, Nathan had little idea how the new adventures would change his life.

Chapter 11

The two men walked casually out onto the porch surrounding the palace. Behind them the sounds of music and people celebrating inside slowly dimmed as they proceeded away from the crowd. Finally, the taller of the two stopped beside the waist tall stone wall and stood looking off to the north. There was a sly smile on El'Azar's face as he stared at the three towers Herod had built for protection. The Towers of Hippicus, Phasael, and Mariamne dominated the horizon and recalled to all Herod the builder. The shorter man moved beside him and looked off to the north as well, searching for whatever his friend was observing. El'Azar waited before he spoke, adjusting his black robe and removing the headpiece that he wore. Like his robe, it was also black and adorned with gold around the edges. It resembled the headpiece of the Chief Priest, Caiaphas, but politically was appropriately three inches shorter. When he removed it, a large red indentation remained on his forehead. He rubbed it vigorously cursing lightly beneath his breath. He was the assistant to Caiaphas and, as the three gold marks on the shoulder of his cloak defined, he was also the Commander of the Temple Guards. He paused and looked carefully around the porch to ensure they were alone and would not be overheard. When satisfied he turned to his friend, and his smile returned. "Every time I look at Herod, I feel I will be sick."

"I thought he was your friend."

"He thinks that too." The smile grew larger. "But I detest the man. He is little more than a lackey of the Romans. We need a Hasmonean back on the throne in Israel—a real Jew."

"Your opinion of Herod is a secret best kept to yourself."

El'Azar turned and looked off again into the fading light. "Perhaps that is a secret that need not be kept much longer." The Chief of the Temple Guards burped loudly and put his hand to his lips awaiting another. He was a man who obviously enjoyed his creature comforts, especially when food or wine was involved.

The shorter man smiled broadly, thinking that for someone so loathed as Herod, his food and drink were more than welcome. "Certainly you are not thinking of confronting Herod."

"Of course not." El'Azar turned his attention to the man before him and winked. "But perhaps it will not be necessary."

"What are you plotting, old friend? Every attempt on Herod thus far has failed with numerous casualties among those who tried to do him harm. I suspect most Jews are simply waiting for him to die of natural causes."

"But there are others who also wish him dead, others who would be more than willing to undertake an attempt on his life."

"Really, now who would be foolish enough to do that?"

"Parthians." He said it with a certain finality.

"Parthians? Do you expect them to send an army to Jerusalem?"

"They don't need an army, just a few determined men, men armed with a bit of good information." El'Azar smiled more broadly as he stroked his short beard. "Information regarding Herod's whereabouts, his habits, his normal travels inside and out of the palace, information about when he might be most vulnerable."

The shorter man's eyes narrowed. "You had best be very careful. As I said, every attempt thus far has failed, and if your name were ever connected to an attempt on Herod, you'd be the next Jew on a cross outside of the city."

"You don't think I'd ever allow my name to become connected to such an activity, do you?"

"Of course not!"

"Of course not." The assistant to the chief priest studied the man before him. "But I do need your help on one small detail."

"How can I be of assistance?"

"I need the schedule for the change of the guards at the palace. Do you think you could get that for me?"

"That should not be difficult."

"And be careful not to raise any suspicion. Be very careful."

"Me? You know I'm always careful." He smiled broadly as well. "Especially when even a small mistake could get me killed."

El'Azar placed the headpiece back onto his head and cursed as he grimaced under the weight. "Did you try the new wine Herod had brought in from Galilee? I thought it was excellent."

"That was good. Shall we try some more?"

"Yes, I think that is a great idea."

Chapter 12

It was one of those beautiful mornings where the temperature is cool and the sky so clear and azure blue. By noon it would be unbearably hot, but at just an hour after sunrise, it was remarkable. Nathan was talking to Gilad on the palace steps when they heard the scream. Both turned and ran toward the courtyard, swords drawn and ready. Nathan quickly outran the older commander; he was younger and Gilad was also encumbered with a bow he often carried. As they approached the noise, they both saw a surprising event. Three of the king's concubines were kneeling before three Parthian soldiers who had climbed the south wall of the city. They were most likely looking for Herod, but, instead, they had encountered three of his ladies. Two of the women were screaming and kneeling, begging for their lives, while a fourth, seeing the guards rushing in from a distance and realizing they were still too far to protect them, did the most amazing thing. She realized she had to delay the attackers for any chance to survive. She looked at the men with swords, stood, and opened her robe, dropping it to the ground. She stood there, naked before the intruders. All three intruders stopped and lowered their swords. They were temporarily stunned and unsure what to do. She was a young, exquisitely beautiful woman with such beauty the men had never seen before. Her curly hair fell across her shoulders and the beauty of her face stopped the men instantly. She had colored her cheeks and her lips with juice from berries. For a moment all three soldiers just stopped and admired this beautiful girl while Nathan and Gilad sprinted across the courtyard toward them. Nathan was faster, but he was still at least thirty yards from the scene, too far to protect the women. He watched as the leader of the soldiers looked at the woman for a moment, then with a decision etched across his face he slowly raised his sword above his head. She stood calmly looking at him, saying nothing. Just as he reached the top of the arc of his swing, Nathan heard a swish pass to his left. The arrow struck the man in his back just before he could swing his weapon. He stopped, slowly turned, and looked at the guards rushing toward them. Another arrow struck the Parthian in the middle of his chest, and he crumpled to the ground. The other two soldiers immediately turned from the women to face the guards as another arrow narrowly missed one of them. As the men approached, Nathan swung his large sword and knocked the first to the ground. He then turned to the second man and they began the dance of death as the two crouched and circled each other. As the downed man rose to rejoin the attack, an arrow caught him in the side, and he fell beside his leader. The final attacker, realizing he was now outnumbered, lowered his sword and raised his hands in surrender. Gilad fired his last arrow, and the man fell with his comrades.

All the women were crying and bending to the ground, except the naked woman in their midst. She stood calmly watching the battle. When it was over Gilad walked over and handed her his cloak. She smiled at him and reached for her own clothes laying at her feet. As she dressed, she studied the face of the man before her, looking into his eyes, and he felt she viewed his soul as well. She held his gaze until he finally looked down. Then she smiled. Nathan kicked each of the three men viciously, and when convinced they were dead, searched the bodies. They were clearly Parthians, part of the great Persian Empire that sought expansion into the Tigris Euphrates river valley. But, as usual, the Romans blocked that goal. Two other guards arrived, breathing hard. Gilad turned to them and gave quick orders. "Find the king and keep him safe. Tell him what transpired here so that he will comply with our procedures.

Also, notify the Roman centurion at Antonia Fortress. They need to ensure this is not part of a coordinated attack. Finally, put all guards on posts around the palace and try to discover how they got in." When they left, Gilad turned to Nathan. "Good work with that sword. One blow to his shield and he was knocked to the ground. That is a powerful weapon. Later, I would like to study it." He turned to the leader of Unit 1 who was arriving with still more guards. "Kalev, I think we have everything here under control. There were three Parthian soldiers." He nodded to the three bodies nearby. "Nathan and I took care of them. But there may be more, so put your men on alert."

Kalev nodded and turned to his friend, Nathan. "I see you still have your victory sword. It seems to have been busy today."

Nathan smiled and gave his friend a hug. "Actually, Gilad's bow did most of the work today. He's deadly with that thing."

"So it appears." Kalev walked over and examined the enemy bodies. "I'll be sure to remember to never displease Gilad." He walked back over to Nathan. "Bring Rebecca, and come over to my house tomorrow night. We will be roasting a lamb and having some wine. Join us."

"That sounds great. Rebecca will be making bread. We'll bring some along. See you tomorrow at sundown."

* * *

Herod arrived surrounded by guards and several of his personal staff as he rushed through the palace toward the courtyard. He went immediately to the young woman adjusting her robe. "Are you okay, my dear? Did those men harm you?"

"No, my King. Your guards protected us and killed them all."

"One of the women said you were naked. Did the Parthians touch you?"

"No, my King. The evil men had sneaked into our courtyard. The guards were running but were too far away. I knew I had to delay the soldiers. It was the only weapon I had."

Herod stepped back and tilted his head as he studied the young woman. "I see." He considered her words a moment and continued with a wide smile on his face. "Quite a weapon, and it worked."

"Their leader had his sword raised, but your commander shot him with an arrow from a distance. That saved me and gave the other guard time to arrive and attack the other two."

Herod turned to Gilad and smiled. "Good work, Gilad. I know I can always count on you. You saved Sabina; she is very special to me. For this great act I will grant you any request you make of me." He waited as Gilad considered his promise.

"My King, I was doing my job. It is my pleasure to protect you and your palace. If I may, I would like to delay that request until another time."

"So be it. Until then I am in your debt." Herod walked over to the dead men and looked at them briefly. "Have these bodies hung on crosses and left there until the birds pluck their eyes from their rotting skulls. Let it be a message to any others who would dare invade my palace." Then he turned to one of his advisors. "A gold coin for the guard and two for the commander." With a flourish Herod turned and marched back into the palace.

As Gilad watched the guards drag the bodies from the palace, he turned and saw Sabina staring at him. She was a slave from Emesa on the Orantes River in Syria. He recalled the first time he had ever seen her. He was walking through the palace one morning when he noticed four women being brought into the building. They had recently been brought to the palace and sold as slaves. As he watched them his eyes focused on the one standing proudly before her captors. She had auburn hair and large dark eyes. Her oval face contained so many normal features, arched eyebrows, slim nose, soft lips, and beautiful white teeth—so normal, but the exact combination and the way they were arrayed composed the most beautiful young woman he had ever seen.

Gilad looked back at Sabina and stood silent, transfixed, staring at the beauty before him. Then, unexpectedly, their eyes met and locked on each other. There was a slight smile on her face, but he was hardly aware as the dark eyes peered at him. He expected her to demurely look away, but she did not. He wanted to turn and walk away from this intrusion, but his legs did not respond. He simply stood, staring, captive to this beautiful creature. Suddenly her eyes grew very large and a look of surprise crossed her face. Gilad's face reflected hers. What had she discovered in his mind, in his soul, to cause such a reaction? As he pondered this, a voice called out behind the women. They all turned to leave, but as she moved, she stopped for only a moment and turned back to face him. And for that one brief moment her eyes locked on his again, and he felt a moment of joy and longing he had never known before. To his surprise she walked over and looked up into his face as she removed a gold chain that hung around her neck. She leaned up as far as she could and placed the chain around Gilad's neck. "My name is Sabina; you saved my life today. Wear this chain so that you never forget my name."

"I am…" Gilad started to speak but she placed a finger on his lips.

"You are Gilad, Commander of the King's Guard, a name I shall always remember."

Long after she had left he stood there until the emotion finally departed, leaving him once again in control in the sunny courtyard, only a man with a job to be done. Over the years he would see her again on occasion and was always surprised how her beauty was enhanced as she grew older. But today, as he watched her leave, he noticed that she had quickly glanced back to see if he were still looking at her. He was.

Chapter 13

El'Azar was sitting at his large, ornate desk of the Commander of the Temple Guards when his guest walked in. There was a dark frown on his face accentuated by the deep furrow between his eyebrows. Even the abundance of food and wine nearby didn't seem to help. He was not happy; he tried to smile, but the frown remained after several efforts to raise the corners of his lips. His short friend frowned as well as he slumped into a large chair covered with cushions across from El'Azar. "What happened?"

"They only sent four men. One was killed by a guard on the outside wall before the others could overpower him."

"Only four?"

"And only three got onto the palace grounds."

"Did they get the times wrong? I thought they were advised regarding the guard schedules."

"They were, but obviously something went wrong."

"Why only four? Why not ten?"

"They felt a small contingent had a better chance of sneaking into the palace." El'Azar stroked his beard and studied a diagram of the palace that was spread across his desk. "Four men probably did have a better chance of sneaking into the palace. Ten would never have made it to within a mile of the building."

"Did the three get into the palace itself?"

"No, they expected to find him in the courtyard."

"He wasn't there? I thought you had his schedule as well, his daily activities. He wasn't in the courtyard?"

"All they found were some of his concubines." Both men stared at each other for several moments.

"Did they kill his women? That would have also made a statement."

"Two of the King's guards surprised them and won the day."

"Two guards defeated three Parthian soldiers?"

"Two of their best." El'Azar picked up the palace drawing and ripped it into two pieces. "Damn Gilad's guards. Someday I'll crush him and take over that entire group."

"Have you tried getting Gilad on board with your plans? It seems he would be a good addition to our team."

"Gilad? That oaf can't be trusted. I'm not sure he has the mental capacity to understand our politics. He's little more than a soldier himself." El'Azar had not gotten over the embarrassing defeat his guards had suffered in the annual competition between his own troops and those of the King's Guards. It had not gone well for the Temple Guards; Gilad's men had easily won every event and therefore the respect of the king and his staff. El'Azar had been humiliated. Even Caiaphas had commented on the dismal showing of El'Azar's men. "Someday I'll get Gilad. It may take some time, but I'll get that pompous bastard."

"What have the Parthians said about the failed mission?" The guest had realized it was time to change the conversation as quickly as possible.

"Nothing; we haven't told them the particulars yet."

"What will you say?"

"We'll tell them their men were met with a much larger contingent of troops who happened to be in the area and were killed in the ensuing fight."

"Won't they question the information your people supplied?"

"Of course they will, and we will do the same, very loudly."

"So you will blame some unknown informants."

"Correct." The commander of the Temple Guards smiled a sly smile. "And two common criminals will die once they are identified as the men who gave the bad information."

"Do you think the Parthians will buy that story?"

"It's the best story we happen to have right now."

"When do you expect to pass that to them?"

"I have men meeting with them as we speak."

"Good luck for your representatives. I'm guessing they aren't very popular in the Parthian camp right now."

"I'm afraid you're right; I have my doubts whether they will even survive the meeting."

* * *

El'Azar was smiling when his visitor walked into his office two days later. The smile was a welcomed change from the despairing looks of the last meeting. The visitor spoke first. "Well, it's good to see you smiling. That's a welcomed change from two days ago. What is there to be so happy about?"

"We discovered why Herod was not in his normal routine the other day."

"Perhaps he was meeting with one of his concubines in another room." Now the visitor was smiling also.

"As a matter of fact, he was meeting with his physicians."

There was a long pause as the shorter man stroked his beard. "Okay, tell me the good news. He has leprosy, right?"

"Almost that good. His health is failing fast. The old tyrant has little time left to live."

A sudden smile erupted on the visitor's face. "Really? How much time?"

"Not much. So, while we failed in our attempt, it appears we get our ultimate wish after all." It seems we may be looking for another king in just a matter of a few months."

"Then we'd better start strategizing real soon."

"You are so right. We have little time to lose."

"Who do you think Rome will choose?"

"Most likely not the person we would like to see on the throne."

The shorter man walked over and poured some of El'Azar's wine into two goblets. "Then we'd better get busy. We've plans to conceive."

"So true, my friend. So true."

Chapter 14

Gilad stood before nine men from his Second Unit and surveyed them carefully. He was a large man, powerfully built. His beard was dark and, like his eyes, foreboding. He had been the leader of the King's Guard for many years, and he held everyone's respect, especially the king, and that was most essential in his position. Gilad knew that Herod was a selfish man and an evil one as well, so he dealt with him with great care. But today he was not concerned with politics; today he was concerned with his men. One of his unit leaders had been ill for weeks, and a new replacement was needed to lead that team. The men were young and strong, and today they would compete for the leadership of that unit.

All of the men in Unit 2 were assembled in a large field just outside the Gate of the Essenes. Each of the men stood with a wooden pole six inches longer than a guard's sword. They were two inches in diameter and were the tools used to practice their craft. Two men at a time would compete until the fiercest fighter remained. He would become the new leader for Unit 2.

The sun beat down on the men as they fought on the dry dusty soil. There were injuries, one serious, as the contests continued. At the end, two men stood alone, Nathan and Tobias. The two men faced each other, and Gilad stepped between them and looked at each in turn. Then Nathan spoke. "I will yield to Tobias." The men watching were all surprised. They knew Nathan was the superior warrior.

"No, you are friends, but you will fight. One of you may lead the rest into battle. Today you fight each other with sticks. Some day you may fight beside each other with swords. Commence!"

The men raised their wooden swords and nodded. Tobias immediately initiated the attack. Nathan stepped back slowly and deftly blocked each blow with his pole. Tobias stepped back two steps and inhaled deeply. Again he initiated the attack. Again Nathan blocked each parry, each blow. Finally the two men stood face to face, their poles locked between them. With one swift movement Nathan shoved Tobias to the ground, on his back. Nathan stood over him a second, then threw his own pole to the ground and turned to walk away. Tobias quickly climbed to his feet, raised his weapon and charged Nathan's back. As Tobias was just starting to swing his pole, Nathan turned and ducked. As he did, he reached up and grabbed Tobias's pole in mid-air. With one jerk he pulled the pole from Tobias's hand and stood, looking at his friend. "From my back?" He threw the pole to the ground and turned and walked away.

* * *

The sound at the door was loud, three sharp knocks. Nathan immediately recognized the visitor and rushed to open the door. His commander stood outside with two guards. Gilad stood above any of the men under his command except Nathan, and he could easily defeat any two of them together. His large frame filled the doorway of the small dwelling; there was a frown on his face. He tilted his head forward and looked out from under heavy eyebrows that matched his thick beard. Nathan stepped aside and motioned for his commander to enter. The two guards stood outside on either side of the door as Gilad entered the room. Rebecca stood and bowed. Gilad looked around the small dwelling and finally spoke. "Bring me the child."

Rebecca stepped back slightly and looked at Nathan for guidance. Nathan spoke, never taking his eyes off of Gilad. "Get Samuel and bring him here." Rebecca looked at her husband for several moments, weighing his words. "Get the child."

Holding the baby close to her breast, Rebecca held the small boy so that Gilad could see his face. Gilad reached for the child, but Rebecca pulled him back and turned away slightly. Gilad withdrew his hand and looked at the woman before him. "Let me see his leg." Nathan nodded to Rebecca and she unwrapped the baby, exposing his wiggling legs. Gilad looked at him carefully, stepped back and turned to Nathan. "I see your hand on your weapon. You are a skillful fighter and a brave man, Nathan, but you are no match for me. Still, I admire your courage." Nathan moved his hand from his dagger and stood straight before his leader. "You did not follow my orders, and much is at risk. Herod is unpredictable; he can be a very vindictive man." He paused for a moment. "And a very dangerous man. He must never know about this child. A man who could have babies killed to protect his throne..." Gilad paused for a moment then continued. "What do you think he might do to someone who disobeyed his orders?" Gilad glanced back at Rebecca and Samuel, then continued. "So, the child may not remain in Jerusalem. If his existence were discovered by Herod, none of us would be safe."

Nathan nodded. "I understand."

"While I admire your courage and skill, Nathan, you disobeyed my orders. That must not happen again. Do you understand?"

"Yes sir."

"You clearly won the contest today, but I am not promoting you to be the leader of Unit 2. I expect my men to follow my orders exactly as directed. Do you understand?"

Nathan nodded, again, clearly disappointed. "I'm sorry I let you down."

"It will not happen again."

"No sir."

"Now, in the morning you will take the baby and his mother away from Jerusalem, and you will never speak of this to anyone." Gilad started for the door but stopped abruptly and turned back to Nathan. "Who should replace you as leader of your unit?"

"Tobias."

Gilad looked surprised. "Why Tobias?"

"He is the strongest and the most respected by the men. They will follow him. He is a man of honor."

"I see." Gilad scratched his beard for a moment, deep in thought, then turned and left.

Rebecca ran to Nathan and put her arms around him. "I'm sorry I've caused you so much trouble. What an evil man."

"Gilad is just doing his job. We protect the king from assassins, and Gilad protects us from the king."

"What will we do?"

"We have no choice. We must do as he says." Nathan rubbed his forehead in thought. "I'll find a place for you in a nearby village."

"How will you live there when you work in the palace?"

"I'll have to live with the guards until I can figure this out. You will be close; I'll visit as often as possible. I'll find a way to be with you." He kissed her on her forehead.

"I'm sorry you lost the promotion; I know it meant a lot to you." As she spoke, Rebecca's eyes were staring at the floor in front of her.

Nathan also stood looking at the floor for several moments before he spoke. "I'm just glad Gilad didn't discharge me. Many men would love to be in the King's Guard."

Rebecca took the baby into the small sleeping room and sang to him as he fell asleep. Nathan listened to her soft voice and the frown began to dissolve from his face. In spite of everything, he figured he was among the lucky. He was loved by this woman who he adored, and he had a family. What else could be more important in a man's life?

Rebecca found him smiling at her when she returned. "Why are you smiling?"

"Did you see Gilad's face as he looked at Samuel?"

"I think he was smiling."

"He was. I think he wanted to hold him." Nathan reached and stroked Rebecca's cheek.

"He would have had to kill me first." Now Rebecca was smiling as well.

"Gilad has no children of his own—no family."

"How sad for him."

"I was just thinking the same thing." Nathan sat slowly, pulled her into his lap, and hugged her tightly.

Rebecca looked at the dying fire and sighed. "I guess I'll have to haul wood again."

Nathan frowned. "A lot will change, but we will manage."

"I wish this had not happened. How did he know?"

"I've been wondering that myself. Perhaps one of the men in my unit mentioned you were with us on the trip back from Bethlehem."

Rebecca looked at him for several moments while studying the dying embers in the small fireplace. Finally she spoke what they both were thinking. "But he asked to see Samuel's leg. He knew about his leg."

Nathan was staring into the fire in deep thought. Finally he spoke. "Did you tell any of the men about Samuel? Could they have seen him?"

"No, I spoke to none of them." She stood and faced Nathan. "None of them saw him unwrapped. I kept him covered from the sun."

"Then who knew about Samuel's leg?" Both looked at each other and spoke the name at the same time. "Tobias."

* * *

Nathan walked into the house and went immediately to the water jug. He drank with large gulps and finally put the jug on the table. Rebecca stood behind, watching him and holding the squirming child. When he turned there was a furrow between his eyes. He was frowning, but as he looked at the two before him, his frown softened. "I am so happy to be home with you."

"What happened with Gilad?"

"We agreed that I will move you to Bethany. I was so worried he would make it farther away."

"How far away is it?" There was concern on her face.

"It's really not too bad. It is about an hour's walk from Jerusalem. It is on the eastern slope of the Mount of Olives."

"Then you can live with us?"

"Most of the time I can. It depends on the shifts I get. If I have the early morning duty, I will have to stay at the palace with the other guards. If I have the later shifts, I can leave Bethany early and arrive in time for my work."

"This will be difficult for you, won't it?"

"Rebecca, nothing could keep me from you and Pumpkin. I will find a way to be with you as much as possible."

"Then we'll just have to make our time together special, however much that time is."

Nathan leaned down and kissed her. "Any time I have with you is special, my dear.

Chapter 15

It was almost dark, and Rebecca was uneasy leaving Samuel alone, but she knew, instinctively, that Nathan needed her. She walked down the dusty road, glad that the coolness of evening was approaching. It had been a very hot day, and she basked in the brief respite that the evening brought. She spotted him under the tree he always used when he had things to consider. Rebecca desperately loved Nathan. He was a good man and a good husband, and she also knew that he desperately loved her. For a woman, that was important. It meant that she was still desirable and still a lover who was needed by this man. He needed her now, but in a very different way. She didn't know what was bothering him, but his silence at dinner had said volumes. She approached the tree and said nothing, she just sat beside him and leaned against the old, gnarled Tamarisk tree he always used for support when he was confused, angry, or lonely. She wondered which of the three concerned him tonight. She was surprised when it was none of these. He was disappointed. She had seldom seen him disappointed in anything. Disappointed? Nathan? That made no sense to her. Without a word, she reached over and handed him a small limb from a shrub near their home. It was a bit longer than her hand and half the diameter of her finger. He smiled, took it and began carving on the end with his knife. When he finished he chewed the end for a moment and then began rubbing it against his teeth. Rebecca snuggled against his shoulder and rubbed his arm. He reached around her and drew her closer. "You seem troubled. Is it because of the promotion?"

"I'm okay."

"No, you're not. You're upset; you feel bad about losing the promotion."

Nathan pulled her even closer and kissed the top of her head. "I'm just disappointed that's all."

"Of course you are. I would expect that. I feel badly too. After all, you gave that up for Samuel and me."

"No, I just did the right thing." He looked up at the stars that were beginning to brighten the evening sky. "Tobias was chosen."

There was a long silence before she spoke. "Well, if you didn't get it, I'm glad it was Tobias. He's your best friend. "

"He is, even though he probably was the reason I didn't get it."

There was another long pause before she spoke. "Most likely."

"I think he wanted it so much..." He failed to finish his sentence.

"If he wanted it that much, perhaps it was right for him to get it." She reached and kissed him on his cheek. "Besides, now you won't have to work late all the time and carry all that responsibility. Everyone knows you are the best guard. You are the one who received the sword from the Primus Pilus. They all respect you, and you know that's true. Would you trade all that for a title and more work, work that would take you away from me and Pumpkin?"

"You're right, as usual." He placed his hand under her chin and lifted her face so he could kiss her properly. "I'm so lucky to have you."

"Yes, you are." She was smiling. "And all Tobias has is more work to do, work you would dread. All that organizing and scheduling."

"You're right, the men all respect me, and that includes Tobias. All he got was more work, and I have my best friend managing the unit. That's not all bad, I suppose."

"See, you feel better already."

He rose and took her hand, pulling her to a standing position. He put his arms around her. "You know, I wouldn't trade this moment for the commander's job, much less a unit leader's job."

She looked at Nathan for a long moment. He could tell she was deep in thought. Finally she took his hand. "Have you spoken to Tobias about all this?"

"No."

"Are you going to be able to forgive him if he were, indeed, the one who told Gilad about Samuel?"

Now it was Nathan who needed time to think. After a moment he nodded. "Yes, I can live with his decision. I suspect it will be more difficult for him than for me."

"Then you have only one thing left to do."

"What's that?"

"You have to make Tobias feel proud of the new job. Then you will truly be his best friend. You gain nothing by making him feel badly about the promotion. Nothing. And you are a bigger man than that."

He looked in her eyes a long time before speaking. "I am truly blessed to have you as my wife."

"And why is that? Because of all my talking?"

"No, because you make me a better man."

* * *

Nathan walked around the west side of the palace and saw Tobias across the palace grounds sitting on a stone bench. He was alone and his head was partially bowed as if in great thought. Nathan turned abruptly and walked toward him. The day was hot, and the sun shone down with the intensity of a great fire. Nathan shielded his eyes with his right hand and studied his friend as he approached. Tobias sat under an old oak tree and was staring off to the south. He was wearing his official cloak but was not armed. Nathan approached and sat on the end of the bench as he looked off to the south. After a few minutes he touched his friend's shoulder and spoke. "What seems to be the problem, Tobias? You are not at peace today."

Tobias turned and faced his friend. "Why do you say that?"

"I have known you for many years, and I know your moods. Something is bothering you. Tell me what it is. I may be able to help you find the solution you seek."

"Nathan, you know me so well. You've been my friend for so long." Tobias turned away and spoke with difficulty. Nathan had to lean closer to hear his words. "I betrayed you, my best friend, and I am ashamed."

"Are you afraid your actions would harm our friendship? If you are, don't be concerned. It won't." Nathan put his hand on Tobias's shoulder. "I know of nothing you could do that would harm the bond we share. We are like brothers, you and I."

Slowly Tobias turned to face Nathan. "It was I who reported your relationship with Rebecca. I told Gilad about the baby."

"Well, Gilad handled it well. He didn't tell me to kill the boy. I just had to move out of Jerusalem."

"But I used that to get the promotion. Otherwise it would have gone to you."

Nathan smiled and patted Tobias's shoulder. "Don't you realize it all worked out as it should? By giving the promotion to you Gilad felt he had punished me enough and so he made no other demands about Rebecca or Samuel. That was the best gift I could have had. And besides, the promotion went to the right man. Each of us has different gifts. I might be the stronger man in combat, but you are far wiser in the politics of the palace.

Your quick wit will serve all of us well in that den of thieves. I would probably say the wrong thing and get all of us fired or worse. Herod is not a man I trust. I am comfortable knowing you are there to deal with him and his minions—not me."

A small smile finally broke on Tobias's face. "You're right about you in the palace. You'd probably have the entire army after you in a week." The smile went away and a serious demeanor returned to Tobias's face. "I really do appreciate what you are trying to do, Nathan. You are a good and loyal friend. You may have forgiven me, but it will take much longer for me to forgive myself. It was a selfish and cowardly act."

"I'll remind you of that if you ever pull rank on me." Both men smiled at that remark, then Nathan stood and he, too, became serious. "Tobias, you will be a good unit commander. I can think of no one who could do that job better. Always remember that I have great confidence in you and your ability to run our team. And you must also remind yourself of that fact. Put away your shame. That has passed. Stand tall and lead us. We all celebrate a strong leader."

"And if we ever get into a battle, I want you at my side."

"I will be there, and you will be at mine."

"That will keep us both safe." Tobias extended his hand to Nathan.

Nathan took the hand but drew Tobias to him and hugged him like a bear. "So it will."

Chapter 16

Nathan walked slowly up the small hill east of Jerusalem. The sun was slowly receding on the horizon, but still the heat was almost unbearable. When he failed to become the leader of a Guard unit, his shifts had become longer and totally unpredictable. He had just finished a ten-hour shift, the same for five days in a row, when he was notified that the king was leaving the city, and he would have three days off. He was all smiles. Three days with Rebecca and Samuel. He pulled a rough thick cloth over his forehead and squinted into the distance, thinking of all the things he wanted to do when he arrived in Bethany. He had a bag of food and presents for his family. It was a heavy bag, but today it felt as light as a feather for the strong young man heading home. Then he heard men shouting and struggling in the distance. Nathan walked faster and approached carefully. A man was on the ground covering his head as three others beat him with sticks; robbers were common on this stretch of the road. "Stop! Leave that man alone."

The robbers turned and immediately saw the large bundle Nathan was carrying. They stood and studied him for a moment, then they nodded to each other as they approached. "We'll take your goods, traveler." The men were young, like Nathan, but they were smaller than he. It was their number that made them brave. Three robbers against one lone traveler gave them the advantage, they thought.

"But there are only three of you. You'll need more help."

The three stopped and studied him carefully. One laughed. "The three of us can carry that pack easily."

"No, I meant you'd need help to get it. I plan to kill two of you and then watch the third running like a scared girl over that hill there."

"You're pretty brave are you? Well traveler, brave isn't enough to beat the three of us."

"How about this?" Nathan drew his large sword and held it high for the three men to see. "I am a member of the King's Guard. We use men like you for practice." Nathan placed the bundle on the ground and took the attack stance. Slowly he advanced toward the three men. "Which of you shall I kill first? How about you? You're the ugliest." He had already seen one of the men draw a knife from his belt. He would be first. The men looked at each other for a moment and seemed to agree that the bundle was worth the gamble. At once the three rushed Nathan. It was a scene he had trained for most of his life, three adversaries rushing directly at him at once. Their goal was to get in and grab him before he could swing the sword. If they were unlucky he might strike one of them, but before he could recover the other two could overcome him. Nathan stepped quickly to the right and swung the sword at the man with the knife. The sword sliced through the man's side just below his left arm. Jumping to his right, Nathan took the attack stance again, the bloody sword poised in the air. The men turned to their left as the sword lashed again, this time into the neck of the second robber. Two down and one running for the hill. Nathan watched the escaping man for only a moment then quickly checked the two on the ground. He didn't want any surprises. Both were dead or dying. As he wiped his blade on the cloak of one of the robbers he heard a loud moan. He turned and walked to the man the robbers had attacked.

"Please don't kill me. They took my money already."

"You're safe. I'm not going to hurt you. Let me help you." Nathan checked the man's wounds and gave him water from his own jug. The man was well dressed, and Nathan noticed a substantial amount of gray hair in the well-trimmed beard. "Where are you going?"

"To Bethany."

"So am I. I'll help you." Nathan looked back at the two dead robbers. "What did they take from you?"

"My purse."

Nathan searched the two bodies. "They have several here. Which one is yours?" The old man pointed to one of the small leather pouches. "Here, take two. They won't need these any longer." Nathan handed the man two of the coin purses and put the others into his pack.

"What about them?" The old man nodded toward the two on the ground.

"Their friend will return tomorrow morning hoping we didn't find their purses. I suspect he may even find a new occupation after he buries his fellow criminals."

"Thank you for saving me. I think they would have surely killed me if you had not come along."

Nathan put his hand on the old man's shoulder. He watched the man carefully. He was bleeding from a wound on his forehead. "Are you able to walk back to Bethany? They beat you badly."

"I'll be slow, but I'll make it. You go ahead."

"We'll walk together. There may be other robbers on this road. Here, drink more water. It's a hot day and you've been injured." He walked back to the dead men and cut a piece of cloth from one of their tunics. "Here, let's tie this around your head to help stop the bleeding."

"Thank you, my friend." As they walked Nathan told the old man that his family had moved there without elaborating the reasons. "My name is Matthias. I owe you my life."

"All you owe me is your friendship. That is payment enough." Nathan put his arm around the old man's waist and helped him along. "Are you sure you can make it walking in this heat."

"I'm old, but I have walked in this heat my entire life. I will be okay, but I may need to lean on you now and then."

"That will be fine, Matthias. And my name is Nathan." The two men turned east toward Bethany and continued their journey. Matthias's injuries were not serious, but they were painful as Nathan helped him along on the road. It was late in the afternoon when they arrived at Mathias's home. It was a beautiful house with a large garden.

"Won't you come in for dinner?"

"Thank you, no. I have been in Jerusalem for a while and am anxious to return to my family."

"Then we will hold this invitation until later. I would like very much to meet your family."

"We shall do that for sure. I am glad to have a new friend in our new town."

Chapter 17

Nathan walked through the door of his new home and stood staring at Rebecca. She was sitting on the rough tile floor, crying. It dawned on him that he had never seen this strong young woman cry except when she had suffered the loss of her husband. She had handled the neglect and scorn of her community and near starvation without one tear. And now she sat on the floor with tears rolling down her cheeks. Nathan ran to her, sat on the floor and pulled her into his lap. "Rebecca, what's wrong?" When she tried to speak, the tears only increased. "My darling, what is the matter?" His voice was increasing in both volume and concern. Finally she pointed across the floor to the small boy crawling toward them. Samuel was smiling as if he had just been given the finest gift. When he recognized Nathan, he began crawling even faster. "What is wrong with Samuel?" It was clear that Nathan was close to panic waiting for an answer from the crying woman in his arms. Finally she spoke.

"He cannot walk."

"But he is only a baby."

"But he tried."

"He did?"

"He'll never be able to walk. How will he ever live like that?"

Nathan pulled her closer and kissed her on the forehead. "Of course he will walk. I will teach him myself."

"But his leg." Her sobs increased.

"You silly girl. I will teach my son to walk. He might not walk the same as everyone else, but he will walk. I promise you that."

She looked up into his eyes. Nathan was smiling as he watched the toddler crawl into his lap beside his mother. Samuel was smiling as well as he tugged on his father's cloak, reaching for Nathan's beard. "See, look how strong he is." Nathan lifted the child into his arms and tickled him affectionately. "He will walk; I'm sure of it."

"But how?"

"Remember the boy who fell from a tree by the well and broke his leg several years ago? Have you seen him recently?"

There was a tentative "yes" from her lips as they reached to kiss her husband under his beard. "I've seen him. He walks like a newborn lamb."

"But he walks! And Samuel will walk as well." The young man lifted his wife's face and kissed her gently. "Unlike the boy with the damaged leg, Samuel will only know the way he first learns." Nathan placed the baby aside and rolled over on top of his wife. He kissed her and tickled her until she stopped weeping. "Come my dear, I am so hungry I could eat a goat. I have fresh meat and even vegetables from the city market. There is so much food I could hardly carry it from Jerusalem."

Rebecca climbed to her feet and helped pull Nathan to his. She enfolded him in her arms. "Nathan, what did I ever do to deserve such a man? Your love constantly amazes me." Tears rose into her eyes again and began flowing down her cheeks. "And Samuel is not even your son."

Nathan's reaction surprised and even frightened her. He pushed her back and spoke angrily to her. "No, don't ever say that again. Never again. Samuel is my son. I love him, and I will raise him. He will always think I am his father." Nathan put his hands on Rebecca's shoulders and pulled her close to his face. "Do you understand?"

"Yes." It was a tremulous answer.

"I will honor Samuel's first father by raising Pumpkin as best I can. But never again say that I am not his father." He paused and wiped a stray tear from her face. "When he is older and ready, we will tell him about his first father, but until then, he is *my* son, and I will teach him to be a man, not a crippled boy."

"I understand."

He pulled her into his arms and held her so close. "I love Samuel as much as any father ever loved his son. I will seek every day to be deserving of you and of him. And by damn, I *will* teach him to walk." When she looked up, he was smiling.

"I love you, father of Samuel. So much that I will make you the best dinner you've had in many days." She smiled at him with an impish grin. "And when we go to bed tonight, I'll give you the best desert you've ever had as well."

Little did they know that night that as they held each other and shared their love, they were starting another life to increase their family and give Samuel a sister to share in his adventures.

* * *

The hot sun beat down upon the thirsty man. Nathan had been making the trip from Jerusalem to Bethany and back for months. He knew every stone along the road. But today in his haste to get home he had forgotten to pack his jug of water for the trip. He peered through the bright sunshine and saw someone running toward him when he was nearing his house. It was Rebecca and she was excited and smiling. It pleased him to know she was so glad to have him home. "My dear, you look so hot and tired."

He grasped her in his arms, but she pulled away quickly. "I'll be fine as soon as I get some water. I hope you have a large container in the house."

"I do." She looked as if she had the greatest news to share as they walked the short distance to the house. Inside she poured water for him and put a wet towel on his face. He sat on one of the two chairs in the room and pulled her to him, but she pulled away. "Be gentle with me."

Nathan looked at her with a perplexed look on his face for several minutes. Then suddenly his eyes widened. "Are you...?"

"I'm going to have our baby." He had never seen such a happy face or such a big smile.

"You're sure?"

"Yes." She put her hands under her belly and stood proudly before him.

"That is the most wonderful news! Oh Rebecca, a new baby in our little house. How wonderful."

"Now we will be four."

"And Samuel will have a brother or sister. I am so happy."

"I hoped you would be."

"Of course I am. A new baby in our house. I will talk to the carpenter. We will need a small crib for this child." He gently put his arms around her and gave her a long kiss. "A new baby, what a wonderful gift."

"Yes, a gift."

Samuel sensed the excitement and crawled quickly to his parents. Nathan picked him up and gave him a very loud kiss on his stomach. "You're going to have a brother or maybe a sister. And after I teach you to walk, you'll have to help me teach the baby to walk someday."

Watching Nathan, Rebecca could hardly contain her joy. Somehow the new child would make them truly a family, and that was something she wanted more than anything in the world. She was barely seventeen, but now she had a family and a man she loved. Now she truly was a woman.

Chapter 18

Jerusalem, 4 BC

It was mid-afternoon when Gilad walked into his office in the palace. His large blue cloak flowed around him like a billowing cloud dancing across his room. Around his waist was a large belt and sash. A sword hung from the belt beside his left hip, and a large dagger was folded into the sash. As he walked through the palace everyone moved aside to let the commander pass. Gilad was well known in Jerusalem, and he was also well respected by the officials he guarded. His very presence exuded power and control. His smile also left those around him with a feeling of security and peace. But this particular afternoon he rushed down the halls as a man with a purpose. He had just been advised that one of his guards had arrived from escort duties with Herod and was waiting for him with news. The young man saluted and stood at attention, waiting for permission to speak. Gilad raised his hand. "Speak, what has brought you back to Jerusalem? Is Herod well?"

"Commander, King Herod is dying."

Gilad accepted the news with no show of emotion. He had been expecting this report for several months. "Is he still at the palace in Jericho?"

"Yes, Commander."

"He always loved that city. He even leased it from Cleopatra until Augustus gave it to him following her suicide. I think he likes the warmer temperature there. It's nearby, but the elevation is much lower than Jerusalem." (Author's note— Jerusalem is about 3000 feet higher than Jericho.) Gilad looked off into the distance for a moment then finally spoke. "How close to death is the king?"

"Archelaus is with him and says it is imminent."

Gilad stroked his beard as he stared at the floor for several minutes. Finally, he spoke. "Report to your unit commander immediately and tell him I want two of his best men, mounted and ready to leave with me for Jericho in half an hour. You are then to remain here and rest from your trip." He started to leave the room but turned back. "And thank you for your diligence in getting this news to me so quickly."

* * *

A young guard stood holding the large horse that his commander would ride the fourteen miles to Jericho. It, like its rider, was large and strong. Gilad had chosen this horse when it was still a young colt. He had looked at the mother and then the father and decided this would be his horse, even if he had to wait as it grew to maturity. On its back was a piece of thick wool with the markings of the King's Guards. On top of that was a piece of leather that allowed the rider to balance on the back of the large beast. Gilad approached, stopped, and admired the animal, as he had done so many times. "What a magnificent beast you are, and how fortunate I am to have you." He tied a roll of personal things onto the back of the horse, swung another around his shoulder, and bounded onto his ride. For several moments he just sat there, patting the strong brown neck before him while the young guard stood silently admiring the two. Two more men rode up and saluted their leader, then the three turned north toward their dying king. The trip took longer than Gilad had anticipated, even on horseback, and he was worried that he might arrive too late to speak to Herod. Darkness was approaching, and the night was troublesome. Clouds had moved into the area and lightening lit the sky intermittently with giant flashes of blinding light. *What a night to die,* he thought. *But this is a man who will leave with regrets. His life was both a success and a monumental failure. He gained so much that this world had to offer, and it all gave him so little joy. Like the magnificent palaces he built, it was all part of a great scheme to protect his rule. But time cannot be stopped by elaborate towers around Jerusalem, or the Antonio Fortress, or the fortress he had built on the mountain at Masada. Tonight the trappings of power will blow in the wind, and his time on this earth will be over.* But Gilad was also thinking of his own lifetime of service to this man. How many times had he fought to protect this king for whom he had so little respect? But soon it would be over. Herod was dying, and Gilad had one last promise to collect before Herod left this world.

Five of Gilad's men were guarding the room where Herod would take his last breath. That gave him instant access to the old king. No one would question the Commander of the King's Guard or oppose him as he entered the room of death; only the man lying on his deathbed had the power to do that, and Herod was in little condition to challenge or defy anyone, even if he wanted. But Herod would not have wanted to stop a visit from his commander. The two men were different, but each had a degree of respect for the other. This was the conflict in Gilad's heart regarding the frail old man lying on his back, staring at the ceiling. He knew what a tyrant Herod had been, and he feared that part of the king. But Gilad and his guards had protected this evil man, and as so often happens, a professional trust had been established between the two. In this relationship each had learned the strengths and also the weaknesses of the other. It was almost as if Herod were the cruel father of a son he learned to respect. And though Herod respected and trusted few men, Gilad was an exception and at the top of that list. And even as Herod knew there was a deep fear and perhaps even hatred for him in Gilad, he also knew Gilad was a professional who wanted to please him as well. Once, in a very close moment after a skirmish with Parthian troops, Herod had put his hand on Gilad's shoulder and told him that he was the brave son he never had. Verbally speaking such words, Herod had surprised them both. Gilad had never forgotten that moment; neither had Herod. The complexity of the personal relationship weighed heavily on Gilad's mind, but equally concerning was the situation of his organization. Herod was his king; he was also his employer. Gilad had almost sixty men in his guard unit. They were his family and depended upon him for their careers in the highly respected King's Guards. It was clear that Herod would soon be dead. His condition had been worsening for months. When that happened, what would happen to the King's Guards? Would there be another king? Would they be disbanded, or would they simply become the Palace Guards? The man who might control their future was most likely the other man in the room, Archelaus, one of Herod's sons.

Gilad entered the room and stood for a moment waiting for his eyes to adjust to the darkness. When they adjusted to the darkness he walked over to the bedside and observed two of the medical men leaving with a large bowl filled with blood. He frowned at them; the blood did not bother him; he had seen enough of that in his life. He just could not understand their medicine. What did blood have to do with an old man dying? The room was dark and foreboding with only a few tapers providing light; it even smelled of death. The walls were made of large carefully chiseled stones stacked perfectly on top of each other. Along the walls were thick wool curtains that opened onto nothing more than the dark blocks of rock. There was only one door leading to the hall outside. Gilad had stopped there for only a moment to speak to two of his men guarding the entrance. Two maids were kneeling beside the bed, wiping spilled blood from the tile floor. Other than them and two additional guards stationed inside the room, there was only

98

Archelaus and a scribe writing on a large scroll on a desk in the corner adjacent to the bed. Gilad nodded to Archelaus, both men wondering if he would be the next man Gilad and his men would guard. Both appraised the other carefully. Archelaus was a slight man and considerably shorter than Gilad. His eyes were a dull gray that matched the skin on his forehead and arms, which Gilad noticed had little hair. Gilad looked down at his legs; they, too, were mostly bare. He then looked into the man's eyes and found them disturbingly empty. He could not determine if what he saw was boredom or perhaps just fear. As Gilad approached Herod, he sensed that he was either asleep or already dead. The man did not appear to be breathing. Archelaus stood and stretched as the commander approached the bed and studied the king. "How is he doing?"

"Not well. I suspect his time is near." Archelaus said it without emotion. There was clearly no love lost between him and his father.

Gilad's heart sank. He was too late. Herod was not even conscious. He was just turning to leave when the familiar voice called out, clear but weak. "Gilad. I'm glad you came. I'm guessing you came for my promise."

"My King, I can come back later. I was concerned with your illness."

"Gilad, we both know this is not an illness. I am just an old man. My time is running out. But I have never forgotten that I made a promise to you some years ago, and I intend to fulfill that. Let it be said that I was a man of my word."

"Yes, my King."

"Herod motioned for Archelaus to come closer. Hear this my son." He waved weakly to Gilad and Archelaus. "Now, my good commander, what is your request?"

Gilad stepped closer to the bed and waited until Archelaus approached. "My King, my only request is that I may be given your slave Sabina and any children she might have had." There was silence in the room for several minutes as the old man thought about the strange request.

"No gold?"

"Only Sabina."

"So be it! As my son is my witness, I give her and any children to you. It is a fitting thing. You will make many male babies with her, and they will grow to be real men." He smiled and looked straight at his son. "We all know there are damned few of those anymore." Archelaus frowned and turned away. He was already aware that Herod's will specified that Rome should divide his kingdom into three parts, one each for three of his designated sons. Herod had made it clear that he did not consider any of his offspring capable of handling the entire country. "Archelaus, my son, when I am gone, honor this promise."

Archelaus did not turn to face his father. His answer was barely audible. "Yes father."

"And add twenty pieces of gold. Sabina is an expensive woman." He smiled, thinking of all the joys he had shared with her. Then he motioned for Gilad to come closer. "Take good care of her Gilad. She is a fine woman but strong in spirit. She will be a good match for you." Then both men were smiling.

"I will take good care of her, my King, and also any children you may have given her."

"She deserves a real man. And you deserve such a woman." He closed his eyes for a moment as a smile crossed his face again. "My blessings on you both."

Gilad turned and nodded to Archelaus and walked out into the hall where his men were standing guard. Gilad stood in the hallway for several minutes breathing fresh air in large gulps. He desperately wanted to rid himself of the smell of the dark room where Herod lay waiting for death. Slowly the stench left

100

his nostrils and a smile began to form across his face. Even his large beard could not hide the happiness that had just entered his mind. He would have Sabina, the woman he had wanted and waited for since the first time he had seen her. Their eyes had met for only a few moments, but in that instant he had known she was the woman he wanted above all others. And now the waiting was over. He turned his head so that his guards would not see that happiness, as well as death, walked the same halls. Death be damned; his life was just beginning.

By morning Herod was dead.

* * *

Herod's body was taken to the Herodium, a circular fortress built on a hill south of Jerusalem where he had won a decisive victory in his quest to become king. He was buried there within the two circular walls he had built. He had been dead four days when Gilad walked into the chief administrator's resplendent office and requested Sabina. Gilad noted that the room was much larger than his own office, and the floors were covered with hand woven rugs from the orient. A large table stood in the center of the room covered with fruit and stacks of dates. Standing by the window was a tall, tanned young woman clothed in a translucent gown. She stood like a statue, not moving. Gilad was not even sure that she was alive. She might well have been a beautiful statue, frozen in time for all to admire. The bureaucrat looked up from his writing and stared at Gilad with contempt. He was a small man with thinning hair that shadowed the top of his shining head. He had to turn his head and look up uncomfortably to see the tall man looking down on him. He studied Gilad's blue cloak carefully for several minutes before he spoke. "And why should I turn over that slave to you?"

101

"Herod gave her to me before he died."

"And how do you verify that?"

Gilad was both shocked and insulted. A bureaucrat questioning the word of the Commander of the King's Guard? He glared at the man for several moments before speaking. "Archelaus was there. He can confirm the gift."

"And why would Herod have given you this woman?"

Gilad looked at the little man for several moments without speaking. He waited until the administrator looked back into his face before addressing the question. It was obvious the large man was getting angry. "It was a promise made long ago. Speak with Archelaus." Gilad's agitation was increasing by the minute. He was not accustomed to being treated with such derision.

"I will certainly do so. You can come back tomorrow for my decision."

"*Your* decision?"

"That's right. I handle all details such as this for Archelaus now, and I will make the final decision."

Gilad's hand went instinctively to the handle of his sword. The administrator noted the motion and moved his chair backward slightly. Gilad stood staring into the man's eyes for several minutes before slowly moving his hand to the belt around his waist and stepping backward two steps. "I'll return tomorrow. Be sure you talk to Archelaus. He was there when Herod made the gift. He will confirm it." Gilad then stepped closer and looked down into the man's eyes. "I expect her here tomorrow, ready to leave with me." Gilad paused for a moment then added. "And Herod also promised 20 bars of gold. You can confirm that with Archelaus as well."

The official nodded slightly, and Gilad turned and left, cursing under his breath. At noon the next day Gilad returned to the office and stood waiting for a long time before he was seen. "I have returned. I assume you have spoken to Archelaus."

"I have, and he knows nothing of such a promise."

Gilad stood for a long time and just looked into the eyes of the man before him. "You did speak to Archelaus?"

"Yes, and he has no memory of such a promise."

"I will speak to Archelaus, personally."

"That will be impossible."

"Why?"

"His schedule is full. There is no time to meet with him."

"Archelaus and I will make that decision."

"No, you won't. I control his schedule."

"Then find time for me to speak to him regarding this matter."

"I don't take orders from you." A small grin crossed the administrator's face. "Actually, you take orders from me now. All palace functions now report to me, and that includes the Palace Guards."

Gilad stood in silence and peered into the man's eyes for several moments. Then he turned and walked out the door. His hand was on the handle of his sword as he left. He could feel the sneer of the bureaucrat burning into his back as he walked from the room. He swore silently, an oath he would not forget.

Chapter 19

Rebecca was crawling across the floor with Samuel when Nathan entered. The spring air that followed the tall man into the room gave it a sense of new life. She was pregnant, and quite large with child, but the humor in the moment was quickly lost when she saw his face. "Nathan, what's wrong?"

"The king has died in Jericho. Herod is dead."

"Was he killed?"

"No, he died in his bed."

"Was one of his ten wives with him?"

Nathan smiled. "No, I don't think that is how he died, but I'm sure several of them would have been glad to kill him, given the chance." He looked at her trying to get up from the floor and reached down to pull her up. "The baby in your belly is growing every day. You are getting heavy. Soon I will need two donkeys just to get you to the market."

Rebecca pushed him playfully then reached up and gave him a kiss. "I love you, Mr. Guard." They both sat down and she reached for the water jug as she spoke. "So, the king is dead. What does that mean to us? Who do you guard now?"

"That is being decided. Since Herod had his sons Alexander and Aristobulus executed three years ago, I can only assume that it will be one of the remaining sons. Gilad told us to just continue with our functions until a new king is named."

Rebecca wanted to sit in Nathan's lap and kiss him, but her stomach made that impossible, so she just reached across the table and held his hands. "How did you feel about Herod? You never talked about him."

"I guess he was like most men, only more powerful. He could be evil, but he also had great dreams for the country. He murdered children in Bethlehem and executed his wife

Mariamne, his mother-in-law, and his brother-in-law. He even had two of his own sons executed by strangulation. He constantly fought to maintain his power. But he also built the urban port in Caesarea, the royal palace in Jerusalem, one at Masada, the theater and amphitheater, and he also began rebuilding the temple in Jerusalem. I suppose he was a complex man who feared nothing, even Yahweh. Some men live with their hearts in control. Others live without hearing the whispers from their souls. I fear Herod was the latter. While he was truly powerful, I think he was never truly happy." Nathan rose and walked around behind Rebecca's chair and bent and kissed her on the top of her head. "But now, however, there is one other item we must consider. Now that Herod is dead, there is no reason for us to remain here in Bethany if we wish to move back to Jerusalem. Once the new king is in place I will talk to Gilad."

"Who do you think will be the new king of Judea?"

"It appears that Archelaus will be our new king."

"What do you know about him? Will he be as cruel as Herod?"

"They say he is weak, but that is something we will not know for a while. Let us hope he is a better man than his father. There are many riots in the streets. I fear we may have an insurrection to deal with very soon."

Rebecca said nothing as she watched Samuel climb up to a standing position then take a few steps toward his parents. After a few steps he fell. Immediately he grasped a small table nearby and climbed up to try again. As she watched her son she spoke. "I have such mixed feelings about moving. This has become my home." She looked up into Nathan's face. "But I know how hard it has been on you walking back and forth to work in Jerusalem."

"It has been difficult."

She waited. When he spoke no more she rose. "Then we will move to be near your work. You have struggled with that long enough. Besides, I want you home more as well." She patted her stomach. "And with a new child coming, I will need your help with these crawling babies."

"That's true, but it looks like this one is getting ready to walk." He nodded toward Samuel.

"Yes, he is. You promised you'd teach him to walk, and now he's on the verge of running."

"Well, he's not quite ready to run, but he will be walking safely soon."

"You promised he would." She hugged her husband. "And now it's true."

Nathan put his hand under her chin and lifted her face to his. He kissed her gently. "I wish I could take credit for Samuel's walking, but other than inheriting my determination, he's done this on his own."

"But you knew he would walk. You knew it; I was not sure."

"Babies learning to walk is the nature of life. I knew that. I also knew it would be difficult for him. His entire life will be more difficult than most. But the same determination he has shown in learning to walk is the same determination that will get him through the difficult times he will face."

"You are a wise man, my husband."

"Right now I am a hungry man."

"Then play with your son while your daughter and I finish dinner."

"A girl? Are you planning to have a girl?"

"As you say, it is the nature of life. We mothers are also wise."

"I never doubted that for a moment, my dear." Nathan was smiling as he knelt beside Samuel who was taking tenuous and awkward steps toward his father.

Chapter 20

Three men walked to the door of the residence in the center of Jerusalem. Two were helping the third who was blind. A long stick in his hand waved in front of him as he walked. They climbed the six stone stairs to the door with some difficulty and were instantly met by a young slave. She showed them in and closed the door after them, peering out for several moments. The group found the food and drink waiting in the large room in the center of the house and began filling their plates. Over the next fifteen minutes more men filed into the room until all seats were filled. The leader rose and waited until the room was quiet. "Gentlemen, it seems our mission has been taken from us. Herod is dead—in Jericho." Several of the men expressed surprise and several clapped their hands in delight. "Let us drink to the death of Herod; may he rot in Gehenna."

"Most likely he will." Several nodded and laughed at the comment.

"It appears that Archelaus will be taking control of Judea. The Romans did not give him the dignity of being called our king. He will be called Ethnarch of Judea, Samaria, and Idumea instead. I have heard that he is a weak man with little backbone. But we cannot be sure. It seems that becoming a king tends to change a man, especially if he is Herodian."

The older man seated near the leader spoke up quickly. Everyone in the room turned to hear what he had to say. "That's right. We really don't know Archelaus, but he is a Herodian, so we need to watch him closely. The real question is Rome. Herod was merely a Roman tool. My guess is that Archelaus will be the same—if Rome decides to inflict him upon us." He turned to the designated leader. "What are our plans for Archelaus?"

"We watch him to determine just what kind of man he is. If he is anything like his father, we go back to our original plans; we kill him." He looked at the blind man putting a large piece of bread into his mouth. "What is the status of our discussions with the new informant? Can we trust him, and will he be helpful?"

One of the men handed a wine goblet to the blind man struggling to swallow his glutinous portion of food. He took a long drink, cleared his throat and spoke. "I have good news to report on that. He is definitely trustworthy. We tested him twice and he proved himself to us. He has been meeting with our fighters to improve their planning and skills."

"What about weapons?"

"We talked about that. They are stored in Antonio Fortress; there is no way of stealing them from there. But he did say there are occasions when weapons are shipped to other areas outside Jerusalem. There might be an opportunity to intercept them once they leave Jerusalem."

"When would a shipment be made? How many men guard such equipment?"

"It is not a regularly scheduled event. We have to wait for him to alert us to a shipment."

The leader continued his questions, repeating an earlier question. "How many men would they have as guards?"

"He says there are generally no more than twenty. The weapons are hidden, and they disguised the caravan as government administrators taking surveys of the kingdom."

One of the men smiled and spoke out. "That's a dumb idea."

"Why?"

"There are lots of people who would want to attack a group of government bureaucrats." Everyone laughed.

The leader raised his hands for quiet and looked at the young man sitting in the middle of the group. "How many men would you need to attack such a caravan?"

"I'll have to study this a bit, but I imagine roughly thirty or forty if we can catch them by surprise."

The blind man spoke up urgently. "There would be a mixture of Roman soldiers and mercenaries according to my contact."

"Then more likely forty since we are still more poorly armed."

"So maybe we should send fifty and restore balance to the armament problem." He spoke toward the blind man in the rear of the room. "Tell your contact we need to know as soon as possible about any arms shipments. It will take time to organize our men and make a plan."

"As I said, these are not regularly scheduled shipments. We may not know until a day or so before they start one."

"Just let us know as soon as you can." The leader turned and poured two goblets with wine. He handed one to the older man seated near him and took a long drink from the other. "Passover starts in two days. Let us all celebrate with our families and friends and pray for Yahweh's blessings, and let us also pray that Archelaus is not made of the same greed and power lust as his father."

Chapter 21

Jerusalem, 4 B.C.

Nathan and Tobias stood on the dusty road outside Jerusalem and stared at the long line of crucifixes that lined the road. Over two thousand Jewish rebels hung there in death. Nathan shook his head in disgust. "Why don't they take them down? Don't they know our tradition prohibits anyone hanging on a tree overnight? They're dead. Take them down."

Tobias wiped the sweat from his forehead and folded the cloth back into his sash. "I think Archelaus is making a statement. Insurrection is not to be tolerated."

"Our ethnarch is a cruel man."

"Like his father."

"Yes, like his father." Nathan looked back at the men following them and resumed his march toward Jerusalem. "His troops killed over three thousand during the Passover riots. When will this ever end?"

"How many people do you imagine Herod killed during his reign? Now we have his sons to deal with. Archelaus is ruling Idumea, Judea, and Samaria and his brother, Antipas, is tetrarch over Galilee and Perea. Philip got northern Transjordan. It must be nice to have a father who is king."

Nathan stepped aside to check the guards following them. "Think about it, would you have wanted Herod as a father? He had two of his other sons murdered."

"I guess you're right. Treachery and deceit seem to follow very closely with royalty."

"Thousands of our kinsmen have died at the hands of these men. The mercenaries have earned their pay."

Tobias gave a signal with his arm and the guards fell into a loose formation behind their leader. "I guess we were lucky that we were not involved in all the killings. Being a royal guard is a much easier job than killing Jews at Passover."

"Or crucifying Jews along the roads to Jerusalem." Nathan looked down the long rows of bodies hanging on the crosses and cursed quietly as he trudged up the small hill toward Jerusalem.

Tobias stepped quickly to keep up with the taller man. "Nathan, when Herod died I was concerned about what would happen to the King's Guard. As bad as Archelaus is as a leader, at least we kept our jobs."

"I was worried about Archelaus, and he has confirmed my worst fears. This is no longer a job of pride for me." The two men walked on in front of the line of guards behind them, checking carefully the faces of the men on the side of the road watching them. Nathan noticed that there was no contempt in the eyes that watched them as happened occasionally in the past. Now all he saw was fear. "The people have been thoroughly defeated. There is no hope in their hearts anymore. It must have been like this on the road to Egypt when our people were taken into captivity."

Kalev marched up to his two friends with anger all over his face. "Have you seen what that monster has done? He's killing his own kinsmen just to show everyone how strong his is." Kalev wiped his brow with the sleeve of his cloak then turned to look again upon the bodies hanging on the crosses along the road. "That bastard! We've got to do something about this. Good men cannot let this stand."

Nathan put his hand on Kalev's shoulder and physically turned him away from the gruesome sight. "Be quiet my friend. We shall talk about this, but in private. Be patient; there are many men who feel as you do, but we must plan before we react." Kalev looked first at Nathan then at Tobias then nodded, trying hard to tame his impatience. "Now, walk with us, but say little. There are many ears in this city."

Tobias watched a group of farmers moving away from the road as the guards passed. He then slowed the march until a stubborn donkey was finally pulled from their path. "I can only think of one thing Archelaus has done right. At least he didn't call us the Ethnarch's Guard."

Nathan smiled weakly. "Yes, Palace Guards sounds much better."

"Indeed, we need some dignity for our positions, but at least it's better than being unemployed, I guess."

"Perhaps; perhaps not." He looked at Kalev who was still scowling.

Chapter 22

Jerusalem, 5AD

As always happens with the passing of time, men grow older and babies grow up to eventually replace them. Nathan was twenty-seven years old when Samuel turned eleven. Samuel's life had been difficult, but with the help of strong parents, he was growing into a fine young man. Often he stood aside and watched the other children chase each other and run among the small houses in his neighborhood. As promised Nathan had taught his son to walk, but it was an awkward pace that set him aside from the other children. The time alone had often caused him to turn his head as tears streaked his dusty face, but that solitude had also been a blessing. The awkward little boy in the village was learning lessons that would remain with him throughout his life, and luckily the example of his father was one that pointed him in the right direction.

The boys were not yet in puberty, but they had already begun noticing the girls. Some handled this new fascination with dignity; others did not. Like all playgrounds, this one had its bullies, and the worst of the group was busily teasing one of the girls. Adriel was not accustomed to such attention and was not sure how to handle his advances, and since he was the biggest boy in the group, he was having his way with teasing her. When she began crying, however, Samuel decided it had gone far enough. He limped over to the crowd of children and walked into the fray. "Stop. Leave her alone."

The bigger boy looked down at the younger, and smaller, boy who leaned precariously on his crutch. "What? Go away Crip. We don't need you around here."

"Go away yourself, and quit being a bully. Can't you see Adriel is crying? You should be ashamed, picking on a girl."

"Maybe I should pick on you."

"That would be a very bad idea."

The bigger boy started laughing as he poked at the shorter Samuel. "Go home. You can't run; you can barely walk. If you didn't have that staff you'd have to crawl."

"You've made a mistake; this staff is not for walking."

"Oh really, then what's it for?"

"It's for bullies like you." Faster than the larger boy could imagine, the staff flashed out and struck him on the neck. Stunned he reached out and grabbed the end of the staff, but with amazing strength Samuel jerked it from the surprised boy's hand.

"How did you do that?"

"When walking is so hard, it makes you strong." The staff swung again and struck the boy on the leg. Immediately, Samuel assumed a very good replica of a guardsman's defensive position.

"I'll beat you up, kid."

"No you won't. That would be the biggest mistake of your life."

"How so."

"I figure it this way. If we fight and I win, you will be the laughingstock of the village—getting beaten by a crippled boy. But then again, suppose you win. You'll be disgraced in the village. Imagine a big kid beating up a smaller boy who is crippled. You'll be scorned by everyone. So, either way, you lose."

The boy looked at Samuel for several minutes. "You're a smart kid. Maybe we can be friends."

"Not if you keep teasing Adriel."

"I didn't mean to make her cry." He turned to the girl who was drying her eyes and nodded. "Sorry." She sniffled a few times and moved over to stand by Samuel. "I'm sorry what

I said about you." He reached out his hand. Samuel looked at it briefly, then took it with his left hand, his right still holding the staff defensively. Adriel moved closer to her defender and watched him carefully. When he looked over, she smiled.

Chapter 23

Rebecca placed her washcloth aside and walked to the window. There was a great deal of laughing and shouting going on in the road just outside the house. She knew the voices; Nathan and Samuel frequently would erupt in great shouts of glee as they played whatever game they chose that day. She squinted slightly and saw the two, shooting arrows at a target Nathan had placed on a small fence across the road. As she watched, she smiled a contented and happy smile. The two men she loved so much were still playing even though both were grown. Well, Samuel was nearly 12; that was getting close to being a man. Later that evening she pulled Nathan aside. "You were teaching Samuel to use a bow?"

"It's not a real bow. It quite a bit smaller than a real one, but it will be sufficient to teach him how to shoot."

"Are you thinking of making him a soldier, or a guard perhaps?" There was a smile on her face as she teased her husband.

"Certainly not. Samuel will never be a soldier or a guard." Nathan put his hand under her chin and lifted her face to his. "No, Samuel is a Levite, but he will not be a palace guard or a temple guard, and not just because of his stature. Samuel has a special heart. He is far too good to be like me."

Rebecca embraced the man before her. She spoke into his chest. "Nathan, you are a good man, a very special man. You are strong and brave, but you, too, have a kind heart. That's why I love you." She leaned forward on the tips of her toes and kissed him gently.

"You and Samuel have made me so happy. My life has been such a joy with the two of you; you know that." The smile on her face suddenly grew larger. "And you can get ready for even more joy in a few months."

Nathan looked at her with a look of both joy and surprise on his face. "Are you sure?" He reached immediately and felt her stomach. Even with all of her clothes, he could feel the small life growing in her womb.

"I'm sure. This is number three. I should know by now." She placed her hands over his as they searched for the first signs of a baby.

"What wonderful news." He was smiling broadly.

"Yes, it is, but now we have one more mouth to feed."

"Do you feel it will be a girl or a boy?"

Rebecca paused in thought then turned to him smiling. "I think it is a girl."

"Another sister for Samuel?"

"Yes, I think so."

"Well, our girl is so beautiful, I think another girl would be wonderful."

"Next time I promise a boy."

"Either child would be fine with me. As long as the girls are as beautiful as their mother and the boys are as handsome as their father..." Nathan brushed a strand of hair from Rebecca's face and smiled at her for several moments before reaching to rub her belly again. "Welcome, my little pumpkin."

Chapter 24

The three young men sat together, apart from the other guards. They were all eating their evening meal at the palace. The long wooden table between them boasted countless scars from swords and knives that had been sharpened there or used there as utensils for meals. This was a place where young men came to eat and share company with their comrades. The walls contained no brightly colored cloth draped to the floor, only an occasional esteemed sword or javelin from some long remembered battle. There were stains of wine and gravy and even of blood on the weathered wood. This was a room for youth and excitement. Adrenalin lived here. Smiles brightened this room, not trappings. It had become a weekly event for all guards to have their midweek dinner together and enjoy the comradery of their fellow guards. The conversation was animated, but quiet. Kalev looked around to ensure they were not being overheard then spoke. "Did you see what that animal did? He murdered thousands of Jews, and left the bodies hanging on crosses along the road to Jerusalem."

"And at Passover. It's hard to conceive."

Kalev looked into the eyes of the other two men, first Nathan then Tobias. "If I had been there, I would have taken my sword and fought the mercenaries who slaughtered our people."

Tobias looked at his friend. "Then you would have been dead today as well as the others."

"Maybe I would, but at least I would feel like a man as I died."

"There has to be another way. The mercenaries are just goons hired to do the dirty work. They are mindless animals." Tobias looked around and scoured the room. "The real problem

119

is Archelaus. He is an abomination. He is the one responsible for our people hanging on crosses outside Jerusalem. He ordered their deaths."

"Then let's kill him. It would be easy for us, after all, we are his guards. Who has better access?" Kalev reached across the table and speared a piece of lamb with his knife.

Tobias looked at Nathan who had been silent in the conversation. "You have a good point, Kalev. But what if we could have him killed without implicating ourselves. Perhaps an enemy group could attack and maybe one gets through and kills our worthless leader."

Kalev looked up smiling. "Now that is a great idea." Then his smile faded. "But how can we make that happen. Why not just sneak into his chambers at night, and kill him with a Parthian sword."

Nathan spoke for the first time. "I can get such a sword."

Tobias pushed his food aside and rose. "Let's keep this to ourselves and give it more thought. Whatever our strategy, it will take much planning. This needs to be well thought out." He reached for his goblet and finished his wine.

* * *

The unit leaders rose from their seats and filed from the morning meeting. Gilad nodded to Tobias to remain. When they were alone he poured some wine for each and sat down, motioning for Tobias to do the same. "I noticed you in a secret conversation last night. What is Kalev upset about now?"

Tobias paused for a moment, but he spoke honestly to his commander. He knew he could trust Gilad and so he spoke freely. "It seems many of our men are upset with the killings ordered by Archelaus."

"I, too, share that concern."

"If he were attacked, I fear some of our men might not defend him well."

Gilad looked at Tobias thoughtfully before speaking. "How many would kill him themselves?"

Tobias was surprised at the directness of Gilad's comment. "There are those who would consider that."

"There are?"

Tobias looked at Gilad for several minutes before speaking. He was clearly uneasy with the direction of the conversation. "Yes."

"Would they be willing to forfeit their own lives to accomplish that?"

Tobias looked directly into Gilad's eyes before speaking. When he did, it was not a timid reply but one of strength. "Yes, they would."

Gilad rubbed his hands together in thought as he stared out the window to his right. Finally, he looked back into Tobias's face. "Well, Tobias, I would not be willing to let them make that mistake. It would be a waste to have good men die just so an evil man would die with them. You must stop them." When Tobias remained silent, Gilad continued. "There is another way, one with less consequences for our friends." Gilad leaned forward and continued with a conspiratorial voice. "There are other men who also want Archelaus dead or out of Judea. Some are very powerful and are pursuing other means to accomplish that."

Tobias was clearly surprised. "I see."

"My desire, like yours, is to see him gone. But I would prefer it be done without losing some of my men in the process. There are things that can only be solved with a sword, but there are also things best solved with quiet voices in the right ears." Gilad downed the rest of his wine before continuing. "Can you convince our young zealots to delay taking action now?" He thought a moment. "Can they be held at bay for at least three weeks?"

"I'll try."

"Good, but they, nor anyone else, can know about this conversation. Do you understand? If this information were known, good men working for our cause would be in jeopardy. They already have risked much, but they are men of courage and conviction. Let's give them a chance."

"I understand."

"And if those men fail, I will be the first to plunge my sword into that bastard." Gilad flashed a wry smile as he spoke.

"Then I will be second." The two men raised their hands and grasped each other's in agreement. "Let us hope the men you talk about will be successful. Archelaus doesn't deserve to live after what he has done to our people."

"I agree. I just hope the Romans agree as well."

* * *

The changing of the guard was scheduled at daybreak. Nathan, Tobias, and Kalev were all there waiting for the sun to climb over the horizon. Kalev carefully moved the three away from the other guards and spoke excitedly to his friends. "I've been working on a plan to have Archelaus hanging on a tree outside Jerusalem within a week. All I need is that Parthian sword you mentioned, Nathan."

Tobias put his finger to his lips and motioned for Kalev to speak more quietly. "If you ever expect to have a chance to do such a deed, you'd better plan carefully and speak more quietly."

Nathan studied Kalev carefully. "Perhaps we can talk of this tonight. You can all join me at my home for dinner."

* * *

When the meal was finished, Tobias turned to Nathan and Kalev. "You are both my closest friends. We are like brothers, so listen to me carefully. I have information that you do not know, and it is information I have promised not to divulge to anyone. Very simply, there are actions being taken even now to rid Judea of Archelaus. It would be wise for us to be patient and give these other actions time to be implemented."

Kalev put his palms together and let his fingers touch his lips. He thought for several moments before speaking. "Can you give us more details about these *other actions*?"

"No. I cannot. Let me just say that I gave my word that I would argue for patience for a reasonable time. You both know I would tell you the details if I could, but I cannot. I have to ask you to trust me as I would trust you."

Nathan looked into Tobias's eyes for only a moment before replying. "That is good enough for me. I trust you. But I do have a question. How long are we to be patient for this other action to commence?"

"Not long. Maybe a month. No longer." Tobias watched as Nathan nodded.

"Okay. One month. If all is the same, then we prepare a plan."

Kalev sat for several moments staring at the table before him. Finally he looked up and spoke. "I hate to wait that long, but I will agree. However, I do have one request. If possible, can you keep us informed regarding the success of the other actions against Archelaus?"

"I doubt I will have that information until it is complete. Until then, it is very important for us to remain silent about this. No one is to know. No one! One slip of this information and good men will die. We cannot speak of this." Tobias searched both of their faces. "Is that understood?" Kalev and Nathan nodded.

As the sun rose, the new detachment of guards marched off to their assigned locations with freshly shined swords and spears. As the leader of Unit 2, Tobias walked around the palace to inspect all of his guards. When he finished he met Nathan under a tree just outside the entrance of the palace. They were alone there. "Thanks for helping me calm Kalev. He's a good man, but a bit impetuous at times. His impatience could be our undoing." Nathan smiled and nodded. Tobias looked directly into his eyes. "I didn't want to go into more details with Kalev earlier, but I know I can trust you completely. The truth is that there is a political move to have Archelaus banished from Judea."

Nathan's face was one of surprise. "Banished? Archelaus? Only Rome could do that."

"There are high level men on the way to Rome even now to try to accomplish that."

"If Archelaus discovers them, they are dead men."

"They are men of conscience, men of courage and integrity. They are risking everything, but they are willing to take that risk for our people."

"When the emperor makes his decision, it may determine the fate of Archelaus or it may settle the fate of those brave men."

"Rome decides. Either he is banished, or those men die. The emperor controls their lives with his decision."

Nathan glanced around to ensure they were not being heard by anyone. "Those men are truly men of honor and courage. That is a weighty decision they made."

"Yes, it is, and that is why we must wait and remain silent."

"Don't worry Tobias. Kalev is quick to action, but he will not speak of this. He knows not to do that."

"I hope you're right."

Nathan picked up a small stone at his feet and threw it against the palace wall. As it bounced off the stones and fell back to the ground, Nathan picked up another and handed it to Tobias. "If we could find a way to propel one of these at a high rate of speed at a distance, we'd have a fantastic new weapon." He watched as Tobias threw his stone at the wall. It was clear he was using this time to consider his next comment. "It was Gilad wasn't it?"

"Yes, how did you know?"

"Gilad is always concerned about his men. If we killed Archelaus, we would be condemned and die as well. If the politicians get rid of him, we are safe." He paused for only a moment. "Besides, who else could have such information and get it to the guards. Gilad is the only one who would be aware of our plans, but how did he know? Did you tell him?"

"No, he saw the same crucifixes along the road to Jerusalem. He has had the same thoughts himself. He assumed, correctly, that some of us might be thinking the same thing."

"Gilad is a good leader." He thought a moment. "He is also a good man."

"Yes, he is, and his ears get far more information about what is happening in Judea than his men. Frankly, he was concerned that we might not protect Archelaus if there were an attack."

"So, he feels as we do?"

"If the new plan fails, we will have another fighter in our band of rebels."

"I cannot think of a better comrade in our quest."

Tobias shaded his eyes and peered toward the corner of the palace where another guard stood on duty. "How are Rebecca and the kids?"

"They're all great. The children are growing so fast. Samuel is a fine young man, and, of course, the girls are beautiful like their mother."

"How do you manage to feed that brood?"

"Very carefully. I help one of the stone masons on my day off now and then. They need a tall man, and it brings in a little additional money. We really don't need very much, but I am a little concerned about when the girls are old enough to need a dowry."

"There's plenty of time for that, my friend. They're still little." Tobias put his hand on his friend's shoulder. "I have no family, so you can count on "Uncle" Tobias when the time comes."

Nathan smiled and put his own hand on Tobias's shoulder. "Thank you, Tobias. But enough talk about the future. Come over to our house for dinner tonight and see those little girls who are quickly growing into young women. They would love to see you."

"I'll stop by as soon as I finish my reports this evening. Till then."

Chapter 25

The men entered the large home from three entrances, not at once but spaced by at least ten-minute intervals between the quiet knocks on the heavy wooden doors. Each was greeted by a facial search, then allowed entry. Doors were quickly closed behind each man that entered. Only once did more than one man approach the door, when one of them was blind. Inside a table was prepared with food and drink. When the last man arrived, the doors were locked and the men all sat, waiting for the leader to start the meeting. El'Azar, the owner of the house, walked into the room and smiled at the group. He looked around and quietly counted those sitting or standing in small groups. They were older men with long beards, mostly white. Five of the men were members of the Sanhedrin, the most prestigious group of leaders in Judea. Their robes were ornate and expensively trimmed so that all who passed knew they were in the presence of men of importance. Others in the room were merchants or men from prestigious families. Some held high positions in the government. Some were Pharisees; some were Sadducees or Levites. They represented Judea and all of the tribes of Israel. All those present were wealthy. El'Azar was a man in his early fifties, tall and a bit overweight—unusual for Judea in 6AD. He was commander of the Temple Guards and a deputy to the Chief Priest, Caiaphas. Caiaphas was not in attendance at the meeting, but it was assumed if El'Azar were leading the meeting, Caiaphas was certainly involved. "Gentlemen, welcome. I'm glad you could come with such late notice. As you know, Archelaus has been banished to Gaul. May his soul rot in Gehenna. Our emissaries and those of the Samaritans were able to convince Rome that Archelaus had to go. They were successful." There were murmurs throughout

127

the crowd as heads nodded and smiles appeared. "But now we have another problem. It seems the emperor has decided to send a Roman prefect to rule Judea." The smiles vanished immediately. "This was not totally unexpected, but we had hoped that a Jew would be put back on the throne here in Jerusalem—perhaps someone in this very room." The murmurs began again but subsided quickly as El'Azar resumed. "Philip and Antipas remain in control of their provinces, but Judea will now have a Roman prefect. That is our problem." Immediately the room was filled with men speaking and shouting over each other.

"Well, he couldn't be any worse than Archelaus. He was a barbarian. We should stone him before he leaves."

"Is the new prefect permanent, or is it a temporary measure until a new ruler can be found?"

El'Azar smiled a thin smile. "That, my friend, is the question of the day. We were not told."

"We don't want a Roman in charge of Judea; he is not one of us; he is a godless gentile."

"Precisely."

"So, what can we do, El'Azar?"

"I called you here tonight to inform you of Rome's decision. I also wanted to alert you all that we must work as a group and strategize together. As I see it, there are two directions Rome can take. One, they put the prefect here permanently. Two, the prefect is only a placeholder until another can be selected to take control—a Jew." El'Azar let his words float across the room as he lifted a goblet of wine to his lips. He held the goblet before his face and peered at it for a lengthy period of time before putting it to his lips. After taking a sip, he continued. "Our strategy depends on which course Caesar Augustus decides to take." He raised his hands to quiet the gathering. "Men of Judea, listen to me carefully. I would like each of you to consider the directions Rome might take. What do you think we should do in either case? Think through this carefully and get back to me individually with your ideas. Once we know what the decision will be from Rome, then we can meet again and decide how we should react." El'Azar pointed to the table filled with food and wine. "So, for now, please help yourselves. Enjoy the meal; there is little else we can do while we wait for the emperor to make a decision."

Chapter 26

Jerusalem, 6 A.D.

Tobias walked around the corner of the palace and shielded his eyes with his hand. He was looking for someone and soon found the object of his search. He walked across the courtyard and sat briefly beside Nathan who was sharpening his sword. Tobias looked at it with some envy. "That is a beautiful sword."

"It is a heavy sword that happens to be quite dull at the moment." Nathan was rubbing a large smooth stone against the edge of the blade. "But it will not be dull long. I intend to make it as sharp as our Jewish swords."

"May I try it?"

"Of course. Who would deny his commander?" Nathan was smiling. He knew he had embarrassed Tobias.

Tobias took the sword and moved away from Nathan in order to swing it safely. He lifted it above his head and then swung it forcefully at waist height. "What a beautiful sword. Where do you think it was made?"

"One of Darius's men told me it was crafted far to the west from Rome."

"The men there must be large and strong. This is a very heavy sword." He raised it in front of his face and studied it carefully. "The metal is strong, but you are right. It is dull. How did Darius fight with such a weapon?"

"Brute strength. I'm sure he must have knocked his enemies to the ground without cutting them at all." Nathan accepted the sword as Tobias handed it to him carefully. "But I will know the true strength of this sword. I'll make it sharp and strong." Nathan resumed his task of scraping the stone along the edge of the sword.

"That is a nice sharpening stone."

"Gilad gave it to me. He agreed that such a sword deserved to be treated as a fine weapon and kept sharp." Nathan lowered the blade and looked at his friend as he blew fine dust from his hands. "But I doubt you came out in this sun to talk about how to sharpen a sword."

Tobias smiled and nodded to his friend. "Let's walk outside the palace and have lunch under the large Sycamore tree where we played as boys."

"That was a long time ago."

"In my mind it was yesterday. I often long for those days of endless play and adventures."

Nathan grinned as he rose to join his friend. "Well, the adventure part is still very real in our lives. We can hardly call these years boring."

"That is true, my friend." Tobias motioned for Nathan to follow and walked back into the palace. It was a short distance to his office where he gathered a small loaf of bread and a large piece of cheese and placed them and a jug of wine in a pack he slung over his shoulder. "I'm hungry, but mostly I'm tired of this office. A little sunshine and peace will be a welcomed change in my day." Fifteen minutes later the two men were leaning against the trunk of the old, scarred tree. Nathan divided the bread and cut the cheese into pieces as Tobias poured the wine into two small bowls. As they ate, Tobias began speaking in an unusually low tone of voice. "Have you heard about Archelaus?"

"No, did the other action succeed?"

"Yes, this time it is Archelaus who will be the victim, not the Jews of Judea." Nathan turned and gave Tobias all of his attention. "Both the Samaritans and our Jewish leaders petitioned Rome to have him removed, and Rome agreed. Archelaus has been banished to Gaul. He was heard cursing in the palace late last night. One of the maids said he and his family were all packing this morning."

"Have you heard anything from Gilad yet?"

"No, and he probably will never mention it again. He is a wise man. We need to be oblivious of all that is happening."

"Do you think Archelaus will go to Rome to address the emperor?"

"I think he is going to Gaul—permanently. It is not wise to question the emperor's decisions." Nathan drank a large sip of the wine and waited for Tobias to continue. "Actually, I *know* that is where he is going. I was called to Gilad's office last night and his scribe ordered me to prepare a team to escort Archelaus and his family to Caesarea where they will embark on a ship to Gaul. When I inquired about the duration of the trip, I was informed that our guards would return as soon as Archelaus sailed." Tobias took a piece of the cheese and put in into the bread he was holding and then took a big bite with wine. After he had swallowed, he continued. "Archelaus is done."

"The scribe gave you the orders, and Gilad was not there?"

"As I keep saying, Gilad is a very wise man."

Nathan raised his head and looked off into the distance. "Well I hardly know what to say. Perhaps there is justice left in this world after all."

"Real justice would be us running him through with that large Roman sword you have. That's what the bastard really deserves."

"It has crossed my mind on several occasions." Nathan turned to face Tobias. "Who will take over Judea now? I hope it isn't another of Herod's kin."

"No, it will be a Roman. I have heard his name, but I know nothing about him. It will be a prefect named Coponius. I know he is appointed by Rome, but other than that, I know nothing of the man."

"Well, it is hard to believe he could be as bad as Archelaus."

"You are right about that."

"Do you think the guards will remain at the palace?"

"I do. It is an item of both safety and also for politics. The Romans like to appear as partners in the government rather than the absolute rulers they really are. They got rid of the Jewish ethnarch; even more reason to retain Jewish guards. It's a big show of unity, Rome and Judea."

"Well, I would like to respectfully request that I not be assigned to the team traveling to Gaul."

"Even though I despise Archelaus, it is our duty to ensure that he arrives alive in Caesarea. For that reason alone Gilad will probably omit both of us from the list of his protectors." Both men laughed as they finished their lunch.

Nathan spoke as he gazed off into the distance. "When will the brutality and the killings ever end? There have been so many men who wanted power over our people. First, we had the Greeks and their allies from Egypt and Syria. They were finally defeated after the priest Mattathias slew the commander from Antiochus IV, and then the priest's son led the rebellion that won Jewish freedom. We were finally free, free to fight among ourselves for many years, only to be conquered again, this time by Rome. And they gave us the likes of Herod and Archelaus. When will we ever find a leader who leads without fear, a leader who doesn't destroy the very people he leads? There has been so much death and so much pain for our people."

"Isaiah and Micah both prophesized such a man will come someday to bring us peace."

"We could surely use some of that. But I suspect he will need an army to achieve that peace, a very big army."

"Isaiah says he will come on a donkey."

"A donkey? Well, I hope he has a very large sword on the back of that donkey." Nathan smiled at his friend. "And I hope he comes soon!"

"We have been waiting for a very long time for this man."

"Yes, we have." Nathan drank the rest of his wine and rolled the remaining bread into a small piece of cloth. He nodded toward the palace. "Well until the Messiah comes, we have a palace to guard, so I guess we had best get back to work."

Tobias smiled. "I was thinking of a short nap beneath this tree before returning."

"Now that is the kind of leader I can follow."

Chapter 27

It was one of those days that is relatively rare in Jerusalem when the air is cool and fresh after a brief rain just before sunrise. The world seemed alive as the guards packed their supplies in the staging area for the long trip to Caesarea as escorts to the deposed ruler. Archelaus and his household had not arrived from the palace, but his emissary, the chief administrator was there with several of his slaves attending to the packing of personal items from the palace. Gilad did not speak as he passed; he only nodded and counted the five donkeys burdened with unknown supplies that the bureaucrat was carefully monitoring. There would be sixteen guards and twice that many mercenaries accompanying the deposed ruler as he left for the coast. The Roman emperor had been quick in his assessment of the situation in Judea, and his decision had been equally quick, and practical. Archelaus was to leave Jerusalem and be replaced by a Roman prefect, in three weeks. The three weeks had passed, the prefect had arrived, and Archelaus was reluctantly leaving the palace, under Roman orders.

Gilad stopped and took a deep breath of the cool air then resumed his trek through the staging ground for the trip. He had been assigned as the commander since none of the centurions wanted the job. They knew Archelaus was a Jew, not a Roman, so they all declined the assignment. It had taken a bit of maneuvering, but Gilad volunteered, and as Commander of the Palace Guards, that gave him standing for the assignment. The senior centurion had great respect for Gilad and had agreed, over the objections of the deposed administrator. Gilad had chosen his men carefully. He had personally selected Tobias and Nathan to assist in commanding the caravan. Kalev was also included. That left Archelaus with guards who despised him and loved their commander, the man Archelaus had cheated out of the only woman Gilad had ever desired.

The commander walked among the men preparing for the trip and inspected the preparations; his outward appearance was one of utter calm and control. Inside, however, he seethed with anger and rage. Sabina had been stolen from him by Archelaus and his chief administrator. Now it was he who was responsible to safely escort them to Cesearea. The anger that boiled inside him was belied suddenly by a small smile that crept across his broad face as he assessed his new command.

The administrator fussed with the personal wagons filled with plundered goods from the palace, but he continually glanced at the five donkeys standing patiently tied to a tree nearby. That attention did not escape Gilad's careful gaze, and neither did the beautiful Emesan slave walking with the administrator's personal retinue. Sabina stopped and turned to look at the large man staring straight at her. For several moments their eyes locked, then she smiled. She had aged in the most wonderful way. Her beauty had grown with a serenity about her that he had not seen when she was just a young girl. As before, so many years in the past, she turned to walk away but stopped again and turned to face him. Only the arrival of the deposed ethnarch on a massive white horse broke Gilad's attention. The guards all turned together to admire the magnificent steed. Nathan gazed at the animal and envied the rider the use of such a fine horse. Tobias smiled. "I guess we will never get to see that beautiful horse run."

Nathan turned to his friend. "Why do you say that?"

"Look at this caravan. It will move at the speed of a crippled goat, and you can be sure Archelaus will never be very far from his protection—us, and we will be plodding along with those donkeys over there."

"You are right, it would not be safe for him to get far from the troops."

"There are few men so hated in Judea or this part of the world. He will stay close."

Nathan smiled a big grin at his friend and commander. "He would also be unwise to venture far with any of us nearby as well."

Tobias slapped Nathan's shoulder. "I can see him riding off with you close by, then you riding back, alone, on that beautiful horse."

Gilad approached and joined the two. He walked close to his men; it was obvious he did not want to be overheard. "Have you noticed the five donkeys the administrator seems to be personally protecting?"

Tobias nodded. "I did, and he ordered me to have three men assigned to protect them along the route."

"Oh really; how interesting. Perhaps we should check just what the administrator thinks is so valuable that it needs three guards. Perhaps tonight after everyone is asleep." Gilad was smiling broadly. Now the tables were turned. Gilad was in charge of the administrator.

Nathan smiled. "I'll be sure to be assigned to the asses tonight."

Gilad smiled. "See you after dark; I'll join you in this little endeavor." He scanned the area carefully. "Have either of you seen the guide who will show us the best way to our destination?"

Tobias pointed to one of the men helping place large jugs of water into one of the small wagons. "I have also brought a guard who has some familiarity with the area as well. I just want to be sure we don't get led out of the way and into a trap."

"Good planning." Gilad motioned for the man. "Let's get this caravan moving. It will be hot today. I'd like to leave before noon."

* * *

The night was clear, and the moon was almost full as it rose over the small hills north of Jerusalem. The caravan had left late, and very little distance had been covered. Their route was to travel first to Jericho, then Archelais, Sebaste, and finally to Caesarea. With the wagons and the supplies, the trip would be long. Gilad walked among the campfires as they began to glow and cast shadows across the dry landscape. They winked in the darkness as men huddled around them for protection from the evening chill. Nathan and two other guards passed on their way to guard the donkeys. In spite of their objections, the administrator had ordered that the animals not be unloaded for the night. He was personally taking water to each of them. As the guards approached, he came forward and instructed them where to stand and how to ensure the animals were not disturbed. Nathan nodded obediently and placed his men as directed. The bureaucrat had built his fire near the donkeys and sat watching them until sleep began to invade his consciousness. As an administrator, he was not used to long treks in the sun and was soon asleep beside the dying fire. Gilad walked past quietly and joined Nathan as they carefully unwrapped the packing on one of the donkeys. As expected there were bags of gold and silver bars and others full of coins from both Rome and Judea. Nathan quickly inspected the remaining beasts. He found the same treasure on each of the animals' backs. Gilad nodded. "As I expected, he's plundered the palace treasury."

"What shall we do?"

"Wait a while then quietly wake the administrator and bring him to the small canyon by the creek. It's the one we passed where the road turns West. Make sure he does not alert anyone else. Bind him and gag him just to be sure."

"And then?"

"I'll be waiting there."

The administrator had given up trying to escape the clutches of the two guards who escorted him to the small canyon near the road. As they walked in the full light of the moon, they saw a small fire burning beside the creek about a hundred yards from the road. Gilad was there, waiting as he had promised. At his direction they untied the man and removed his gag. The commander handed him a small bowl of water. "Here drink this."

"How dare you treat me like this. I'll report you to Archelaus immediately."

"That will be interesting. What do you think he will do? It is I who command the troops in this caravan. They all report to me." Gilad waited for a reply. When there was none, he continued. "It seems your plot to steal the treasury has been discovered. One of the donkeys reported you, so we investigated. It seems you took all of the treasury. Did you leave any at all?"

"What is it to you? It all belonged to Archelaus."

"Not really. It actually belongs to the new Roman Prefect, Coponius." Gilad's eyes glared as he stepped forward; the administrator stepped back immediately. "And, I might add, we have a Roman prefect because you and Archelaus made such a mess of your jobs of managing the country. Now we have a foreign government running things, not a Jew." He stepped forward again, and the man stepped backward again. "And it is your fault." Gilad pointed his finger at the little man and spoke more loudly. "Well, what do you have to say for yourself?"

"You can't do this to me! I'm a government official."

"The correct verb is *were*! Now you are little more than a common criminal, a thief stealing the wealth of the country you were supposed to protect and manage. You even helped Archelaus plan the murder of thousands of your own people. What kind of man are you?" Gilad pulled his sword from his scabbard and pointed it at the frightened man. "Sit, now, or I'll slit your throat." The man's eyes were very large as he did as instructed and sat near the small fire. Gilad pulled a leather folder from his tunic and extracted two small scrolls. "Sign both of these—now!"

"What are they; I can't read them in this light."

"You don't need to read them, just sign them."

"And if I don't?"

"If you don't, I'll chop off your right hand and you'll never sign anything again." Gilad raised his sword. The large image and the dark glaring eyes hovering over the bureaucrat were enough to send a slight shiver up his back.

"Okay. I'll sign." Gilad handed him ink and a quill.

"When you took the gold, did you even think of those who would not be paid? The cooks, the gardeners, my guards?"

"My job is to look after Archelaus. The others would have to take care of themselves."

"Stand up you piece of camel dung."

As the administrator climbed to his feet he sneered at Gilad. "You know I'll deny signing those papers, whatever they were. Furthermore, I will see you and all of your men crucified along the road to Jerusalem—just like the others who defied us." The bureaucrat was regaining his courage.

"I had planned on your lies." Gilad smiled back at the defiant man. "You are truly a fool. Don't you understand that I have killed men I did not know simply because they attacked my king, an evil man for whom I was responsible? How much more would I do to an evil man in order to protect those I love? You may have been clever in the politics of the palace, but you made a major mistake; you forgot you were dealing with a military man who lives by his honor. You insulted me, and that was an insult to both my personal honor as well as my position. That was a major mistake, almost as dangerous as your taking Sabina for your own. But that was the greatest mistake of all, and for that you will die." Gilad stepped forward quickly and thrust his sword into the administrator's stomach. The man's eyes grew large as he realized what was happening. Gilad pulled his sword free and wiped it on the administrator's cloak as he fell to the ground. He turned to Tobias and Nathan. "He will die slowly. Then take four of the donkeys and the body and return to Jerusalem. Leave the body along the road with this sword nearby." He handed them a Parthian sword after he had smeared it with the official's blood. "Take the gold and silver and return it to the palace. Put it in my office and have two guards protect it until I return and the new prefect arrives. I will personally return it to his control."

"What about Archelaus?"

"Unfortunately, he must be spared, at least for the moment. Rome is watching him closely. They don't like him any more than we do, but they have alliances that depend on the man living."

"Then he gets away with the murder of thousands of people."

"Maybe not. I suspect living in Gaul without the fortune he plundered from our people may be a punishment in itself. I don't think he will enjoy his life in Gaul."

"What if he regains power?"

"If he does, I will kill him myself. But for now, he lives; that is my decision. Any questions?" There were none, so he continued. "One last thing. Tonight I want half of the gold and silver on that last donkey taken and hidden nearby. Do not keep any of it with you. Understand?"

"Yes sir."

"If there is a search, I don't want any guards found with treasure. We can recover the gold later. Now go about your work. Be the professional guards you are trained to be." With a salute they were off.

* * *

The sun climbed slowly in the eastern sky as the camp awoke and fires began to send columns of smoke into a teal blue sky. The escorts and those in Archelaus's party alike stood around the fires as the slaves began making bread and meat for breakfast. Large cloths were spread on the dry ground and soon covered with stacks of bread, fruit, and stacks of meat. Breakfast would be consumed and the camp dismantled before the caravan continued. As men were beginning to climb from their tents, an uproar began among the small group of slaves the administrator had brought. They could not find their master. Soon a small group of mercenaries, guards, palace slaves, and Archelaus were standing in the middle of the camp shouting. Gilad approached. "What is the problem here?"

One of the slaves ran forward. "The administrator is not in the camp. He is gone."

Gilad stood before the slave. "Where did he go?"

"We don't know."

"When was he last seen?"

One of the guards stepped forward and spoke loudly. "We saw him last night. He came and took some of the donkeys and said he was following orders from Archelaus, so we allowed him to move them."

Gilad addressed his guards. "Why did he want the donkeys in the night?"

The guard shook his head. "They were his donkeys, so we figured it was okay. Maybe he wanted to give them some water. Maybe he wanted to unload them. They still had heavy packs on their backs."

Gilad then questioned his own men as they had rehearsed during the night. "What was loaded on the donkeys?"

"He never told us. He let no one approach the animals."

Gilad turned to Archelaus who was standing in the midst of the crowd. "Do you know what the donkeys carried?"

Archelaus stared at the men. "The donkeys are gone?"

"All except one."

"I have no idea what he loaded on the beasts. It might have been personal items from the palace." The deposed ruler was clearly confused and visibly upset.

Gilad turned to Tobias. "Send three men back toward Jerusalem and three ahead on the road. Try to find the administrator. This is not a safe area to be transporting anything from the palace. Find him and bring him to me." Gilad glanced at the ex-ethnarch's face; the color had drained as had his finances. "Give the other donkey to Archelaus's slaves. They should give the beast some rest and remove the load it carries until we leave." As everyone turned to obey the orders, Gilad turned his back to Archelaus and smiled at Tobias, who saluted and turned to direct his men.

It was late morning when Gilad motioned for Archelaus to approach on his horse. After he dismounted the two men walked aside to confer out of hearing range of the soldiers. Gilad handed Archelaus part of the administrator's robe with blood smeared on it. "It appears he was killed by robbers, or perhaps Parthians. The goods were gone. All of the donkeys were missing." Archelaus looked at the ground and said nothing. "Tell me Archelaus, what was really loaded on those donkeys? Why would your administrator leave with them? That seems strange to me."

"I have no idea what he was doing. Perhaps he stole the items to sell in the market." Archelaus looked up into Gilad's eyes. "There was no trace of the donkeys?"

"Whoever killed him obviously took them. I suspect they will be the ones profiting in the marketplace tomorrow." Gilad studied the ex-ruler's eyes. "It's too bad about your man. He should have known better than to start out alone on these roads."

"Agreed."

Gilad knew Archelaus's concern for his administrator was insignificant compared to the loss of his fortune. Now he would enter Gaul with only one donkey to sustain his lifestyle. Gilad smiled inside, knowing that lifestyle was now changed substantially, and even the load on that one remaining donkey had changed substantially.

"I'll report all of this to the new prefect when he arrives. He may want to investigate further." He watched the ex-leader's face carefully. "I hope your administrator didn't have money from the treasury on those animals. If the new prefect arrived to find his treasury has been looted, I suspect he would be quite angry. I can only imagine the report he would send to Rome."

"A report won't be necessary. It seems the thief has already received his punishment." Archelaus was clearly uneasy with the direction the conversation was going.

"Yes, I suppose he has." As Archelaus mounted his horse and rode off, Gilad turned and walked to the administrator's tent. He leaned down, looked inside and motioned. After a few moments Sabina walked out, holding a small child. Gilad approached and handed her one of the small scrolls. "Can you read?"

"No. I was never taught to read."

Gilad looked around; he had not anticipated this situation. Tobias stepped forward quickly and took the scroll. Clearly and slowly he read the scroll. When he finished Gilad took her hand. "What this means is that you are no longer a slave. You are a free woman. It verifies that Herod gave you to me and that I have freed you." He looked into her eyes and continued after several moments. "Herod also left enough gold and silver to support you and his child throughout your life. It is now in my office at the palace, being guarded by my men. That is also explained in the scroll. It is official; you are free."

Sabina looked up at the man still holding her hand. "I can go wherever I want and live wherever I want?"

"Yes."

There was a long pause as the woman considered what she had just learned. "Where is your tent?"

There was a puzzled look on Gilad's face as he pointed to some tents in the distance. "There."

"Then, if you will have me, I will live in that tent." She looked up into his face and paused a moment. "But Gilad, you know that I am not pure..."

His finger pressed against her lips and stopped her from speaking further. Very deliberately he removed the gold chain that was still around his neck and carefully placed it around hers. "You have looked into my soul, and you know that I love you. Come into my tent, not as a concubine, but as my wife. I welcome you and your son, but from today he will be my son. We will never speak to him of Herod. Sabina stood on the tips of her toes and reached and kissed the large man before her. Nathan watched from a distance and smiled as he saw the look on Gilad's face. He had never seen such joy there before.

* * *

Gilad and his men were packing their equipment carefully. Tomorrow they would deliver Archelaus to the palace in Caesarea where he would wait for the next Roman ship headed west. His new home would be far from Judea and the people he had brutalized. The deposed ruler climbed from his horse and walked over to the guards. He stood for some time looking at Nathan and his weapon. Finally, he walked over and pointed to the sword. "I have heard many stories about your sword. May I see it?" Nathan pulled it from its scabbard and held it in view. "I like that. It is a remarkable weapon. I'll take it."

"No, you won't." Nathan stepped back two steps, holding the sword pointed at the ground, but with a tight grip on the handle.

"What do you mean no? You are simply a guard. I am the..."

Gilad stepped forward and spoke with authority. "You are a man looking for a home, just like any other man. This man," he pointed to Nathan, "is a guard in the palace in Jerusalem. There are only two ways he gives up his sword. I am his commander, and I know that sword was a gift from a Roman centurion. Since our new leader at the palace is now a Roman, I find it unwise to order him to relinquish his weapon. The other way would be for you to defeat him in battle; then you could take the sword as a trophy." Gilad reached and withdrew his own sword. "If you would like to try the second approach, I would be glad to lend you my sword." Gilad smiled at Archelaus. "But I must remind you that Nathan is the best swordsman in Judea." Gilad held his sword, handle extended, toward Archelaus for several moments then put it back into its scabbard. "Good choice, but I expect you have disappointed my young guard." Several of the men laughed out loud as Archelaus turned and walked away.

* * *

Gilad, Tobias, Nathan, and Kalev stood on the road leading to the harbor and marveled at the port. It was the largest artificial harbor built on the Mediterranean. The harbor was over one hundred feet deep and protected by a seawall that was nearly 200 feet wide. Herod had decreed a one hundred sixty acre site complete with warehouses to store goods, and a hippodrome, theater, and amphitheater for entertainment, all named in honor of his friend and benefactor, Caesar Augustus, who had deeded the anchorage of Strato's Tower to Herod in 30 BC. Gilad stood for several minutes just watching the activity taking place as ships were being loaded and unloaded. Then he turned to his men. "Herod might have been an evil man, but he certainly knew how to have things built. This is an amazing port." The men only nodded as they looked out onto the sea and the ships. "Tomorrow we leave for Jerusalem. It will be a quicker trip without the wagons and goods." He smiled. "We also don't have to accommodate the administrator."

Tobias grinned. "No, I suspect his accommodations have been taken care of by now."

"Okay, men, back to camp. I'm anxious to leave this place. Our responsibility for Archaleus is done. I hope his ship sinks at sea."

"That would be justice, to be sure."

147

Chapter 28

The two men sat leaning against a fence that had long since outlived its purpose. They sat silently watching the sun slowly sink into the western horizon. They had become good friends, Matthias and Nathan, not so much because Nathan had saved his life on the road to Jerusalem, but rather because they were both men of quiet strength and courage. When Matthias turned to the younger man he smiled. "You are very quiet tonight. What are you thinking about? Are you enjoying visiting Bethany again?"

"All day long I have been walking in the sun. It is so hot here. I was thinking of an afternoon several years ago near the base of Mount Hebron. There were eight of us on a special assignment, and it was late in the year and quite cold. We built fires to keep warm, but the cold soaked through our cloaks and blankets. It was terrible, except for one thing. I went down to a spring nearby to fill my jug. Then I knelt and drank some of the water. It was so cold and tasted so good. That was what I was thinking about. How I wished all day long to have a drink of that cold water."

"Yes, cold water on a hot day is a precious luxury to be sure." Matthias watched his younger friend and made a calculated guess. "How is Samuel doing? I notice that he is growing into a fine young man. Except for his leg, he seems very strong."

"He is, but I worry about him. He's growing up, and he has no occupation to look forward to. He certainly cannot follow in his father's business."

Matthias sat looking off into the distance for several minutes before speaking. He smiled as golden rays streaked across the sky and blended abruptly with the dark blue shades of the evening. There were only a few clouds hanging in the sky, moving slowly like leaves on a placid stream. "Has he mentioned this to you?"

"No, but I know Samuel. I am sure it is on his mind. The other boys are working with their fathers or family. I just don't think he's ready to talk to me about it yet, and I have no idea what I can say when he does. He probably thinks it would hurt my feelings if I had no job for him to move into."

"He is a thoughtful boy. You have done well raising him, Nathan. There is no better measure of a man than his sons. And if that is the measure of a man, you are tall among your neighbors."

Nathan shifted his weight against the rough timber of the fence and threw a small rock into the distance. "Perhaps I should initiate the conversation; Matthias, do you think that would be a good idea?"

"I'm curious why you ask me that question."

"Well, you're older, and you have raised three fine sons of your own." Nathan smiled broadly. "And you are the only friend I have to talk to right now. I trust your wisdom."

"What does your heart tell you to do?"

"It keeps telling me I have no idea what I am talking about. I have spent my entire working life guarding the king or the palace. I know that, and that is all I know." Nathan threw another small rock, this time with more force."

"You will know when the time is right to talk to him, and I believe that time is soon. Your worry is evidence enough for that."

"But what do I say?"

"Perhaps a good place to start is to explain your purpose and then ask him what he likes to do. A man spends most of his life working; it might as well be something he loves."

149

Nathan's face spread with a smile. "You are a very wise man, my friend." He reached and put his hand on Matthias's shoulder. "Tell me, did you do the same with your own sons?"

"Only after my father recommended that we pursue what they really enjoyed doing in life." Both men laughed briefly. "And when Samuel comes to you someday about his own son, you will know just what to tell him."

Nathan's face suddenly turned dark. "Children, sons, for Samuel. I never thought about that. Do you think…"

"Of course. He is certainly capable of fathering a child. And if whatever venture he chooses is profitable, there will be many families with daughters available for a fine man like him, even with his limp."

Nathan broke into a smile again. "Grandchildren, how wonderful to think about. But how can you be sure?"

"I heard Jesus talking about faith as small as a mustard seed." He looked off at the horizon for a moment then struggled to stand. "Samuel will be a great father, and you will be a fine grandfather."

"Jesus? I have not heard of this man. Who is he?"

"He is a rabbi and a great prophet."

"A prophet?" There was surprise in Nathan's voice. For a Jew to call a man a prophet was a strong pronouncement. There had been few of them in many years.

The old man looked at Nathan and smiled briefly. "A prophet and much more. Some even say he is Elijah, returned from the dead. He has a very large following."

"What more can you tell me about this man? What is his message?"

"He teaches about Yahweh and heals the sick who come to him."

"It sounds like he really is a prophet, like Elijah."

150

"I think he may even be greater than Elijah. I have heard that he heals the lame and gives sight to the blind, and some say he has even raised the dead."

"How can that be?   Raise the dead?"   Nathan's skepticism was evident in his voice.

"I don't know, Nathan; I cannot understand this either. That is why I want to find him and see what kind of man he really is."

Nathan looked at Matthias for several moments before speaking. "Do you think He could be the Messiah prophesized in the Torah?"

"Perhaps. We have waited for the Messiah for a very long time." Matthias stopped and looked into Nathan's eyes. "Perhaps we can seek Him and hear Him together."

"That would be difficult with my schedule, but if you do pursue Him, please keep me informed. We have waited a long time for a great leader; we have certainly had enough cruel ones."

"That is so true. I'll let you know what I learn. Surely our people need such a man." Matthias slowly climbed to his feet and stood with Nathan as they watched the final rays of the sun, then both men turned for their homes.

Chapter 29

Matthias grabbed his robes and pulled them up to his knees as he hurried to catch up to Nathan who walked at a fast pace toward Jerusalem. "You walk very fast for an old man to keep up."

"I'm sorry, I was just thinking about my day at the palace. I've enjoyed our visit, but it is time for me to get back to work."

"It must be a fine place to work."

"I suppose. But we have many responsibilities as well as guarding the palace and those within. This week we are learning to ride horses. Gilad thinks we should all possess that skill." Nathan slowed for Matthias to join him. "In fact, we are all going to learn to swim as well." Nathan smiled. "Like there would be water for swimming here in the desert."

Matthias was working to control his breathing as he joined alongside Nathan. "I think it is a good idea. You may go out to the sea someday—or maybe in the river."

"I guess you're right. What I wish they would do is teach us to read."

"Do you want to read?"

"Yes, but mostly I want Samuel to learn; it might be important in his life. It would offer more opportunities, and he could learn more about the world."

Matthias stopped and drank from his water jug. "It is hot today." When he finished, he resumed his trek alongside Nathan. "Did you talk to Samuel about his future yet?"

"I did. We had a nice talk."

"What are the things he likes to do?"

"He likes animals, but a shepherd's life would not work for him."

Matthias thought for several minutes then spoke. "He seems to like to grow things. What about farming?"

"I thought about that. It is a possibility, but harvesting and planting would be difficult."

"Well keep thinking. There must be something. If we cannot find an answer, we can ask the smartest people in our village."

Nathan turned to Matthias. "And who would that be?"

"Why our wives, of course."

* * *

The wind was blowing hard against the small house when the knock on the door disturbed the family dinner. Nathan opened it carefully and found one of Matthias's sons standing outside. "Come inside, quickly, the wind is howling tonight."

The young man nodded slightly to Rebecca then gave Nathan the message. "My father would like to speak to you after you have your dinner if it is convenient. He says it is important."

"Tell your father that I will be there as soon as we finish our meal, and thank you. You are a brave young man to come out in this weather. You could have been blown away."

The boy's cheeks reddened as he smiled. After he left Rebecca cleared the table. "I hope everything is okay. What could be so important that it could not wait until tomorrow?"

"I don't know, but I'll find out soon enough."

When Nathan walked into Matthias's home, the smells of dinner lingered in the air. Matthias welcomed him to a seat and poured a goblet of wine. "I think you will like this. Wine is a rare delicacy." Nathan took the wine and waited to hear what had prompted the summons. "I think I may have found the answer to your question about Samuel." His wife turned from

153

her chores and scowled at Matthias, who laughed in return. "Well, let's just say I had a lot of help—as I mentioned earlier—you know about wise people." He bowed deeply to his wife. "I, we, think he should raise grapes and make wine." Matthias stood before Nathan and watched for his response.

Nathan's expression was initially one of surprise. Then slowly it changed to one of agreement. "That is a great idea. Now all I have to do is find a lot of land and figure how to get grape seedlings."

"Not a problem. I know someone who has a vineyard and would let Samuel manage it."

"And who is crazy enough to let a young cripple man manage his vineyard?"

"Someone who got it in a trade and has no interest in doing all the work it needs to make it operational."

"And you know someone like that?"

"I do."

"Who? He must not be very smart to do something like that."

"Well, you're right about him not being very smart, I guess."

Nathan was shaking his head. "Who?"

"Me."

"You?"

"You know that old vineyard up on the side of the hill south of town?"

"The one with all the weeds and needs a lot of work?"

"That's it. I've actually owned that for two years. I got it in a trade for some donkeys I raised. Probably a bad trade for me at the time, but it seemed the right thing to do back then." Matthias drank his wine and grinned at his friend. "It's going to take a lot of work, but if Samuel wants to do the work, he's welcome to it."

"Matthias, you could sell that vineyard. It must be worth something."

"Not much, and I'd like to see someone develop it and make it productive. It will give Samuel something to work on, and he can make it his own project. I'd like that." Matthias poured a bit more wine in both goblets. "And, of course, we would all get some free wine each year. I'd really like to do this for Samuel if he would like to give it a try. After all, I am his uncle."

"His uncle? Samuel has no uncle." Nathan placed his goblet on the table and leaned to hear Matthias's response.

"Well, he has called me *Uncle* for many years, so I just take that as a fact."

"You and Tobias." Nathan was smiling broadly. He just nodded to his friend. "Thank you, Matthias. This is a grand idea and a wonderful gift. I know Samuel will work hard to get it in top shape for you. It will give him something he can work on to make his own success in life." The two men raised their wine into the air and toasted the fellowship of friendship among men. They both also realized that they were starting a young man on the road to his future, a young man with limitations, but also with a bright mind and a good heart.

Chapter 30

Jerusalem, 8 A.D.

Nathan and Samuel climbed the small hill and stopped near the top. Samuel had just turned fourteen a few months earlier; Nathan was thirty-two and still in his prime. He watched Samuel struggling up the hill but did not stop to help. He had determined that he would treat Samuel like any other young man. He chose not to treat him differently in order to make him strong. It was far too easy to live one's life on a foundation of excuses. That was no way for a man to exist, and Nathan was determined that Samuel would be a man, a strong man, albeit one with a limp. When they arrived at the top of the hill, the old vineyard spread below them. It had obviously been deserted for several years, but the plants were still alive. Nathan looked off into the distance and estimated the distance to their home, about a mile. It would not be easy for Samuel, but it was certainly something that he could manage. "Samuel, what do you think of this old vineyard?"

"Looks deserted, and it needs a lot of work."

"Do you think it could ever be a working vineyard again?"

"Sure, but it would take time." Samuel looked down at the land below them. "It's a good-sized vineyard. With the right care, it could produce a lot of grapes."

"And the grapes could be converted into wine." Nathan was watching the boy carefully.

"That's true."

"Would you be willing to take on this job, to make this old vineyard productive again?"

"Do you think someone would be willing to hire me? I'd work really hard."

"I know you would son. That is why I brought you up here today. This land belongs to my friend, Matthias. He'd like you to take it over and make it productive."

The boy's face broke into a large smile. "Really? He'd like me to work for him?"

"Actually, son, he wants you to handle it all for him. Just take it and make it a real vineyard again. And if you like, he has a friend who will teach you how to make wine after the vineyard starts producing enough grapes." Nathan was watching Samuel carefully, trying to look very serious, but inside he was smiling as much as his son. "Matthias is too old to do this kind of work, but he might come up now and then to help a little. Basically, it would be your responsibility to run the vineyard."

Samuel leaned on his staff for a few moments in silence, then limped over to Nathan, threw the staff on the ground, and grabbed his father with both arms in a big hug. "Thanks, *Abba*. I won't let Matthias down, or you."

"I know you won't son. I have great faith in you." Nathan picked up the staff and handed it back to Samuel. "I think we can also get some help from your friends. They know nothing about vineyards, I suspect, but with your supervision, I'm sure they can share the work." Nathan walked over to one of the old plants and studied the vine carefully. "Besides, I've always wanted to learn about winemaking, so I can be of some help when I'm not at the palace or on some assignment."

"Do you think you might have more time at home, *Abba*?"

Nathan looked around to ensure they were alone on the hillside. "It's not probable that I will have less work to do. Now that Archelaus has been banished to Gaul, we have a new Roman Prefect to control Judea. Some see this as a major insult to the Jewish people."

"What is your opinion, *Abba*?"

"In truth, most anyone is better than Archelaus. He was an evil man and had thousands of Jews murdered. We really don't know much about this Roman, but generally the Romans tend to establish order in society, even if it is accomplished with brutality. We have been told that we will remain as Palace Guards, so at least I still have a job. I suppose we will learn more as the new prefect establishes his government." Nathan paused for a moment and then continued. "But we have learned one thing from all of this drama with Archelaus. Rome wants stability in Judea and is willing to listen to our leaders. That is good news for everyone."

* * *

Nathan stood at the entrance to the vineyard and admired the gate that welcomed them. It was grand and spanned the entrance with a large plank supported by two tall logs. The inscription simply said, Matthias's Vineyard. Samuel had been working on the vineyard for almost two years, and the results of his work were evident. Rebecca, the other children, Matthias, Matthias's family, and Adriel all started spreading blankets and food under the sycamore trees that shaded them from the sun. It was late fall and the grapes were ready to be picked. But first there was a celebration for the harvest. Samuel climbed down the hill and met everyone at the gate. He was beaming. In his hand he held a cluster of grapes. They were plump and ready for harvest. "Look, Uncle. They're beautiful."

Matthias took the grapes and studied them carefully. "Perfection. Samuel, I am so proud of you, son. You have done a remarkable job with this old vineyard. It looks great."

"Well, I've had lots of help."

Matthias smiled. "But it was your project, and you managed it well." He turned and surveyed the large assortment

158

of baskets stacked under one of the trees. "I see you anticipate a good crop."

"Come and look at the vines, Matthias. They're covered with grapes. We may even need more baskets."

"Are you ready to make your own wine this year?"

"I am. I learned a lot from your friend last year. Now I'm ready to try it myself."

"Would you mind if he came by to help you again this year? It would be your work, but he could watch and give advice if you need it."

"I would welcome that. I want to make enough wine for the entire town."

Matthias smiled. "You may just do that, Samuel, but first there is something to be done." The old man smiled as he clasped Samuel's shoulder. He turned as two men approached walking up the road. They smiled at Matthias as they passed and walked directly to the gate. They carried a large piece of wood that they began to attach over the gate. Inscribed on it were the following words: *Samuel's Vineyard*.

Samuel looked at Matthias in utter surprise. "*My* vineyard?"

"Yes, Samuel, it's yours. You have brought this old vineyard back to life and made it fruitful. It is only right that you should have it." He raised his first finger on his right hand and smiled as he spoke. "But! The prior owner does get first choice at the new wines each year—and at a reduced price." The old man grabbed Samuel and hugged him. "I'm very proud of you, Samuel. You have worked very hard, and it is evident for all to see."

Chapter 31

Samuel watched his father sit heavily into the chair in the main room of their house. "You look tired, *Abba*."

"It's been a long day. Tobias decided we needed more drills, and then we did a forced march for two hours to support the new prefect's family. I'm getting a little old for such things."

"Why don't you leave the Palace Guards and do something else, something a bit easier?" Samuel handed his father a goblet of wine. "Try this, it's a new batch I just made. It's not great yet, but with time I think it will improve."

Nathan took a swallow and immediately broke into a smile. "Son, this is actually quite good. You've learned a lot about grapes and wine. Has your mother tried this?"

"She likes it too." Samuel smiled. "She suggested that perhaps you should stop being a guard and help me in the vineyard."

"Maybe soon I will do that, but not yet. Most of my life has been as a guard, and it's all I know."

"How did you get into the King's Guard in the first place? How does one do that?"

"Well, for me it happened because I was the biggest and strongest boy in the village, and I am also a Levite. One day a large rock had fallen onto the road. The king just happened to be there and saw me lift it and toss it into a ditch beside the road. I guess he was impressed."

"And so you became a guard for the king."

"Yes, and it was considered a big honor. It has been a tradition that Levites make up most of the King's Guard, so my family was very proud. I recall my father bragging to everyone who would listen that his son was a guard for the king." Nathan finished his wine and then continued. "I guess I have to admit that I was impressed with my position as well. I also had two of my best friends, Tobias and Kalev, joining with me. That was an extra benefit."

"Was it hard to learn?"

"Not so much. They taught us the art of combat. They also taught us how to act and dress to exact standards that would match our status in the country. Being a King's Guard was a real honor, so we had to behave in a way that reflected well upon the king."

"Was the combat part hard?"

"Not really, not physically. I was strong. But we were entering the warrior class. We were supposed to be the elite fighters in the country. That is why we constantly worked so hard to learn our craft. It was our job to defend the king and anyone he assigned for our protection."

Samuel took the goblet and refilled it half way. "Warrior class. I guess I never thought about it that way."

Nathan took the goblet and set it aside on a small table by the window. "Well, the warrior class is made up of men who serve others in their city or country. They are men who fight to defend the nation and its citizens. Our history is filled with strife, and I doubt that will ever end. We are Jews, and there are many people who hate us. Long ago we learned that weakness is an invitation to destruction. Strength is the opposite. Enemies seldom attack a strong nation. So, if the need arrives, that is when the warrior class rises to defend their fellow Jews. Think of it as a service to others."

"*Abba*, do you think it will ever come to pass that the warrior class will no longer be needed?"

"Most likely not, but we can hope for that. It would take a complete awakening of the human spirit. Unbridled ambition, greed, hatred, fear, misunderstanding--all these and more must first be overcome. And, oh yes, religious differences would also have to be set aside for the development of a meaningful peace. So, I suppose the warrior class will remain in this country, but it is a shame that it is necessary."

"We have many enemies in this world, don't we?"

"Yes, but we have also dealt with them very harshly on occasion in this never-ending struggle. Jericho was a good example of Jewish ferocity and strength."

"Do you think something like that could ever happen again?"

"Only if our leaders and our people become weak. Unfortunately, in war the barbarians generally win."

"Like Jericho?"

"Like Jericho."

"Have you ever had doubts about your role in life? Have you ever wished you had done something else?"

"There is one great sadness in my career. I have often regretted that the men we protected were evil men. Herod was such a man. We stood guard over him and his family, and he was a man without honor, an evil man with no scruples at all."

"But you protected him." It was a statement, not a question.

"Yes, my son. We protected him. That was our job, to protect the king, not to judge him." Nathan stroked his beard for several moments in silence. "By the time I was your age, we all began to realize that the leaders we protected were generally evil men, men with power who knew how to use it to ensure their position of leadership." He turned to his son and smiled. "There was a time when several of us conspired to kill Archelaus. Now there was a truly evil man, and a stupid one as well."

"But you didn't do it?"

"Gilad discovered our plot and convinced us to wait. Archelaus was deported to Gaul a few weeks later, saving us the trouble of killing him. Gilad knew it would have cost our lives as well. He would not allow that; he was a good commander."

"You've always admired Commander Gilad, haven't you?"

"Yes, he is like my second father. In some ways even closer. He leads us as guards of the palace, but he loves us like sons. It is a very strange, but wonderful, relationship."

"Like ours."

Nathan smiled at his son. "Like ours."

Chapter 32

Samuel struggled down the hill among the lush vines growing in his vineyard. He moved slowly due to the large armload of weeds and trimmed vines but mostly because of his crippled leg. He didn't see the young woman standing below him, smiling. When she spoke, he stopped abruptly and lowered his burden to the ground. "I've brought you something to drink and some fresh bread I made this morning. I also brought some honey."

"Oh, do you think I need something to make me sweeter?" Samuel was smiling as he took the water and drank it in large gulps. "Come, let's sit under the trees and rest. It's a very hot day."

As they sat in the shade, Adriel spread honey over the bread and handed a piece to Samuel. He took it and tasted the sweet honey. "This is very good. Did you bake this yourself?"

"Yes, but I had some help with the honey." He had a questioning look on his face. "The bees." Samuel laughed and continued eating. Adriel studied his face. "Why did you decide to make wine and work in a vineyard? Climbing this hill each day must be difficult."

"Not for me. Working on a hill is easy. I just have to be sure that my right leg is downhill. Then my left leg is perfect for the slope uphill."

"You're so funny." She grinned as she punched his shoulder lightly.

"Crying over difficulties seldom helps. Laughter makes them easier to bear."

"Speaking of easier to bear, let me help you with those vines."

He looked at her carefully. "Are you sure?"

"I'm strong. You'll see." He watched her as she walked up the hill and gathered almost half of the vines. She stood and waited until he had climbed after her and recovered the remaining load.

"You're right. You are strong." Together they worked most of the afternoon. As the sun began to sink into the mountains behind them, Samuel gathered his tools and took her hand. "I'll walk you home." He smiled and added, "If you aren't in a big hurry; you're not only strong, you are also very fast."

"Actually, I'd prefer a slower pace. It gives us time to talk."

"I know. It's hard to converse when cutting vines."

"Are you going to the wedding tomorrow?"

"Of course. The groom is my friend. I assume you will be there as well."

"I will." She took his hand, and they turned toward her home.

* * *

The wedding ceremony was beautiful as the bride and her kin paraded toward the bridegroom's home. Food and wine had been lavishly provided by the bridegroom's family, and there was music for dancing and revelry. It was a time of joy and celebration. The wedding agreement had been signed and the traditional wedding tent had been erected for the couple's wedding night. Friends, family, and even strangers arrived to join the festivities.

As the celebrants drank wine and ate the foods arranged outside the home, the music began, and soon people were dancing and singing together. There were two *kinnors*, a *nebel*, a *lyre*, and two *khalils* to entertain the friends and the families of the bride and groom; no expense had been spared. Off to the side, Samuel watched, seated under a small tree in the yard. The bridegroom was a friend and the bride was an acquaintance. He nibbled on freshly baked bread, dates, and figs and watched with a smile as the dancers moved about the yard in unison. When Adriel walked over and sat beside him, his attention changed immediately as he turned and focused entirely on her. "Hello Adriel. Are you enjoying the celebration?"

"I suppose."

"Did you get some of the wine? It's very good."

"I did, and it's wonderful. Someday you will make wine like this, Samuel."

He looked at her in silence for several minutes before continuing the conversation. "You don't seem happy today. Can I get you something? The food is wonderful."

"Thank you. I'm fine. I've had enough. It is very good."

"Why aren't you dancing?"

"No one asked me." Adriel looked down at her hands. "All the other girls got invitations. I did not."

"I'm sorry that I can't oblige and dance with you. I'd like to if I could."

"That's okay. I'd rather sit here and talk to you anyway." She brushed her long brown hair back from her face and watched him carefully as he spoke.

"The bridegroom is my friend. He seems very happy today. It is a big day in his life."

"Well, he is marrying the prettiest girl in the village. He should be happy."

"Do you know her well?"

"In this village everybody knows everybody. I've seen her around, but we've never been close friends." Adriel did not look into his eyes.

"Then why do you say she is the prettiest girl in the village?"

166

Adriel turned abruptly and looked directly into Samuel's eyes for a long time before speaking. "Don't you think she's beautiful?"

"I really don't know her well enough to make that judgement. My friend is a good man, and he loves her, so I suppose she's a wonderful person. But I don't know her well enough to gage her beauty."

"You are a strange and very thoughtful man, Samuel." She glanced down and continued. "I like that about you."

Samuel reached and put his hand under her chin and raised her face. "When we were little and the other children were playing, I was learning to walk upright. Later when they were chasing life and each other, I was alone and had time to learn what life is all about, and I decided that beauty is not about the shape of one's nose or face. Beauty is about the size of one's heart. External beauty fades as a person gets older, but the true beauty inside only grows. And so, my dear girl, she may or may not be pretty, but *you* are the most beautiful woman in this village—in my unchallenged opinion. Your beautiful eyes are large and dark, filled with the peace and mystery of the night. Your hair shines so in the morning sun, like a thousand rays on a sunny beach in the morning. But your true beauty is in your heart. That is what captured me."

Adriel's eyes were wide as she wiped them. "You really mean that don't you."

"Yes, I do. I've known that I've loved you for a very long time."

Adriel put both of her hands on Samuel's shoulders and reached over and kissed him. "I love you, too, Samuel."

Samuel smiled at the young woman beside him. "I know you do; I've known that for some time as well." He kissed her back. "I was just not sure you had realized that yet. It's not easy to love a crippled man."

"You silly man. Do you really think that makes any difference to me? I love you, and I'm very sure about that."

"Are you sure enough to live with a man with my limitations?"

"Samuel, when I'm with you, I don't see a man who is crippled. I see a man with a warm smile and a great heart, a man I've learned to love. I'm so sure that I'll even help in your vineyard, when I'm not tending to children." There was a bright smile on her face. He returned the smile promptly.

Suddenly a dark shadow crossed her face and she looked as if she might cry. She started to speak but her lower lip quivered violently. She stopped, wiped her eyes then turned to face him with tears coursing across her cheeks. "I'm sorry, Samuel, but I cannot marry you, even though I love you dearly." She tried to look at him bravely but quickly dissolved into tears.

As Adriel buried her face in her hands, Samuel gently placed his right hand under her chin and lifted it so he could look into her eyes. "Are you afraid your family will not approve of a man who is crippled?"

"Oh no. That is not it at all." She spoke the words quickly and decisively. "Both of my parents love you, Samuel."

"Then what could possibly keep us apart?"

He could feel her pain as he looked into the fear on her face, but all Samuel could do was hold her hands and wait. She hung her head for several moments in silence. When she looked up, she spoke very quietly as she rubbed her eyes in an effort to stop the tears that continued to streak the dust on her cheeks. "There is something you must know that could affect your decision to marry me." He watched her carefully. Obviously, what she was about to say was of great importance to her. He could tell it was something that she feared. "If we were to marry, when my mother and sister come to get the sheets from our wedding bed, there will be no blood on them. It is traditional

168

that the bride's family do that to prove their daughter was a virgin." She raised her head and looked directly into Samuel's face. Suddenly she was a strong young woman making a statement of great import. She looked directly into his eyes then spoke. "I'm no virgin; there will be no blood." Samuel reached and took her hands but said nothing. After a moment she continued. "When I was thirteen I was raped in Jerusalem during the Passover celebration. It was an older boy. I was so ashamed that I told no one. There was so much blood in the temple from the sacrifices; I told my mother that was what was on my clothes. I knew my family would be disgraced as was I. I just couldn't do that to mother or my father, so I said nothing." She looked at him bravely, but the tears flowing down her cheeks betrayed her courage.

Samuel took her face into his hands and kissed her gently. "I love you, my dear. There is no chance I would ever dispute our marriage like that. I will be the luckiest man in Judea to have you as my wife." He wiped the tears that were forming in her eyes. "And as for your family, it will be easy enough to get some blood for our sheets. They will never know, and you will never have to explain. We will give them that honor. It will be our secret."

"Samuel, you are such a good man, and I do love you so much."

"I am a blessed man, my dear. A very blessed man." Very gently he held her face in his hands and kissed her again. "I'll talk to my father and ask him to talk to yours if you'll have me as your husband." The smile on her face was all the answer he needed.

Chapter 33

Adriel sat under a flowering tree at the base of the vineyard and watched as Samuel carried a load of cumbersome poles up the hill to support the new vines. She smiled; she was carrying new growth as well. She rubbed her belly and hummed a lullaby to a baby who might be listening to his or her mom. As she leaned against the tree trunk and let her mind wander, she watched her husband. She was so familiar with his movements. It seemed he moved more to each side when he walked than in the forward direction in which he was trying to maneuver. It had become familiar to her. She didn't see her husband as a crippled man, but rather as a very successful and strong man who had overcome a great impediment in his life. As she watched, he mistakenly stepped on a loose rock and began to fall. The suddenness frightened her as she watched Samuel toss the poles to his left as he fell to his right. She had almost climbed to her feet when she saw him tuck his right shoulder and roll twice down the hill. Then he rolled back to a standing position; there was a smile on his face as he stood and turned to see his wife scrambling up the hill. "I'm okay. Don't worry. I'm okay." Adriel ran up the hill and grabbed her man, hugging him tightly. Then she stepped back and looked him over.

"How did you do that?"

"Do what?"

"You just fell and rolled over like an acrobat. I've never seen that before."

"My dear, I've done that so many times. It is a trick my father taught me when I was a boy. I guess he figured I'd have more than my share of falls, so at least I would be able to avoid getting hurt so much."

"He taught you well."

"Actually, I think he learned it from his military training. If you fall in combat, it is wise to get back up very quickly. A man on the ground is vulnerable."

"Your father is a good man. You are so lucky to have such a father."

"When I was young I would try and fail at so many things that are normal to most people, but my father would always tell me: 'Get up son. Stand up, and stand tall.' I must have heard that a thousand times."

"You fell that many times?"

"Yes, but I got back up a thousand and one times. My father never let me be weak; he never let me think I was weak. He knew he could not heal my leg, so he worked on my mind and my heart instead."

"He was truly a good father."

"He is a great father. He taught me a so many important lessons in life. Excuses are for weak people. Strong people don't need excuses. They just get back up and try again. I owe whatever persistence I have to him." Samuel looked up the hill at the vineyard. "I love him for that."

"Then I love him too. He helped you become the man I love."

* * *

The sun was high in the sky as the old man walked slowly through the vineyard. Matthias's eyes were dimmed with age, but he could still feel the size and the firmness of the grapes. He held two to his nose and sniffed them carefully. Then he punctured the skin with his fingernail and tasted the ripening grapes. They were not sweet, but the pungent taste was just what he was seeking. With a smile he turned and called for Samuel to join him. Soon the two men were climbing up the hill, talking about grapes and wine. Matthias waved his arm to sweep across the entire vineyard. "You have worked so hard, and the vineyard is doing very well." He paused and took Samuel's arm, stopping him as he hobbled along beside the old man. "But, Samuel, grapes are just part of the business of making wine. Many good grapes have been wasted because the owner of the vineyard only knew grapes—not the secrets of making truly fine wine. The wine you are making is good; now let's make it excellent."

"I agree, Matthias. That is why I asked you to come here today. I have so many questions."

"As I expected. But I hate to disappoint you my son. The problem is that I know little of the process of making wine." He could vaguely make out the frown that was forming on Samuel's face. Before Samuel could speak, Matthias continued. "However, you may recall that I mentioned a man who can help you. And if I can persuade her, his wife probably knows more than he does about turning the grapes into a good wine."

"I remember. Are they nearby?"

"No, but if I ask, they will come." The weak old eyes sparkled as the old man grinned broadly. "How about next week. That should give you time before all of the grapes are harvested."

"That will be wonderful."

Matthias reached out and searched for Samuel's shoulder. Samuel stopped walking so that it could be found. "Samuel, there is another thing that you should be thinking about; well, actually two. You will need help for the harvest. There is more here than you can pick yourself."

"I agree. I have already gotten promises from my family and some friends."

"That is good. But you also need to ensure you have the crushing vats and sufficient containers to produce the wine as well. But don't worry, my friend will help you understand all of that." Matthias lifted his face to the sun and felt its warmth penetrate his frail old body. He smiled. He still had much to offer his village; he still was a man of wisdom and respect. The vineyard had become his project, his and Samuel's. Samuel was crippled, but he was still very strong and could work long hours when needed. A deep friendship had developed between the two. Samuel was like a sponge; he could absorb huge amounts of information and process it quickly. When Matthias tired of teaching, Samuel would entice him again with countless questions. Together they had built a very fine vineyard. Now, God willing, they would produce a fine wine as well.

Adriel stood at the gate to the vineyard and watched the two men climbing down the hill. One was bobbing sidewise as he walked, the other reached to touch the vines as they passed to ensure his balance as well as his direction. She almost laughed. What a pair. What an unlikely pair. An old man nearly blind and a young crippled man building a vineyard and now setting out to make wine. She felt a sudden kick in her tummy and turned her attention to that tiny indication of life within her. Softly she began to sing to that little spark of life that kept reminding her that it was alive and growing inside. The lullaby was soft and sweet. She looked again at the two men and laughed out loud. Then she spoke to her baby. "My dear little child. Your father is going to make the finest wine in Judea. I have no doubt about it at all. That wine, like you, will be a wonderful gift to this world. And these two silly men who stumble around in the vines will someday stand among their peers and raise their heads with success from their labors. And on that day you, like your mother, will honor them both." She rubbed her belly gently. "But for now, my child, go back to sleep and continue to grow. I have work to do, but I will sing for you again later tonight." As she turned to return to her house, a dark thought drifted into her mind. And like things that frighten us, it brought excitement, but not an excitement born of joy. Instead it was a fear that climbed from the recesses of her mind and invaded her day, dismissing any joy that had brightened the sky. She stopped and put her hands back on her belly as she looked down at her extended stomach. "My dear child, I pray to the God of Israel that you will be whole and beautiful, but I also promise you that however your tiny body develops, I will love you and protect you." She smiled a thin smile and patted the tiny foot she felt poking into her womb. "Like your grandmother, I will defend my baby and rejoice in your being, however God designs you for this world. Your father has proven that a cripple can be a joy to all who know him. He will be your example; however you are made." She looked off into the distance for several minutes, then raised her head. "Oh my God, bless this child. Give this baby first the heart of its father; with that, this child can face this world, regardless of how its tiny legs may be formed."

Chapter 34

The two men sat across from each other at the polished table surrounded by soft cushions. They were Sadducees, descended from Zadok, King David's high priest. The Sadducees were few in number but their control over the priesthood gave them power and prestige among the people. Even though Herod despised them because they had supported the Hasmoneans he had defeated to become king, he was wise enough to leave them in the temple where he could watch them carefully. Both of the men at the table had a sprinkling of white in their beards. El'Azar, the Chief Priest's second in command, was balding as well. Spread across the table was sufficient food for two families; the two dined slowly on the fruits, breads, and roasted lamb. In addition to the food there were several jugs of wine sitting nearby on the floor. The older man stopped eating for a few moments and addressed his friend. "Well, El'Azar, how did your meeting go with the new Roman prefect?"

El'Azar was a man greatly respected by the "right" people in Jerusalem. He was a high ranking official in the temple and Commander of the Temple Guards, positions held almost exclusively by Levites who were loyal to the high priest and the Sanhedrin. El'Azar enjoyed his food and drink, and it showed in his waistline. His long nose was accentuated by a receding hairline that extended almost to the middle of his head. He was shrewd, ambitious, and totally unscrupulous. Finally, he leaned back, took a drink of the wine, then addressed his friend. "Our new prefect is like all other Romans, arrogant and slow of thought. He treats us like children. Do this; do that. Report to me when it is done; report to me if it is not done. He has just arrived, and already I can hardly stand to be in the same room with that man."

"You sound angry." His friend was smiling inside. He knew El'Azar would tell a good story to his friends, but he bet inside the prefect's office it was all 'Yes, of course. I'll be glad to take care of your demands—immediately!'

El'Azar reached for a cloth and wiped his mouth and his well-trimmed beard before answering. "I am tired of being treated like a commoner. After all, I do have a position of responsibility, and if the damned Romans were not here, we would all be treated with more respect." The temple official drank more wine then leaned back on his cushions. Without looking up from the food, he raised his hand and beckoned for one of his slaves to bring more wine. After it was poured he took a sip, smiled in appreciation of the purple drink then continued his discourse. "What we really need is another Jew in charge, not the Romans. When Herod was alive we were all better off. We weren't being directed by a godless gentile. That's what we need—another Jewish king."

"Well, if Archelaus had not failed so miserably, we might still have a Jewish leader. Many say even a Roman is better than Archelaus. Didn't Herod have any decent sons? Were all of them as dumb or as ruthless as Archelaus?"

"I hear Antipas is about the same. Why can't we have another Hasmonean king as we did before Herod? Then we were a wealthy nation, and the temple took in great sums of money. But look at us now, bowing to a Roman, a non-circumcised gentile." El'Azar munched on a fig for a few moments and continued his rant. "And the Romans take our taxes. Before, we collected the taxes ourselves and got to keep a portion of the money for our own purses; now we turn them over to our lords from the west to pay for the soldiers who oppress us."

"Well at least the Romans are efficient, and actually they really are smart as well. Like you say, they even have us pay for their armies. How efficient is that? I guess we just have to learn to live with it. For certain we cannot drive them out."

El'Azar growled, then burped several times. After he calmed his stomach he looked up with a sly grin on his face. "Maybe there is a way." The conspiratorial look on his face served only to excite his colleague.

"What do you have in mind?"

"What if we could get another Jew into the palace? While we cannot defeat the vast Roman legions, what if there were enough insurrections and attacks to get the emperor's attention. What if he could be convinced that putting a Jew in charge would help keep the peace in Judea? That would certainly be a big benefit for Rome. And what if the Parthians were unsettled during all this with a few attacks here and there? I would think an argument could be made to Tiberius that perhaps a Jewish king on the throne who was completely loyal to Rome—as was Herod—might be a good idea, and perhaps they could be convinced to reinstate a new Jewish king, a return of the Hasmonean Dynasty, for example." El'Azar smiled another of his sly grins. He knew the Sadducees were always supporters of the Hasmoneans and benefitted greatly from that relationship. He also considered the possibility that perhaps a Sadducee might make a good king. All he needed was concurrence from Rome. "How does that sound?"

"Dubious for sure. Who would be fool enough to lead such an insurrection? That is a quick way to get executed. Like you say, we cannot defeat the Romans." He smiled as he took another piece of bread and wiped it in a small bowl on the table. "Certainly you are not thinking about leading such an endeavor yourself."

"Of course not. Like you, I know better, but the rebels need a leader, and I know a young man who could be persuaded to take that responsibility."

"And why would someone agree to do that? He'd have to be a complete fool."

"Agreed." El'Azar fished around one of the plates and came up with a date which he put into his mouth whole. After a polite period of time he spit a large seed into an ornate bowl on the table. It created a ping which signaled that the discussion could continue. "But what if that person could be convinced that he was entitled to the throne himself? And what if he were given enough resources to build a small group of men who were willing to support him?"

His colleague was becoming more and more interested in the direction of the discussion. He was having fun sparring with his friend, but suddenly he was seeing the puzzle pieces fall into place. "Let's see if I understand you. You say there is a man who could be convinced that he is entitled to take the throne and would therefore be willing to lead the insurrectionist attacks to get Rome's attention. And who would that be?"

"One of Herod's sons."

"His sons are already in positions of power somewhere, or dead."

"Not all of them."

"Who?"

"One of his bastard sons. A young man filled with the enthusiasm and the vigor of youth—without the benefit of the wisdom that comes from experience and age."

"You think you could convince him to do this?"

"I've been watching him for some time. I think he has the temperament to attempt such a plan. We simply tell him we want to get Rome's attention to have them allow a Jew to return to the throne. We'll tell him he is the chosen one, and that we will support him. All he needs to do is carry out an attack now and then and not get caught. In the meantime we stir up the Parthians and we have a perfect storm. Parthians and insurrections in Judea—I think there is a good chance Rome will concede that a Jew might have a better chance of success than an "outsider" from Rome. We must, of course, promise the new king will be perfectly loyal to Rome, as was the case with Herod." The Temple Guard commander leaned back and watched his friend, waiting for the excitement he knew would come.

"You know, I think you may have a good plan. This could work. Have you implemented any of it yet?"

"For now it is just a plan, but I have made arrangements to meet with young Doran. He is the bastard son of Herod and one of Herod's slave girls. All I have to do is convince him he has royal blood flowing through his veins." El'Azar stopped suddenly and turned to his friend. "You must never mention this to anyone. What we are discussing is a dangerous proposition." It was obvious he was realizing he had spoken more than he had intended, or perhaps it was the wine that was speaking. In either case, he was treading on dangerous ground.

"Of course, I would never mention anything we have discussed, and you are right, in the wrong hands, this information could be dangerous, indeed."

"There are only a handful of men aware of my plan. These are important men, powerful men. It would not be wise to anger them."

"I understand." The man drank more wine and watched El'Azar carefully. "Just how old is this young man?"

"Twenty-nine."

"That's not young."

"No, it's not, but to me he seems a child. Still he is young enough to have a healthy degree of naiveté as well as fire in his belly."

"And you think you can use that naiveté to recruit him."

"Oh yes, I'm sure I can. I'll offer him a great position in my organization. Then I'll take him under my wing and groom a new king. And once the Romans agree that we need a Jewish king, we report Doran's activities or kill him ourselves and put someone appropriate on the throne." El'Azar smiled. "Like, perhaps, the person who might report the traitor to the Roman authorities."

"I see you have thought this through carefully."

"Yes, I have. All we need is two men to start the plan moving forward: Doran and a candidate for the new king."

"Have you thought much about who that might be?"

"Indeed, I have." El'Azar was tired of taking orders from the Chief Priest. Maybe it was time for the Chief Priest to take orders from him. With that thought he smiled and poured more wine.

Chapter 35

Rebecca and Adriel moved around the crowded kitchen stirring a large pot of lamb, beans, garlic, and onions and arranging the table for the evening meal. Adriel wielded a wooden spoon with her right hand and held her extended stomach with her left. She was in her final month of pregnancy and working around her was an invitation to be bumped repeatedly. Rebecca smiled as she watched her daughter-in-law. She remembered her first child and the many feelings a new mother experiences. There was the fear, of course, but there was also a feeling of complete responsibility that possessed her mind and heart. A new life was within her, and for the rest of her life she would be inextricably bound to that tiny heart beating within her womb. Rebecca remembered being worried that she would not know how to care for that new life. How would she ever mother anything so precious when she was just a bit older than a child herself? She remembered envying the older women who felt so comfortable in their roles as wives and mothers. She had felt so unsure, so unready for the new role, and especially the overwhelming responsibility. And then after the pain of giving birth they had placed the tiny, crying infant in her arms, and the world changed forever. Adriel looked over at her smiling mother-in-law and guessed at what she was thinking. As the two women looked at each other a bond stronger than most will ever experience was formed between the two. Adriel pondered in her heart the journey that Rebecca had taken in her life, and in that moment she understood the older woman's smile as they both watched the continuation of life in her belly. Certainly, it was beautiful, but the degree of that beauty was something Rebecca fully understood, and Adriel had yet to experience.

The table was filled with breads, cucumbers, figs, and dates as the iron pot of stew cooked over the fire. The men of the family would soon be home. Samuel had spent the entire day at the vineyard, talking with one of Matthias's friends about grapes, and Nathan's guard duty was due to end soon. Adriel dropped the spoon she was using to stir the stew and was awkwardly trying to reach it on the floor. It made Rebecca laugh as she retrieved it and handed it to the younger woman. "Soon my balance will return." Adriel smiled as she took the large wooden spoon.

"Don't be too sure. You will have a baby on your hip for several years. That will be yet another balancing trick to learn, until she learns to walk. Then you will be running around all day long trying to prevent disasters." She smiled and reached to pat Adriel's arm. "But you will love it. Trust me." Abruptly Adriel turned her face from her mother-in-law. There was a small movement in her shoulders, then more rhythmic movements. She was crying. "My dear girl, what is the matter? Are you worried about having this baby? You will be fine."

Adriel turned her belly sidewise so she could hug her new relative and her new friend. "I'm just so worried about the baby. What if..." She broke into sobs as she clung to Rebecca.

"Oh, Adriel. Are you afraid your child will be crippled like Samuel?" The young woman simply nodded into Rebecca's shoulder. "My dear girl. This baby is going to be fine. I promise you. She will be beautiful."

"How can you be sure?"

"Well, I've had a brood of babies myself. I also know that crippled parents don't have crippled children."

"But how do you know?"

"Women just know things like that. We've been creating children for this earth for a very long time, and we have the most amazing intuition." She stroked Adriel's hair and kissed her on the top of her head. "Women just know things." Rebecca gently pushed the younger woman to her arm's length. "Like I know this child will be a girl."

"A girl?" Adriel wiped her eyes and took Rebecca's hands. "You're sure?"

"I'm sure. And I'm also sure she will be beautiful, just like her mother." A small smile was forming on Adriel's face. "Now, go over there and sit down and let me finish this dinner. We have two hungry men coming home soon, and they will be ready to eat, along with these wild children running around the house. So rest, you have a very important job to do very soon, and you will need your strength."

"What if I'm not strong enough? Some mothers die." There was a slight tremor in her voice.

"Adriel, look at me." Rebecca took Adriel's face in her hands. "You are going to do fine. You are a strong young woman. Women have been giving birth since the beginning of time. It is a beautiful gift that God has bestowed upon us. Only we can carry a child and deliver it into this world. It is the most amazing and beautiful act you can imagine." Rebecca smoothed a few stray hairs that hung across Adriel's forehead. "And my dear, you are about to experience the most wonderful event of your life; you are about to discover what love is really all about. Trust me, it will change your entire life in such a beautiful way that you have yet to understand."

Adriel rose from the chair and put her arms around the woman standing before her. "Thank you, Rebecca. I've been uneasy about all this, and my mother is gone. I miss her so much."

"I know, but you are going to be fine. I'm now your mother too, and I'll be here with you, and my dear, your mother will be here as well. Trust me, you will feel her strength and her love when you hold this new child." Rebecca forced a small laugh. "And I'm an expert. Just look at these children running around this house. Three are grown and the last two, well, they surprised us."

There was a commotion at the door as Nathan and Samuel arrived together. Nathan had a large smile on his face. "Guess who I found along the road? A man with a jug of wine. And just in time for dinner."

* * *

It was late in the evening when Adriel's labor pains began. Rebecca had insisted that she and Samuel stay with them until the child was born. When she first heard Adriel cry out, Rebecca jumped from her bed and ran into the other room. Immediately she knew the baby would soon be born.

It is generally assumed that men pace while awaiting their first child, but when the man is lame, a hard chair by the fireplace has to suffice. Nathan looked over to see his son, his head supported by his two hands, his elbows on his knees, staring at the floor. With a smile he walked over and put his hand on Samuel's back. "It's going to be fine, son."

"I just wish I could help."

"That's not your job. Your job comes later. For now we just have to wait. Rebecca is in charge now, and she knows what she's doing."

Later in the night a woman's loud cry came from the back bedroom, then the comforting voice of Rebecca, coaching her daughter-in-law through the age-old process of bringing new life into the world. With each cry, Samuel's head drooped closer to the floor. Finally a distinctive cry emanated from the back room, a different voice, a small, but strong, voice. Samuel jumped from the chair and tumbled onto the floor. Before Nathan could even stand, Samuel was up and limping toward the back room. He met Rebecca at the door. The smile on her face told him all he wanted to know. When he entered the room only two candles illuminated the face of his wife. She looked tired, but she was smiling broadly. In her arms was a small bundle making strange sounds. Adriel looked up at her husband for only a moment, then her eyes went automatically back to the baby in her arms. Nathan and Rebecca joined the two smiling parents as Adriel unwrapped her new daughter. Slowly she moved the cloths down to expose the child's legs. They were both normal and wiggling in the candlelight. All Samuel could say was, "She's beautiful." Then he reached and kissed his wife on her forehead and added, "Just like her mother."

Chapter 36

Jerusalem, 28 A.D.

Sabina walked into the main room of the home she and Gilad shared. It was a pleasant home, furnished well and full of light. Like the people inside, it spoke of happiness and love. There were several other rooms as well, two bedrooms and a large dining room near the cooking area. The back door led to a small courtyard where many happy evenings had been spent after long hot days. She spoke Gilad's name as she entered, not because she was uncertain of his presence, but as an alert that someone was entering the room. Gilad's eyesight was failing rapidly, and that precipitated a personal struggle for a man so strong and proud. As his eyesight dimmed, he became increasingly dependent on those around him. Going blind was difficult, but becoming dependent was far worse for a man like Gilad. "Gilad, my husband. I have food and drink for you."

"I'm not hungry."

"Nonsense, you are always hungry. You are a big man, and you need your strength."

"For what purpose? I can barely see across the room."

Sabina walked to the large man and held his face with both of her hands. She leaned close to talk to him. "My dear, you need your strength for that which does not require your sight. When you hold me in the night neither of us can see." She smiled at him, and he smiled back. "That what you do best requires no light at all, only me." She leaned even closer and kissed him on his forehead as a large grin spread across his face.

He scooped her and placed her in his lap. "I'm going blind, yet I am the luckiest man in Judea, simply because I have you as my wife."

Sabina took his hand and placed it on her breast. "You can use your sense of feeling as your eyes dim." She watched his face for any reaction then continued. "And I will be your eyes, and like your own eyes, I will never leave you."

A tear rolled from Gilad's left eye and dropped onto his beard which was as white as snow. Gilad would soon be sixty-two, and the stress of his life was wearing on things other than just his eyes. His hands would often swell and become hard to move, like both of his knees. His body was engaged in a battle, and it seemed time was winning. He was frustrated to sit each day with little he could do but talk to Sabina, whom he loved dearly. But Gilad was a man of action. He had always been one who walked quickly and with purpose in his steps. Now they were slow, and every movement was a portent of some crashing disaster. He had fallen numerous times, and his body ached, but it was his pride that pained him most. But life still held one great pleasure that made Gilad glad to wake each morning, his love for Sabina. Their life had been a wonderful adventure that Gilad had not even envisioned in his most extreme moments of fantasy prior to her entry into his life. She had brought him a joy and peace that left him smiling constantly. She had also brought him a son, Doran. Doran knew that his real father had been King Herod, and Gilad had told him many tales of courage and wisdom about his father. They were mostly false, but it was important that the boy learn pride in himself and his heritage, so Gilad the warrior became Gilad the storyteller. It was a character shift that was totally surprising and unexpected, but welcomed. Late into the evenings the three of them would sit around the fireplace and share stories of their lives and events that occurred inside the palace of Herod the King. In time there were others around that fireplace as the deep love of Sabina and her husband grew and remained vibrant throughout their lives together. Gilad had remained the commander of the Palace

Guards until the betrayal of his eyes became apparent to all. At his final day with the guards, Gilad had named Tobias as the new commander. He also promoted Nathan to be the leader of Unit 2. Sixty-three guards stood in a long line to salute their leader as he left. Even the Roman prefect and three centurions were there for the ceremony. The large man stood tall and walked along the men, accepting their salutes. Tobias was at his side, insuring he would not stumble on his last day at the palace. Gilad's eyes were especially dim on that day, partly because of his infliction and partly because of the tears that occasionally escaped and ran down his cheeks. He had spent his life leading the men who protected the king, the prefect, the palace. Now that phase of his journey was over. It was time to find new and different paths to explore. But Gilad knew those paths would require someone else to hold his hand.

Sabina kissed his cheek and was just rising from his lap when Doran walked into the room. "My son, how was your day at the palace?"

"Okay, just like every other day—stand around and guard the stairs leading into the palace."

Gilad sensed the frustration and turned toward the sound of his adopted son. "When you entered the Palace Guards I told you there would be days of little to do, but there would also be days of great danger and excitement. Personally, I preferred the boredom."

Doran smiled at the large man sitting beside the dinner table. "You were right about the slow days, but thus far there have been few days of significance to lend excitement to my career—which is moving very slowly, I might add."

"Are there no chances to be promoted into a leadership position?"

"All of the unit leaders are older. Those of us in our twenties are still considered children."

Gilad reached and put his hand on the table and slowly rose. "I became a unit leader when I was nineteen, then commander when I was twenty-three. Times have changed." He stood straight and started to walk toward his son. Sabina immediately moved beside him and took his arm. "Thank you my dear, but I can still see well enough to walk around this house." He reached for her, located her neck and pulled her to him for a kiss. Then he stood directly across from his son and lowered his head. "Would you like me to talk to Tobias?"

"No, absolutely not. I will earn my own promotions."

"I understand, and you're right. Any interference on my part would only make your career more difficult." Gilad smiled. He had expected that reaction from his son, and he was pleased that he was right. "Patience my son. Now come and tell me all about your training. Is Nathan still teaching the sword fighting course? He's the best I've ever seen, except me, of course." There was a smile on his face.

Doran walked forward and guided the old commander toward the table. When they were seated, Sabina brought both of them a mixture of wine and water and placed bread and cheese on the table before them. Very soon they were deep into the intricacies of protecting a palace and the weapons and tactics that were used to ensure its safety. There was a connection between the two that was wonderful for her to watch. Doran had been lucky to have such a man raise him. Certainly his real father had not been a man she would have wanted instructing her son. Unlike Gilad, Doran was not a large man, but his mind was quick, and his will was great. Together Doran and Gilad made a good pair and the affection they shared was apparent to all.

* * *

189

Three days later the sun was just sliding below the dark trees that covered the low hills to the west when Doran walked into the house. There was a large smile on his face. "I have news, but it will have to wait until after our meal."

Sabina smiled at her son. "Does this have anything to do with a certain young woman who lives nearby?"

"Mom!"

A voice boomed from the first bedroom, demanding attention from all in the house. "Your mother is right. It's time you started thinking about a wife and a family."

"All in good time."

"Well this is a good time. My beard is white, and I want to be able to see my grandchildren before I die, so you need to get busy." The voice was one of command, but it was also filled with mirth.

"I'll think about which young woman will be lucky enough to get me later; first I have other news, but after dinner. I'm starved."

Sabina placed large plates of lamb, bread, vegetables and fruits on the table. In short order, she was refilling the plates as the two men talked and ate. She smiled as she refilled their wine goblets as well. Gilad had been a brave leader for the Palace Guards; he had also been wise with the money Archelaus and his administrator had stolen from the palace treasury. He had recovered the 20 pieces of gold Herod had promised him, and a bit more as well. Secretly he had also stashed a considerable amount of gold in a safe place to assist any of his men who might be injured or killed while serving under their commander. A new child among his guards' wives, a new wedding of one of the younger guards, an emergency of any kind—there was always a generous gift from their commander. Gilad looked after his "family" at the palace. And when the new prefect was briefed on the recovery of the treasury, he immediately rewarded Gilad and his guards with a sizeable amount of the money. The prefect was a wise man—these were the men who would guard him and his family—best to keep them happy.

When the table had been cleared, the two parents sat before their son and waited for his announcement. He smiled and looked directly at Gilad as he spoke. "I've been offered a leader's position with the Temple Guards." He watched Gilad's face for several moments then continued. "My pay will be a third more, and I'll be in charge of ten other men."

Gilad stroked his beard several times then smiled at his son. "What good news, Doran. I had hoped you would remain a Palace Guard like me, but a Temple Guard is a position to be proud of as well. And, since we all trade our time for pay, a third more is significant. Congratulations son."

"Thank you, *Abba*."

"They were smart to get you. I've heard that our training at the Palace is much better than that for the Temple Guards. Now you can help them raise their standards."

Doran frowned. "You don't think their standards are good."

"They're much better today. They just hired a real professional into their ranks. Good for them; good for you." Gilad smiled a large smile. "You know I'm teasing about the Temple Guards. I'm sure they are as professional as the Palace Guards. And now you are in a leadership position. The head of their organization had better watch his job. Now he has some real competition."

Doran walked over and hugged the large man across the table. "I love you, *Abba*."

"And I love you too son. And I'm also very proud of you as well."

Sabina joined the celebration. "Now that you are becoming a rich man, what about those grandchildren. One of my friends has a beautiful daughter about your age."

Gilad interrupted with a big grin. "I've heard about her…"

Sabina punched her husband on the shoulder playfully. "Gilad, don't you dare!"

The very next morning Doran approached his leader at the palace and told him that he was moving to the Temple Guards the following day. Kalev congratulated him and began training his replacement that afternoon.

Nathan and Doran stood in Tobias's office as he finished writing on a large scroll rolled across his desk. As he finished, he looked up and smiled at the two. "Welcome, Doran, I hear you have good news to share."

"Yes, Commander. I have been offered the position of one of the leads of the Temple Guards. Commander El'Azar of that organization made the offer three days ago, and I told him I would take the post."

"Unit leader! That is a prestigious position, Doran. I am very proud of the work you have done here, and I wish you the very best. It is good that we maintain a close connection with the Temple Guards. Now we will have one of our own as a leader there. It will benefit both organizations." Tobias walked around the desk and put his hand on Doran's shoulder. "I'm sure your father is as proud as we are."

"Yes, he seems very pleased."

Kalev put his hand on Doran's other shoulder. "You have been a good guard for us here at the palace. I will hate to lose such a good man, but I am also pleased to see the opportunity you have before you, and though you now work at the temple, you know you will always be a member of the Palace Guards as well. Congratulations."

El'Azar watched the new leader of Unit 3 of the Temple Guards report for duty. He rose from the large desk in his office and walked out to greet his newest recruit. "Welcome to the Temple Guards, Doran. I have heard many good things about you, and we are very pleased to have you in our organization."

"Thank you, Sir. I am happy to be here."

"Come, let me show you around the temple. It is very large and has a very long history in our nation. As you know, the original temple was built by Zerubbabel (between 520 and 516 BC). When Herod decided to rebuild it he decided to use the same soft white stone that Solomon had used. He needed a thousand wagons just to carry the stones and ten thousand skilled workmen to handle the construction. He also had a serious problem since only priests were allowed inside the sacred building. That was solved by training a thousand priests to do stonemasonry work. The courtyards are still under construction, but you will see just how magnificently the temple has been constructed. There are stones in this wall whose weight ranges from 2 to 400 tons."

"It is certainly a majestic complex."

"It is, and there are nine gates leading inside. All of these must be guarded." As they walked through the Shushan Gate, Doran looked at the colonnade of tall Corinthian columns, each over 38 feet and carved from a single block of white marble. There were 162 of these just on the south side called the Royal Porch. El'Azar pointed to that area. "That is where the money changers and the sellers of sacrificial animals conduct their business. They provide the opportunity for the people to participate in the worship ceremonies held here. The animals are then slaughtered just beyond the Court of Israel." The two men toured the entire structure and El'Azar explained the various parts of the temple itself. They toured the Women's Court, the oil store, the Nicanor Gate, and the Court of Israel. Then they climbed the twelve steps that led to the sanctuary itself. Doran looked up at the 148-foot structure and touched the thick white walls, which, like the roof, were covered with gold. Even the spikes were made of gold. They crossed the porch and stood before massive doors that led to the Holy Place. The golden sculpted vine above the doors represented Israel triumphant. El'Azar explained that inside the Holy Place was a table where the menorah stood with its seven branched lamp. Beyond that was a giant curtain that extended from floor to ceiling separating the Holy Place from the Most Holy Place, the Holy of Holies, a place where even the high priest only entered on one day each year, the day of Atonement. El'Azar could easily assess that the young man was impressed. Smiling, he turned and led Doran back to his office. When they arrived a lunch had been prepared and was waiting for them. Doran was clearly awed. The temple was the center of Jewish life, and he was now assigned to guard that heritage.

* * *

Gilad and Sabina watched with pride as their son explained the excitement of his day. Doran's excitement was obvious. The temple had a way of impressing anyone who entered its gates. Gilad joined the discussions and explained how the Ark of the Covenant, so important to Jewish history, was once held in the Most Holy Place but had been stolen or destroyed when Nebuchadnezzar's troops had conquered the city in 586 BC. Gilad, Sabina, Doran, and four other younger siblings sat around the table until late in the night telling stories of their Jewish history, stories passed down from generation to generation for many years. Now Doran would have the opportunity to be a part of that history in a very special way.

* * *

Doran stood at attention as El'Azar cleared his desk of several stacks of maps he had been studying. They had been carefully drawn on thick sheets of parchment and colored to give them beauty as well as functionality. The older man turned and motioned to a chair near his own. "Please, take a seat." He poured two goblets of wine as the two made themselves comfortable. "I have heard very good reports on you, young man, but then, I was not surprised. As you know, I'm sure, there are two kinds of men in this world, those who merely participate on the edges of life and those who make a difference, the men who guide the others, who drive society forward. I knew you were one of those who will be a leader in his life. It was inevitable, of course, since you have royal blood in your veins." El'Azar stopped and sipped his wine, looking carefully over the rim of the goblet to assess the impact of his words on the young man before him. He was pleased with what he saw.

"Thank you, commander. I appreciate this opportunity to be a leader in your organization."

"Doran, I fully expect someday you will command this entire organization—as a starter for your real calling." El'Azar knew he had advanced farther in the conversation than he had intended and had done so very quickly, so he immediately backed away from the thrust of his words. He was planting seeds. Now it was time to let them germinate before advancing again. He had time for his purposes, but what had pleased him most was the look on Doran's face, the sudden sparkle in his eyes. Now El'Azar knew his plan was viable, no, more than viable, it was certain—he just needed time.

* * *

The days turned into months as El'Azar slowly coaxed his new protégé toward a dream that was in reality little more than an illusion. First, he built up the image of greatness that was not something deserved but bestowed by birthright. And any man with royal blood flowing through his veins not only had the opportunity for greatness, he also had a responsibility to achieve that greatness. To do less would be an insult to himself, his heritage, and also to those who cried out for his leadership during the difficult occupation of the Jewish homeland. Israel was waiting for a great man to stand up and, like Moses, lead the people out of bondage, a bondage inflicted by Rome. Slowly, but consistently, the message was delivered, first with subtle insinuations, and finally with the accusing voice of one opening the doors of darkness in another man's mind. It worked far more successfully than the old Sadducee could have imagined. And as he celebrated his success with yet another goblet of wine, he smiled with quiet satisfaction. He had succeeded; he had only missed one key item in the complex plan he had woven. He had overlooked one very important trait in Doran's life as he celebrated the birthright of the Herodian blood line—Doran's affection for his other father, Gilad. El'Azar was a political animal who had won his advancements through deceiving other men less skillful in that art. Gilad, however, was a military man who lived by his honor and his duty. The two were very different. El'Azar made one other mistake, he assumed the old commander of the Palace Guards was slow of thought, less capable than himself. He was wrong on both of these assumptions.

196

Chapter 37

Jerusalem, 30 A.D.

Procula walked through the palace with all the dignity of her husband's office. Her husband, Pontius Pilate, was Governor of Judea under Tiberius Caesar. Like all politicians he was constantly balancing many issues and many enemies. He had to carefully manage the local Jewish leaders, and the enmity between him and Herod Antipas, ruler of Galilee, was a constant irritation. Procula's clothing was not like that of the common people in Jerusalem or especially those of the small towns nearby. Her gown was crafted from fine silks brought by traders from the East. But she possessed another rather distinct characteristic other than her wardrobe that set her aside from the citizens in her country. For a woman she was tall. Her beautiful figure and graceful demeanor were made for palaces. Even her name meant "crown." She had been blessed with great beauty, but most important of all, Procula had yet another characteristic that set her apart. She was inquisitive, and she was extremely bright. Pilate had learned long ago that it was a wise man who took counsel from someone much smarter than himself, and there was little doubt that Procula was the smarter of the two. But she still had the impediment of being a woman. That was a major obstacle for someone of her intellect. The value of women in both Roman and Jewish society was only slightly higher than that of children, and children were not valued very highly, so even the wife of a governor had to be aware of her place. Therefore, Procula stood silently as the ruling men of the country discussed the issues of the day, but in the evening, when she had Pilate alone, her wisdom and intellect would change the trajectory of the nation's course. Hours during the day were spent listening, and a few minutes of talking in the evening were enough to guide her fearful husband as he struggled to make decisions for the country—and also for his own career. Pilate liked being a ruler. He liked the power, but mostly he liked the adoration. Like his wife, he wore the finest robes and dined on the finest foods and drink. Even the religious leaders paid him his measure of respect. Like him, they understood power, and like him, they courted it carefully and constantly.

Procula sat very still and listened as a messenger reported on the new rabbi that was traversing the country. There was much excitement about this man. He was said to be able to heal people simply by touching them. One report stated that he had actually raised a man in Bethany from death. Procula considered the details of the reports, but what amazed her most was the zeal of those reporting the news. One of the men she knew well. He was a man of truth and a man of keen judgment. She watched him carefully as he reported on the latest teachings of the new young rabbi. The messenger's face, his voice, his eyes, all were alive with some new understanding that had changed the man. Even her maids were discussing this new phenomenon. The new rabbi, the man named Jesus, was gathering a broad group of devout followers, and his teachings were not what one might envision. He was teaching the people about their God and about love, not rebellion or war. Love your neighbor as yourself; love your enemies. What strange messages.

It was getting dark and the evening breeze was finally cooler. Pilate was sitting near the open window with stacks of scrolls on the small table nearby. He had forsaken the work of the country for a glass of wine and a moment of peace and serenity. Procula walked back into their bedroom and put on a very thin gown of almost transparent silk. She smiled, knowing that Pilate's peace would soon be forgotten. As she walked through the palace, she heard a commotion from the area where food was prepared. She approached quietly and stood behind a large column, listening to two of her maids talking excitedly.

"I tell you, I saw it with my own eyes. The man was lame. He had been lame for many years. Some of his friends took him to Jesus but could not approach for all the crowds, so they lowered him through the roof of the house. The rabbi took pity on the man and told him to rise and walk. The man bowed to the rabbi and rose and walked away. Everyone was amazed. We all saw it. All He did was tell the man to rise and walk—and he did. Then He taught us about the scriptures and about loving each other. He made every one of us feel important in the eyes of Yahweh. My heart burned in my breast as I listened to Him talk."

The second maid was excited. "How many people were there?"

"More than I could count. People came from villages far away—just to hear Jesus speak."

"I would love to see Him. Where does He live?"

"He is from Nazareth, but He travels around the country giving the people the good news."

"The good news?"

"He talks about how Yahweh loves us, and how we should live to find happiness and salvation from our sins. It is all so wonderful."

"How can I hear this man? Can you discover when He might be in this area? I'd love to hear Him."

"One of my friends knows some of His followers. I'll ask them to get us information so we can attend one of His gatherings."

Procula backed away quietly and determined to speak to the young maid alone in the morning. She simply had to hear this man. Certainly no one could do the miraculous things the maids were saying, but it would be very interesting to see what was exciting so many people in the villages. If, indeed, this Jesus were a fraud, it would be interesting to see how He had fooled so many people, for His popularity was increasing daily, and the people flocked to hear His message. It might be very useful to know just what that message was all about. It might also be wise for her husband to be aware of this new rabbi. Could He be a threat to Pilate's position?

* * *

Pilate took his goblet of wine and walked out into the early evening air. The night was glorious. The heat of the day had cooled as the sun set slowly in the distance. Overhead the stars were out in profusion and peace seemed to float in the air. The prefect saw his queen sitting by one of the small pools near the edge of the palace wall. He walked to her and touched the small hairs that grew just behind her ears. She was not a young woman any longer, but her beauty still beckoned to him and reminded him that he was not only a governor but also still a man. "You are quiet tonight my dear. Are you troubled?"

She turned and looked at her husband with a peaceful smile on her face. "No, my husband, I was just thinking about the day."

"And what was so interesting about your day to cause such a quiet reflection?"

"I went to hear this new rabbi, Jesus, today."

Pilate watched the woman with surprise in his eyes. "Did you take the guards as I suggested?"

"Yes, I followed your orders." Her tone teased him. "I was safe."

"And where did you go to see this man?"

200

"He was in Bethany. He went there to visit a friend who was sick."

"I've heard He can heal the sick. Did He help His friend?"

"The friend had died before Jesus arrived."

"That's too bad that He was too late to heal him."

Procula turned slowly and looked at Pilate for several minutes before she finally spoke. "No, but He raised the dead man to life."

Pilate stood quietly for a moment. "He raised a man from death? Oh come now! Surely the man was only pretending to be dead."

When Procula looked up, her eyes were filled with tears. "The man had been dead for several days—in his tomb. The people of the town had seen him dead. They all were convinced."

Pilate was clearly not convinced. "Really! Raising a dead man? There must be an explanation."

"Jesus wept when He heard His friend was dead. Then He walked to the tomb and called for him to come out." She lowered her eyes as she continued. "And the dead man walked out, still covered with the wrappings of death. Everyone was astounded." She raised her head and looked off into the distance as the sun sank into the horizon. "Especially me!" Pilate stood speechless, watching his wife. Then she continued. "I heard Jesus speak. It was as if the entire world stopped to listen. His words entered my ears, but they also entered my heart. He's special, my husband. He's a wise and wonderful man."

"He may well be a problem, my darling."

"A problem? How? He talks of love and forgiveness. How can that be a problem? Why would anyone dispute His words?"

"The chief priest and his band of thieves came to see me about this Jesus. They fear Him."

"Fear Him?"

"He teaches a new kind of law, and the priests feel the law is their purview. They don't like anyone challenging their authority, their power."

"You should have expelled them long ago, my love."

"It's not that easy. They exercise great power over the people. In their society, they are the arbiters of right and wrong. They own the people."

"Own! I don't like that term."

"They promise the people things that can never be delivered, and when disappointment arrives, they say it was the will of Yahweh. They have an answer for everything." Pilate looked into his goblet for a moment, took a sip of the liquid, and continued. "And the priests hate me, a Roman, for sharing a small part of that power."

"But you have soldiers and the backing of Rome."

"And they have the people—and God, so we keep a fine balance. I don't challenge their authority, and they don't challenge mine." Pilate breathed a small laugh. "We have meetings with much talk, but no one is listening. We all simply nod and smile at each other."

"You are a patient man, my dear." Procula brushed a strand of hair from Pilate's face.

"True, but it is wearing thin, very thin."

"Well, when you finally reach the end of your patience, join me and listen to Jesus. It will restore your peace. He even preaches that we should love our enemies."

"Well, that settles it. If He means I should love those self-righteous, pompous priests, He does not have a message for me." Pilate reached and put his arm around his wife and pulled her closer. "Peace I could use, but listening to some rabbi will not give that to me. I'm tired of the entire lot of them."

"Well, you and Jesus share your opinions of the priests and Pharisees. He disparages them constantly, and they hate Him for it."

"A truthful man has few friends in this world. Trust me, it is dangerous to criticize the Pharisees and priests." The governor finished his wine and set the goblet beside the pool. "My dear, you are so beautiful. Have some wine and come to bed. We've talked enough tonight. None of this discussion is of any importance in this world, but this wine is special, special indeed. It may be the only thing remembered of this hot, dry day, certainly not the preaching of some poor rabbi from Nazareth."

* * *

Rebecca carefully reached and stirred the pot boiling over the small fire. She was just turning for a rag to wrap around the metal handle when Nathan raced through the door. He was visibly excited. "Rebecca, I heard Him. I saw Him heal people. It was amazing."

"Nathan, calm yourself, and give me a kiss." He swept her up into his arms and kissed her quickly. "Now tell me what all of this excitement is about."

"Jesus! I saw Jesus today." Nathan was speaking quickly; his eyes wide with excitement. "He spoke to a large crowd, and He healed people." He looked around the room for his son. "We've got to get Samuel to Jesus. He can heal Samuel. Where is he?"

"First of all, sit down and tell me about how you saw Jesus." Nathan carefully removed his cloak and hung it on a nail in the back of the door. As he sat at the table, Rebecca placed a cup of water in front of him. "Drink, then tell me about Jesus. I have heard so many things; I want to know what you actually saw and heard."

"Pilate's wife had seen Him once in Bethany and wanted to hear Him again, so a detail of guards was selected to protect her while she was in the city. Jesus had come to Jerusalem from Capernaum for the Feast of Tabernacles. I was one of those chosen to accompany her."

"I see. Well tell me, how was the governor's wife? Is she as beautiful as everyone says? And why did she want to see Jesus?"

"At first I thought Procula just wanted a chance to get out of the palace for a while. But then I listened to her talk to one of her maids about Jesus. She was really anxious to see Him and hear Him."

Rebecca smiled as she handed Nathan some bread she had dipped into the small black pot. "And you didn't answer my question about her beauty."

Nathan smiled. "Well, she is pretty, almost as pretty as you, but not quite." They both were smiling. "Rebecca, I'm serious. I have never encountered a man like Jesus before. When He talked, it was as if the world stopped and listened. He talked of Yahweh and how He loves us. He talked of how we should love those around us, and how we should love ourselves. But then, late in the afternoon, the people started bringing their sick to him. He had such compassion for those suffering. He healed them and told them to go in peace. It was just...amazing." Nathan touched Rebecca's face and looked directly into her eyes. "And then I thought of Samuel. Maybe Jesus would heal him too."

Rebecca found a piece of cloth and wet it in a large clay bowl. She returned and began wiping Nathan's face. After a while she bent and kissed him. "I have never seen you so excited, except perhaps on our first night together as husband and wife." She smiled as he grinned at her. "But Nathan, let's not build up Samuel's hopes. He's learned to live with his limitations. He's happy; let's not risk that with expectations that may not be realized."

"No, Rebecca, you don't understand. I saw Jesus heal a man crippled from birth. I saw Him restore a blind man's sight. I *saw* it with my own eyes! A young boy was possessed by demons. Jesus simply ordered them to leave the boy, and they did. He was healed!" Nathan reached both of his hands to hold Rebecca's face. "We must get Samuel to see Him. And I want you to hear Him as well."

Rebecca freed herself and walked back to the pot hanging over the fire. "How did the governor's wife hear about Jesus? What prompted her to have such a desire to hear Him?"

"She had heard so much about Jesus..."

"Everyone has." Rebecca stirred the pot while she watched her husband. "What did she think of the rabbi?"

"She was amazed, like everyone else."

Rebecca returned to their table, and the two sat as she poured water and put bread on their plates. "Tell me more about Jesus. What does He say to the people?"

Nathan drank some of the water then spoke in a quiet voice as he looked off into the fading light in the room. "He speaks with authority, but He is gentle with His words. He speaks of peace and love. He calls Yahweh our Father. The people bring their sick to Him; today He healed many, young and old alike."

"Are there many people in the crowd?"

"Yes, when He was near Magdala there were thousands. I'm told He took a few fish and loaves from a small boy and fed the entire crowd. Then they gathered many baskets of what remained. As the crowds grew He had to go out onto the lake in a boat and speak to the crowd on the shore."

"I can see He has touched you. He must be very special."

"When He spoke, my heart burned within me. None of us spoke when we traveled back to the palace. Even the Governor's wife was silent, weighing His words." Nathan turned and smiled into the eyes of the woman he loved. "We have had so many years of oppression and killings. But this man brings hope for a better life, a life of love and peace. I have to find a way to get Samuel to Him."

Rebecca looked down, her head bowed. "Oh Nathan, you are such a good man. You love Samuel so much. Yahweh gave Samuel a difficult road, but he has struggled through it, largely because of you. He loves his vineyard, and he is happy. Don't give him hopes that cannot happen."

Nathan smiled at the face he cherished. "You are right about my love for Samuel. I love him almost as much as I love you. That is why I will find a way to take him to Jesus. I won't talk about healing; I'll just talk about His message." He thought for a moment. "And actually, that may be more important anyway. The healing is only for the body. His message is for the soul."

Chapter 38

Nathan sat outside the Palace Guard's headquarters and waited. He could hear loud voices in the commander's office, but he could not understand what they were saying. When the two Roman administrators left, he was advised that the commander would see him. He walked in and saluted, standing smartly at attention. Tobias was writing on a scroll and took several minutes to complete his work. Finally he looked up. "Good morning, Nathan. It's good to see you." Tobias rose and walked around his desk, his light blue cloak spotless. He looked at Nathan's and saw a large spot on the left shoulder, an obvious reminder of his granddaughter who spent many evenings sleeping on her grandfather's shoulder. Tobias smiled.

"And good to see you as well, Tobias."

"I understand you wanted to take the day off today for personal reasons."

"That is correct."

"May I ask what those personal reasons are, because I have an important task I need you to accomplish?"

"I wish to take my son to see Jesus." He said it simply without further explanation.

"I see. And how is Samuel doing? He must be in his thirties now, not old like you and me."

"You are right about us being older. But the years have been good to both of us."

"In many ways you are right." Tobias looked at Nathan for a long time before continuing. It was as if he were balancing his thoughts and his words carefully. "You have a family. Five children. That is a great reward in this life."

"I have been blessed; it is true." Nathan could see the pain displayed on his friend's face. "And you have become the Commander of the Palace Guards. That is quite an honor."

"Yes, I suppose it is."

"What is it you wish me to do?"

"We have many new recruits who are still rather clumsy with their swords. If we ever had a determined attack, I'm not confident they could do the job required. Have you seen that as well?"

"I have. We have instituted a very thorough training program in Unit 2. It is working well, and I am pleased with the results I am seeing in the newer troops."

"I have heard the same reports." Tobias walked to the table below his window and poured two goblets of wine. He handed one to Nathan. "As a result, I would like you to start a training program for the entire Guards detachment. You are unquestionably the finest swordsman in Judea." The commander peered over his drink at Nathan. "I told Pilate that we would begin this afternoon, and the prefect has advised me he will be coming to see our progress—today." As an afterthought he added, "I had hoped it would be later in the week."

There was very clear disappointment on Nathan's face when he finally spoke. "As you wish. I'll call the troops together, and we will begin immediately."

Tobias studied Nathan's face before he spoke. "Tell me, Nathan, why do you want to see this rabbi Jesus?"

"He is a very special man, Tobias. I heard Him speak when I was on the escort team for Procula, Pilate's wife. I had little interest in another rabbi, but as He spoke, His words pierced my heart, and suddenly I began to understand His message. Then I saw Him heal people just by touching them. I could not believe what my eyes were seeing. It was amazing."

Tobias stood, watching the man before him. "And you thought about Samuel." Tobias approached his friend and put his hand on his shoulder.

"Yes, I thought about Samuel."

"I have little use for the priests and Pharisees, as you know; I guess that is the one thing I share with this man, Jesus. But as for healing people and the story about raising a man from death...I have difficulty believing that."

"I would feel the same had I not seen it with my own eyes."

"Interesting." Tobias stepped back with his right hand on his chin, thinking. "Well, perhaps later we can go together to see this rabbi. I would like that. I had paid little attention to Him until what you have just told me. There is no one else I would believe but you when told a dead man was raised. So, if you will allow me to join you, we both will see Jesus, and we can take Samuel as well. But for today, the prefect will be expecting to see our troops learning swordsmanship. I told him how good you are with a sword. He was even aware of the Primus Pilus's gift to you of the special sword."

"I will have the men ready just after noon."

"That will be fine, but before you leave, I have another item I would like you to consider. I spent some time with Gilad last night. He was helping me with the new guard schedule, but he also seemed worried about Doran."

"Is there a problem with Doran?"

"He's not sure. He has just seen a change in his son over the past few months, and he is bothered by what he is witnessing."

"Is Doran having problems with his position? Do his men respect him?"

"Yes, they respect him; it's not that. It's almost the opposite. It's like his pride has clouded his judgment. Gilad says

209

he constantly talks about Herod, calling him his real father. He once said that Herod's blood was in his heart and made him strong. Things like that."

"It doesn't sound like the Doran we knew here at the palace."

"No, it doesn't."

"Maybe he is focused on a young woman."

"That is a possibility. Or maybe some young woman is focused on him." Both men smiled.

"Well, he always listened to Kalev. Perhaps he can spend a little time with him and discover what is in his head. Probably it's just the impetuousness of youth. He's still learning his way as a leader of men."

"You're probably right. Sorry to have to change your plans today."

"That's all right. I can find Jesus later. I'd better collect the men. We'll need better practice poles if the new prefect comes to review our training. I'll see you on the training field."

"Thanks, Nathan. If anyone else could do this as well as you, I would not have asked." Nathan nodded and turned for the door.

* * *

Nathan sat opposite Rebecca and Samuel as they completed their dinner. "So, I had to start the entire program with only a few hours' notice."

Samuel smiled at his father. "Well, at least Tobias recognized who was the expert swordsman in the Guard." He reached across and took the final piece of lamb on Nathan's plate.

"But I had planned that the two of us would go to Bethany to hear Jesus. As I've explained, He has a message of hope that I want you to hear. He is a man with a great heart and a great message." Nathan glanced at Rebecca and continued. "Samuel, this country has suffered such oppression and death at the hands of so many different leaders and oppressors. Perhaps the answer is finally here. Jesus's message is one of love and hope and peace, all of which is so needed today. I can't explain His message well enough. It is so important to me that you hear it. Over a thousand men stood on the side of a mountain and listened to Him speak. No one made a sound. Every man present felt Jesus's words in his heart. I just can't explain it. You must hear Him yourself. Tobias has even agreed to go along as well."

"I've also heard the stories about Jesus. What about mother?" He turned to Rebecca. "Won't you join us? I've heard that Jesus was in Bethany three days ago. If we leave tomorrow early, we may get to see and hear Him."

Rebecca looked at both of the men at her table. "Well, since we have older children in the family, I guess I could get away for a day. Besides, who would prepare the food and carry the water?"

Nathan smiled at his wife. "You know who will carry the heavy water!"

"The same man who will drink most of it, I imagine."

Samuel laughed at his parents and handed a piece of bread to one of his younger siblings racing around the table. "I wish I could run that fast."

Rebecca spoke immediately. "You do very well; when you were a small boy I had a very difficult time catching you as you raced around our yard."

Samuel smiled. He had heard that story before, and he doubted it now as much as the first time. The story said far more about a mother's love than about how fast he could move as a child. He knew the fierce determination and love in his mother's heart, and he marveled at the woman who had borne him. She was as strong as the mountains—especially when it came to her family. He looked next at his father, a strong man in battle, and also a man with a great heart. When he was younger Samuel had assumed that Nathan was his natural father. Later he learned about that night in Bethlehem and he then assumed Nathan married Rebecca out of pity or concern for her wellbeing. Over the years he had witnessed one of the greatest loves he could imagine. It was so obvious how Nathan loved Rebecca. Perhaps the marriage was, in part, the result of compassion, but in time it was definitely one of great love. He understood that because he also had a woman he loved. He rose from the table and kissed his mother on the top of her head. "I've got to get home. Adriel is making dinner." He smiled broadly. "I get to eat twice tonight."

Nathan looked up at his son. "You be sure to tell Adriel her dinner is the best."

"Now *Abba*, there you go in the teaching mode again. Of course I would say that." He stopped at the door. "Tomorrow morning at daybreak, I'll be here with as many supplies as I can carry."

"Your mother and I will be waiting, but Tobias will not be along tomorrow. He has a meeting with the prefect; he'll join us later on another trip." After Samuel had left Nathan turned to Rebecca and pushed a small patch of white hair from her brow. "Thank you."

"For what?"

"For coming. You know I may need to assist Samuel along the way. And you know I would have difficulty if I were also trying to carry most of the supplies."

"Silly man. You know why I'm coming along—to keep you two out of trouble."

"Right!"

212

Rebecca began clearing the table. "Besides, I, too, have heard stories about Jesus from my friends. I'd also like to hear Him." She grinned at Nathan. "While I take care of my men."

After the table was cleared and the washing was complete, Nathan and Rebecca checked their children and then climbed into their bed. Rebecca cuddled next to her husband and kissed his shoulder. Nathan responded and pulled her close into his arms. He kissed the top of her head and stared into the night sky outside the window. "This is my favorite time of day, lying here holding you as we fall asleep."

"I know, it's also mine." She snuggled closer and tucked her head on his shoulder. "There were years, when the children were small, when I was so busy at this time of night. I hardly know how we had time for each other. It seems there was an endless stream of babies demanding my time."

"Well, there must have been some time for us." Nathan grinned into the night. "We did keep having more babies."

Rebecca playfully punched him in his ribs. "Yes, I do recall those times as well."

"You make it sound like something far back in the past." He reached and touched her breast.

"Go to sleep you silly man. You know we have a busy day tomorrow." As she said it, she put her arms around his chest and squeezed him affectionately. "Do you really think we can find Jesus?"

"I hope so."

"I know how much you want Samuel to see Him, but don't get too disappointed if we fail."

"If we do, we will simply keep trying." Nathan lifted her chin and kissed Rebecca. "We will simply keep trying until we succeed."

"You never give up do you?"

"Never. I am a guard in service of my country. We never quit."

Rebecca rolled away from her man and prepared for sleep. Staring out the window at the stars she responded. "No, you never quit, my love. If persistence is a virtue, you are the most virtuous man in all of Judea." Then a moment later, "And your son is just like his father." She listened for a reply but only heard the soft snoring of the man next to her.

* * *

The sun was barely rising in the eastern sky when Samuel appeared at the door. As usual, he was smiling. He went straight to his mother. "Mom, sit down." He sat opposite her and looked into her eyes. "Last night Adriel told me she is going to have another baby." He was smiling from ear to ear.

Rebecca stood and moved toward him quickly. As he tried to rise he stumbled and fell. She grabbed him, and they both tumbled to the floor. Both looked at each other for a moment then they both began laughing. "Oh Samuel, I am so happy. A new baby in our family. You must be so proud." He nodded without speaking. "You are a fine father." She glanced up at Nathan who was responding to the sound of the crash. "Like your father." As they both climbed to their feet, Nathan grabbed his son and hugged him with great force. "Son, I am so proud."

Rebecca was counting on her fingers. Samuel laughed. "See *Abba*, *Ima* is already counting the months."

Three of the children in the house walked into the room and began searching for food. Nathan put the smallest into a chair at the table. "See son, see what you have to look forward to...more mouths to feed." He was smiling as he handed a piece of bread to the child.

"I'm happy, and Adriel is too." Samuel looked at the supplies stacked next to the door. "How much of this will we carry? There is a lot of food here."

Nathan looked at Rebecca and began sorting through the items. "We will only be gone for a day, and we can replenish our water once we get to Bethany, so I guess we could leave some of this behind. Besides, we can go to Matthias's house if we need anything more. I'm sure he would be glad to help us." Nathan placed two jugs of water in the bottom of his pack. On top of that he placed bread, cheese, dates, and some dried figs from a shelf near the fireplace.

Rebecca spooned three plates of stew into bowls and gave each of the men one along with a piece of bread. "Eat this and drink some water before we leave. You'll need this; we have a long walk today."

Samuel limped over to the table and sat to eat. Nathan stood near the door sorting the things he might need. He looked at his large sword and paused. After a moment he placed it back in the corner and found the smaller Jewish version. He saw Rebecca watching him. "Just in case. You never know who you might meet on the road to Bethany."

"Well, be sure to put it under your cloak when we see Jesus."

Nathan grinned. "I won't need this if we find Jesus, but it might be useful on the way."

The road to Bethany was one Nathan knew well. He had walked it so many times when King Herod ruled Judea and he and Rebecca had hidden in the small home near Matthias. The sun was high overhead as the three traveled toward the small town. There was not a cloud in the sky and the wind had retreated to someplace far away. They pulled their shawls over their heads and squinted their eyes from the glare as they walked together. After the first mile the conversations ceased, and each paced their own stride to accommodate each other and also the heat of the day. The three miles were not difficult for a young, strong man, but for a man nearing fifty helping a grown man with a crippled leg, it was a bit more difficult. Rebecca walked easily and paced the two men as they proceeded on the dry, dusty road. They were not yet halfway there when she noted that Nathan's face was quite red. He was working hard to assist his son. "Look, there is a tree ahead beside the road. Let's take a short rest. I need some water, and I expect both of you do as well." Nathan helped Samuel down the slight incline to the tree. The shade was a welcomed relief from the sun's hot rays, but the heat of the day remained. Nathan dug through the pack and retrieved the water jugs which they all shared. He then handed Rebecca and Samuel pieces of bread and cheese. As they relaxed beside the tree, Nathan stretched his right shoulder and groaned slightly. Rebecca noticed but said nothing.

Nathan looked up at the angle of the sun and encouraged his family to climb back onto the road. Samuel did quite well on the flat road, but the rough trail to the road was a bit more challenging. Both of his parents stood on either side and helped him along. The day had been clear and hot as they started their trek, but then a slight wind began to blow in from the northeast and increase as they continued. The dry terrain around them became the birthing area of yet another sandstorm that caused them all to huddle together and cover their heads and faces as sand and trash attacked them from several different directions. The trek that should have taken a couple of hours grew to over four before they reached Bethany. It was just past noon when they reached the outskirts of the small town. The wind had finally given them some relief, and they arrived tired, but excited. It was a town they all knew quite well, and it held many memories for all of them. For Samuel

216

they were memories of growing up and playing in the fields. For Nathan it held memories of walking along the dry roads heading to his home and the family he loved after a long day at the palace. For Rebecca the memories were of waiting for the man she loved to return to her and the children. There were memories as well of babies crawling on the floor and long summer nights together holding each other as they talked of their future together. As they approached the village, Nathan pointed toward the southwestern edge of town. He knew Matthias would welcome them, if he were not in the crowd around Jesus himself. So it was that as the three approached the house of Matthias, Nathan's heart sank a bit as he saw his friend rushing to greet him. Matthias embraced Nathan first. "My friend, Matthias. How are you? I have missed our visits and our talks."

"As have I." Matthias embraced the rest of the family then turned again to Nathan. "What brings you back to Bethany? Is everything okay in Jerusalem?"

"We have come to see Jesus. I had hoped one of your servants could direct us to the place where He is teaching. I assumed you would be there yourself."

"I'm sorry, Nathan, but Jesus left yesterday afternoon. He has gone to Peraea. While He was here Jesus healed a blind man who had been blind from birth. As one might expect the Pharisees were displeased because the healing was performed on the Sabbath. For them, the law was more important than healing a blind man. They know that Jesus has come to change the law. He is a direct threat to all they profess. Jesus has many enemies in Jerusalem; they are accusing Him of blasphemy. So, He left and crossed the Jordan into Peraea. It was wise to avoid the Pharisees and the priests. They fear Him, so they will seek to harm Him."

217

"We missed Him." There was defeat in Nathan's voice. He turned and looked at his wife and son as his shoulders physically slumped.

"Don't worry *Abba*. We'll get another chance." Samuel walked over in his unusual gait and put his hand on Nathan's shoulder.

Matthias approached Samuel and clasped both of his shoulders. "Of course you will. But I know you are all tired, so come into my house and eat and rest." He looked over at Nathan and could see the disappointment in his eyes. Beside him stood Rebecca, her arms around her husband. She was looking up at him with both concern and love on her face. Matthias smiled at the two. "Nathan, you are a man greatly blessed. Now come inside, and I insist you stay tonight. You can return to Jerusalem tomorrow."

* * *

"You mustn't feel badly, Nathan. You did all you could to get Samuel here. There was no way we could have known Jesus left yesterday." Rebecca reached and combed his hair with her fingers. She turned and pulled a small jug from the pack she had carried on the trip. He watched as she poured a small amount of oil into her hand and then began rubbing it into her feet. The hot, dusty road had left them dry and slightly burned from the sun's relentless rays. Nathan smiled until she reached for one of his feet. "Here, let me rub some oil into your feet. They are as dry as a lizard's back in the desert."

"A lizard's back?" He smiled at his wife.

"Sure, a lizard's back. Have you ever seen a lizard in the desert?"

"I hadn't thought of that comparison."

218

She playfully hit his leg with the jug. "Give me your foot. I refuse to sleep with a man whose feet feel like a desert lizard." Nathan smiled and surrendered his feet while sitting on the floor. After Rebecca finished rubbing them with oil and a cloth, she climbed into bed and reached for him to join her.

"I just feel like I've failed you both. It was such a hard trip today." Nathan pulled Rebecca closer as they lay together, looking out the window to a clear night with more stars than they could count. "But I was surprised at how strong Samuel is. He did very well on the walk. I really didn't have to help much at all."

"He's a strong young man." She snuggled her head on Nathan's shoulder. "And he is a good man as well."

"Yes, he is." He was smiling in the night, and though Rebecca could not see his face, she knew he was smiling proudly.

"You did a fine job raising our son, Nathan."

He kissed her on the top of her head. "And you are a great mother. I remember when the villagers urged you to leave him in the desert. I think you would have fought the entire village for your son. I was so impressed with your strength."

She ran her hand across his chest. "Yes, I would have fought them all."

"That's why I stayed—to save the entire town from the mad woman in the small house south of the town."

His teasing made her laugh out loud. "You are a silly man." She kissed him on his shoulder. "And you have been a great father to all of our children."

"They are quite a brood. We've been away just one day, and I miss them already."

"I know." She pulled her right arm from under his neck and leaned up over her husband. "Now turn over and go to sleep. We have a trip to make tomorrow. And if I remember well, I think you have to work tomorrow evening at the palace."

He pulled her face down to his own and kissed her. "Good night, my dear." She smiled in the night, looked up again at the stars, and then snuggled next to her husband for sleep.

Chapter 39

The young soldier frowned as he emptied the two pails he was carrying and turned to re-enter the large gate to the Antonio Fortress. On either side of the great door stood three Roman soldiers armed with swords and spears. They appeared bored and spoke quietly to each other until an officer passed. Then they stood straight, at attention. When he left, they resumed their conversations. The young man stopped just inside the gate and placed the two pails he was carrying on the ground. As he wiped the sweat from his face, he glanced around at the huge military complex. Originally it had been a Hasmonean fortress called Baris, built just northwest of the temple on a large rocky scarp. After defeating the Hasmoneans and taking control of Judea, Herod the Great had it rebuilt. It was then renamed for his friend, Mark Antony. Currently it was a Roman fort, known by all as the place where the high priest's vestments were kept between festivals. Herod had instituted this rule, (much to the chagrin of the chief priests), and the Romans had continued the practice. The young man moved into the shade and placed his right hand on the immense stone blocks that were used to make the fortress impenetrable to foreign invaders. His feelings were mixed; he felt safe and even important to be a part of such a mighty and powerful army, but emptying piss buckets was not the kind of glory he desired. A centurion approached with a distinctive stride, one he recognized, so he quickly retrieved his two pails and proceeded toward the northeast corner of the fortress. Down a dark hallway in the corner of the building was the armory, a room filled with weapons. The armory was a crowded room with surprising light from two windows carved into the thick stone walls. Each was protected by iron bars to ensure no enemy lucky enough to scale the walls could gain entry. Inside two other men were sorting a stack of spears newly delivered from Rome. The older of the two looked up and smiled at the frowning face in the door. "Finished your important task, I see." The unhappy soldier tossed the two wooden pails into a corner and wiped his hands on the bottom of his cloak. He said nothing but walked to a large table in the center of the room and picked up a sword and a large sharpening stone. As he raked the stone along the blade, a centurion strode into the room and stopped beside the table. His legs were spread apart and his fists were on his hips. He was the epitome of military rank. The three men immediately stood to attention and snapped their fists to their chests in salute.

"I want a full accounting of our equipment in the armory. Count every spear, javelin, sword, dagger—all of it. Then report to me by mid-afternoon. Questions?"

"No, Centurion."

"Good." He started for the door but stopped and looked back at the three soldiers. "Do any of you read and write?"

The younger man held up his hand. "I do, Sir."

"Good, I expect the report to be legible; it will be passed along to higher authority."

"Yes, Centurion."

After the officer had left, the older soldier looked at the other two. "What was that all about?"

"Who knows? Probably just another exercise to keep us busy."

"Well, let's keep them happy. Get some parchment and let's begin." The older man paused and turned to the young soldier. "I didn't know you could read and write."

"My mother taught me when I was a child. She said it might be useful someday."

"Well, bless your mother. She was right; today is the day."

* * *

The last entry was made on the parchment and the three soldiers stood and looked at the beautiful document. There were words and numbers, and beside each column there were small drawings of the weapons listed below. It was a magnificent artifact, or at least that was the assessment of the older soldier. All three turned and looked out the window above them, searching for the position of the sun. From their angle it was hard to discern the time, but they estimated it was still roughly mid-afternoon. The older soldier put his hand on the younger man's shoulder. He was smiling as he spoke. "Well, it appears you may not be collecting piss much longer. You have gained the centurion's eye. Men who can read and write are far too valuable to be left to such menial tasks." He turned and looked at the young man for a moment as if considering his next statement. "And *you* must take the list to the centurion."

"Me?" There was surprise in the response.

"Yes, you." A small smile broke across the older face. "You are the only one who can read. He might have questions." He picked up the document and handed it to the prior bucket tender. "And one other thing. While there, pay attention. It would be good if we had some idea why the sudden interest in how many swords and spears we have. Is there a big battle being planned? Are the Parthians moving toward the Euphrates again?"

"I understand." There was a smile on the young face.

"And one more thing. Clean up your uniform. You wouldn't want to get piss on the centurion's nice new armor would you?"

All three men laughed as the young soldier brushed his uniform.

* * *

The two weapons experts listened carefully as the young soldier described his trip into the offices of the military hierarchy. "The centurion had another request. He wants to know how many wagons we have capable of carrying heavy weapons."

"Wagons?"

"Wagons capable of a journey as far as Samaria and back."

"How interesting."

"And animals to pull them."

"Not slaves?"

"He feels the weight would be too great for that distance."

"If weapons are the cargo, he's right."

The young man produced another parchment with words and numbers that were obviously added quickly. It was barely readable. "He says for us to start staging the following equipment."

"Can you read that?"

"I can."

"Good. Let's start that as soon as we've had our meal. I'm hungry."

There were soldiers of all ranks standing in line waiting for their evening meal. Bread and a thick gruel were served along with several dates for each. A mixture of wine and water were also allotted to each of the mercenaries in the fort. As the older soldier rose to leave, he complained that he was still hungry. He walked to the large gate and stepped outside where several merchants sold various things the soldiers might buy. After a quick search, the soldier approached a young boy selling bread. A small coin was passed between the two and the soldier returned with a small loaf of bread and some olive oil. He was smiling as he split the bread among the three men. The young boy was also smiling as he walked quickly back into the heart of Jerusalem. He had a message for a very important man waiting in the temple.

"What have you, my boy?" The coin was passed to the well-dressed man in flowing robes. He studied it carefully. "A *Greek* coin, I see." He stroked his beard for several minutes. "So he wants a meeting. I wonder what news he has for me." He smiled to himself. "I'd better get more coins for my friend in the fortress—especially Greek coins."

Chapter 40

Tobias sat at his desk studying reports from his unit commanders while Nathan and two others sat across from him on a long bench against the wall. Their robes were basic tan and brown robes, standard Guard uniforms. Tobias, on the other hand, wore his resplendent robe of light blue color. It had dark blue stripes around the neckline, down the front, and at the hem of the garment. A gold chain hung around his neck with the emblem of the Palace Guards attached. Five gold buttons were attached to the top left breast to signify all of the units he commanded. Like everything in his life, it was spotless. Nathan looked at the uniform and felt a slight twinge of jealousy. Looking down at his own, he noticed several stains and even a small tear at the hem. He smiled and reaffirmed to himself that Tobias was the right man for his job. The Commander of the Palace Guards shouldn't have baby stains on his robe.

Tobias moved the reports to the side of his desk and rose, standing before his commanders. "We need to be very careful. The Roman Prefect, Pilate, was appointed to his position by Sejanus, who was the Regent of Rome, not by Emperor Tiberius. As it so happens, Sejanus was later executed by Tiberius along with a number of his colleagues. We also have heard that Tiberius is condemning many of Sejanus's appointees. What this means for Pilate is not clear. It does, however, mean that it is possible we could see abrupt changes here. Whether Pilate remains in control is questionable. Should some of Tiberius's men seek Pilate, we will be in the middle."

One of the unit commanders spoke up abruptly. "I wish Rome would get together on who runs things. Every time they have a change in government, the entire world gets thrown into the maelstrom."

"You're right, but our job is to protect the palace and whoever lives there. For now that is Pilate." Tobias paced back and forth as he spoke to his men. "No one will speak of this meeting. Is that understood?" When all nodded he continued. "I will monitor events and keep you advised, but in the meantime, go about your jobs as you have always done. We guard the palace and all who live there." He paused briefly then continued. "If anything changes, I'll let you know. Any questions?"

As the men filed out, Tobias motioned for Nathan to remain. When they were alone, he spoke frankly. "I'm worried. If a fight starts in Rome, we will be involved almost immediately. We may end up guarding one of the men Tiberius wants removed."

"That is an ominous position to be in, to be sure." Nathan watched Tobias carefully. "What is your plan?"

"I don't have a plan. I haven't decided how to handle this yet. I guess it depends on how events play out. Tiberius is the man in charge in Rome. He may just order Pilate to return to Rome. Or maybe he will have him remain in charge here. Hopefully it will not resort to conflict here, but if he sends men for Pilate, I'll try to secret Pilate and his family out of the palace, maybe to Caesarea. If we do that carefully, we may avoid being drawn into the fray. I don't want us in the middle of Roman politics."

"The important thing now is to be informed. As Commander of the Palace Guards, I would suppose you have good communications with both Pilate and Rome."

"With Pilate, yes. Rome—not so much." Tobias poured wine for both and sat beside his old friend. "I have an appointment with Pilate this afternoon. You can be sure this will arise as a topic of conversation." Both men sipped their wine. "There is a lot going on just now. We have Pilate's precarious situation with Rome and the ongoing resentment of Herod Antipas in Galilee, and now we have Jesus criticizing the religious leaders while the Chief Priests and Pharisees strut around like scolded children." Tobias looked over at Nathan. "And worst of all, both of us have gray hair now. We are becoming old men."

"Not old, just experienced."

"Well, we had better use that experience to keep the peace around here. Passover is coming soon, and we have much to prepare. Finish your wine and we'll make a plan." The Commander of the Palace Guards pulled a cord hanging from the ceiling and a young man entered. "Bring food. We may be working late tonight." He turned to Nathan. "I hope Rebecca won't mind too much if you have to miss dinner."

"That will be okay. She's understanding."

"You are fortunate, Nathan. Rebecca is a fine woman." Tobias lowered his head in thought for a moment. "You know there were times earlier when I thought she was a mistake for you. I was wrong."

Nathan smiled at the commander. "You are a good man and a good friend, Tobias. And I understand your earlier position about Rebecca. Now we both have had many years to realize what a good woman she really is. I was fortunate."

"She has made you happy. That is a rare gift in Judea these days."

Nathan looked into Tobias's eyes. "Have you ever regretted not having a family?"

"Children, yes. A wife? No." Tobias playfully hit his friend's shoulder. "You got the last good woman in Judea; what was I to do?" An orderly walked into the room with food and more wine. "Well, back to work. How do we keep the politicians safe and happy—not a small job at all." Tobias rolled a large scroll onto the table and placed a piece of fruit on each corner to keep it flat. "We now have seven units of six men each, a third

228

less than Herod demanded. How do we best allocate those resources to protect the palace?" And so the planning began.

Chapter 41

Darkness had settled over Judea as the small contingent of men filed into the large home on the outskirts of Jerusalem. The *haverim*, or meeting of devout leaders in the area, would have seemed normal as the men met regularly to discuss important things concerning their community and their faith. The only difference tonight was that several young men patrolled the area and two stood alert at the door. There were no strangers allowed in this meeting. As usual, the men shared personal stories as they ate their dinner of bread, vegetables, and lamb. There was no wine served tonight, only a thin tea boiled over an open fire. When the men finished eating and cordial discussions ceased, an older man stood and addressed the group. "Are we alone?"

A voice from the door answered promptly. "We are safe. Everyone is identified, and there is no threat outside."

"Good, then let us begin." The leader was tall but slightly bent as he stood. His beard was almost completely white. He introduced another, younger, man who stood and faced the group. "I'm sure you have all heard about the death of John the Baptizer. His head was delivered to Herod Antipas on a silver platter."

All in the room were shocked. This was news they had not heard. "How did that happen? Why would Antipas do such a thing?" The man paused for a moment then added. "Not that I am a follower of that wild man." Others in the room nodded agreement, but still they were shocked at the evangelist's death.

"It was Herodias's doing. John had criticized Antipas for marrying her, his brother's wife. It is against our law, and he spoke boldly. She hated him for it. Her daughter, Salome, danced for Antipas at a party he held for some friends, and he promised her anything she wanted as tribute." He paused for a moment as the message was consumed by the men in the room. "She asked for John's head." There was a sudden silence in the room. "The voice in the wilderness has been silenced." The men looked at the floor together. "That is how low this country has fallen. This is how depraved our leaders have become."

"Where did this happen?"

"At the Machaerus Fortress, where Antipas had held him prisoner for two years."

"All the more reason for our meeting tonight." He waited until all of the assembled men nodded and gave him their full attention. "We have received information that a shipment of arms will be transported to Samaria in the near future. Our source in Antonio Fortress says it will include swords, javelins, bows, arrows, and knives. According to him the plan is for the caravan to travel first to Jericho to collect tax money then proceed with the weapons to Samaria."

One of the men in the back of the room stood. "When will this take place? And how many soldiers will be in the caravan?"

"Our source doesn't know the size of the contingent of soldiers; he will be one of the men arranging the weapons for shipment. He may not even know the date until the night before the shipment leaves. But this should not be a problem. The caravan will stop in Jericho for at least a couple of days before moving on to Samaria. That will give us plenty of time to assess their strength and prepare an ambush."

"You are right, we should know the number of men involved before they leave Jericho."

"We need to start assembling our forces immediately. Regardless of their numbers, we just plan for a large force and take enough men to defeat them."

One of the other men spoke up. "And how many men is that?"

"More than we have available." The man standing looked down at the floor before continuing. "We will need help if we decide to attack."

At that point an older man in the rear of the room stood and held both of his hands high in the air. His face was worn from many years and though he was bald, his beard was thick. It was also totally white. The entire group suddenly fell silent as he spoke. "Men of Judea, I have spoken to the leader of a sizable Parthian force to the north. They are willing to join us if the battle is with Romans." The room remained silent as he stood waiting for any comments. "They would want some of the weapons and gold, but that is a small price to pay for success." He looked slowly around the room then sat down. The man who started the meeting stood again. "What discussion do we have? Are we willing to join forces with the Parthians? They are not our friends, but we do share a common enemy."

From the crowd: "But can we trust them? They are idol worshipers and unholy men. There is great risk dealing with them."

The bald man stood again and addressed the crowd. "I have nurtured this relationship for several years in case we needed it. I have met with the Parthian leaders several times and feel them to be honest men. Their hatred for the Romans is considerable. They would have little to gain by betraying us, but they would have much to gain by defeating a contingent of Roman soldiers and collecting a portion of their weapons. And as far as any gold or coins, they would certainly want a small share of that as well, but mostly they are looking for a victory to enhance their own status among their fellow Parthians."

Another man stood and faced the group. "And what is our purpose in this raid? What do we seek to gain, for we will most certainly suffer losses as well. The Romans are known to hire men who are willing to fight."

Another voice from the room spoke loudly to be heard. "Will we be facing mercenaries or Romans?"

The leader raised his hands to quiet the room. "I have a source within the palace who has heard some of the plans. He is not certain, but he believes the convoy will consist of mostly mercenaries with perhaps a few Romans in command."

"Do you believe your source? Just how reliable is he? How does he get such information?"

"He is a trusted spy. He has access to the Sanhedrin, and they have their spies everywhere." The man paused for a moment for effect then continued. "He is one of the Temple Guards."

There was sudden silence in the room. "One of the Temple Guards? Do you trust him?"

The leader waited for that information to settle in the group then continued. "Yes, and he will lead the attack. If he is first into the battle, that is all the commitment I need." The leader paced the room for several moments staring at the floor in thought. Finally, he raised his head and continued his exhortation to the group. "There is no certainty regarding the money, and that is of minor importance to us. Like the Parthians, we seek to make a statement to the Roman invaders that we are men who are willing to fight them, but we need more weapons to do that effectively. With this one battle we can accomplish both goals; we get their taxes and their weapons, and we send them a message." The conversation eventually turned from facts and clear planning to stories of emotion, injustices seen and suffered by all. In time the men stood and held their fists in the air and declared their own honor and willingness to fight for their freedom and their country. As the fervor rose, clear insight into the actual battle was lost. In the end, emotion won out over judgment, and a decision was made to enter into the unholy alliance with the Parthians. In time they might become enemies as well, but for the present they both hated the Romans more than each other. As the evening proceeded wine was brought, and any reservations remaining were drowned in the dark liquid.

* * *

Eight days later a young Jewish boy walked into Antonio Fortress with a large stack of freshly baked bread wrapped into a small net. The smell wafted throughout the area around the entry gate as soldiers moved along with their daily orders. The boy selling bread smiled as a thin man wearing a worn Roman uniform approached and took a loaf of the bread and bit a large chunk. Smiling he handed the boy some coins and lifted the entire net onto his shoulder. They smiled and gestured but spoke little. Then the boy carefully counted the coins and nodded as he left. The soldier also nodded and moved his fingers to carefully measure the heavy item carefully wrapped in parchment in the bottom of the net. His grin grew substantially as he walked back into the fortress. There was enough gold there to make him a wealthy man—for at least several months.

As the boy walked outside into the bright sun, he counted the coins again, but in a different manner this time. He separated them into two groups in his palm. Among the coins were three Roman coins with Caesar's face stamped on them. Three days. The weapons would be leaving the fortress in three days. He quickened his pace. He had important news to report.

The old man carefully studied the coins the boy had given him and turned to the bearded young man standing beside him. "He's right, Doran. Three days and approximately twenty

234

soldiers in the caravan. Prepare a message for our Parthian allies. They need to depart soon to meet us as planned."

Chapter 42

A young male slave walked into El'Azar's bedroom and handed him a note. The Commander of the Temple Guards studied it carefully and finally tossed it aside. "Why can't we teach people to write? This means nothing to me." He motioned to the young man to approach closer. "Bring the messenger inside; I will talk to him."

The young visitor stood in the spacious room and studied all of the furnishings El'Azar possessed. He had never seen such opulence. Two slave girls had lit enough candles to light half the city, and there were three couches forming a private area before the fireplace along with several paintings and exquisite rugs hanging along the walls opposite the fireplace. A large wooden desk, covered with parchments and scrolls, stood along the wall opposite the door. Two comfortable chairs sat to the right of the desk with a small table between them. In the far corner was a marble statue of a half nude young woman. Her white flesh shone in the light of the candles around the room and reflected from the freshly oiled tile floors. It was obvious that El'Azar knew how to live well and enjoyed that pleasure.

El'Azar quietly entered the room and stood behind the young man, silently watching him. The commander was proud of his home. It was a measure of his success, and his success had been great. He only answered to one man, the Chief Priest, and he answered to him on very few occasions. Caiaphas was far too busy on mundane things to participate in the schemes of his main lieutenant, schemes the lieutenant did not want the Chief Priest to be aware of. Even a priest needs enforcers now and then, and it was well understood by both men that it was generally best if the Chief Priest were not aware of all of the actions needed to enforce his office. When the young man realized he was not alone in the room he turned quickly, his face burning. "Commander, I have news."

"Go ahead. Speak." El'Azar said it with authority. He knew it was important to maintain his position.

"I was advised that the convoy to Jericho will be a mixture of Jews and Romans."

"Jews? I do not understand." The commander was obviously surprised. For just a moment the cool composure was shaken.

"I was told to inform you that some of the Palace Guards will be a part of the convoy going to Jericho. It is speculated that they will collect and guard the taxes that are being sent to Jerusalem."

"Then the rumor regarding the taxes is correct?"

"According to our sources, that is true."

El'Azar's left hand went immediately to his chin, and he began rubbing his well-trimmed beard. "Do we know how many Palace Guards will be along?"

"I'm told there will be between ten and twenty."

The older man studied the younger as his mind originated a plan. "Can you read?"

The young man was surprised by the question, but he paused only a moment. "No Sir; I cannot."

"Do you know our unit commander named Doran?"

"Yes Sir."

"I want you to take a note to him, but do not mention the Jews on the caravan. Do you understand?"

"Yes Sir."

El'Azar smiled as he wrote in beautiful script, confirming the tax revenues as part of the convoy leaving Jericho. Then his smile widened as he described how those funds were to be handled. "And remember, not a word about the Palace Guards." He looked straight into the young man's eyes for emphasis.

"Yes sir; not a word."

"Good; now be on your way." As the young man departed El'Azar poured himself a goblet of the new wine he had recently purchased from a new vineyard in the area. As he savored the dark liquid, a smile grew across his face. He was calculating the amount of taxes that might be collected in a town the size of Jericho.

Chapter 43

The tall thin man walked through the center of Jerusalem as a man with authority, and, indeed, Caiaphas had plenty of authority. He was the Chief Priest at the temple and the titular head of what little Jewish leadership existed. He was the son-in-law of the famed Chief Priest Annas and had been appointed his successor in A.D. 18 by Valerius Gratus, the Roman Governor. His robes and his headdress were signs of his status and his wealth. The soft black fabric was lined with broad gold trimming that added to the weight of the garment, but it was a weight willingly borne to signal the leader of the Jewish Temple, the titular leader of the Jewish people. Caiaphas was of normal height, but his thin frame and his tall headdress made him appear much taller. His black headpiece towered eight inches above his dark, glaring eyes. Beneath that crown the black wool extended down in three large flaps that flowed to his thin shoulders, covering his gray streaked hair. Like the robe, gold thread was woven in long broad stripes around the borders of the headdress. On top a three inch diameter golden jewel shaped like a large tear drop pointed toward the sky. As he walked through the streets with his head held high and his eight aides in tow, the people stepped back, and many bowed as he passed. He was an important man, one that held his nervousness carefully in check. It was not the weight of his garments that caused the deep furrow between his eyes. He was losing control, and it was becoming evident to those around him. The Chief Priest had the Romans to deal with, and he was acutely aware of their brutality. He had witnessed the death of thousands of his countrymen at their hands. He also felt the displeasure of some of his own countrymen who felt he was too agreeable with the Romans; after all, it was a Roman who had decreed his position as Chief Priest. Some had even suggested he was their lackey. Then there were riots over the beheading of John the Baptist by Herod Antipas and also a new rabbi from Nazareth going around inciting the people and chasing the money changers from the temple. He feared them all—the young rabbi, the Romans, and even his own people. He feared them, and he trusted no one, not even his second-in-command who was first on his list to visit this day.

El'Azar stood as Caiaphas entered his office. The Chief Priest's retinue waited outside. "Good morning Caiaphas. Would you care for some wine? Some food?"

Caiaphas looked at the feast on the table across from his lieutenant's desk. "No thank you. It is too early for me to have wine. It would only dull my senses, and I have much to consider this day." He looked at his assistant's robes and furnishings. The light green robe and even his sandals were color coordinated to match the appointments in the room. Unconsciously Caiaphas looked down at his own sandals; they were not nearly as nice as those of his advisor.

"You seem concerned. What is it that bothers you?"

"Everything. The Romans are still overly demanding. It seems all they want is our money for their projects. Then there is this new rabbi chasing the money changers out of the temple. Just who does He think He is?" He selected a chair across from El'Azar's desk and settled himself near the wine.

"Are you talking about the Nazarene?"

"Yes, that's Him. He constantly criticizes us and the Pharisees, although I tend to agree with Him regarding certain of the Pharisees." A small grin spread across his face.

"He seems to be gathering quite a following."

"That concerns me. We both know how paranoid the Romans are. When people start talking about a Messiah they get nervous, and when they get nervous, Jews die. We've seen it before."

"Yes, sadly we have." There was a slight smile on El'Azar's face as he watched his leader pace around his office. "And what is the third thing that disturbs your sleep at night?"

"I'm not even sure I can trust my own people in the Sanhedrin. There are probably men there who would betray us all for the right amount of gold. I fear that I am not in control of that group, and they are a powerful group to be sure."

"I understand your concern, but I'm convinced it is overrated. The men in the Sanhedrin respect you. They respect the position of the Chief Priest. You are the last remaining Jewish semblance of government that exists in this country. You are our balance to those infernal Romans who oppress us all."

The grin on Caiaphas's face disappeared and was quickly replaced by a deep frown. "Balance? Balance?" His voice was rising as he spoke. "There are many who suggest I bow too deeply to the Romans. How can I be sure there are no jealous conspirators among the Jewish hierarchy? How many yearn for my position? Who are my enemies? Who are Judea's enemies?"

El'Azar walked over and plucked several items from the table behind Caiaphas. He handed a large brown date to his leader and then put another in his mouth. After a moment he spit a large seed into an ornately decorated bowl on the table and addressed the pacing man in his office. "Caiaphas, Caiaphas, relax. You have so many things to contend with. Let me do my job as your assistant. You worry about the rabbi from Nazareth, and I'll manage our colleagues in the Sanhedrin. I know them, and they know me. I'm convinced they are dependable allies; after all, we all share the same goals." El'Azar was smiling as he turned his face from the Chief Priest.

241

"You're right. I guess I must worry too much. There are just so many issues to deal with every day. How did Annas handle this load?"

"Most likely he had a good steward like me to help him. Now, stop your pacing and enjoy this food and wine. You need a break from the stress, and my office is your refuge."

"Well, I know you'll keep me advised if needed."

"Of course. Now have some wine."

Caiaphas nodded and held out his goblet.

Chapter 44

Nathan was walking around the courtyard adjacent to the palace in Jerusalem, checking that his men were in place and alert. It also gave him time to exercise and stretch his legs. As he grew older, he found he was still vigorous, but in the mornings he tended to be a bit stiff. Walking helped warm his muscles and quicken his steps. As he walked across the flagstones, he saw Tobias walking toward him at a fast pace. Nathan stopped, turned, and approached his friend. "Good morning, Tobias." Nathan knew he was not in hearing distance of any of his men, so he used the familiar name instead of "Commander."

"I assume you've heard about the Baptizer."

Nathan shook his head. "I have. What a brutal thing for Antipas to do, and all for a dancing girl."

"Herodias finally had her way with John. It's not wise to criticize the leader's wife."

"No, it isn't. It seems all those Herodians are a blood thirsty bunch."

"Like father, like son." Tobias tried to change the somber mood as he watched Nathan's frown. "I see you are obeying Passover rules and staying away from the inner portions of the palace."

"Well, it isn't Passover yet, and you know I really don't worry too much about our religious rules, except for the Seder meal. I always enjoy a feast." Nathan smiled as the two walked toward the palace steps. "You seem to be in a hurry. Is everything okay?"

Tobias looked around to ensure they were not being overheard. "We have a special mission tomorrow morning. An emissary from Pilate is going to Jericho to collect taxes. Pilate has asked that we escort him and ensure the funds are returned safely. I'd like you to command that group."

"He's not sending his mercenaries?"

"I don't think he trusts them with that much money, so he's sending us along to accompany them and watch over his interests."

"Smart man. I would do the same if it were my money. I hope this has been kept secret. There are many who would risk death to steal such a fortune."

"The plan is to also carry a load of weapons from Antonia Fortress to Samaria. First, we go to Jericho, collect their taxes, then proceed to Samaria to deliver the weapons. I'm guessing about two weeks in all."

"This could be dangerous."

"It is. And we have been secretly alerted that some of the insurrectionists plan to take the weapons on the way to Samaria. They probably don't know about the taxes, but there are many in the fortress who know about a shipment of weapons."

"And they'd be glad to alert anyone who would be willing to pay them even a small amount of money." There was derision in Nathan's voice.

"We have been told that they plan to attack about two hours outside of Jericho where the oak trees are thick, just below the road. I think you may know the place. It's north of the town."

"How did you get this information, Tobias? Can we believe it?"

"The Sanhedrin has spies everywhere, and generally they are dependable." He smiled a wry smile. "And we also have spies—in the Sanhedrin."

"I find it strange that the Sanhedrin did not furnish this information to us directly. Why did they not alert us? Why did we have to discover it from one of our spies?"

"I've had the same concern. It's one that needs further examination. Normally I would expect the Sanhedrin to protect tax money for the Romans."

"Protect money for the Romans?"

Tobias laughed. "The Sanhedrin will gladly protect Roman taxes because they get a portion of the money themselves. When it comes to gold, our Jewish leaders are willing to negotiate with anyone. If protecting Roman interests coincides with their own, they would be more than happy to send us out to fight the rebels, but of course they would deny any participation in the battle—on either side."

"But this time they didn't inform us of the ambush."

"No, they didn't, and that is worrisome." Tobias stroked his beard in thought then continued. "We also don't know if the entire Sanhedrin is aware, or perhaps just a small group. That's something I need to investigate."

"If the entire Sanhedrin has this information and did not inform us, we have a serious problem. I guess it is all a balancing act for them with Rome on the one side and the Jewish people on the other."

"And either is expendable if it furthers our leaders' own goals."

"And that means we are expendable too, right?"

"I'm afraid so." Tobias walked along with Nathan as they approached the center of the palace where Pilate's own personal garrison was located. "We don't know how many men we might face on the road, so I have scheduled another unit to accompany you."

"That's sixteen men. That won't be enough."

"You're right. How many would you feel adequate?"

"Perhaps thirty. No less. And they would have to be trained fighters. I would not want to be outnumbered."

"I have an idea. I'll ask Pilate for an additional thirty of his personal soldiers. Surely they can be trusted, and you will be along to ensure the money is safe."

Nathan stopped walking and turned to Tobias. "You said Jews negotiate well. Tobias, I am depending on your negotiating skills to ensure I command *all* the troops. I would not want one of Pilate's men making the decisions along the road to Samaria. They don't know this country like we do. Remind Pilate of that, and no *Joint-Command*. We both know that doesn't work."

"I agree. Pilate was a military man early in his career. I suspect he will agree with that." Tobias stopped talking as a Roman soldier walked by at a distance. After he had passed, Tobias continued. "I'll send replacements for your men this afternoon. Tell them to prepare for two week's journey and a fight along the way—nothing more."

"What about the weapons?"

"They are being loaded at the Fortress. I've instructed that slaves be included to attend to the animals and the supplies you will need for the trip. They will meet you just outside the gate just before sun-up tomorrow morning. We'd prefer that few people are aware of your departure."

"Will the weapons be covered?"

"Yes, of course. They will appear to be blankets and other merchandise. The javelins will be placed in the bottom of five wagons; the swords, arrows, and shields will then be covered by tents and other supplies."

"One last item. Pilate's soldiers. If Pilate approves his troops for the trip, they are not to know anything about where we are going or the money we will be bringing back. Just have them armed and at the gate for departure in the dark. And tell him half should dress as mercenaries. The other half should dress as slaves. I'll brief their leader along the way as needed. Be sure to tell Pilate that we want men with battle experience." Nathan scratched his beard momentarily then raised his right forefinger. "And, if Pilate has a centurion named Cyprianus in his unit, ask him to send that man as commander of his troops. I knew Cyprianus when he was a unit leader; now he is the centurion in charge of the Fifth Century of his Cohort. He has eighty men assigned. Pilate should be able to spare thirty."

"You want the Romans to dress as mercenaries and slaves?"

"All but the officers."

Tobias nodded. "Of course, deception. They will not expect a large force of trained soldiers."

"Exactly. Just be sure Pilate and the centurion agree and comply."

"It's his money we're protecting. I don't expect any arguments from him, and I'll inquire about Cyprianus. I recall him. He was the soldier you fought outside Jerusalem. The centurion who became your friend."

"He's the only centurion I trust."

Tobias stopped and looked off into the distance as if trying to cover everything in his mental checklist. "I'll insist on Cyprianus. Oh, the emissary. He will be traveling with three assistants. I'll ensure he is there on time as well."

"Good point, and also add an extra wagon to carry the money we collect in Jericho."

"What about robbers on the road?"

"Robbers would have to be very foolish to attack forty-six armed soldiers."

"No one said thieves were smart." Tobias was not smiling as he spoke. He rubbed his left shoulder a moment then turned back to Nathan. "And let's both keep this information between us. I wouldn't want anyone to know where we are going and why, just in case the spy is wrong about an attack already being planned. The less the enemy knows about our plans the better."

"I agree. There is no reason to tempt fate, especially when we are transporting Jewish taxes." Nathan grinned broadly. "If our friends discovered we were working for the tax collectors, no one would ever speak to us again." Both men laughed then embraced before they departed.

As the sun sank below the horizon, Rebecca tucked her children into bed and then climbed into her own next to Nathan. "You seem rather quiet this evening. Are you worried about the trip? Will it be dangerous?"

Nathan pulled her right hand to his lips and kissed it. "No, I'm just concerned to be away from you and the children so long. It won't be dangerous."

She sensed he was not being truthful. "Will you be taking your large sword?"

"Yes."

"Good." Now she knew her intuition had been correct.

* * *

Nathan sent three of his men with torches to check the donkeys and the equipment. It was still dark, but he wanted everything checked twice. He had personally talked to his men and counted the supply animals before the Roman contingent arrived, but only two of the wagons had arrived. Two men were dispatched to the Fortress to check on the remaining supplies and the arms that were to be delivered in Samaria. Surprisingly, the emissary and his assistants preceded the Roman soldiers who arrived an hour before the sun was climbing into the sky. Nathan went out with two of his lieutenants to meet the heavily armed soldiers. There was a big smile on his face as Cyprianus stepped forward. "It is good to see you again, my friend."

Nathan saluted the Roman officer. "And you too. Have you been briefed on this mission?"

"No, I was only told to be here and be ready for a long walk and a fight. I understand my superiors insisted we be part of this mission." He glanced back at his men. "And I was given very specific guidance regarding how the soldiers would dress." He grinned at Nathan. "I salute your planning. We will appear to be a much smaller force."

"Regarding the trip and the fight, I'm afraid both of those await us. Come with me; I will brief you as we begin. It is important that we depart Jerusalem before sunup." As the men walked along, Nathan and Cyprianus moved to the front of the troops and walked alone to talk. Nathan looked at his friend and spoke quietly. "It appears that we both have aged since our first meeting."

"Yes, and that is better than the fate of many of our friends."

"That always seems to be the fate of soldiers, it seems."

"But we have been fortunate." Cyprianus shifted his weapons as they walked.

Nathan noticed and turned, motioning to one of the slaves. "Take the officer's pack and put it on one of the donkeys—and protect it as you will protect my own." The young man rushed and took Cyprianus's pack. The Roman kept his sword. When they were alone again, Nathan continued to speak in a low voice. "Were you told that I would be in command of this mission?" He said it simply, without softening the fact that he was to be in command, not Cyprianus.

"Pilate, himself, advised me of that fact. I told him I had no problem working with you and following your orders on this trip. He knows I hold you in high esteem, as I do."

"As I do you as well. But both of us are military men who know that there can only be one commander, and I know this country better than you." Nathan walked on for several minutes without speaking. "But I value your military experience, and we can work together to plan and execute this mission."

"What do you know that I have not been told?"

"We are to collect taxes at Jericho and then proceed to Samaria to deliver weapons to your troops there. Then we return to Jerusalem."

"Do you expect thieves will attempt to steal the money?"

"This trip has been planned under utmost secrecy, but we have been advised that a group of rebels will try to take the weapons we are transporting just north of Jericho."

"Is that intelligence good?" Cyprianus stopped, turned, and watched Nathan's face carefully.

"We think so. Our source is a good one." Nathan weighed how much of his information he was willing to disclose, but he trusted his friend, so he continued. "If the information regarding the location of the attack is correct, it will occur at a point where the road curves around a small hill, about half a day's walk outside Jericho. There are oak trees to the right of the road and a small cliff with large rocks on the left. Attackers coming from the trees will be below us; they will be moving uphill. If there are men on the cliffs, they will have the advantage with their arrows."

"If you were planning this attack for the enemy, would you select that location?"

"I would; it's perfect for an ambush."

"Where would you put your men?"

"Both places. On the cliffs and among the trees. If they all come from above, we would simply move into the trees and regroup. If they all attack from the trees, we have the advantage of being above them. They would be wise to attack us from the cliffs with arrows then have another force move up from the trees. We would be caught between them."

"I agree." The centurion seemed concerned.

"I know those hills. I spent a summer there as a boy, and I know a way to send some of our soldiers around behind the men on the cliffs. If we can take them by surprise, we will have a big advantage over those from below."

"If they don't just run away."

"You're right. They might just retreat in haste."

Cyprianus patted his sword. "Do we know what kind of weapons they have?"

"I would expect swords, bows, and spears—the same as us, but they are not trained fighters. They will be men with great passion but lesser skills in fighting."

"That will be unfortunate for them." The Roman glanced back at the soldiers following behind them. "It is good that we have this information in advance."

"Yes, information is often the most important asset in any battle."

"That and sharp swords."

"I hope your men are ready for a fight."

"My men are always ready for battle. Woe to those who attack us."

* * *

The soldiers stood beside the road waiting for their commanders to decide on their encampment for the night. They could see the city of Jericho before them, only a short walk away. The late arrival of the weapons wagons had delayed their departure, but they had made good time since the trip was downhill from Jerusalem. There was little banter among the troops as there had been earlier in the day. They were tired, and they were hungry. At noon they had taken a short break and had just enough time to eat a little bread and some dates. Then they were off again. At mid-afternoon the primary emissary had asked for a break. He was an older man and had walked as far as he could go for the day. As the men huddled around the man, Cyprianus walked to the rear of the column and surveyed the troops. He also stopped and had a brief discussion with one of the soldiers. The soldier nodded, then saluted as his commander walked to survey the rest of his men. They loaded the emissary into one of the wagons and continued toward Jericho.

As the sun sank further into the horizon, men began gathering wood for campfires. Soon the hillside was sparkling with the lights of many small fires. Guards were posted and given strict orders to stay awake until their replacements arrived around midnight. Nathan, Cyprianus, and the other leaders sat around their own fire and discussed strategy for the anticipated battle. A young shepherd walked into the camp and was brought immediately to Nathan. As he approached, Nathan rose and embraced him affectionately. "How are you my friend?"

"I am well, and I have the news you want."

Nathan led the man to his campfire and ordered food and drink for the new arrival. "How many are there?"

"I counted fifty-four."

"That many?" There was surprise in Nathan's voice.

"There may be sixty. I could not count all of them as I walked along with my sheep."

"That is more than I expected." Nathan looked at Cyprianus; there was concern on his face. "I would not have expected that many rebels in one attack."

The young shepherd looked at the men around the campfire. "There are Parthian fighters along with the rebels."

"Parthians!" Cyprianus sat up straight. There was a grim look on his face. "I should have known." He tossed a stick into the fire. "Strange bedfellows for the rebels."

One of the other men stood and faced the group. "All they have in common is that they all hate the Roman alliance."

Nathan held his hand up to silence the men. "Okay, there are sixty of them and forty-six of us. All we need is a good plan to defeat them." He drew a picture of the curve in the road into the sand beside the fire. The men all moved to get a better view of his map. "Here are the cliffs beside the road. Part of the enemy force there will be watching the road with probably no more than a sentry watching their flank. Those in the trees will be hiding until we are close. When they advance from the trees they will have to climb a small hill below the road. It's a small hill, but it will slow them enough for our archers to catch them in the open." He drew more marks on the ground then turned to his friend Kalev. "Kalev is a unit leader, like me, in the Palace Guards, and like me he knows this area well. We played here as boys. He will lead eighteen men around the hill and surprise the archers on the cliff. They won't be expecting an attack from their rear; Kalev is familiar with a hidden path among the rocks that few men know. If the surprise works, the enemy on the hill will be unprepared and left with a cliff behind them and no place to regroup. We will continue the ruse of slaves tied behind the wagons until the enemy start their attack. They will suspect a smaller force, and that will lure them out into the open grouped together instead of spread formation. As they climb the hill, our archers and Kalev's men will fill the air with arrows. When the enemy approach the road, we attack with swords and javelins as they climb the last embankment." He turned to one of the Phoenician archers. "When our troops engage with swords, have half of your men join our attack with javelins. The remaining can use their bows to pick off any who are still climbing the hill." Nathan turned to Cyprianus. "Any additions or suggestions my friend?"

"I think your plan is a good one, but I don't like the numbers."

"I may be able to get some more men in Jericho, are any of your troops stationed there?"

"Unfortunately, they were all called north to repel a major Parthian force on the border. There may be a few remaining, I'll see when we enter the town tomorrow."

* * *

Normally a contingent of Roman soldiers would draw the attention of the populace of any town in Judea, but as the men marched into the southern entrance to the town, they were surprised to see the citizens standing in the center of the road waving their arms in excitement. Nathan stopped the soldiers and walked ahead to speak to one of the older men watching the celebration. When the man finally turned to him, he pulled the man aside and spoke. "If I may ask, what is all the excitement about? The people are acting very strange."

The man stared at Nathan, then looked at the soldiers and wagons waiting down the road. "We have just witnessed a miracle. It was from Yahweh!"

"A miracle?"

"Yes, do you know about Jesus?" The old man's eyes sparkled.

"I do."

"Then you will understand. He passed this way earlier this morning, and as He was leaving the town a blind man called to Him from the side of the road. He called 'Jesus, Son of David, have mercy on me!' There were those who tried to silence him, but he shouted even louder. 'Son of David have mercy on me!'

The man's name is Bartimaeus; I knew his father, Timaeus. Bartimaeus had begged on that corner of the road for many years. Then Jesus asked him, 'What do you want Me to do for you?' and he replied, 'Rabbi, I want to see.' And Jesus told him his faith had healed him. And Bartimaeus began to jump into the air; his sight was restored."

"And you saw all of that yourself?"

"Yes, I was there."

"And you know this man, Bartimaeus?"

"All his life."

"Then you have been blessed. Is Jesus here now?"

"No. He left with His disciples and a large group of followers early this morning."

Nathan bowed his head as he turned. "Thank you for the information. I wish I could have been here to see Him."

"I believe He is the promised one we have been waiting for." The man said it quietly so that only the two of them could hear his pronouncement.

Nathan turned back and faced the man, thinking *You may very well be right*.

The centurion walked to the front of the caravan and met Nathan as he returned. "What is the excitement all about?"

"A very big celebration. A blind man's sight was restored."

"Well, that is certainly something to celebrate."

Nathan waved for the men to proceed and motioned for Cyprianus to follow as they entered the town.

* * *

Nathan refused to sleep in an inn while his men were camped just west of the town. He sat around the fire and chatted with his troops. Finally, as darkness overtook them, he

255

doubled the men standing guard and collected the remaining soldiers around his fire. In great detail he and Cyprianus explained the plans for the anticipated battle the next day. They had been able to recruit three Jewish fighters and the four remaining Roman soldiers in Jericho. The odds were improving, but were still not satisfactory to Cyprianus. Just before the men climbed into their tents to try to get some sleep prior to the battle, the centurion pulled Nathan aside. "I just wanted to let you know I sent a messenger ahead to Samaria and asked for twenty more troops. I have no idea if the messenger got through or if the troops are available, but I did ask for them." Nathan put his hand on the Roman's shoulder. "I'm glad you did. Let us both hope he was successful. Tomorrow we will know."

*   *   *

As Nathan and Cyprianus discussed their strategy, less than ten miles away a group of Jewish rebels and a band of Parthian soldiers did the same, and like their enemies, they, too, drew maps on the sand. The two leaders, one Jewish and one Parthian, eyed each other suspiciously as they mapped their plan of attack. Neither trusted the other, but both knew they would fight together the next morning, side by side. The older Jew led the discussion. "We know these hills well; there is one place that would give us great advantage for an attack." He drew a line in the dirt and made it curve sharply. "It is here, at the curve I showed you today that we will attack." He emphasized the word *will* to indicate it was his decision to make, with no questions.

The Parthian leader watched the tip of the sword marking in the dirt and simply grunted. "Agreed!"

The Jew continued. "We will have most of our men hiding in the trees east of the road. The remaining men will hide atop the cliffs to the west. The Romans do not expect an attack, so they will march straight along the road until directly below the cliffs. At that point our archers will have the advantage and rain death upon them. While they try to regroup and focus their attention on the cliffs, we will charge from the trees and attack from their rear, again catching them by surprise."

The Parthian raised his hand to be heard. "I agree, but we must be swift attacking from the trees. When our archers catch them by surprise on the road, they will quickly regroup and retreat down the hill toward the trees. We need to catch them on the road before they can regroup and begin a retreat. Everything depends on surprise. If we can catch them while they are concentrating on the cliffs, we will have a great advantage." He scratched a line from the trees to the road on the sand map. "And we need a signal for our archers to stop firing their arrows lest they hit us as well."

The Jewish leader pulled a long ram's horn from his pack. "This shofar will be our signal. I'll blow it twice as we approach from the trees." The Parthian nodded. The Jew turned to a man standing beside him. "You are a military man and know of such things. Have we forgotten anything?"

"I am not a strategist, merely a guard, but I have studied this area and this attack for several days in my mind. I think your plan is a good one." He turned to the Parthian. "I'm glad you mentioned the archers stopping as we attack on the ground. I would not want to be killed by a Jewish arrow." Both men smiled briefly. He then turned to one of the younger men standing nearby. "Tell me about the convoy. How many men and what were they wearing?"

"I'm guessing about thirty mercenary soldiers and a large group of slaves tied to the carts."

"Slaves?" The guard was surprised.

"Yes, some appeared to be women."

"So the mercenaries even managed to bring along their entertainment." He grinned. "Perhaps we should attack at night while they are preoccupied."

The Parthian nodded and smiled. "After we have chased the mercenaries back toward Jericho, maybe we will be the ones preoccupied tomorrow evening. And maybe they even brought wine for the party. We can use that as well."

The Jewish leader did not join the laughter. Instead he raised his hand for silence. "We need to be in place by mid-morning, so have the men eat and cover their fires then get some rest. Ensure all weapons are ready, all arrows in place, and all subordinate commanders are briefed on the plans." He rose and stood in the flickering firelight, looking up into the clear night sky. "Get your sleep. Tomorrow we fight." As the men dispersed, he stood longer. Finally, he bowed his head. "Great Yahweh in the heavens, look down on Your Jewish fighters tomorrow. Like Job, give us victory over our enemies that Your people might live in freedom to worship You more fully; hear my prayer Yahweh." He then looked up again into the sky at the myriad of stars above. *Surely*, he thought, *a god with so much power over the heavens and the earth can grant so simple a request. We fight for His people, so we fight for Him as well.* He turned and began shoveling sand over the dying fire. He looked at the diagram on the sand one last time and started to erase it. Then he stopped. They would win tomorrow; he was certain. The map would be insignificant as they celebrated their victory after the battle. He dropped the shovel to the ground and picked up his sword. Like the map, the shovel would be unimportant tomorrow, but the sword would be the instrument that would give them success over their oppressors. He looked at it for several moments then kissed the blade and carefully put it into his scabbard. One last glimpse at the stars and he climbed into his tent for sleep.

* * *

It was mid-day as the Rebels began taking their positions along the small cliff and in the trees along the creek in the valley beyond the road. One of their men had climbed to the highest point along the hill and had signaled that the convoy was proceeding in their direction. Earlier, one of their spies had reported that he had counted eighteen troops and a dozen slaves headed in their direction with five wagons pulled by donkeys. The troops were spread before and behind the wagons. The slaves were tied and following the last wagon in two columns with a few soldiers trailing behind. The caravan was moving slowly. As they approached closer the sentinel signaled to the leader below. Sixteen soldiers and half a dozen slaves and non-combatants were approaching. Twenty-five insurgents were crouching on the ridge with bows and spears; over three dozen more were hiding among the trees. Nervously they nudged each other and smiled false smiles. They knew that some of them would not survive the day, but the weapons were essential to their purpose, a purpose that was worth the risk they were facing, and it appeared that the odds were in their favor. Two dozen Roman troops and a few slaves would be easy pickings.

Kalev and his men walked carefully along the rocky path and stayed out of view of the enemy soldiers. Two men dressed as humble shepherds preceded them to scout the trail. As they approached the site of the ambush, the two "shepherds" spotted two sentries guarding the back of the formation on the cliffs. The two Herodians watched the sentries and quickly discerned that they were watching the men on the cliff prepare for their attack instead of protecting their position. Quickly and expertly the two Palace Guards pulled their swords from their cloaks and killed the two. With a wave of an arm, they motioned for their men to continue up the trail. Soon all of Kalev's men were crouched in place, less than fifty yards from the men they were to attack, all of whom were watching the road below them. They were anticipating their enemies; no one was watching their rear flank. Kalev crawled farther up the rocks until he could see the caravan approaching. When it was just entering an archer's range, he gave his men a signal, and eighteen fighters rushed down a small embankment toward the men hiding on the cliffs. The Zealots and Parthians were caught completely by surprise. Immediately there were shouts of anger and screams of pain as the Romans and Herodians slashed their way through the enemy troops. As those in the ambush tried to climb to their feet, they were easy targets for the archers and then the advancing troops running at full speed. The eighteen were outnumbered for a short while, but soon there were bodies and wounded men falling and leaping off the cliffs.

Like all battles, things never go exactly as planned. Nathan knew that if the surprise attack from his own soldiers did not succeed, they would be easy targets on the road between two forces. With that in mind, he had slowed the caravan to give the second force more time to get in place behind the enemy on the ridge. And as always, timing is the key. They were about one hundred yards from the combat zone when a shriek arose from the top of the small ridge. His sneak attack was underway. The enemy were not ready for an ambush from their rear and were being forced off the hill onto the road below them.

When it became obvious that the battle was raging and that their men were losing, the enemy in the trees charged from their hiding places and began racing toward the road below the cliffs. There were screams of anger and defiance as they rushed toward the smaller force moving in their direction along the road. Above it all were two loud trumpets from the enemy's ram's horn. Nathan and Cyprianus led the column, followed by six soldiers, then the donkeys and wagons, the slaves, emissaries, and finally another eight soldiers. As the screams echoed from the trees, the "slaves" tossed off their ropes and their cloaks, revealing Roman armor. Tents and supplies were tossed to the ground as the "slaves" grabbed bows and stacks of arrows from the last wagon. Within seconds arrows were being fired in volleys toward the attackers rushing up the small hill. Unlike the Roman soldiers with their large shields, the attackers were unprepared for the arrows raining down upon them. Men screamed in pain and fell to the ground as the archers continued their withering attack. Still the horde continued up the hillside. Nathan and Cyprianus readied their twenty troops for battle and marched toward the embankment the enemy would have to climb to enter the road. As the first Parthians broached the road, javelins flew through the air and sent five bodies back down the hill. Still the enemy climbed onto the road to fight. Eight Roman soldiers stood together and lowered their large rectangular shields and charged into the fray. They moved together and rammed the first attackers on the road with the scutum in the centers of their shields, these large metal protrusions knocked the enemy off balance and left them easy targets for the Roman Gladius short swords. Still the enemy poured onto the road to join the battle.

Nathan turned toward his colleague. "We are outnumbered. There are more than we thought."

Cyprianus glanced up the road to the north. In the distance he could see dust rising from just over a small hill. He dodged a sword and screamed at Nathan. "Help is on the way."

Men were fighting at close range with swords while bodies and spears fell from the cliff. It was a horrific battle as the outnumbered guards and Romans fought bravely. Three men rushed Nathan and Cyprianus. The first swung his sword, but Nathan's blocked the blow and staggered the attacker. Nathan was just raising his sword to continue the fight when he happened to look to the left. He heard a voice he knew cry out in the attack. He stopped in the middle of his arc and stared in open disbelief. Doran stood three feet away sparring with Cyprianus. For a moment their eyes met, and Nathan uttered unspoken words. Doran blocked a blow from the Roman and stepped back a step. As he did, a Parthian on the ground swung his sword and hit Nathan's thigh. Nathan grabbed his leg and bent over in pain. The attacker rose and raised his sword above Nathan's back. Before he could strike, a familiar voice screamed "Noooo!" Suddenly Doran lunged forward and struck the Parthian before he could finish Nathan. Cyprianus, totally confused, immediately lunged and speared Doran with his sword. Nathan, holding his bleeding leg, turned to see the young man lying on the ground mortally wounded. Two guards saw Nathan's wound and stepped beside him to protect their leader as he knelt beside the man who had just saved his life.

"Doran, what are you doing here? Why are you with these brigands?"

"Nathan, I did not know you were leading this caravan. If I had known, this would not have happened. I would have told you."

"You would have told me? You were with these men? Why?"

"You fight for Judea. I fight for Jews." Blood trickled out of Doran's mouth; he turned his head and spit more on the ground. He was obviously dying.

"You never told me." Nathan pulled the young man into his lap and held him as he breathed his last breath. A loud moan came from Nathan's lips as he laid the body on the ground. It was the first time he observed his own wound. It was a long cut into his right thigh, and fairly deep. He pulled a piece of cloth from his sash and tied it tightly around his leg. With some effort his rose and picked up his sword to rejoin the battle. One of his men was fighting two enemy soldiers. Nathan's large sword removed one of them immediately.

As Nathan pulled his sword from the Parthian and glanced up the road to the north, he heard the sound of men shouting and running toward the battle. He glanced quickly at their standard as they approached. They were Romans. The insurgents were now the lesser force, and they were caught between the soldiers from the caravan and those rushing toward them from the north. Many of the attackers realized the situation was hopeless and ran back toward the trees to escape. Those who stood and fought were quickly killed or captured. As the sounds of battle died around them, Nathan and Cyprianus began to assess their men. Bodies were strewn around the road and some still hung from the small trees along the cliff above. Nathan counted over thirty insurgents dead, six of his own men and twelve Roman soldiers. The Roman officer that had arrived to support them approached. "Shall we chase those fleeing to the east?"

"No, let them go, but gather their weapons left behind and put them in one of the wagons. They will take the message of this defeat to their comrades. We'll leave the bodies of their soldiers stacked here along the road for them to bury later. Another message." Cyprianus put his hand on the other Roman's shoulder and then hugged him. "You arrived just in time."

"We marched fast-paced then ran the last mile. I knew time was of the essence."

"Well done, my friend. You saved the day."

Nathan looked at the two Romans embracing each other. "I'm glad you requested more troops."

"We were lucky my messenger got through." Cyprianus turned to Nathan. "You are a brave leader, my friend, but not a military strategist. Roman officers have very simple rules. If you think the enemy has thirty men, you bring sixty. If you think he has sixty, you bring a hundred and twenty. Always fight with superior numbers if possible. That is how we always win. To lose means death. To win means death to your enemies. We don't fight to lose. We always fight to win."

"Wise words, indeed."

"I was not at all certain my man could get through to Jericho. Luckily, he did. I was as surprised to see the additional troops as you."

The second Roman officer interrupted. "I have support wagons following for our wounded and dead."

"I hope you have enough."

"We do. We don't want the enemy to know how many men we lost in this battle. Yet another message."

"Well done." Suddenly Cyprianus pointed at Nathan's leg. "How bad is your leg? There is a lot of blood there." Both men looked at Nathan's right thigh. Red blood was flowing down beyond his knee.

Nathan took another piece of cloth from his sash and wiped the wound carefully. "It doesn't look too bad. I'll have it checked in Jericho. What is the status of the prisoners?" He pulled the cloth around his leg tighter and walked carefully to see how strong it was. "But before the prisoners, let us see to our own wounded." Nathan and the centurion walked among their men sitting beside the road being attended by their comrades while the extra wagons were being loaded with wounded and dead soldiers to be returned to Jerusalem. Nathan called one of the soldiers over and spoke to him privately. The soldier nodded and promptly loaded Doran's body into the wagon with the dead guards. The two leaders stopped to talk with each of the wounded men, then finally turned toward the prisoners on the other side of the road.

As they approached the bound men, Cyprianus stopped Nathan and turned to face him. The centurion placed his hand on Nathan's shoulder and looked directly into his eyes. "Who was that back there? That enemy soldier I was fighting saved your life."

"He was the son of a very close friend, the man who commanded our guards for many years. I still find it hard to believe he was with the Parthians. It makes no sense at all. There is much I need to investigate and understand."

"In the battle I struck him. I did not know who he was. I'm sorry if he was someone you knew."

"You could not have known. I was shocked myself." Nathan turned back to his friend and stared for just a moment. "I would prefer that this not be discussed with anyone else."

"I understand." Cyprianus nodded and turned to his lieutenants guarding the prisoners. "What is the status?"

"We have five captives with minor wounds and eight wounded severely. My men finished the eight and any who could not walk." The soldier looked back at the men tied and laying on the ground. "I think we got their leader."

"Bring him here." Nathan limped forward carefully as the men dragged the man onto the road to face their commanders. "Stand him." Two of the Romans grabbed the man and stood him before the two victors. "What is your name?"

"Barabbas."

Chapter 45

The two men stood in the door and spoke quietly to Sabina. Immediately she cried out and sank to her knees before them. Tobias reached and helped her stand, and the two helped her into the main room of the house. Gilad came rushing into the room and stumbled over a chair that had inadvertently been left in the middle of the floor. Nathan reached to grab his old commander but fell with him as his injured leg gave way. Both men ended up sprawled in the middle of the floor. Tobias helped Sabina to a chair and turned to the two men crawling to their knees. Gilad sat up and shouted. "What has happened?" Before either of the men could answer Sabina ran and sat beside him on the floor. She was weeping as she brushed his hair from his face.

Finally Nathan spoke. "Gilad, Doran is dead." There was a long silence in the room as the words sank into Gilad's mind, then his heart.

"My son is dead? How did this happen?"

Nathan looked at Tobias for help but found none there. Tobias just put his arm around the large man's shoulder and helped him to his feet. As the two men moved to a chair by the table, Tobias answered the question. "He was killed in a battle near Jericho. He fought bravely and saved Nathan's life." He could think of nothing else to say, and the silence returned.

"Why was Doran in such a battle? He is a Temple Guard. Why would he be fighting with Palace Guards?" More silence. "Tell me why." Nathan lowered his head, signaling Tobias that he had no words to utter. "And don't lie to me. You both owe me too much for that."

Tobias straightened his shoulders as he stood before his old commander. "He was with the attackers. We think he was

266

a spy sent by the Sanhedrin and somehow became involved in the battle. As I said earlier, in the battle he saved Nathan's life. Nathan was injured, and Doran killed the man who had the advantage over him."

"Who killed my son?"

For the first time Nathan spoke. "It was in the midst of the battle. I was down when Doran struck the enemy soldier. I could not see who struck Doran. Swords were everywhere. It was impossible to know."

"I see." Gilad stroked his beard. There were tears in his eyes as he turned to Nathan. "Were you injured badly?"

"I will heal. But if it had not been for Doran, I would have been among those lost in the fight."

"Where did the battle take place?"

"We were just north of Jericho at a place with cliffs on the west and an oak forest on the east of the road."

"I know the place." Gilad reached out and felt around for Sabina. She immediately went to him and sat beside him, holding his hand. "How many men did you lose in the battle? Who attacked you? And what was their purpose?"

Tobias pulled a chair before Gilad and began speaking, slowly and deliberately. "We were tasked to take some weapons to Samaria and to stop at Jericho on the way to collect tax revenues to be returned to Jerusalem. As usual, the Palace Guards were chosen to lead the mission because we were trusted, and the mercenaries were not. When we heard there was to be an attack, Nathan decided to ask for additional soldiers to support his men."

"Wait." Gilad's mind had reverted to his days as a commander. For the moment he was in charge, and the two men before him were young guards in his command. "How did you know there was to be an attack? Who informed you?"

"Our spies."

"Which spies? Where did they get the information?"

"From members of the Sanhedrin."

Gilad's voice rose with excitement. "The Sanhedrin knew about the attack?"

"Yes."

"And they advised you?"

"No. It was one of our spies in the Sanhedrin who advised us."

Gilad's voice suddenly dropped in tone and volume. He was almost whispering. "So they knew but did not officially advise you." It was as if he were only talking to himself. "Those bastards."

Tobias looked over at Nathan who was limping across the floor. "I, too, have reached the same conclusion. It is possible that only a few men in the Sanhedrin knew about the attack. Now it seems that many did not. I have a lot of questions to ask of our leaders. Who knew? How did they know? Why did the entire Sanhedrin not know? And why were we not advised? Why did we have to discover the attack through a spy?"

Gilad released Sabina's hand, then struggled to stand beside the table. Slowly he began to pace the floor. Nathan quickly moved the errant chair that had caused him to fall earlier. It was clear Gilad was thinking, putting pieces of a mental puzzle into place. "Now it makes sense." He was still talking only to himself. Everyone else in the room strained to hear his words. "Doran told me he was working on a special mission for El'Azar. I thought it was something for the temple. He said he might be gone a few days. Of course." The big man began stroking his beard violently as he paced around the room in thought. "El'Azar is ieutenant to Caiaphas, the Chief Priest. He also is Commander of the Temple Guards, and Doran worked for him; he gave Doran orders, and Doran was at the battle, so El'Azar had to know. Why didn't *he* alert you there was a trap?"

Tobias spoke with the authority he now held as Commander of the Palace Guards. "That is exactly what I want to know. Something is strange in all this. I'm going to question El'Azar, but first I want to do a little investigating to discover just how deep this treason goes. It seems obvious El'Azar knew, but what about Caiaphas? How much did he know?"

Gilad stopped his pacing and turned to face the two men. "It doesn't matter. You cannot touch Caiaphas or El'Azar—the Chief Priest and the Commander of the Temple Guards are untouchable. Caiaphas has been the Chief Priest since the death of Annas. His position is inviolate." Gilad walked across the room and felt his way to his seat. He sat into his chair and his head sank to his chest. "Doran told me how El'Azar had insisted he had royal blood in his veins and that he had a special mission in life. Now it is beginning to make sense." Gilad reached out and found Nathan's shoulder. "Tell me honestly, Nathan; tell me the truth because this is very important. When the battle started, was Doran fighting with you or against your forces?"

Nathan looked at Tobias a long time. Finally Tobias nodded affirmatively. When Nathan spoke, it was just above a whisper. "He was fighting with the enemy."

"Were all of the enemy Jews?"

"Some were Parthians."

"How many Parthians?"

"About half."

"I see." Gilad began pulling at his beard. Sabina sat watching her husband, trying to understand the military mind of the man she loved. "There is only one answer. Someone in the Sanhedrin decided to embarrass the Romans. That was so important that they were willing to invite Parthians to join the ambush to ensure they had sufficient manpower to win. Only two questions remain. Just who was involved in the Sanhedrin and why did they suddenly want to attack a Roman caravan? What was their purpose? Since the weapons were Roman, it's possible they didn't even know Palace Guards would be involved. My guess is this was a message for Rome."

"The entire mission was kept secret, or so we thought."

"They even knew the very day you would be passing the battle site." Gilad turned his face to the floor as he continued. "There are no secrets in Jerusalem. Everything is known. You are not the only ones with spies."

Tobias nodded. "Yes, they knew our plans, but they didn't know we knew theirs."

"Reward your spy. He saved many lives. If you had been ambushed there unaware, they may well have won the day."

"That's true."

"What is your plan, Tobias?" Gilad was now acknowledging Tobias's rank as the new commander.

"There is much I need to learn, Gilad. It seems that perhaps El'Azar may have had some role in this attack, but it is difficult to determine. Before we can accuse anyone, we have to be certain what happened. And I intend to discover that truth."

Gilad spoke and his voice rose as he spoke. It was a deep pain that echoed with his words across the small room. "And why didn't my son tell me, his father, what he was doing? How could he have been persuaded to join Parthians in a battle against his own people?"

Nathan stood and put his hand on Gilad's shaking shoulder. "Gilad, he didn't know we would be there. He thought the caravan would only be manned by Romans." Nathan looked back at Tobias for only a second. "He told me that before he died." Nathan's voice began to break as he continued. He was clearly in great pain himself. "He told me he was fighting for Jews."

Silence filled the room as Gilad nodded. Tears were streaming down his face as Sabina rushed to him. Finally the large man got control of himself and stood, addressing the two men he had trained since they were boys. "Thank you both for coming to bring this news in person. I also want to thank you for your honesty with me. It was important that I understand what happened. You both are like sons to me, and I am so proud of the men you have become. One last request—did you bring his body back to Jerusalem?"

"We did, and we have prepared a proper burial." Tobias stood silent then continued after several moments. "What was said here will remain in this room. Our report will show that he was fighting for us and spying on the enemy before the battle."

"Now I just want to find the men who know that is a lie."

"We will find them, Gilad. We will find them."

* * *

Nathan and Tobias sat under a large oak after Doran's burial. Both were silent for a long time. Finally Tobias spoke. "Did you see Gilad's face during the burial?"

"It was as white as his beard."

"Did you see the furrow between his brows and the anger on his face?"

"I did. I'm worried about our old commander."

"As am I."

"Have you had any luck determining who was behind the raid on our convoy?"

"I have a list of people to talk to and others to threaten. My plan is to start tomorrow. I'll need your help."

"I'd like to volunteer for the second group, those who need a bit of persuasion."

"You don't get to have all the fun yourself. Maybe we could work on that as a team."

"Sounds fair to me."

Nathan moved uncomfortably and removed a bloody cloth from his leg. "Damn, this thing just won't heal." He looked at it carefully. The leg was swollen and red. Carefully he placed another cloth over the wound and tied it tightly.

"That doesn't look good. Have you seen one of the court physicians yet?"

"I did, but it seems there is nothing to do but wait for it to heal. I just wish it would do so promptly. It seems to be getting worse instead of better."

The two sat in silence and watched several of the Temple Guards pass. Doran had many friends among his contemporaries. When they had passed Tobias spoke in a low voice. "So, we've concluded that someone in the Sanhedrin knew about the raid and wanted to keep that information secret. We don't know how many men knew, but we are confident that El'Azar was among those who did."

"It is possible that perhaps he was the only one."

"That is possible, but unlikely in my opinion." Tobias grimaced as Nathan tossed the bloody cloth aside. "The remaining question is the motive. Why would leaders in our community launch an attack against that convoy? Was it the weapons or the money? Perhaps it was both."

"I think Gilad might be right. It was a strike against Rome and maybe for the weapons as well. But for what purpose? Even if they win the weapons, they cannot defeat Rome. That is a reality we have learned to live with for the present. Why would a lamb attack a lion?"

"Not to defeat the lion." Tobias pulled at his beard for several moments. "But perhaps the lamb was simply trying to make a point."

"A point? That is a sure way to be eaten by a lion."

Tobias smiled as he looked around at his friend. "What would frighten the lion?"

"Nothing!"

"True, but would an attack in Judea cause concern in Rome?"

Nathan's eyes widened. "Yes, we are the buffer between Rome's empire and the Parthians. Rome wants stability in Judea."

"Therefore, an attack, even an unsuccessful one, would get Rome's attention." When Nathan remained silent, Tobias continued. "And who would benefit from that concern or be harmed by it?"

"Well, I would think Pilate would be on the list of those who would be embarrassed. In fact, he would probably be at the top of that list."

"With that in mind, who would benefit?"

"Anyone who is Pilate's enemy or anyone who might..." Nathan's voice rose as he finished the sentence. "Anyone who might replace him."

"My brother, I think we may have just discovered the motive that cost a lot of good men their lives."

Nathan's face reflected pain as he rose. He took a few awkward steps on the injured leg before turning back to Tobias. "So what is our next move? Shall we drag El'Azar out of the Temple and beat the truth out of him?"

"He's far too important to do that. Gilad was right; he's untouchable, but I'm working on a plan that may well solve our problems with the Temple Guard's commander." Tobias shifted his sword to a more comfortable position and continued. "First, we need to chat with that poor excuse for a man and see what we can learn. We have time, and we have to be very thorough and careful. When he realizes we suspect him, he'll probably panic and make a mistake." A grim smile crossed Tobias's face. "Or maybe we'll just ambush him some night and coerce his confession."

"Then I'll let you try my sword."

"I'd like that. Doran was a fine young man and a friend."

"More importantly, he was Gilad's son. That alone is enough for me."

"True, but first I want to learn of this scheme and all who were involved."

"Good plan. But I am tired. I think I'll go home and clean this wound."

"Give Rebecca my regards."

"Remember you will have dinner with us tomorrow."

"That I would never forget."

Chapter 46

Doran had been buried only two days when Gilad decided it was time for answers to many of his questions. He was a big and physical man, but Gilad also had a very keen intellect and a wisdom few understood. He had been sitting for several days thinking, thinking and analyzing what little data he had. Tobias and Nathan had supplied what they knew, but much was still missing in the puzzle he was trying to solve. Now the big man was weaving the facts he had into a tightly knit fabric that included everything Doran had discussed and things he had not wanted to discuss with his father. Gilad divided the death of his son into several alternative scenarios. Finally he rose from his chair and began swearing. All of the paths his mind had taken ended in one name: El'Azar. Gilad was convinced he was behind the attack and therefore responsible for Doran's death. What he didn't yet understand was why. What was his motive? Gilad stood and turned until the light from the front door was evident. He faced it, took four regular steps then turned ninety degrees to his right. He had to relieve himself, and that was twelve steps forward then four to his left. He bumped into the table and stepped back one step then resumed his trek. When he returned he knew he was not alone. He could smell her, and it made him smile. "Hello dear."

"I was outside in the garden when I heard your cursing. Are you all right?"

Gilad stood silent for several minutes before speaking. As he stared at nothing he tugged on his beard and started across the floor. When he answered his wife, his head was bent forward and the words were barely audible. "Yes, Sabina. I'm okay. I just realized that I have a task to perform at the palace.

Could you get a message to Kalev for me? He and Doran were very close friends, and I have something to give him."

"A gift for Kalev?"

"Yes, Doran's dagger. I'd like to give it to him. I think Doran would have wanted him to have it."

Sabina walked over and put her arms around her husband. "Gilad, I know how difficult this has been for you, for both of us. But promise me when the pain in your heart becomes too difficult, promise me you'll tell me. It's a pain we both share, but together, the load is far less heavy. You know how much I need you to lean on in my grief. Well, you can also lean on me as well." She reached up on the tips of her toes and kissed Gilad in the middle of his chest.

"I already depend on you just to navigate my own home, but the darkness in my eyes is insignificant compared to the darkness in my heart."

"I know, my dear."

"Be sure that Kalev gets my message. Tell him I'd like to talk to him as soon as he is available."

* * *

Kalev had to stand in the doorway for several moments as his eyes adjusted to the darkness in the house he had come to visit. After a quick visual search he spotted his old commander leaning on the window casing in the main room. His head was raised as if he were staring at the sky. Kalev was unsure how to address Gilad. He knew Gilad's eyesight was slowly ebbing, but he didn't know how far the loss of sight had progressed. He took a deep breath and marched across the room and stood at attention behind the large man staring out into the night. With a loud slap to his chest, he saluted his old boss. "Commander!"

When Gilad turned, there was a broad smile on his face. "Kalev, it is good to have you in my home."

"I received a message that you wanted to see me."

"Well, actually I am having a bit of difficulty seeing you right now, but I would recognize your voice anywhere." Gilad stood for a moment, and it was obvious he was deciding something in his mind. "I would like to have a brief conversation, but I would also like a walk. Would you be kind enough to join me for a short walk?"

"Of course, Commander."

"I am no longer a commander, Kalev. My beard is white, my eyes are dim, and I spend most of my days sitting in this house, but it will be good to have a short walk with you." As the two men left the home, Gilad called out in no particular direction. "Sabina, I will be back shortly. I am taking a walk with Kalev."

The evening was pleasant. The skies were clear, and a slight breeze from the northeast cooled the countryside. Gilad inhaled deeply and smelled the fading day; he put his right hand on Kalev's left forearm, and the men walked to the south, with the wind at their backs. When they were a distance from the house Gilad stopped abruptly and turned to the younger man. "Kalev, I asked you to come here for two reasons. First, I wanted to give you Doran's dagger. I know how much your friendship meant to him, and I'm sure he would want you to have it. When you were his leader, he admired you very much." He pulled the knife from his sash and held it out to Kalev.

"Thank you, Commander, and to me you will always be *Commander*." Kalev took the extended weapon and put it into his belt. "I think you know how much I valued my friendship with Doran. He was a fine young man. I will treasure this dagger."

Gilad leaned forward and one would have thought he was studying something on the ground. After a moment he stood straight and put his hand on Kalev's shoulder. "The other reason I wanted to talk to you is because I need your help with something. It's a matter I did not want to discuss in front of Sabina. It must be just between the two of us. Is that okay with you?"

"Of course."

"Is anyone within hearing distance?"

Kalev turned and scanned the street. "No, we are alone."

"Do you know the circumstances surrounding Doran's death?"

The younger man stood silent for a moment. "Yes."

"Then I'm sure, as Doran's friend, you must be as confused as I am regarding his actions. They made no sense to me at all in the beginning. But as I began putting the pieces together, I began to see a picture of deceit and lies that led Doran astray. He was still a very young man. I feel that inexperience was used against him to perpetrate some kind of plan that I still don't understand." He waited for a moment then continued. "But I think I know from whence it came."

"You do?"

"I've been recalling all of our conversations over the past few months, and a trail is emerging in my mind. I just need a bit more information, and that is why I need your help."

"I'm here when you need me, Gilad. What will you have me do?"

"Take me to El'Azar."

Kalev nodded silently. "You think he was behind the ruse?"

"I do."

"He is a ruthless man and also very clever."

"You're right, Kalev. And he has the power of the Chief Priest behind him, not to mention the Temple Guards."

"This won't be easy."

"Correct; it will be difficult, and I can't even find my way to the Temple."

"Are you going there to confront El'Azar?"

"If you will direct me to his door that is exactly what I have in mind."

"Maybe I'd better go in with you. My eyes are still good, though I'd never be a match for your skills with a sword."

"No Kalev, this is not an attack mission. I simply want to talk to him to see what I can learn. First, I want to know what drove so many of our people to join with our enemies and then attack our own caravan. It's the motive I want to understand. How many well-placed Jews knew about that raid? Who were they? Why did they plan such a disaster? Why did they join forces with the Parthians? Once I know the answers to those questions, we will figure a way to serve up a little justice to El'Azar."

"Be careful Commander. He is a respected member of the hierarchy—and he has the Temple Guards to protect him if necessary."

"Kalev, if I were twenty years younger, I would simply walk over there and kill the lot of them. But I am an old man now, and I have to use my head instead of my sword. But trust me, I will have El'Azar before this is over. He killed my son."

Kalev was silent for a moment, staring off into the distance, thinking. He knew what he wanted to say, he just didn't know how to do so without embarrassing the man holding his arm. "Gilad, might it not be wise to let Tobias handle this? As Commander of the Palace Guards he has an interest in this matter that would allow him access without arousing too much suspicion initially."

"You are right, Kalev. Tobias is a wise leader, and I'm sure he will handle this well. I simply want to ask a few questions as any father might in such a situation. I fully intend to coordinate with Tobias. Like you, I have great respect for him, and I'll be very careful not to interfere with his investigations. Hopefully I can assist them." Kalev could feel the older man's grip tightening on his arm. "Don't worry, I have no plans to walk in and kill El'Azar. One cannot kill what one cannot see. I simply want to talk to him to understand what Doran was doing, what El'Azar knows."

Kalev nodded and put his hand on Gilad's shoulder. "I would be honored to be your eyes in this endeavor. If needed, I can also be your sword."

"That will not be needed; I simply want to talk."

The two men turned and began the short walk back to Gilad's home. As they walked the wind was now blowing in their faces. It was a clean, cool breeze that stimulated both men, in spite of the discomforting cloud of rage that lingered over the larger of the two. "Stay for dinner and be sure to comment on the dagger. Sabina knows nothing of what we have been discussing. I'd like to keep it that way."

"I understand." Kalev stopped the larger man in the middle of the street and leaned in close. "What about Tobias and Nathan? Shall I tell them of our conversation?"

"No, not yet. We'll brief them when I have the answers I need. Until then, let's keep this between the two of us." A slight smile crossed the older man's face. "We'll need them in the second part of our plan, but that comes later."

"As you wish."

Chapter 47

Nathan was preparing for bed when the insistent knock came from his front door. He looked at Rebecca for only a moment then limped to the door. When he opened it, a young guard stood there, obviously upset. "Come quickly. Our commander says it is urgent and to come armed."

"Where are we going?" Nathan turned and gathered his cloak and his sword.

"To the Temple."

"The Temple?" Is Tobias there?"

"He is on his way even now."

"What has happened?"

"I don't know. He received a message from Kalev and said it was urgent and to find you as quickly as possible." The young man paused then commented. "Our commander was very upset."

The two men passed the huge stones comprising the exterior wall of the temple. Some of the massive stones were as large as 39 feet long, ten feet high, and 13 feet thick, a formidable wall for any invaders to attack. It was a structure of both strength and ornate beauty, like the God of Israel it represented. Nathan raced to keep up with the younger man as they entered the bronze "Beautiful Gate" and crossed into the Women's Court where they met Tobias, Kalev, and two other Palace Guards who were walking rapidly toward the inner courts. Nathan looked at his friend and saw the anguish on his face. Tobias simply looked back and said one word. "Gilad." Tobias's face was partially cloaked in the darkness, but Nathan could see his eyes and the tightly drawn mouth. The expression was of both intense sadness and extreme anger. "Gilad is in grave danger."

"Gilad? Are you sure?"

Kalev approached from behind the two and began speaking quickly, with great emotion in his voice. "Nathan, Tobias, Gilad asked me to escort him over to the Temple this evening. He said he wanted to talk to El'Azar. He felt Doran's death was precipitated by something to do with El'Azar, and he was looking for information. He asked me to wait for him outside the Temple; he told me they would talk alone; I was concerned but knew Gilad had no sword, he said he only wanted to talk. That was two hours ago, and he has yet to emerge. When I tried to search for him four of the Temple Guards stopped me. They said he was not in the temple and had not been there all evening.

Nathan's eyes grew very large, and a panicked look crossed his face. "Where did you leave him? In El'Azar's office?"

"No, El'Azar was going to the Chamber of the Hearth where the priests on-duty reside. I left Gilad at the base of the Nicanor Gate."

Without a word Nathan turned and began running toward the stairs that led into the Court of Israel. Somehow the pain in his injured leg disappeared as he awkwardly ran toward the entrance. The young messenger ran with him, easily passing the older man with the large sword. It was dark in the Temple and only a few torches were lit to shed enough light for the men to proceed. The young guard started up the stairs, but Nathan stopped abruptly behind him. There beside the stairway lay the body of a very large man with a snow white beard and hair. Nathan recognized it immediately and turned to kneel beside the corpse. His mouth opened to scream, but only a hoarse sound emanated from his lungs. "Gilad!"

The young guard had not noticed the body as he rushed toward the stairs. Only the light from the four eighty-six foot tall lampstands in the Women's Court lit the area. As he started up the stairs, two of the Temple Guards suddenly blocked his way. They took note of his tan cloak, obviously a palace guard. "And what are you doing here this time of night, boy? Don't you know only men are allowed into the Court of Israel? Women, girls, and little boys are not admitted—only men." They laughed at the young man standing before them. His face had only three scraggly brown hairs growing from his chin. The Temple Guards both sported full, dark beards.

"I'm here to find Gilad, the first Commander of the Palace Guards."

"That so? Well he's not here and you aren't entering the Court of Israel behind us. Understand?"

"Move and let me pass."

"We aren't moving for any Palace Guard, so what are you going to do about it, boy?"

As the men laughed at the youth before him, Nathan stepped into the light of their torches. His face was one of complete rage. His neck, his shoulders, and his face were red, not from the kiss of the sun but from an anger that grew deep within his breast and boiled to the surface with the blood of a seething rage that threatened to erupt at any minute. There were tears in his eyes. One of the men had drawn his sword, and Nathan saw there was blood on the tip. Very quietly he spoke, but the words were spit from his mouth as he attempted to control his anger. The men looked down at him as he stood below them at the bottom of the large curved steps. Nathan was a large man, but his beard had streaks of white interspersed with the deep brown. He was older than either of the two he was facing. "I'll tell you what he's going to do. As his commander I am going to order him to hold my cloak while I kill you both. I know he would like that honor himself, but the man you have killed here was my friend and my brother at arms, so I claim the right to avenge his death." Nathan turned to the young guard. "If, by chance, they get lucky, then you can kill them both for me."

"Oh really, you think you're that good do you?" The larger of the Temple Guards drew his sword.

Nathan pulled his sword from his scabbard then threw the scabbard and his cloak to the young man beside him. "You will soon know how good I am. Are you brave enough to try me one at a time, or are Temple Guards cowards who only fight two against one? Either is fine with me."

As Nathan spoke Tobias stepped into the light of the torches. He looked at his friend holding his sword before the two Temple Guards. "As Commander of the Palace Guards I insist on killing at least one of these cowards who murdered an old man who was almost completely blind. What kind of man would do such a thing? And he was only armed with a small dagger. What cowards you Temple Guards must be."

"We are Levites, no one calls us cowards."

Nathan stepped toward the men and climbed the wide stairs to stand at the same level on the steps. "You are no Levites. A Levite would never kill an old man who is blind. No Levite would ever stoop to such a deed and dishonor his heritage. I know, because I, too, am a Levite. You embarrass our clan, but tonight that stain will be erased, and there will be two less Levites in Jerusalem. You have murdered a great man, one who could have defeated ten like you when he was in his prime." Nathan raised his sword and moved toward the two. When Nathan was at their level on the stairs, the men saw for the first time how large he was. They both stepped backward immediately. "So, now you will face another man with white hair in his beard. But my eyes are still keen and my strength still with me. Now you will fight a real man. I'm not like the men you normally challenge, thieves who steal the priests' money. I am a warrior who has seen battle." He was standing eight feet from the two as he spoke.

The larger of the Temple Guards lunged forward and swung his sword at waist height. Nathan blocked it with a blow that staggered the man. The guard grasped his right hand with his left as he tried to recover from the strength of the blow. His hand felt as if it had been struck by lightning. He looked at his sword and a large piece of metal was missing where the two swords had collided. The impact had travelled through his sword and had stunned his hand. Nathan advanced carefully, glancing back only momentarily at Gilad's body lying in a pool of blood. Tobias saw the anger in Nathan's eyes; he knew the love all of the men had felt for Gilad, especially Nathan. With a scream, Nathan advanced on the man swinging the large sword faster than the man could dodge. The man stumbled backward and crouched again in the defensive position two steps lower down the stairs, but the onslaught of the large man and the flashing sword were more than the man had ever encountered. There were tears and rage on Nathan's face as he expertly managed the large weapon. The Temple Guard went down before him, his sword rattling down the stairs. Tobias watched carefully, his sword in his hand, keeping his eyes on the second of the Temple Guards. Nathan moved quickly and stood over the injured man, his sword pointed at the man's throat. Then the silence was split by a mournful sound as Nathan bellowed from somewhere deep inside. There were no words, just the primeval sound of a suffering man with no words left to speak. The Temple Guard lay on the steps attempting to cover his head with his arms. When Nathan spoke, the words coming from his mouth were barely audible. It was almost a whisper. "You will die for what you have done tonight. But I will not allow you to have the traditional ceremonial burial of the Jews, because when I leave I will carry your head with me in a basket, and the rabbis will not bury a body that is so perversely mutilated. They will put what is left of you in a hole somewhere in the desert. Next week your head will be hoisted on a spear and left at the gate to the temple for all to see. The sign below it will proclaim that you were a coward." He waited for a moment to let his words sink into his enemy then thrust his sword into the man's chest. ·The second Temple Guard's face turned suddenly white as Nathan turned his bloody sword toward him. The man looked as if he might vomit at any moment. "Now it's your turn. You were ready to fight a man just beginning to learn about swords. Well, now you can face an expert instead. Draw you sword or I'll kill you with it still in its scabbard. Even that would be more honorable than killing an old blind man."

Tobias stepped between the men and raised his hand. "No! Wait!"

Nathan stepped back one step. "Why prolong his death? See, he has already drained his bladder." The man looked down and saw a large growing stain on his tunic.

Tobias turned to the remaining Temple Guard and spoke with authority. "I know you would not have killed an old man without cause or orders from your superiors." Tobias looked back at the body on the floor. "And I know Gilad was a man of honor who would have never given reason to be killed. He had no issue with you. So, I want to know who ordered his death." He stared straight into the man's eyes. "Speak, or I will kill you myself." The man closed his eyes tightly. It was clear he was weighing his options when suddenly Nathan turned and swung his sword at the body at his feet. With a loud chop, the head of the first Temple Guard flew across the stairs and rolled to a stop on the floor between Tobias and the frightened guard. Instantly the man began speaking very quickly, his eyes large and filled with fear. "El'Azar, it was El'Azar. He told us to kill him." As the man spoke, his eyes never left the head laying on the floor before him.

"Why would El'Azar want Gilad dead? He was a harmless old man."

"I don't know. He just said it was important. We didn't even know who he was." The man explained how Gilad had come to speak to the priest and there had been loud words, an argument. Then El'Azar sent a message by a servant with orders for them to carry out.

"And you killed a hero to the Jewish people…" Tobias looked into the man's eyes in silence for several moments, then he leaned close to the Temple Guard and spoke very quietly to him. "How many of you were involved in killing this man?"

"Just the two of us."

"Only two?"

"He was old and unarmed." The Temple Guard's voice trembled as he spoke.

"And he was also blind…" Tobias's words trailed off as he drew his sword and with one quick movement thrust it into the man's chest. With a jerk he withdrew the sword and wiped it on the dying man's cloak as he sank to the floor. Tobias turned to Nathan and put his left hand on Nathan's shoulder. For several minutes they just looked at each other in silence. There were still tears making small streaks down both of their faces. Finally Tobias spoke. "We have as much information as these killers could give us, and we now know El'Azar ordered the killing." Tobias breathed in deeply and paused for only a moment. "And I swear by my honor that El'Azar will die for this deed, but for now we must think clearly. We have two things to do immediately. First, we take these two to the place in the temple for slaughtering sacrifices. We'll leave their bodies there. It is up the stairs and then turn right. It is the last chamber on the left." He was looking at the two young guards who had accompanied them. "Then we must get Gilad out of the temple without being seen." He motioned, and the men began dragging the two dead Temple Guards up the stairs. "Use their cloaks to wipe any blood on the stairs. There will be enough blood as you approach the Place of Slaughters." He paused then looked at the head below his feet. "And put this in a basket and bring it with us. We'll take care of it later."

Nathan put his sword back into its scabbard and attached it to his waist. "What will we do with Gilad's body?"

"We will say he died in his sleep. I will talk to Sabina. She'll support our story."

Nathan looked up the stairs and slowly withdrew his sword again. "Why don't we just kill El'Azar now? I would like to feel my blade entering his heart, if he has one."

"There will be time for that later, but not now. We need to understand much before we kill that snake. Besides I have no desire to fight the entire Levite community tonight. There are many Temple Guards, and I suspect El'Azar has most of them protecting him right now. We'll get him, but on our time, not his."

"When they find the two we killed, he'll know we are after him."

"Maybe not. He won't be sure what we know. Perhaps we killed them in a fight without asking who ordered Gilad's murder. We will act as if nothing happened. He will probably sweat a bit, but he will finally assume we know nothing about his role in this. Then we will show him that military men value their honor more highly than his thieving priests." They both turned to the body behind them. "Now help me lift Gilad. Damn, he was a heavy man in life and equally so in death." Tobias turned to the young man holding Nathan's cloak and handed him his own as well. He knew that both he and Nathan would both soon be covered in their old mentor's blood. "After you deposit the bodies, bring these with you to the palace."

Nathan spoke as he lifted Gilad. "I'm glad it's you who will explain this to Sabina."

"Why do you assume it will be me?"

"Because you are the commander, and it's your job." He paused a moment. "I'm not sure I could do that."

Tobias only grunted as they raised Gilad's body and started across the Women's Court. Their burden was heavy, and they had to traverse over two hundred feet to the Eastern Gate of the temple without being seen. From there another three hundred feet to the Shushan Gate in the eastern temple wall. Only the shadows from the Temple Guards' torches and the tall lampstands in the Women's Court betrayed the dark shadows moving slowly toward the stairs exiting the dark, cold building. Precious blood had been spilled, and the bleeding was far from over.

Chapter 48

Nathan limped across the courtyard and turned toward the palace. His leg still had not healed as he had hoped, but he was on his way to plan a trip to Ephraim. The Chief Priest and his associates were concerned about Jesus. They were aware that he had left Jerusalem and Bethany and had travelled to Ephraim. Then their spies went suddenly dark, and they had no information regarding his whereabouts or what he was doing. They hoped he would simply head north to Galilee and stay away from Jerusalem and the Temple. If, instead, he intended to return to Jerusalem for Passover, they wanted to be prepared. Information was what they needed. Caiaphas knew that it would be risky to send any of the religious leaders to find Jesus in case they were identified. He feared it might be dangerous for them to be caught in the throng of followers that pursued Jesus wherever He went. It would also denigrate the entire priestly staff if they were caught spying on this new threat to their control over the Jewish people. Most importantly the Chief Priest also knew he had to keep this assignment out of view of Roman eyes. Pilate must not know their plan. They had to find a way to rid themselves of Jesus, but they did not want Pilate involved until they were ready. Caiaphas had a plan that involved Pilate, but it was best advanced by surprise. But now he needed information, information that no one in the temple could gather. That left one group available, and he was on his way to request that help.

When Caiaphas walked into Tobias's office, he was easily recognized by the guards meeting there. Nathan rose to welcome the esteemed member of the Sanhedrin. The older man nodded slightly and quietly asked if they could talk alone. Tobias was not in Jerusalem and Nathan had assumed his position until his return. They walked out into a sun filled yard and walked slowly across to the garden Herod had built so long ago. Nathan was limping, but still he could keep pace with the Chief Priest. Finally, the dignitary spoke. "We have a special request of utmost importance, a request that must never be disclosed to anyone."

Nathan listened to the man and realized it was an assignment to find Jesus. The Sanhedrin wanted to know where He was and what He was doing; how large was His following? What was He saying? Immediately Nathan accepted and agreed to send three men to find and track the movements of the young rabbi. What he didn't explain was that he would be one of the three, but his purpose was not that of spying on Jesus. His reasons for finding Jesus were his own, personal reasons from deep within his heart. He would also warn Jesus.

* * *

Rebecca looked at her husband and just shook her head. "No, you cannot go to Ephraim, and you cannot go to Bethany either. Your leg has not healed. It is getting worse. Last night you had a fever, and now you can hardly walk. How will you go to Ephraim? It is a long journey. You must stay here and rest. Send some of the younger men."

"I know I can't take Samuel that far, but if I can just talk to Jesus maybe I can get Him to see Samuel the next time He comes to Jerusalem."

"My dear husband. I know how much you want to help Samuel, but your heart is now larger than your head. There is no way you can make that trip."

"But of course I can." With great effort Nathan walked across the floor and sat before her. "See, I can walk just fine."

"Look at your leg." Blood was slowly seeping through the bandage and the entire leg was swollen and red. Rebecca stood over him and pointed to the injury. "Your assailant must have rubbed his sword in manure before the battle."

"There will be three of us, and I can get a donkey or maybe even a horse."

"Who would give you a horse?"

"The men who made the request have great wealth. I will talk to them about a horse tomorrow, and if not a horse, a donkey."

Rebecca placed her hands on either side of Nathan's face. "My dear, I admire your persistence and especially your love for Samuel, but sometimes your stubbornness is just more than I can take." She kissed him gently on his forehead. "We need you here. We don't need you trying to travel half way across Judea trying to find Jesus. Your leg will not allow that. Use your head, and stay home. Surely Jesus will return to Jerusalem for Passover. You can find Him then."

When Rebecca left for the well, Nathan watched until she was out of sight. Then he hobbled over to the fire and placed the blade of his dagger into the coals. When the blade was white, he put a piece of firewood into his mouth, bit on it as hard as he could, and slowly slid the white-hot blade into his wound. Rebecca was halfway to the well when she heard his scream.

* * *

The sun was slowly creeping across the tile floor toward her bed when Rebecca opened her eyes and sat upright. She felt the other side of the bed. Nathan was gone, and the bed was not warm. She put her face into her hands and wept.

Chapter 49

Rebecca stood outside the palace gate and waited as the young guard left to find Tobias. It was unusual for a woman to come to the palace without permission, but all of the guards knew Rebecca. They also respected her husband. He was a man greatly admired by all of them. Tobias ran the last twenty yards when he recognized Rebecca. He was even more distressed when he approached and saw that she was crying. "Rebecca, what is wrong? Has something happened to Nathan?"

"I tried to stop him, but he left early this morning for Ephraim."

"Ephraim? Why would he be going to Ephraim?"

Rebecca watched to see that they could not be heard then explained about the visitor from the Sanhedrin. Tobias cursed and rubbed his hands together rapidly. "So, he went in search of Jesus." He said it without question.

"Yes."

"He still thinks Jesus can heal Samuel, doesn't he?"

"Yes."

Tobias cursed again and slammed his right fist into his left palm. "He is in no condition to make that trip. I've been watching his leg; it is not improving. If there is any healing to be done, the first should be Nathan himself."

"I know."

The commander raised his head as if looking off into the distance, but his eyes were closed in thought as he calculated his decision. Finally he looked back at Rebecca and said firmly. "Don't worry. I'll send my best men to find him and return him to Jerusalem." He reached out and patted her arm. "Go home; I'll take care of Nathan." He forced a smile that she knew was to calm her. She could see the tension in his face as well.

* * *

The slow, steady bouncing of the donkey's pace forced Nathan to moan softly with each step. He reached forward and touched the neck of the animal and stroked it gently. "You are old and tired like me, yet you still carry me toward my destination. Thank you for your patience." He could smell the distinct odor of the little animal beneath him as it plodded along. He glanced at the two young men accompanying him on his trip to Ephraim. They were strong and able, but they walked along slowly, patiently, just like the donkey. They had yet to learn of pain; theirs was the strength of youth. He recalled that time of life when there were no mountains too steep, nor journeys too long. He had been a strong young man, like the two walking along beside him. He smiled. Someday, they too, would be old and tired. Someday, they too, would taste the silence of pain. But not now. Now they just walked and waited patiently. Nathan knew they were afraid. They did not fear enemies or animals; they feared what was happening to him. Like all of the young men in the guard unit, they had heard stories of his great courage, but now they were left to escort an old, injured man to another city. He knew they had seen his leg. They knew he was struggling with a fever that left him so weak he could hardly hold the rough rope that was around the donkey's neck. He looked quickly at his leg when they were not aware. The infection was growing and the blood that oozed from the wound was no longer bright red, it was turning brown as his body tried desperately to heal itself. It was a losing battle, and Nathan was aware he would not be able to continue much longer. Ephraim was roughly two days journey from Jerusalem, over difficult terrain. The three men had been traveling almost a day and a half, but Nathan knew he was less than halfway to his destination. He had selected the young men who would accompany him based primarily on their strength; he knew they might have to help him along the route. He signaled the two and stopped to drink from his water jug. The water was hot, but he knew he had to drink water often. He could feel the fever increasing. He climbed painfully from the back of the patient animal and grasped the hair on the animal's neck to help steady himself. Slowly he stood upright and raised his face to the heavens. He felt the tug in his chest. It seemed to be growing in intensity over the past few days. He understood what it meant, but he was not afraid, only disappointed. He had not been able to help Samuel make the necessary journey to see Jesus. He looked off into the distance and thought about the things he had heard Jesus say, the wondrous things he had seen Him do. That day on the hillside as he listened to Jesus's words with Pilate's wife, Nathan's heart and mind were opened, and he could feel his heart burning inside him. Today that heart was tired, and his vision was blurred, but his yearning for Jesus remained. He had failed in his quest for Samuel, but Nathan was not a man to quit. His body was weak, but his will never faltered. He knew he needed two things. He needed a short rest, and he needed help. So, for the first time in many years he prayed as the small donkey stood patiently beside him. "Yahweh, my God, and the God of my people, I beseech you to allow my son to see Yours. Give me that gift I pray. I have lived a long life, and you have blessed me with love and happiness beyond measure. Please, I ask of You, give me this last request." He raised his arms in supplication and bowed his head. A soft wind ruffled the edge of his cloak and he felt his strength returning. "I do not deserve the blessings You have given me. I am a sinful man, but You know that Samuel is a good man. He has struggled throughout his life and has been a blessing to all who know him. I beseech You, great God of Israel. Let Your Son touch mine. Touch his heart and mind and soul. Let him walk in Your light, and if Your will is that he remain a cripple, then give him strength to carry on with joy in his life. Thank You for all of Your blessings, I pray for only this one last gift. Let my son meet Yours." Nathan looked out at the horizon, but it seemed to be moving slowly back and forth. He blinked his eyes and looked again. They cleared for a moment, then he collapsed, his fingers leaving long scratches on the patient beast's neck.

* * *

The first face he saw when consciousness returned was Rebecca. She was placing wet cloths on his head. He peered at her for several minutes as the vision finally cleared. She spoke first. "You silly man. I told you not to try to make that trip. I told you to stay home." There was a mixture of anger and love in her voice. He smiled a weak smile. As she moved from his line of sight he saw Tobias, Samuel, and several of his children.

Tobias spoke next. "Whatever were you doing taking a trip on that leg? You're lucky we found you when we did." They gave him water and continued to put wet cloths on his head. He could feel the heat and the dizziness of the fever, and he longed to close his eyes, but he fought to remain awake. Nathan's body had many scars; he had lived the life of a guard and had fought many battles. But now, for the first time, he realized he was in serious trouble. He saw Rebecca and Tobias standing aside talking and motioned for his son to come closer. Samuel changed the wet cloth on Nathan's head and reached for another. "Be strong, *Abba*. We will get the fever down, and you'll be okay."

"I'm sorry, Son."

"Sorry, about what?"

"I tried, but I never got you to see Jesus."

"There will be more opportunities for that. You just get better."

"I want you to promise me something."

Samuel took Nathan's hand. "Sure *Abba*."

"Promise me you'll see Jesus. Promise me that." Nathan coughed slightly and then motioned for Samuel to come closer. "Son, the reason I first wanted you to see Jesus was so He might heal your leg. I have seen Him do such things. Then I listened to His message; it is far greater than the healing." Nathan's eyes were pleading as he held Samuel's hand. "Promise me you'll find Him." Nathan looked deeply into Samuel's eyes. "And take Tobias as well. He's a good man; he just needs to see Jesus to understand. Promise me."

"I promise, now you rest and get your strength back."

Nathan closed his eyes and smiled weakly as Samuel walked over to his mother and Tobias. For the first time Samuel noticed how old Tobias looked, standing next to Rebecca. Both had the wrinkles of age and though Rebecca still had mostly brown hair, Tobias's hair was mostly white, like his beard. Rebecca offered the two men food and insisted that Tobias try some of Samuel's wine. Finally, he rose and took Rebecca's hands in his own. "When we were young Nathan and I played together, and then we became guards for Herod together. We fought together; we traveled together; we became men together. Then he found something special. He found you, Rebecca. He found love. And you found him as well. How fortunate for both of you. You have loved him dearly all these years, as he has loved you." Tobias stopped for a moment and gathered himself to continue. There were tears in his eyes. "Well, I loved Nathan too. He was a special friend who never let me down. I envied what the two of you shared. I never found that in my life, and once I even betrayed him, but he forgave me and remained my friend. We have all been blessed by him."

There were tears in her eyes as well as Rebecca stepped forward and put her arms around the sobbing man. "You have been a very special friend, and Nathan has loved you as well. He has enough love for us all."

Tobias took a deep breath and straightened his shoulders. "I'll stop by in the morning to see how he's doing." He turned and slowly walked out the door. Tobias walked only several steps then stopped. He looked off into the evening sky and studied the stars that appeared as scattered grain upon the threshing floor. *What beauty*, he thought. He turned and looked at the worn wooden door behind him. He was a wise man, and he had experienced much in his life. He recognized the threat of the infection in Nathan's leg. He, himself, had fought such infections several times in his life and had scars to prove it. But he had been young. Nathan was older now, and he was weak, weaker than Tobias had ever seen his friend. He looked into the night and prayed for the first time in his life. When he finished he raised his eyes to the stars again and marveled at the night sky. *What beauty God had created. A God capable of that could surely manage to heal one man's leg.*

Rebecca stood alone in the room with Nathan. Tobias and the grown children had all left for the evening, but Samuel remained, resting on the floor of the main room. Nathan was breathing with shallow breaths and occasionally he would gasp for air. She felt his head and reached for more wet cloths to help cool him. His temperature was still very high, his head hot to the touch. For a long time she sat beside him and just watched him, but finally the fatigue of the day overcame her, and she lay beside him, her left arm across his chest. In her mind she thought back over the years to the first time she had lain with Nathan. They both had been so young, and he was so nervous. Together they had explored the beautiful world of sex and then the deep love of a couple facing the world with their own family around them. She had worried about Nathan and his work as a guard for the palace. Occasionally it was dangerous, but he always seemed to escape the battles with little more than minor bruises and scratches. This time was different. The wound was serious, but it was the infection that represented the larger threat. She felt her eyes closing, but Nathan moved slightly, and she jerked back into consciousness. She thought about the days together with their children, the many days of laughter and the nights they held each other close in this same bed. She reached and felt his head again. It was still very hot. She rose and poured fresh water into the bowl by the bed. Then she began putting the cool pads on his forehead. Just after midnight, in the early morning, Rebecca's eyes closed in sleep. The events of the day had exhausted her, and the tension only made that worse. Finally sleep overtook her, and she rolled close to Nathan and slept.

It was about two hours before sunup when she woke with a jerk. She realized she had been asleep and quickly felt Nathan's forehead. The heat was gone. Excited she sat up quickly as her head cleared. Then she realized what she had felt. Nathan's head was cold. Her eyes opened quickly as she reached to feel his chest, his neck. Slowly she turned and put her hands to her eyes as she wept. He had died during the night. Tears flowed from her eyes as she reached and kissed him on his forehead and combed his hair with her fingers. "You were a good man, Nathan. You were a great father, and you were a wonderful husband. I shall miss you, my dearest. May Yahweh hold your hand this day and take away all of your sorrows." She patted his hand as she talked to the body of the man she had loved for so long. "Our children are grown; they will be fine. You trained them all to be strong, but you forgot to teach me how to live without you. I hope where you are is a place of peace."

299

Finally, Rebecca rose and walked to the small window and peered outside. It was still dark; morning was hours away. She walked to the doorway to the main room and heard Samuel's light snoring. She decided not to awaken him. Let him sleep. The pain of loss could wait. She turned back to the bed and sat beside Nathan's body. She could think of nothing she could do, so she put more cool towels on his head. Finally she lay beside him and looked out the window at the stars awaiting the sun's rays to send them into hiding. Tomorrow would be another day. People would go about their lives. Some would argue; others would touch with affection. But for her it would be a different day; it would be a day without Nathan—the first of all the days remaining in her life. How would she live in a world without him? How could the sun dare to shine tomorrow? How could she ever find joy again? The thoughts climbed from the deepest caverns of her soul and left her cold, afraid, and so very sad. Then she thought of Nathan and how he had loved her and how he had loved life. *Get up Samuel; stand tall, be proud.* How many times had she heard those words? Now that voice was speaking to her. *Get up Rebecca; the sun will rise tomorrow, and you must face it with courage and a smile. That is what I want, and it is right for you.* There were still tears streaking the dust on her face, but somewhere in the night she found his strength, and a small smile formed on her face as she repeated his words aloud. He had been strong; now it was her turn to find that strength. She looked out at the darkness again. All she had to do now was wait for the sun to rise and help her face the day.

* * *

Adriel walked into the small home with freshly washed cloths. Nathan had to be prepared for burial and as daughter-in-law, it was customary that she assist. It was decreed in their

300

faith that the burial be within 24 hours of the death, so there was little time to spare. As she entered she heard Rebecca talking and stopped to see to whom she was speaking. Nathan's body was laid on a table in the middle of the main room and Rebecca was already preparing it for the ceremony that would occur that afternoon. Adriel watched as the older woman carefully combed her husband's hair. All the while she spoke to the body as if he might answer or take her in his arms.

Rebecca laid the comb aside and touched a scar on his right shoulder. She examined it carefully. "I recall that one very well. I told you the oil would help, but you didn't believe me." She touched a smaller scar on his chest and rubbed it with her finger as if to heal the damage done by some enemy sword. "You had that one when we were first married." She stopped and smiled. "You were such a handsome young guard. You felt you needed to heal the world—especially mine." She wiped her eyes and patted his arm. "And you did. You saw a skinny little girl with a crippled baby all alone in this world, and you just had to step in and take care of them. And you did. I never understood that, but I was so glad you came. What would have happened to us without you?" Rebecca dipped her cloth into the bowl of water and began to wipe the body very carefully. "What a silly man. You always thought you had fooled me, but I always knew it was you who saved little Samuel when the soldiers raided the village. You thought that silly mask would keep your secret. But I always knew it was you. I recognized your voice immediately when you returned." She stopped and looked straight ahead for just a moment, in thought. "Perhaps that is why you needed to take care of us." Then she resumed her washing of the body. "But love changed both of us, didn't it? So quickly I learned to love you, and somehow I feel you felt love for me even earlier." She put the cloth in the bowl and reached and brushed the hair from his forehead. She lingered there and touched the wrinkles on his face. "You were such a handsome man, and I was so proud to be your wife." She brushed at her own eyes again and then in a very small voice began to cry. "I tried to make you proud as well. I really did. But I was just a silly girl." She leaned over and kissed his cheek. "You were so proud of your family. You sacrificed everything for me and your little pumpkin and then the rest of the children. I'll never forget how you patiently helped Samuel learn to walk. I never knew who was more proud, Samuel or you." She stopped speaking, and the tears came more rapidly. Suddenly, overcome with grief she just stepped forward and hugged the cold body on the table. "Oh Nathan, I was so blessed to have you, but how will I live without you? You taught me how to love you, but you never taught me how to let you go."

Very quietly, Adriel put the cloths on the chair by the door and stepped back into the heat of the morning. There were tears coursing down her own cheeks as she left the little house behind. She would return later; there are times to share and times to be alone, and when a woman is saying goodbye to a man she has loved for most of her life that is a private time only the two of them should share together. The necessities of the day could wait.

Chapter 50

Caiaphas sat at the end of the long table and watched the last of the Jewish leaders walk out the door. A team of young slaves began clearing the remnants of the feast and removing bowls and goblets. Only El'Azar remained. They sat in silence, waiting for the table to be cleared and the slaves to leave the room. El'Azar reached for one last morsel before the last girl could complete her work. He stuffed it into his mouth and washed it down with a large sip of wine. Together they waited until the door was finally closed and the room was theirs. Caiaphas's dark eyes glared as he brooded in his chair. "How dare my own countrymen accuse me of complicity with the Romans! Such an insinuation is an insult. Don't they understand that it is my responsibility to ensure the Roman legions camped nearby stay out of our city? We have all witnessed what the Romans are capable of, and there is no way on this earth we could stop whatever plans they devise. It is a reality we might not like, but it is reality nevertheless."

The Temple Guard Commander refilled his wine goblet and watched his leader carefully over the brim of the ornately decorated vessel. "They're just nervous. Perhaps they're listening to those who declare that the Nazarene is the Messiah. As His miracles grow, so do His followers."

"We both know that is a great danger to our people. When members of the Sanhedrin are becoming followers of this so-called Messiah, we are at risk. The Romans are aware of the Torah. They have studied our Scriptures and understand what a Messiah would entail. They might be cruel, but they are no fools."

"I agree, Caiaphas, but what are we to do?"

"I have been questioned several times regarding this new preacher. I was particularly surprised when Pilate, himself, asked me about Him."

"Pilate is concerned with Jesus?"

"He had many questions; questions I could not answer."

"That is serious. Did he seem concerned? Does he consider Jesus to be a threat to Rome's rule here?"

"Pilate is a Roman; he doesn't divulge what he is thinking. One does not rise in the Roman hierarchy by being transparent."

"You are right. Only cunning men survive in that environment. Clever men who are also brutal men."

Caiaphas rose, stretched, and began pacing around the table, his magnificent robes flowing behind him, while El'Azar watched the garments with envy. Caiaphas abruptly stopped his pacing and spun around and pointed to his lieutenant. "We need more information about Jesus. Where is He at all times? What is He saying that could be held against Him? How many are in His inner circle? We are nearing a collision, a collision of this man and the security of our people. He is a great danger to us, and He must be dealt with. We cannot let one man jeopardize Judea." The Chief Priest reached for his robes and swung the garments around behind him then resumed his pacing. He was mumbling to himself, but El'Azar was listening carefully to his leader's plans. There was a good chance they might coincide with his own. "Maybe he will simply go back to Galilee. That would solve everything. Let Antipas deal with Him. Maybe we could convince Antipas to handle Jesus."

"Don't count on Antipus to do anything right. He's unpredictable and inept, and that's a bad combination."

Caiaphas frowned. "So, what do we do about Jesus? He's a threat to us and to the Jewish people, and the crowds are growing around Him. On one occasion the crowds were so large they say He had to go out into a lake on a boat to preach to the people."

"Then we just arrest Him and get Pilate to crucify Him before His followers become an issue." El'Azar watched Caiaphas carefully. When he saw a sly smile on the Chief Priest's face, he knew he was on the right track.

"Do you think we could get Pilate to do that?"

El'Azar patiently lowered his head for several seconds. When he looked up his narrow eyes were cold. "Of course we can." He rose and stood just in front of Caiaphas. "Listen, Pilate is in no position of strength. Vitellius had him sent back to Rome after he ordered the attack on Mount Gerizim. He was strongly reprimanded before he was sent back. Then there is his relationship with Sejanus. It was Sejanus who gave Pilate his post here. We both know what happened to Sejanus and a good number of his colleagues. I'll bet Pilate has spent a lot of sleepless nights waiting for Tiberius's troops to knock on his door as well."

Caiaphas stood with both of his fists on his hips. He was clearly agitated. "And the meaning of all this history?"

"Consider this Caiaphas, who got Archelaus banished? Jews! Rome wants peace in Judea. We are their buffer for the Parthians. They won't permit an insurrection, but they still want us pacified. They need us." El'Azar waited for Caiaphas to catch up with his strategy then continued. "Pilate fears we could get him removed just like Archelaus. So right now, we have the power. He's tenuous in his position at best. Tiberius is not his benefactor. I'm guessing we could get most anything we want right now if Pilate thought we might complain to Rome. He's most likely just trying to hide here until this Sejanus affair is forgotten."

Caiaphas stood with his eyes suddenly glued on his Chief Assistant. "You're right. He is in a very weak position. The strength is, indeed, in our hands, not his." Caiaphas removed his headpiece and scratched his head. "Do you think he recognizes this shift in power?"

"Of course. I'll bet he was thinking of this long before we did. Pilate is a crafty politician; he understands power, and he knows we have influence in Rome. Archelaus's fate will attest to that."

"You're right, so first we just have to find Jesus and arrest Him then tell Pilate he should crucify Him." El'Azar walked back to the table and poured another two goblets of wine.

The Chief Priest was suddenly animated and excited. "We need information on Jesus and His followers. We need to find Him. We need a reason to send Jesus to Pilate—any reason."

"You're right about that, Caiaphas. We approached agents who were not associated with the Temple to do just that. We had to find men who could not be seen as working for us and men who could be blamed with success or failure, but they failed. Perhaps there is another way..." The commander paused for effect and watched his leader for any signs of displeasure. "Perhaps I could arrange a conspirator in his ranks. Surely one of his followers could be turned."

"A spy?"

"A traitor!"

Chapter 51

The entire assembly of palace guards, with the exception of those on duty, stood outside the small house along with many friends and family to pay their last respects to a man they had admired and loved. Tobias walked over and talked to his men as they began leaving. Rebecca sat inside with Samuel and his siblings. Samuel rose to meet him as Tobias turned toward the door. He motioned and the two men walked outside. Tobias nodded as the two proceeded down the road a bit. One was wobbling back and forth as a cripple would; the other was slightly bent in his back and walking slowly as an older man. Tobias spoke first. "Samuel, if there is anything I can do to help Rebecca just let me know. You know how I loved your father; he was my best friend in this world, like a brother. He was a fine man, one who will be missed by many." Tobias was having difficulty speaking. His affection for Nathan was real and evident.

"My father loved you like a brother, Tobias. You two were always close."

"We saw much of life together. There couldn't have been a better man to accompany one on this journey we call life. I was fortunate to have him along."

"You know he felt the same." The two men walked on for a while before Samuel turned and spoke to his adopted uncle. "I made *Abba* a promise before he died. But I will need your help to fulfill that final debt."

"What is that, Samuel?"

"He asked me to promise that I would see Jesus." Samuel stopped walking and looked directly into Tobias's eyes. "I told him I would."

"I see." Tobias stopped as well and stroked his graying beard for a moment. "That may be difficult; Jesus is in trouble with the Chief Priest. I suspect Caiaphas will soon have Him arrested."

"Arrested? Why?"

"It is all about power and how men achieve and maintain it. Right now there are many in the Sanhedrin who fear Jesus. He is a direct threat to their power." The older man turned and started walking slowly back toward the house. Samuel followed, listening carefully. "Jesus has achieved a wide following, and some are afraid He might give Rome the excuse to tighten its control over the region. Others are simply jealous and afraid of the message He preaches. Either way, the powers that be are not happy with Jesus and His followers. When He chased the money changers from the Temple, He harmed the treasury of the priests. That will not easily be forgiven."

"Can they arrest Him for that?"

"They could, but they won't. They need a much stronger accusation for their purposes."

"Like what? Jesus has not harmed anyone."

"True, but he has called Yahweh His Father, and claiming to be the Son of God is ample grounds for the Sanhedrin to have Him crucified."

"Would they do such a thing?"

"They are politicians, and such men are capable of anything."

Samuel waited until the older man was finished talking before he broached the question in his mind. "Will you help me see Him?"

"Of course; I'll try. It was important to Nathan, so it's important to me. I'll ask some questions tomorrow and let you know what I discover. It will be difficult with the Passover crowds, but we shall try."

"Thank you, Tobias. This was the last thing I promised my father. It's very important to me to comply with his last wish."

"I understand. Rest well tonight. Tomorrow we shall seek Jesus if it's not too late."

"Does Caiaphas really hate Jesus that much?"

"There are many conflicting concerns in Caiaphas's mind. He is concerned about the role of the high priesthood in Jerusalem. Jesus has accused them of grasping for money and power. Caiaphas also feels it is his role to prevent more bloodshed from the Romans. He has personally seen the brutality they are capable of, and he wishes to avoid that happening again. He knows that any sign of an insurrection could incite Rome's ire, and he wants to avoid that. I'm sure he is torn between many different pressures that he faces. I don't envy him today. He stands at the threshold of a mighty force that he does not fully comprehend."

"Will they imprison Jesus, or will they try to kill him?"

"I don't know, but as commander of the Palace Guards I have access to those who have the information we seek. That is where I will be going now."

"Thank you, Tobias. I appreciate your help."

"Be ready to leave tomorrow as soon as I notify you."

"Tomorrow will be a special day; I feel it."

"Let us hope so, but there are many dark clouds on the horizon."

Chapter 52

The young Roman soldier stood at attention and saluted his centurion. "Sir, the Commander of the Palace Guards is here to see you."

"Show him in." Cyprianus rose to meet his friend. His sparsely furnished office was located in the old fortress, not because of necessity but rather by choice, Cyprianus's choice. He greeted Tobias warmly. "Tobias, what brings you to the fortress? It most definitely is not the food!" Both men smiled at the comment. "And this office is not nearly as fine as what you have in the palace."

"One of the few benefits of serving as a Palace Guard."

"From the look on your face, I assume this is not a social call. Do we have another convoy to escort into rebel territory?"

"I certainly hope not." Both men sat at the centurion's bidding as a young slave brought wine and two goblets into the room.

As the Roman poured the wine, Tobias addressed Cyprianus's first question. "I need to talk to you about the battle outside Jericho. I also need our conversation to be confidential, for no other ears. Is that agreeable?"

"Certainly, what do you need to know?"

"The issue is not what I need to know, but rather what I have learned about the attack."

"Go on."

"Our spies learned of the raid before we left. The information came from certain members of the Sanhedrin. I assume Nathan told you that."

"He did."

"Well, as it turns out, the Sanhedrin never officially informed us of the attack. They assumed we left unaware of what was to ensue. That is a great concern to me. Since then we have discovered that the entire Sanhedrin was also not informed. It seems a select group of its members were involved in the treason."

"I see." Now Cyprianus was leaning close toward Tobias, squinting in thought as his Jewish friend continued.

"When we became aware of a possible link between some members in the Sanhedrin and the impetus for that battle, one of our prior commanders became involved due to the death of his son on that road."

"That would be Doran?"

"Yes. He was Gilad's son."

"Nathan and I discussed this in some detail. Nathan was very upset over Doran's presence in the battle."

"He fought on the other side, didn't he?"

"Yes." The centurion lowered his head and spoke in a lower voice. "In the midst of the battle, Nathan recognized Doran, and that momentary delay caused him to be wounded. When the Parthian was going to finish Nathan, Doran killed him, saving Nathan's life."

"And what happened to Doran?"

"I killed him. I had no idea who this enemy combatant was, and in the midst of battle I struck him with my sword."

Tobias leaned back and took a sip of his wine. "That is understandable. You did what any of us would have done in those circumstances. It is certainly unfortunate, but it is understandable." Cyprianus only nodded. "I appreciate your recounting that for me. Nathan only spoke of it briefly before his death."

"Well, it is finished now."

"Perhaps not." Tobias watched until Cyprianus raised his head and looked him in the eye. "Old Gilad was in great pain over the loss of his son, and he began to understand some comments Doran had made in the past few weeks before the battle. As a result he went to visit El'Azar, the Temple Guard Commander, to discuss what might have inspired Doran to take such a foolish role with the Parthians and the insurrectionists. El'Azar was Doran's immediate boss at the Temple. He is also a member of the Sanhedrin—a member who knew about the attack." Tobias stopped talking and looked beyond the Roman to the hills in the distance.

"What did El'Azar say to Gilad?"

"We don't know. El'Azar had him murdered on the steps of the Nicanor Gate."

"Are you certain it was El'Azar?"

"If you believe a man with a sword to his neck, then it was El'Azar. We found the two men who killed old Gilad."

"You found the men who did that? Where are they now?"

"Nathan and I killed them both." It was said as a matter of fact with no emotion. "But only after they confessed that their boss, El'Azar had directed the murder." He paused only a moment. "I had no reason to doubt their word. Fear has a way of eliciting the truth."

The centurion stood slowly and took a long drink of his wine. "So now you are going to kill El'Azar." It was a simple statement.

"I learned a great deal from my old commander, Gilad. He was like a father to all of us young guards. He loved us, and we all loved him. He always fought for his men. He always defended the King's Guards and later the Palace Guards." Tobias lowered his head as memories flooded his mind. Finally he looked up. "A good commander always finds a way to win with the least risk to his men. That is what Gilad told me the day I put this blue cloak on my back. I've never forgotten." Cyprianus watched Tobias and waited. He knew Tobias was leading him toward a conclusion that was firm in Tobias's mind, one that would soon be solid in his own as well. He had worked with Nathan as a close comrade, and as such he had also become friends with Tobias. Both were men of honor, and that was a major attribute in any man—especially when being evaluated by a Roman officer. After a moment Tobias continued. "Here is my plan. We are convinced that a small group of men in the Sanhedrin were a part of the conspiracy to have your convoy attacked. We believe El'Azar was one of the leaders and that he convinced Doran that he should participate. As a result of that group's actions, three of my friends have died, Gilad, Doran, and Nathan. I intend on avenging their deaths and to stop such suicide attacks in the future."

"With a sword? If so, you can count on mine and those of my cohort."

"My plan does not require a sword; not our swords at least. A war between the Temple Guards and the Palace Guards would not be a good solution. Killing him alone would not enable us to know the others involved. Here is my plan. When Pilate has his routine meeting with the Jewish leaders, he will have the entire Sanhedrin there and perhaps a few others. That is when we take down El'Azar and perhaps identify most of the others involved—and we can do it without one blow from our swords. I just need you to convince Pilate to support our plan—without complete knowledge of what we are doing. I would rather he not be involved other than one innocent statement." Tobias walked to the window and peered out for several minutes, thinking, deciding whether divulging his plan was wise. Finally, Nathan's earlier words of praise for this Roman swayed his decision. He turned with a sly smile on his face and relayed his plan.

Cyprianus smiled as he nodded. "Well done, my friend. Well done."

313

The Jewish leaders exited the Temple and turned southwest toward the Palace where Pilate lived when he was not in Caesarea. They walked in small groups, mostly defined by the color of their beards. The first group had thick beards of black and deep brown colors, then came those with streaks of gray invading the dark shadows at their chins. Finally, lagging in the rear were the men with beards the color of clouds on a sunny day in Judea. Caiaphas, the Chief Priest, was in the middle group, and everyone there deferred to his opinions and positions. They were the leaders of Judea, the Sanhedrin, and their meeting earlier in the day had one purpose, to discuss their positions when they would meet with Pontius Pilate, the Roman Prefect, to discuss his latest construction project. The men of the Sanhedrin had all learned to admire the Romans' abilities to build infrastructure that actually worked. In most cases it was not only effective, it was also magnificent to behold. What concerned these Jewish leaders most, however, were the taxes the Romans needed to pay for the work. For two hours they had discussed and plotted on the best way to achieve their goals. Now they were ready to negotiate with Pilate.

Pilate stood at the East wall of the palace and watched the entourage that approached. He almost wanted to laugh. What a sight to see the many different colored cloaks waving in the afternoon breeze. And the beards! As a clean-shaved Roman, he could not understand why these men wanted all that unruly hair around their faces. In the beginning he had found it repulsive, but more recently he only found it humorous. Cyprianus stood beside him. "Here come your staff."

Pilate laughed out loud. "So be it. And if this is the best I can get, I am in real trouble." He made fun of the old Jewish leaders, but Pilate also realized that these men were shrewd

314

beyond measure. They might be old and funny to watch as they trundled along toward the palace, but they were also highly intelligent men, men with great purpose, men willing to do whatever was necessary to further and protect that purpose.

"I see you have managed to have them come to you rather than your making the trek to them."

"That was necessary. They would not want a non-Jew defiling the Temple, so it is necessary that they come here—to my courtyard—which they contend is not really a part of my house. Therefore, they are not defiled by meeting there. What nonsense."

"Nonsense to us."

"But not to them."

The centurion stepped closer and spoke lower as though someone might overhear them. "Are you in agreement with my request about the announcement?"

Pilate knew men; he had spent his entire life maneuvering and dodging through the many traps of Roman politics. He understood men well; it had been a great benefit in his life, in his career. He knew that his centurion and the commander of his guards had been plotting against some or all of the men walking toward his meeting. He was not totally sure what the plot entailed, but he had great respect for both of these men. They were honorable men; they were also brave men—and what a remarkable and rare combination among the elite of Rome or the leaders of Judea. His decision had been immediate. Though he was not aware of the details of their subterfuge, he knew their target was also his, so he would play their song and watch to see who would dance. These were two men he felt he could trust, and there were few on that list.

As the last of the older men arrived, Pilate stood on the top step of his courtyard and held his hands in the air. "Men of Jerusalem, I welcome you to my courtyard, and I welcome this

315

time to speak of things that require the attention of the leaders of this city. Shall we begin?"

The meeting droned on through the afternoon with many proposals and counter proposals. Pilate explained the infrastructure project and the need it would fill. Then the Jewish leaders inquired how it would be funded, and the debate began in earnest. In time a compromise was met. The leaders would agree to the project for half the money requested. Pilate frowned and complained, all the while knowing he was getting as much as he needed. He had doubled his request, which the Jewish leaders understood. So, when the final compromise was agreed, everyone got pretty much what they wanted. And there was also some extra money for some temple projects that Caiaphas had requested.

During the meeting Tobias, Kalev, and Cyprianus stood back and observed. Secretly they were watching each of the men in attendance, watching how they reacted to the discussions, when they smiled, when they frowned. Tobias had instructed his colleagues well. Cyprianus would speak at the end of the meeting and there would be two reactions among the Jewish leaders to the centurion's words. Some would be surprised; their eyes would grow larger. Some would become instantly angry; their eyes would narrow. The three men standing in the background were watching for narrowed eyes and angry faces. After almost two hours of negotiating, the group was tiring and ready to leave for their evening meals. Pilate walked back up the seven stairs and stood with his hands raised for the second time that afternoon. Within a few moments everyone turned to give him their attention, and the group became silent. "Leaders of Jerusalem, I thank you for your time and your suggestions regarding our new project. I think we are in agreement. I will have a scribe put our words on a scroll, and I'll send a copy to Caiaphas, the Chief Priest, tomorrow."

There was much nodding of heads and several of the men were turning to leave. "But before you leave, one moment more." The men turned back for the final words of their Roman governor, the man representing the government that had dominated them for years. "My chief centurion here in Judea, Cyprianus, has a brief announcement to make to all of you."

Cyprianus squared his shoulders, stepped to the second step below Pilate and turned to the crowd. "As many of you know, we had a convoy of men travel to Jericho and Samaria two weeks ago. We had just collected tax monies from Jericho and were traveling north toward Samaria when we were attacked by a group of brigands and Parthians." He paused watching the increased interest in the men standing slightly below him in the courtyard. "Fortunately, we were alerted about this raid before we left Jerusalem. That information was key to our success in the battle that ensued. We knew when, and we knew where the attack would take place, and that made all the difference in our tactics which proved so successful in the battle. We only lost a few Romans in the fight, but the enemy was taken by surprise when we attacked from their rear and caught them unaware. We decimated their ranks, and they lost many men that day." Tobias and Kalev were both carefully watching the faces of the men in the crowd as Cyprianus spoke. Three of those men had lost sons in that battle, and several others had lost family members. Among the surprised faces they could also see eyes narrowing and furrows forming between eyebrows. "That success was possible because of your help in stopping this unwarranted attack, and I'd like to publicly thank the Commander of the Temple Guards for supplying us the information that allowed our success. Had it not been for his warning and specifics, many of my men would have been left dead on the side of that road instead of the enemies of Rome and Judea." He stopped and scanned the crowd, gesturing with

317

his right hand toward the stunned man in the middle of the courtyard. Several men nearby could be seen reaching for their daggers in complete reflex. It was totally silent for several minutes while every face turned to stare at El'Azar. The blood drained from his face as he stood before his compatriots. He knew immediately that he had been discovered and betrayed. Tobias, standing behind Pilate stood looking into El'Azar's eyes, a small smile on his face. There was no need to protest; El'Azar knew it would do no good. He had just been handed a death sentence. A death at the hands of his own colleagues, a death as a traitor to his cause. Cyprianus and Tobias mentally noted the glares that were directed toward their target. A list would later be made, a list of men with narrowed eyes and angry faces.

As the Jews departed, Cyprianus and Tobias stood monitoring the last of the group leaving the palace. Pilate stood beside them. When a slave closed the large palace door behind the suddenly silent group of old men, Pilate turned to the two smiling men watching the exodus. "I'm not quite sure I understand all that happened here today, but my inclination is to congratulate you both. I have never seen such a reaction to an announcement." Both Cyprianus and Tobias nodded. Neither spoke. Pilate looked over the wall at the men leaving the palace. "If I am correct the man walking alone toward the temple is the Commander of the Temple Guards. And if I apply my experience to what I have just witnessed, I'd guess the Temple will be looking for a replacement very soon."

"I'm guessing you're right." The centurion's smile grew larger on his face.

"Come into my chambers, and let's have some wine. I'm not quite sure why, but I feel like a celebration right now."

The centurion and the Commander of the Palace Guards both turned and followed Pilate into the palace. "I'll drink to that."

* * *

Two days later it was announced that the Commander of the Temple Guards had died in his sleep. If so, he must have fallen on his sword in the night; one of his slaves said there was a lot of blood in his chambers. Tobias stood in his office staring out the window. He was talking to his sword as he sharpened it vigorously. "I'm sorry I did not give you a chance to split his heart. I would have preferred that, but the job is done, and the traitor is dead." He held the sword up so the sun could shine on it from the east. It flashed in the bright rays and caused him to squint his eyes. Satisfied with the blade, he returned to his desk and placed it in his scabbard. There was a slight smile on his face. He had only one regret. Tobias had two new red stripes sewn into his blue commander's cloak. He had wanted to explain the two stripes just before he would kill the despicable man who had orchestrated the death of his two closest friends. But it was not to be. Gilad had been right; he was always right. The action had been clean; no loss of men; no stain upon the Palace Guards. He had avenged the death of the two men he had called family and one of their sons, but the pain of that loss remained a weight in his heart that he knew he would carry for the rest of his life.

Tobias wiped his eyes, then walked to the window to stare at the rising sun for several minutes. After watching the sunrise he found a basin of water and washed his face. Using a comb made from bone he brushed his thick hair back across his head. He glanced out the window one more time then reached for his sword. He still had one very important promise to keep. First, he had to find Samuel, then Jesus.

Chapter 53

The young boy stopped and bent over to catch his breath as he stood before Samuel in the middle of the vineyard. Samuel hobbled over and put his hand on the boy's shoulder. "Rest, my boy, then you can tell me your message." He signaled to one of his workers in the vineyard. "Please bring this boy some water."

When the boy had rested he stood and spoke. "Are you Samuel, son of Nathan?"

"I am."

"My Lord, Tobias, Commander of the Palace Guards, sends a message. He says you should come at once to fulfill your father's request." All the while, the boy was looking at Samuel's leg. Samuel watched his eyes and understood his concern.

"Go to Tobias and tell him I shall come with all haste." He looked at the boy for a moment. "But first drink the water and rest under one of the trees. You will surely arrive before I can." The vineyard was outside the city and the trip would take two hours if he were walking, but with a small cart attached to one of the donkeys, he could be there in just over an hour.

* * *

Samuel watched the people scurrying along the road before him. They had all heard about Jesus's entry into Jerusalem. He watched an old man walking past, quickly. He was old, but he stood erect and walked proudly with the surging crowd. Samuel envied the man. He could walk—really walk— while Samuel moved along slowly in a small cart attached to a tired old donkey. For the first time in his adult life he felt pity for himself even though Nathan had taught him the waste in

320

doing so. "A man must not dwell on his limitations" he had said so many times. "A man should, instead, concentrate on his opportunities. Stand up; stand tall; be proud." But how does one stand tall in a cart behind a donkey? A crowd of people moved along the road before him, but Samuel only watched one head in the crowd, that of the old man who had passed him along the way. He was losing sight of the white beard and hair now, the distance had grown too far, and the man was swallowed by the throng of people walking to see Jesus. Samuel heard them shouting in the distance. "Hosanna! Hosanna! Blessed is He who comes in the name of the Lord!" The sound was a deafening roar ahead, happy people rejoicing at the sight of Jesus. Slowly the old donkey plodded along. Nathan had already decided that hitting the animal to try to gain more speed was useless. There they were, an old donkey and a crippled man, moving at the speed of a snail, going to see Jesus. Samuel lowered his head and closed his eyes. He listened carefully to the screaming crowd. He strained to hear anything Jesus might say, but he could not. When he opened his eyes and looked up, the back of the throng was moving farther away, not closer. He knew he was too late. He pulled on the reign and stopped the beast before him. He raised his hand to shield his eyes from the sun as he watched the procession moving along the road toward Jerusalem. From a distance, his hand raised above his head might have been mistaken for a wave as one might gesture to a friend far away, a friend who was leaving.

* * *

Rebecca heard him talking to the old donkey before she saw Samuel's face enter her door. She ran to him and hugged him, holding him a long time in her arms. "Oh Samuel, I have missed you."

"I know mother. I've been working in the vineyard day and night recently."

"How is it going? Have you added more vines?"

"I have. I was able to buy some special vines from a merchant last year, and they are doing very well. I can't wait to see what they add to my wine."

Rebecca stepped back and looked at her son carefully. He looked tired. "Come, have some dinner. I cooked too much for myself. Now that most all of the children are grown, I need very little food in this house." She motioned toward the table. "But I know you did not come this far to tell me about some new vines."

"I came to see Jesus, but I was too late." He hung his head slightly. "Seems I'm always late."

"He's in Jerusalem? How did you know?"

"Tobias sent a messenger to alert me, but the crowds were everywhere, and I couldn't navigate them very well in a silly cart." His face was filled with the look of discouragement.

Rebecca went to him and put her arms around her son. "Don't be discouraged. We'll go tomorrow to see Him. I'll go with you."

Samuel kissed Rebecca on the cheek and smiled. "You are a special woman and a very special mother." Rebecca turned her attention to the fire and a big black pot that hung over the dying embers. As she spooned food onto a plate she suddenly stopped, staring over Samuel's shoulder. Tobias entered the room. Two of his guards waited outside.

Tobias walked directly to Samuel and patted him on his back. Rebecca placed the plate before Samuel and immediately began filling another for the commander. Tobias's attention was directed at Samuel. "I'm sorry you didn't get close enough today."

"How did you know?"

"My messenger followed you." Tobias looked at the food and smiled at Rebecca, then turned again to Samuel. "But no fear. Now that He is in Jerusalem, we will find Him for sure. I have three of my men scouting the city even now. Just stay here tonight, and tomorrow I will personally take you to see Him. That is a promise." He said it in a grand way, and even Samuel had to smile. "I will find the best time and the right place, then we will march right in and see this man some people call the Messiah."

Samuel turned to the older man and questioned him. "Do you think he could be the Messiah?"

"Well, Isaiah said he would ride in on a donkey, and Jesus certainly did that today. It's not what most people wanted, but that is what Isaiah prophesied." Tobias suddenly spoke very quietly, almost as if he were speaking only to himself. "We have waited a long time for the Messiah; I had hoped for a great man on a large horse leading a grand army, but perhaps Isaiah was right, perhaps it will be a man on a donkey. I can only hope this is the man." He paused for a moment then turned to Samuel. "Your father listened to Jesus and saw Him perform miracles. He was convinced this is the man of whom Isaiah wrote, and for that reason, I would like to accompany you and also see and hear this man. I have always had doubts, but I want to see Him for myself."

Rebecca smiled at the two. "Then you both better eat your dinner. You will have much to do tomorrow."

Tobias reached and touched her arm. "Bless you, Rebecca." Then both turned to their food and raised their cups to Rebecca.

Chapter 54

Pilate walked onto the palace patio and sat beside his wife. She turned and studied his face for several minutes then reached and touched his forehead between his eyebrows. Procula rubbed gently. "You have a deep furrow, my dear. It seems this job is not agreeing with you. You look worried."

Pilate took her hand and pulled it to his lips. He kissed it gently, then settled himself on the small bench. The sun was just going down, and night was falling quickly. He watched the horizon as it slowly faded from sight as he rubbed the back of his neck. "You are right as usual, my dear. This job would age any man. I'm somewhere between Rome, the cursed Jews, and even Vitellius."

"What is the Imperial Legate to Syria doing now?" She smiled at Pilate and moved closer to him. "Is he still angry because you sent the army to break up the demonstrations on Mount Gerizim?"

"I tried to explain that my intelligence indicated a demonstration on that mountain that might lead to conflict. Rome has made it very clear that I am to ensure there is no insurrection here." Pilate lowered his head and studied the wooden bench as he continued. "I can't allow a demonstration, but I also can't use force. I'd like to see *Vitellius* run this district. These Jews would eat him alive."

"Well, at least Sejanus supported you when Vitellius removed you and sent you to Rome to explain your authority."

"Vitellius is a fool. I told him that damned centurion misinterpreted my orders. I didn't mean for him to slaughter all those people." Pilate shook his head. "He even killed most of those captured after they surrendered. Damned fool. How am I supposed to run a country with commanders like that?"

"Well, at least there was no insurrection. Rome should have been happy about that."

"Insurrection? It turned out that a Samaritan prophet led them all up on Gerizim to see some old relics Moses was supposed to have left there."

"Relics from Moses?"

"That's what he told them." Pilate stood and paced around the patio for several minutes thinking. "Perhaps he should have told us what he was planning. It would have saved a lot of lives if he had." Pilate looked out as the last rays of the sun colored the sky, leaving streaks of red and orange slowly fading into the darkness. "Can you imagine the people believing some self-proclaimed prophet telling them he has relics from Moses?"

Procula watched her husband and tried to ease his apparent discomfort about a failure he had ordered. It had been costly for his career and had almost cost him his post. "Well, Rome sent you back, so Sejanus must have had confidence in you."

Pilate smiled for the first time that evening. "I'm guessing he couldn't find anyone willing to come to this outpost. He had no option but to send me back." He rubbed his right hand vigorously as he spoke. The smile disappeared as quickly as it had arrived. "But that is of little significance now. Sejanus was executed by Tiberius last month." Pilate stopped his pacing and stood looking off into a sky filled with stars. "Displeasing Tiberius was not a wise act for any man, even Sejanus."

Procula turned and looked at her husband in shock. "Sejanus was executed?"

Slowly the governor turned and faced his wife. "I'm guessing he was assuming far too much control of Tiberius's government. Tiberius settled in Capri and spent little time managing the Senate and internal affairs. He preferred foreign affairs and the Legions. Someone had to step into the void in Rome—and that was Sejanus, but in doing so he must have overstepped his authority and assumed more control than Tiberius was willing to share. There are some who say he was plotting to take over the Senate and the government." Pilate walked over and sat again next to his wife. "I just got the notice of his execution three days ago."

"What does that mean for us? Sejanus is the one who appointed you to this post."

"I don't think it will be a problem, but I have to be very careful until we see what changes Tiberius might make. For now I just have to ensure that there are no insurrections or demonstrations against Rome here. If things here remain quiet, I think we will stay."

The beautiful woman seated beside Pilate reached and put her hand on his arm. "If we are asked to return to Rome that really wouldn't be so bad. This is not a prized location for someone with your experience."

"You are right dear. Dealing with the Jews is tough enough, but living in Jerusalem has not been much fun either. Thankfully we get to spend as much time in Cesearea as we do here. I can only take dealing with the Sanhedrin for short periods of time."

"It must be difficult trying to please the people Rome conquered."

"And according to Rome, I have to make them *like* me."

"Are they really all that difficult?"

"Difficult? We bring a bunch of soldiers marching into Jerusalem with Roman standards leading the troops. The Jews see the banners and designate them as idols offensive to their God. They were simply cloth banners bearing the insignia of our troops and Rome." As he talked, Pilate's voice rose with anger.

"Why are they so sensitive to Rome's insignia? Rome rules this place." Now Procula was also getting agitated.

Pilate calmed himself and reached to put his hand on Procula's knee. "Actually, it's almost humorous. The people filled the stadium and bared their necks for the soldiers to kill them. In the end the Emperor, himself, intervened and had us remove all the golden shields and the emperor's name."

"What did you do then?"

"I recognize one-upmanship when I see it. I just appropriated the funds from their temple treasury." Pilate resumed pacing around the patio. "I know how to get to these Jews. I took their money. I'll bet the Jewish leaders were really upset about that." He smiled, "But I fooled them. I used the money to build an aqueduct. Rome loves aqueducts. So far no one has complained to Rome about their money."

"Sometimes you men are like little boys, always playing games."

"True, my dear, but the silly games we played as boys were only practice for the serious games we play as men." He turned and faced the beautiful woman before him. "As boys we mocked the losers; as men we kill them."

"Maybe the boys are more mature than the men."

Pilate nodded. "You may be right, my dear."

Chapter 55

Jerusalem, 33 A.D.

Tobias stood and stretched his aching back. Age, it seemed, had ways to find the weakness in every man. His, it seemed, was his back. As he grew older, the pain intensified when he tried to do too much, but generally he could just work his way through it. He bent forward at the waist and tried to touch the ground between his feet. If he stretched a bit he could touch the floor with the tips of his fingers. Five stretches, then he resumed his pacing around the small office. For a moment he stopped and turned to look at the walls adorned with trophies from prior victories; most had belonged to Gilad. Tobias frowned and cursed silently. He had meant to send those to Gilad and replace them with more current items. He reviewed the weapons, arrows, and even a Parthian shield with great scars that adorned the wall behind his table. Finally he peered out the window into the darkness. There was not even the sliver of a moon to light the way to men rushing through the city, men intent on deeds Tobias needed to understand and plot.

When he heard the footsteps of one of the young guards running across the flagstone courtyard and up the tile steps, Tobias quickly adjusted his cloak and turned to face the open door. The young man rushed in and saluted as he waited to calm his labored breath. After a moment he spoke, quickly. "Commander, I have tracked the men who arrested Jesus as you directed. They arrested him in the Garden of Gethsemane and took Him to Annas's house."

"Annas? The High Priest? Hmmmm. That is Caiaphas's father-in-law. I wonder why they took him there." The young man did not reply as Tobias continued to wonder out loud. "But this is troublesome; Annas is a strong ally of Rome."

The young man dared a question to his commander. "I don't understand, Sir."

"Annas is a Zadokite, a Sadducee. They were banned as high priests by the Hasmoneans. Only since Herod was king have they been allowed back as priests. They are very political and very close to Rome, as was Herod." The young man looked confused. "And only Rome can order an execution. The Sanhedrin does not have that power." Tobias turned and walked back to the window and looked again into the darkness, darkness that he likened to men's souls when they killed innocent people for political reasons. After several minutes of thought he turned back to the young guard. "Does Jesus remain there now?"

"He was released to the Temple Guards to be beaten then returned to Annas's home. I was told that the entire Sanhedrin was called to question Him there."

Tobias recoiled at the mention of the beating at the hands of the Temple Guards. He had little regard for that group and considered them little more than thugs. They were certainly below the professionalism of his troops, but they were experts in ways to beat the victims they were given. "Did you leave another man to watch while you were reporting to me?"

"Yes, Sir."

"Good, return and continue your watch. If they move Jesus, come immediately and let me know. Also, gather any information you can about the Sanhedrin's actions or what their role might be in this arrest."

"I understand."

"Good, now go." The young man saluted, turned, walked to the door then sprinted toward the courtyard. Tobias returned to his table and poured half a goblet of wine and downed it quickly. He didn't taste the quality of the wine or enjoy the aroma it presented. His mind was concentrating on

329

the events of the evening. What was the priests' purpose? Would they be satisfied with just a beating for Jesus, or was their intent more sinister? Tobias was a pragmatist. He cared little for the priests and the Pharisees. Mostly they irritated him, but he was able to keep that irritation hidden. He tolerated them, and they ignored him. He liked it that way. Suddenly one of the candles flickered and a ray of light reflected from the blade of a Parthian sword hanging on the wall. Tobias looked at it for only a moment before remembering that it was the sword Nathan had proposed to use to kill Archelaus. Tobias's head drooped instantly at the thought of Nathan. He looked at the floor as memories flooded across the landscape of his mind. So many memories when they were young and strong and fearless. That was so long ago, and he missed those carefree days. Then the world was exciting with so many new things to experience and learn. But now he was beyond those sunrises and sunsets that had framed his life. Now he was beset with responsibilities and purpose. Now it was his job to understand and fight the evil that had been a scourge in this country for so many generations. It was a task of giant proportions, and he was becoming old and tired.

Tobias poured another goblet of wine and downed it more slowly than the first. He savored the wine and reflected on the man who had produced it. Samuel was remarkable. He had been given a very bad start in life, but he had not let that stop him. He refused to be a victim. Tobias smiled. Of course he had been strong. Nathan had demanded that he stand tall and be a man, regardless of his limitations. He tasted the wine again and spoke quietly to himself. "This is good. Nathan would have liked this." Finally, he walked to his desk and sat in his chair. He could feel the weariness in his limbs. It had to be the wine. It also had to be the hour. It was already past midnight, and he had a promise to keep.

* * *

The sun climbed slowly on the horizon and sent bright rays into the commander's office. Tobias shook his head gently and opened his eyes to the daylight. He had been sleeping in his chair and his back was sending countless messages to his brain that sleeping in a chair was not a smart idea and that Tobias would pay a price for that this day. Tobias walked to the window and stared at the dawning morning. He had just started his stretching exercises when the young guard from the prior evening arrived at his door. Quickly Tobias straightened his cloak and stood straight before the young guard. Neither acknowledged the slight groan from the commander as he straightened his posture.

"Commander, Jesus is being brought here to the palace by the Temple Guards and the chief priests."

"Now?"

"Yes Sir."

"Who is leading this entourage?"

"Caiaphas, Sir."

"Of course. I should have known it would be Caiaphas." Tobias turned and spoke to the wall, to himself. "There is only one reason to bring Jesus to the palace—Pilate."

"I'll watch and let you know where they take Him, Sir."

"They will take Him to the Praetorium. Passover started at sundown; the High Priest will not enter the home of a Roman today. They will meet in the Praetorium, the special courtyard for such things." The commander paced across the floor for several minutes. Finally, he addressed the waiting guard. "Do you know if Pilate is aware that the priests are bringing Jesus to him?"

331

"I am not aware of Pilate's knowledge of these affairs, Sir."

"You've done good work, but we are not yet through this day. I will be in the Praetorium when Jesus arrives. I'd like you to stand outside and continue to observe and follow if they move Him again."

"Yes, Sir." As the guard left, Tobias straightened his clothing and brushed his graying hair. He looked at his sword briefly then reached for it, studied it carefully for a moment, and attached it to his belt. After all, he was the Commander of the Palace Guards. He walked out into the hallway that led to the Praetorium, wondering what this day would bring. He felt a great sense of foreboding. He knew he was dealing with men he did not trust. He was a warrior by training; they were politicians, despite their titles as priests. Tobias was an older man and had experienced much in his life. Of one thing he was sure, warriors and politicians didn't mix well. Warriors fought and killed men openly in battle. Politicians had far more subtle ways of disposing of their foes, ways that left little evidence, but ways that were equally deadly.

* * *

Tobias met the entourage at the entrance to the Praetorium. There were a group of Jewish leaders and chief priests, with Caiaphas leading the crowd. When Tobias stood in the entrance Caiaphas stopped and put both of his hands on his hips in a stance of defiance. He looked at the Commander of the Palace Guards with utter contempt. Tobias stood expressionless. "Good morning, Caiaphas, what brings so many esteemed leaders to the palace at this early hour? The sun is barely rising in the East."

"We demand to see Pilate."

332

"Demand?" There was sarcasm in Tobias's voice. He looked straight into the High Priest's eyes. "Is that the word you would like relayed to the prefect?"

Caiaphas lowered his gaze and removed his hands from his hips. "Just tell him we need to talk to him immediately."

"Is this something that can wait until after the prefect has risen and dressed for the day?"

"No, it isn't." Impatience was growing on the priest's face and in his voice. Tobias recognized this and reacted accordingly. He could push the high priest, but only so far. He was nearing that point, and discretion won over against his great dislike for the man standing before him.

"No problem. I'll alert the prefect that the leaders of Judea's religious traditions wish to speak with him as soon as he can make himself available." He started to turn but stopped and faced the group of men again. "I'll tell him you are waiting outside."

* * *

Pilate and Tobias walked down a long, polished marble hallway replete with statues lining the polished floors, but neither man noticed the opulence or the beauty around them. They were deep in conversation about the purpose of the meeting they were walking toward. Pilate was in no hurry to accommodate the Jewish leaders he despised. They had made it clear to him that he was beneath them; they would not even step into his home without being defiled. "I'm glad you kept them in the Praetorium."

"That was their choice, not mine. They are concerned about entering your home during the celebration of Passover."

"Right, they are so holy they cannot visit a Roman palace." Pilate laughed to himself. "And what do you think these holy men want a defiled Roman to do?"

"Something they cannot. They want you to murder an innocent man."

"And what man is that?"

"A young rabbi who preaches love and peace to the people."

"Jesus?"

"Yes."

"I know of Him. He doesn't seem to be a threat to anyone. What has He done to deserve a Roman crucifixion?"

"He has displeased the Jewish religious leaders."

"Did He kill someone or raise an army to lead an insurrection?"

"No, he preached peace."

"That's all?"

"He also healed people and spoke of love for all men."

"Procula has heard Him; she thinks He is a good man with a wonderful message. She specifically spoke to me of Him. I think she has become one of His followers." He paused for a moment then continued. "She once went to hear Him speak. When she returned, she was changed."

"One of my friends was one of the guards who accompanied her when she went to hear Jesus. You may recall Nathan; he was the guard the Primus Pilus presented a sword after an attack on him and Herod. When he returned, he, too, was changed."

"Have you heard Him?"

"No, I have not, but I would like to. There is something special about this man who can change people so profoundly."

"I just wish He had the same impact on the Chief Priest and all of his minions." Pilate shook his head and muttered to himself. "No wonder the priests want to kill Him. He's a good man, a real threat to their control over the people."

Tobias stood back while Pilate and Caiaphas argued over the arrest of Jesus. When the priest mentioned that Jesus was from Galilee, Pilate saw a way to end the discussion and send the troublesome religious leaders on their way. Pilate raised his hands and waited for quiet. "Jesus is from Nazareth; he is a Galilean; therefore he belongs to Herod Antipas." Pilate smiled inside. He had escaped Caiaphas's trap. "Antipas is in Jerusalem. Take Jesus to him."

Walking far more quickly than when he had come, Pilate turned and nodded to Tobias. The two men left quickly, leaving Caiaphas and the others standing alone with their bloodied prisoner. When the men were out of sight from the religious leaders, Tobias nodded to Pilate and turned toward his own office. Pilate nodded in return. "Thank you, Tobias. This is a strange world we live in now. I appreciate the work you do here."

The commander walked into this office and immediately wrote a quick note to Samuel. It said simply: *Things here not good. The chief priests have arrested Jesus. Stay with your family. I'll keep you advised.*

* * *

Antipas looked at the religious leaders with clear contempt. Unlike Pilate, he had no responsibility to accommodate these men. He also knew he would never agree to kill Jesus or any other preacher in the hills around Jerusalem. He had gone down that path already with John the Baptist, and it was not a mistake he was about to make again. Like Pilate, Antipas had heard of Jesus and demanded that Jesus perform some miracle for him. But the tired and injured man before him

335

simply stood before him, quietly awaiting His fate. Eventually Antipas wearied of the affair and sent Jesus back to Pilate.

* * *

The sun had barely climbed over the horizon and started to warm the countryside when Caiaphas and his band of religious leaders and Temple Guards returned with Jesus. Pilate's escape had not worked. As Caiaphas had known, Antipas was too smart to persecute another preacher. John's death had been a huge mistake in his eyes. Little did Antipas understand the purpose of John's life or his death.

Pilate stood before men he despised, but he understood their political influence in Rome, and he had already caused the displeasure of the Emperor once. The execution of Sejanus and some of his appointees had been a clear message for Pilate. He understood he was not in a position of great strength; he was certain of that. So was Caiaphas. Eventually Pilate agreed to take custody of Jesus, even though Procula warned him against that. His intention was to have Him beaten and then released, but Caiaphas and his men had arranged for a crowd of their followers to intercede. They demanded that Jesus be crucified. In the end Pilate conceded to the priests' demands and washed his hands of the whole affair, blaming the Jews for the decision he implemented.

Tobias and several of his guards stood behind the proceedings, listening. The face of the commander was one of both sadness and anger. Jesus would die, and there was nothing he could do about it. Tobias understood Pilate's predicament. He also knew Pilate was an ambitious man with little strength of character, and that he would finally acquiesce to the demands of Caiaphas and the crowds the priests orchestrated. Pilate would be the arm that would wield the Jewish leaders' sword.

Tobias turned and walked away alone, wondering what Nathan would think if he were alive. Could he be watching from somewhere beyond mortal sight? If so, what must he be thinking now? The Commander went to his office and poured a goblet of wine. Then he thought of Samuel. How would he explain the events of the day to him? He set the goblet aside and reached for his sword. As he was attaching it to his belt, he stopped. Slowly he put the sword aside and reached for the large sword that was hanging on his wall. It was heavy and strong, like the man who had carried it for so many years. He attached it to his belt, adjusted it on his hip and walked out of the palace. He was looking for another strong man, one who walked with a very distinctive limp.

Chapter 56

Samuel stood with his head bowed, looking at the floor. Finally, he raised his eyes and stared straight into those of Tobias. "Thank you, Tobias. You are a true friend. I appreciate your help in my attempts to see Jesus."

"I'm glad Nathan is not alive to see what is happening." Samuel only nodded. "Nathan always talked about a new leader and a new way of life. So many had hoped that Jesus was the answer to that prayer."

"My father never gave up."

"No, he didn't."

"It was a lesson he taught me, so I will be there when they crucify Jesus today."

Tobias was clearly shocked. "Samuel, are you sure you want to do that? The religious leaders have their gangs out today. They are aware of the crowds that welcomed him into the city, and they fear those followers. It will be dangerous."

Rebecca put her hand on Samuel's shoulder and hugged him. "I agree with Tobias. I don't think you should be there. It will be awful; you don't want to see that."

"I told *Abba* I'd see Jesus. This is my last chance." Samuel grabbed his crutch and started out the door.

"Wait!" Tobias walked alongside the crippled man struggling down the road. "I'm going with you."

"You don't have to come, Tobias."

"You made a promise. So did I. I told your father I'd help you see Him, so I guess we walk together." Tobias slung a small pack onto his back. "And I remembered to bring water."

There was an overwhelming sadness as the two men approached the path to Golgotha. Twice they were met by Roman soldiers as they proceeded. In each case Tobias had

338

insisted he was in the employ of Pilate. They all knew him, yet they still held the two men back. Only a few people had been able to skirt the guards and approach the procession along the dusty path. Frustrated, Tobias had pulled the sword from his belt and held it high above his head, pointing down toward the earth. Both soldiers stopped, studied it for only a moment, then they saluted and let them pass. Tobias turned to Samuel. "It still has its magic. Your father would be proud." Samuel gave only a nod as they continued toward the path of death. Tobias put his hand on the crippled man's shoulder. "I'm sorry it has ended this way. They're going to kill an innocent man just to protect their power." He paused a moment to catch his breath then continued. "And it was the Sanhedrin who did this, not the Romans. The chief priests and their like are responsible for this death. The Romans are simply the instruments who carry out their bidding."

Tobias saw three condemned men approaching with Roman guards urging them on. He had planned well and had placed themselves on the path fifty yards ahead of the group that was slowly climbing the hill. He stopped Samuel and looked into his face for several moments. "Are you sure you want to see this? It will be a memory that will linger in your mind for the rest of your life. The men who have had Jesus are little more than animals. He will not be the man you expect when He comes into view."

When Samuel spoke his voice was not strong, but his words were clear. "I made a promise. It is not what either of us wanted, but it's all I have. I'm sure *Abba* would understand." He thought for a moment then continued. "Besides, Jesus deserves to have someone here to mourn His death. Someone on this path must care. He deserves to know that." Then he looked straight into Tobias's eyes. "That is what my father would have done. He would have been here."

"You're right, and like your father, I have lived the life of a warrior. I have seen much death and suffering. But this today is perhaps man's worst sin against another man." He paused and put a hand on Samuel's shoulder. "Samuel, you are a good man, a kind man. You need not see this. I'm sure Nathan would understand."

"We tried to see Jesus for so long, and always we failed. I know it grieved *Abba* that we couldn't seem to make it work. But today, I *will* see Him. Maybe I will touch Him. I will fulfill my promise."

"Just know that I will be beside you. We will stand together."

Samuel's head turned quickly at the words. "Yes, we'll stand—*tall*—together."

Chapter 57

Pontius Pilate walked slowly to the table filled with food and drink and poured a large goblet of wine. It had been a long and troubling day, a day he had wanted to avoid but could not. He downed the wine quickly and then poured another. When he turned he saw Procula standing in the door, watching him. Her face was white; her eyes were large and questioning. "What have you done, my husband?" There were small white lines etched over her cheeks where tears had left their salty trail. "Why did you condemn Jesus?"

Pilate sat heavily on a large cushion and placed his wine goblet on the floor. He then buried his face in his hands. "It was the Sanhedrin. Damn Caiaphas, he had his people in the crowds, demanding that Jesus be crucified. I offered to free Him, but they just shouted louder, 'Crucify Him! Crucify Him!' I had no choice." He lowered his head and stared at the floor. Something in his heart, his very soul cried out, but he could not understand what it was saying. He only knew it was the most mournful sound he had ever heard.

"You had no choice? I cannot believe you let Caiaphas win like that. You know Jesus was an innocent man. The priest just wanted you to do his evil work for him." Another tear sparkled in the late sunlight as it rolled over her cheek and down onto her fine linen robe.

Pilate raised his head suddenly. He had never heard his wife speak like that to him before. That was upsetting, but more troubling was the knowledge that she was right. Caiaphas had, indeed, won, and the governor felt both shame and defeat. Slowly he turned his face from her and drank the remaining wine in the goblet as he walked to the stone wall that ran along the walkway by his living quarters. For a long while he stared off into the distance, trying to make some sense of what had just happened in his life. And why was his heart so heavy? Another preacher wandering around the villages was silenced. How could that possibly be important? He shook his head. In another week it will all be over, and He will be forgotten. Surely it was as simple as that. He turned and forced a smile, but Procula was gone. When he looked back the sky was turning dark.

*   *   *

Caiaphas stood before the assembled Jewish leaders. Most had participated in the trial, but none were going to Golgotha. All eyes were focused on him as he stared at the floor below his feet. Finally, he raised his head. "We did our duty for Israel today." He scanned the eyes staring into his. "It will soon be over." The priest looked back at the ground briefly and then turned to leave. He had noted that the faces staring back at him were dark. He had expected nods of congratulation and friends slapping his back, but all he saw was a confusion as deep as his own. He had won. Then why was there no joy in the victory, or was there a victory to celebrate after all? Caiaphas looked up at the dark clouds that covered the sky and felt a strange foreboding as he examined the darkness deep in his heart and made a startling discovery. The confusion in his mind was only surpassed by a profound sense of loss in his soul.

Chapter 58

The team of soldiers walking with the procession blocked the view of Jesus from the crowd as the condemned man approached. Samuel put his hand on Tobias's shoulder to steady himself as the group drew closer. Leading the group was the *exactor mortis*—the centurion in charge of the execution. He was holding a sign stating the charge against Jesus. It said simply: *Jesus the Nazarene: King of the Jews.* Following was a centurion and several soldiers with whips. Some in the crowd were jeering Jesus; others were weeping and calling to Him. Then Samuel saw His face. For a moment he stood transfixed, watching the bleeding and battered man stumbling along with the large *patibulum* crossbeam on his back. Jesus was barely capable of walking, much less carrying the large wooden beam strapped to his shoulders. Unlike the centurion and the soldiers who walked erect, Jesus moved under the weight of the heavy plank, struggling and stumbling and finally falling. Samuel knew the pain of falling and the rejection of the crowd's insults and instinctively reached out to help the bleeding man as He tried to rise from the dirt. Samuel was focused on the face before him; he didn't see the fist of the centurion that struck him on his neck, but he felt the impact as it drove him to the ground. "Back! Back you cripple! Get back!" Samuel tried to rise but the man hit him again and began to pull his sword from its scabbard. As he did, Tobias drew Nathan's sword and stepped between the two. The centurion looked into the eyes of the man in the blue cloak and then at his sword. Slowly he lowered his own and saluted.

Samuel reached his right arm to balance himself and tried to climb to his feet. He felt unsteady and his head was spinning as he tried to rise, his eyes desperately trying to focus on the world around him. He climbed to his one good knee but fell backward into the dirt. Desperately he reached to steady himself but with no success. He lay there dazed and confused. Then his hand felt the splinters on the beam of the *patibulum*. He lay on his back and felt the rough wood with his fingers. Then he felt something wet and slick across the heavy beam. He raised his hand; it was covered with blood. For just a moment the world stopped its frantic pace, and in that peaceful silence Samuel heard the voice he knew and loved so well. It was both gentle and also insistent. "Get up. Stand tall, son; stand tall." Without even thinking he replied as he had so many times in his life. "Okay, *Abba*." Slowly he rubbed his eyes with the back of his hand, and when they cleared, he turned and found himself looking directly into the eyes of Jesus, eyes filled with compassion and love that were suddenly staring back into his own. A whip cracked beside him and Jesus began climbing slowly to his feet with the heavy *patibulum* on his shoulders. In that moment the confusion in Samuel's head disappeared as he, too, started to stand. But something was different. It didn't feel normal. The angular stature of a cripple was gone. Samuel climbed to his feet and stood erect; he stood tall and looked down into the eyes of the Roman centurion who stood, stunned, looking back at him. Tobias followed the soldier's eyes and dropped the sword to his feet. All three men were looking at Samuel's legs. They were the same; the deformity was gone. The heat, the dust, the smell of blood, all disappeared in that moment.

The centurion looked up into Samuel's face, his mouth open in a silent cry. He, too, dropped his sword and stepped backward several steps. "How did this happen?" Then all three men turned and looked at the bloodied man carrying the large beam toward Golgotha. Samuel stood fixed, looking at his left leg, then back at Jesus. His eyes filled with tears as the procession moved along the path toward the *staticulum*, the eight-foot-tall wooden pole on which the *patibulum* would be fixed.

Tobias stood with his eyes wide. For a long time he could not speak. Finally, he looked up into Samuel's face. "Nathan was right. What he said is true."

The centurion abruptly turned and began running up the small hill toward the slowly moving entourage, while Samuel reached and touched his restored leg. Tobias stepped aside and watched as Samuel took several tenuous steps. For the first time he walked erect; the old crippled gait was gone. "Tobias, get your sword and put it in your scabbard; then follow me." Samuel turned and began following the procession, as Tobias hurried to catch him.

* * *

As the crossbeam was heaved into place, many in the small crowd watched with tears in their eyes and pain etched across their faces. It was the third hour when they crucified Him between two common thieves. In the sixth hour the entire land fell into darkness. In the ninth hour Jesus breathed his last and the curtain of the Temple was torn in two from top to bottom.

In that darkest moment, the centurion standing below the cross slowly scanned the crowd until he found the two men he had encountered on the path to Golgotha. For a long time he looked at Samuel's face, each peering into the other's soul. Then his eyes moved down to Samuel's legs. Finally, he looked up to the man hanging above him on the cross and fell to his knees proclaiming; "Surely this man is the Son of God."

Epilogue

Adriel stood in the door and looked up the road to the northwest. The baby in her arms was cooing sweetly as it sucked on her left breast. She smiled and kissed the soft hair on the top of his head. Then she looked again at the road, trying to focus on the people walking in the late afternoon. She was worried. She had urged Samuel to remain home, to avoid the dangers of the evil men in the city. Only Tobias's reassurance that he would accompany Samuel had given her comfort. Tobias was old, but he was Commander of the Palace Guards; he wore the robe and the sword to prove it. No one would dare harm them. She studied the groups of people walking in the distance. She could not discern their faces, but that was not what she was seeking. They all walked normally. The awkward gait of her husband was not among the travelers. All afternoon she had returned regularly to the door to peer at the road. As the sun moved across the sky, her pacing, as her concern, had increased. When the entire sky had turned dark during the day, she had nearly panicked. What strange things were happening to her normally peaceful environment? Adriel looked down, the baby was asleep, her nipple still in his mouth. She studied her new son; he was beautiful, like all her babies. She had worried about them. She couldn't let Samuel know, but deep in her heart she feared they might be born crippled, like their father. Rebecca had assured her that such things seldom happened, but only after three children were born with kicking legs did she banish such thoughts from her mind. She walked back into the house and carefully placed the sleeping child in the small bed beside her own, then she looked out the window to count, once again, her laughing children playing in her courtyard.

As the day lengthened, Adriel's trips to the door increased, like the small wrinkle between her eyes that grew deeper with each passing hour. Her anxiety was growing, but then in the distance she spotted the official light blue cloak of the commander of the Palace Guards. It was late afternoon and the dust on the road dimmed her sight. She stepped forward as her hands automatically continued to knead the dough she was holding. Then the fear struck deep inside her heart. Samuel was not with Tobias, only a tall man walking at his side. She froze in place, her hand ceasing their constant work on the dough. She stepped forward slowly, watching Tobias. She could finally see his face. Yes, it was him; then she focused on the man beside him. She squinted and peered closely at the broad shoulders, the shape of the head, then the eyes. He looked like Samuel. It *was* Samuel! The bread dropped to the floor as she stared. He was walking normally, no bobbing to the side with each difficult step. Adriel moved forward a step, then two, then she grabbed her garment and lifted it to her knees and began running.

When Samuel saw her, he also began running and embraced her, lifting her into the air, swinging her around in the process. When he finally placed her back on the ground, she stepped back several steps, looking at his legs. He smiled broadly and raised his cloak to his knees. Her eyes were wide with wonder as she slowly reached out and touched his left leg. When she looked up there were tears in both their eyes and many questions in hers. "How did this happen?" was all she could say.

"Jesus!" was his answer as he pulled her to him.

*   *   *

Total darkness enveloped the room; even the window that opened to the skies was black. Samuel lay there staring into that darkness, weighing the events of the day. His body was tired, but his mind would not be still. There were so many mysteries to consider and attempt to understand. He turned to the window and tried to find one small light from the skies, even one small star sparkling from the heavens, but he could not. *Perhaps*, he thought, *the darkness of evil has conquered the whole world*.

Then a small sound broke the quiet of the night and Samuel smiled. It was his new son, lying in a crib near the end of his bed. The world was in darkness, but that small sound brought him hope. The arm across his chest moved, and Samuel lay very still until he was certain that Adriel was asleep. Then his mind returned, again, to Golgotha. Tobias was right. What he witnessed there today would be with him for the rest of his life. And what would that life be like with a healed leg when all he had known before was deformity? But he knew his memories of today would not be of blood and suffering; instead, what he would remember forever was the moment his eyes met those of Jesus. As Samuel finally drifted into sleep it was with feelings of peace. Nathan's wish had been fulfilled.

Bibliography

Lawrence, Paul (2006). *The IVP Atlas of Bible History*. Downers Grove, Il: InterVarsity Press. ISBN-13: 978-0-8308-2452-6

Achtemeier, Paul J. (Ed.) (1996). *The HarperCollins Bible Dictionary*. San Francisco: HarperCollins Publishers. ISBN 0-06-060037-3

Burge, Gary M. (2015), *A Week in the Life of a Roman Centurion*. Downers Grove, Il: InterVarsity Press. ISBN 978-0-8308-2462-5

Metzger, Bruce M. & Coogan, Michael D. (Eds). *The Oxford Companion to the Bible*. New York: Oxford University Press. ISBN 0-19-504645-5

O'Reilly, Bill & Dugard, Martin (2013). *Killing Jesus*. New York: Henry Holt and Company. ISBN 978-0-8050-9854-9

Currid, John D. & Barrett, David P. (2010). *Crossway ESV Bible Atlas*. Wheaton Il: Crossway. ISBN-13: 978=1-4335=0192-0

Douglas Fain is a graduate of the Air Force Academy and holds graduate degrees from Georgetown University and the University of Southern California. He flew more than 200 combat missions over Southeast Asia and was awarded a Distinguished Flying Cross for Heroism, a Distinguished Flying Cross for Achievement, fourteen Air Medals, and an Air Force Commendation Medal. He is the president of CEBG, Inc., an international consulting company, and has worked in more than 30 different countries in that capacity. He has taught for four universities in both undergraduate and graduate programs as an affiliate faculty member and was a candidate for the U.S. Senate in 1992. Doug has served on several boards and is the author of four novels and co-author of one professional text. He lives with his wife in Evergreen, Colorado.